'I loved this story'

'A fast-paced detective story'

'Great story and full of twists'

'Each book gets better and better'

'Suspense all the way through'

PAUL GITSHAM started his career as a biologist working in the UK and Canada. After stints as the world's most over-qualified receptionist and a spell ensuring that international terrorists hadn't opened a Child's Savings Account at a major UK bank (a job even duller than working reception) he retrained as a science teacher.

Also by Paul Gitsham

The Last Straw

No Smoke Without Fire

Blood is Thicker than Water

A Case Gone Cold

The Common Enemy

A Deadly Lesson

Forgive Me Father

Silent As The Grave

Paul Gitsham

ONE PLACE. MANY STORIES

HQ
An imprint of HarperCollins*Publishers* Ltd
1 London Bridge Street
London SE1 9GF

This paperback edition 2020

1

First published in Great Britain by
HQ, an imprint of HarperCollins*Publishers* Ltd 20

Paul Gitsham asserts the moral right to be
identified as the author of this work.
A catalogue record for this book is
available from the British Library.

ISBN: 9780008389147

MIX
Paper from
responsible sources
FSC™ C007454

FSC
www.fsc.org

This book is produced from independently certified FSC™ paper
to ensure responsible forest management.

For more information visit: www.harpercollins.co.uk/green

This book is set in 10.8/15.5 pt. Minion by Type-it As, Norway

Printed and bound in Great Britain by
CPI Group (UK) Ltd, Croydon, CR0 4YY

To my number one cheerleaders, Mum, Dad and Cheryl. If you find one of my business cards or flyers in an unexpected place, it was probably them…

Prologue

The teenage boy walked carefully, balancing an overfilled mug in each hand. The kettle had boiled only moments before and his mother had called down the garden, asking if his father wanted coffee. There had been no reply, but in twenty years of marriage Aileen MacNamara had never known her husband refuse a hot drink. So, curious to know what his father had been doing all evening, the fourteen-year-old had poured himself one as well and set off down the path.

The garage door was a sturdy, wooden affair, the handle missing for as long as the boy could remember, the hasp for the padlock its replacement. Looping a free finger around the metal bracket, he unhooked it then pulled as hard as he could. The door, warped from years of hot summers and cold winters, resisted before screeching open with a sudden jerk, spilling scalding liquid all over his hands. The teenager swore quietly.

Niall MacNamara had patrolled the streets of Coventry for over twenty-five years and had seen—and heard—it all. Nevertheless, he had zero tolerance for foul language in his home and his son wasn't in the mood for a lecture.

The garage was dark, filled with tools and gardening implements. A spate of recent vandalism had prompted Niall to enlist the help of his two sons to clear enough space for him to park the family car in there overnight, but it was a tight fit.

1

The boy started to cough at the same moment he saw the hosepipe snaking from the rear of the car and in through the partially open driver's side window. With an incoherent shout, he dropped both mugs, forcing himself around the car's bonnet to the driver's side. After yanking the hosepipe from the window, he pulled the door handle. Locked. Through the clouds of exhaust filling the car, he could see his father, head slumped forward in the driver's seat. Choking, the boy cast his teary eyes around wildly before spotting a claw hammer hanging from a hook. With so little room to swing it took three desperate attempts before he shattered the window, all the while screaming for his mother. After pulling the door lock button, he opened the door. An empty whisky bottle rolled off his father's lap and clattered onto the concrete floor. Reaching in, he took the keys from the ignition. But he knew it was too little, too late.

Tuesday 10th May 1988. After tonight, nothing would ever be the same again.

Twenty-Two Years Later

The scrum of press outside the prison gates was more like that await-ing the appearance of a pop star than a convicted murderer. An explosion of flashbulbs greeted the arrival of a black Jaguar. Some of the dozen or so uniformed police officers, who were stopping the pushing reporters from getting too close to the prison gates, broke off to form a similar line around the rear doors of the luxury car.

Parked one hundred metres away, DCI Gavin Sheehy looked on with incredulity at the spectacle. All of the major national broadcasters were present, along with several noted international ones. Reporters earnestly spoke into cameras or radio microphones. Recognising one of the BBC's most famous radio presenters, Sheehy reached for the car radio, selecting Radio 4. Sure enough, the anchor of World at One *was reporting on the release of the prisoner, before handing over live to the presenter.*

"The scene outside Wormwood Scrubs prison is unlike anything we've ever witnessed before. Vinny Delmarno, the notorious crime lord sentenced in 1988 to life in prison for ordering the killing of a rival drug baron and accused—although acquitted—of dozens of counts of racketeering, money laundering, drug dealing and prostitution, is due to be released any moment on parole.

"Most prisoners slip out of this back door with little more than

a carrier bag, the clothes they wore when they came in, the address of a local bail hostel and forty-six pounds to help them start life again. Vinny Delmarno will have no need of any of these. It is alleged that whilst he was one of the most successful crime lords of the Seventies and Eighties, he also owned—and some claim still owns—a string of apparently legitimate businesses across the Midlands and the East of England. All of these businesses and his palatial Hertfordshire home were signed over to his ex-wife in an entirely uncontested divorce settlement weeks before his successful conviction. Rumour has it that he and his wife have reconciled over the past twenty-two years and that he will be returning to the couple's former home as soon as he is released."

The anchorwoman broke in, "This has caused some controversy, hasn't it, Mark?"

"Indeed it has. Politicians from all sides of the House are questioning if there is any way the state can seize these assets, even though they were legally awarded to his ex-wife. The shadow Home Secretary has claimed that the divorce was clearly a sham and that therefore his assets should be used to repay the millions of pounds of back tax that it is alleged he avoided through money-laundering schemes. It should be noted, of course, that despite his conviction, he claims to be innocent of all these charges and that he was the victim of a conspiracy.

"When he is released, any moment now, it is expected that he will give a statement repeating those claims."

Suddenly the press started snapping pictures again and even from his distant vantage point, Sheehy could hear the increase in volume from the waiting press. A moment later it became clear why, as a small side door started to open.

Sheehy's breath caught in his throat. It had been a long time since he had last set eyes on the man. He wasn't prepared for the shock.

4

Delmarno was a small, dapper man in his mid-fifties. His silver hair had been expertly coiffured and his thin pencil moustache trimmed neatly. The fitted suit that he wore was certainly not the one he'd worn in court; its cut was clearly contemporary. But then he had been a very different man back then.

"In many ways it is a big surprise to see Vinny Delmarno here today. When sentenced back in 1988, he was believed to be within a year of dying from kidney failure. In fact, that was put forward in mitigation by his defence team when the judge sentenced him. Six months into his sentence, however, he received a controversial life-saving kidney transplant. Questions were again raised in the House of Commons and the House of Lords as to whether a convicted murderer should be given such treatment on the NHS. The then Health Secretary acknowledged such concerns but stood alongside the Home Secretary and the Prime Minister in claiming that denying prisoners such a life-saving operation would be a slippery slope."

The anchorwoman cut back in again, "I believe that Mr Delmarno's lawyer is about to read a prepared statement."

A taller man, in an equally expensive suit, was now standing shoulder to shoulder with his client. He paused whilst the various camera crews jostled for the best position and microphones were thrust under his nose. Clearing his throat, he began, "I am going to read a short statement on behalf of my client. He will not be answering any questions.

"This day has been a long time coming, but finally my freedom, wrongly taken from me, has been returned. For over twenty-two years I have languished in prison for crimes that I did not commit, the victim of a conspiracy concocted at the highest levels. In that time I have maintained my innocence. During my incarceration I have been comforted by the support of my family and friends, who have stood by me and championed my innocence, and I cannot thank them enough. In a moment I will be driven away to be reunited with loved ones and I look forward to embracing my son and rebuilding my life. I feel only sadness that I could not do the same to my dear parents, both of whom passed away during my imprisonment.

"On the advice of my lawyers, I will not be saying any more other than that I will be turning all of my energy towards overturning my conviction and seeking redress for this appalling miscarriage of justice." The lawyer paused briefly, before continuing, "Those responsible for this cannot hide for ever. We know who you are and we will have justice. That is all."

Behind the wheel of his car, Gavin Sheehy's hands shook. Suddenly and without warning his stomach lurched and he yanked the door open just in time. He was still hanging awkwardly out of the car, dry heaving, as the Jaguar roared past. The rear windows were blackened, yet he felt the man's eyes burning hatred through the smoked glass.

PRESENT DAY
SUNDAY 25TH MARCH

Chapter 1

The body had been concealed well enough for it to remain unnoticed for at least a couple of days, Detective Chief Inspector Warren Jones decided, as he bent his six-foot frame under the branches of the flowering bush. Nevertheless, after a string of warm spring days the smell had finally attracted the attention of a middle-aged couple out for a post-Sunday lunch dog-walk.

The two witnesses were now busy giving their statements to Detective Inspector Tony Sutton on the other side of the line of blue-and-white crime-scene tape. Both walkers were wearing disposable plastic booties, their shoes impounded by the forensic team to check for any trace evidence they might have picked up and to distinguish their footprints from any that may have been left by the killer or killers.

"It looks as though he was initially stabbed over there on the footpath, then dragged through the grass and hidden here at the edge of the forest."

Crime Scene Manager Andy Harrison used a white-gloved hand to point out the red, bloody smear to the paper-suited detective. A similarly clad CSI squatting carefully amongst the long grass was filling a series of clear plastic evidence bags with bloodstained vegetation.

"And what about the dog? I'm assuming it's the victim's?" Warren gestured at the black-and-white furry form lying next to the old man.

"It's early days and we haven't moved either body yet, but I can't see any obvious stab wounds. We'll get a vet to perform an autopsy to work out how it was killed. The dog's still wearing its lead, but the victim isn't holding it. We had a look in the pockets of his windcheater but didn't find any doggy treats or other evidence that he was walking a dog, so I'm not yet prepared to declare him the owner. If it's been microchipped that could help us link them. Not to mention help you identify the victim if needs be."

"And you didn't see a wallet or phone or other ID?"

"Not unless he keeps them in his back pocket, which he's lying on. We haven't even found a set of house keys."

Warren stared at the body thoughtfully. "No wallet or phone suggests robbery, but why would they take his keys?"

The Yorkshireman shrugged, his protective clothing making a rustling noise. "Not really my place to say, Guv, but if he left the missus at home when he went out to walk the dog he may not have had them on him."

Warren conceded the point with a small nod of his head. "It's possible. But something doesn't seem quite right. He's an old man, shabbily dressed, not obviously wealthy and he had a dog—not your usual target for some opportunist mugger. And why conceal the body afterwards? If it was a case of 'stab first, ask nicely for his wallet after' then we're dealing with somebody pretty brutal here—especially if they did the dog as well. Would they have taken the trouble to conceal both bodies?

"And if it was a mugging gone wrong, I'd have expected them to flee the scene immediately, not risk exposure by taking the time to hide the victims."

"Like I said, not really my place to say."

Warren sighed. "You're right. I should stop speculating and wait for your findings."

Harrison picked up on the hint. "We'll probably finish processing the scene tonight and get the bodies removed before morning. I imagine the post-mortem will be tomorrow afternoon. I'll get you a preliminary report before close of play tomorrow."

Warren glanced at his watch—just after 6 p.m. He sighed and pulled his mobile phone out of his pocket. It was going to be a long night; he'd better phone his wife, Susan, and tell her he wasn't going to be back in time to go to the pub quiz. It looked as if he'd be sleeping in the spare room again tonight.

MONDAY 26TH MARCH

Chapter 2

The 8 a.m. briefing was full, the room crammed with most of Middlesbury CID's detectives. Standing next to the projector, Warren stifled a yawn and took a swig of his coffee before calling for quiet. Leaning against the wall, looking similarly worn out, was Tony Sutton. However, standing at the back, fiddling with his Blackberry, Detective Superintendent John Grayson was as shiny and well-groomed as always. If past form was anything to go by, he'd probably nip out to the barber and get a quick trim and tidy before the upcoming press conference.

The station's senior detective had appointed Warren lead investigator as usual—where possible Grayson tried to avoid doing any actual detective work, Warren had soon learnt—but he would of course be available to talk to the press at any time, skilfully taking any credit for the team's successes whilst cannily distancing himself from any failures.

This was largely fine by Warren, who hated being in front of the camera, but at times—usually when he'd had less than three hours' sleep—it did irritate him that his team's efforts seemed to be mostly laying the groundwork for his superior's next promotion and the securement of an increased final salary pension.

Warren clicked the handheld presenter and two photographs

appeared on the screen behind him. On the left was a greyish, blue-skinned headshot of the old man from the park, his snow-white shock of hair lying limp and greasy, a couple of days' stubble covering his chin. The skin had a slightly puffy appearance from the early stages of decomposition, the effect being to smooth out the lines and creases that would otherwise bear witness to this individual human's story.

On the right was a more vibrant picture of the deceased, taken the previous Christmas. In this image the man's face was a mass of deep wrinkles and smile lines, his skin tanned the dark bronze that comes from a life spent working outdoors. The picture had been cropped, but it was possible to make out decorations in the background. The big grin and slightly unfocused eyes painted a portrait of a happy man, enjoying the festive season with loved ones.

"Reginald Williamson, aged sixty-eight. Found dead, body concealed under a bush next to his dog, just off a path at sixteen-twenty hours yesterday afternoon by two members of the public walking their dog on the western edge of Middlesbury Common." Another click revealed an aerial photograph from Google Earth, annotated with the position of the body.

The common was situated on the edge of Middlesbury, abutting a small wooded area that served as a divider between the small market town and the adjacent farmland. Although the land was popular with dog-walkers, joggers and local kids, the area where Williamson had been dumped was in a secluded corner. It was inevitable that the body would be found sooner, rather than later; however, its concealment had probably gained the killer—or killers—at least a couple of days' head start.

"Preliminary cause of death is a stab wound to the chest. Cause of death for the dog is unknown. Initial analysis points to the victim being attacked on the pavement here—" Warren used the laser pointer to circumscribe an area of pavement on the photograph "—then dragged through tall grass into the edge of the woods and dumped out of sight under this bush."

Warren cycled through a series of photos of the crime scene, highlighting the bloody trail and the body's final resting place. "The victim's pockets were empty, suggesting robbery as a possible motive. A leather wallet with his fingerprints and cards but no cash, was found in a litter bin about eighty metres from the dumping spot. However, forensics have been unable to identify any other prints."

Warren paused. "It's early days, but something doesn't feel quite right. Our victim lived alone since his wife died three years ago yet we found no house or car keys on him. His niece, who reported him missing, went around to the house Sunday morning and found it locked. His car was still there, so the robbers didn't steal it. She went into the house and said that nothing was obviously missing.

"His mobile phone is also unaccounted for. His provider shows that the handset went dark at about twenty-thirty hours Thursday evening, although we don't have any other data from them yet. Either it's been destroyed or the battery was removed. His niece says it wasn't worth stealing though. It was an old Nokia brick that he'd owned for ever."

Detective Sergeant Hutchinson raised a hand at the back. "Does that tie in with the time of death?"

"We don't know yet. The PM is scheduled for this afternoon. They'll try and get an accurate time for us; at the moment we're operating on a time frame of about forty-eight hours. What we do know is that nobody had seen him since about 11 p.m. Wednesday night when he left his local—the Merchants' Arms. Apparently he was in the habit of taking his dog for a long walk most evenings, often up the common, then stopping in for a nightcap.

"Regulars didn't think anything of it when he didn't come in for his evening pint on the Thursday, but when he didn't show on Friday or Saturday either, a couple called his mobile but were diverted straight to voicemail. One of them bumped into his niece Sunday morning and mentioned it, so she took the spare key she keeps for emergencies and went around to see if he was all right. There were pints of milk on the doorstep and Friday's newspapers stuck in the letter box. That's when she started to worry and reported him missing."

Warren looked around the room. "I want you to all keep an open mind. Don't just assume it was a random mugging gone wrong—start canvassing his friends, family, neighbours. Let's see if he had any unusual visitors or mentioned anything that was worrying him. Dig into his background and look at his lifestyle.

"Meanwhile, let's see if we can scare up any witnesses. It's been a pleasant few days. There were bound to have been a few folks in and around the park in the hours before and after the murder. Did they see anyone or anything suspicious?"

As the meeting broke up Warren crossed over to Tony Sutton, who made a sour face before commenting. "It sounds as though your gut's asking the same thing mine is. 'Why would someone kill a retired gardener in a public place, then conceal the body and try to make it look like a mugging gone wrong?'"

Chapter 3

The first twenty-four hours of any murder investigation are crucial. Assuming the clock had started the moment the couple found the body, over sixteen hours had elapsed. Add to that the time that the body lay concealed, and several days had probably passed. It was now almost nine o'clock on a Monday morning and the world was awake and at work; Warren was hopeful that this would mean things would start moving faster. The killer—or killers—had a large head start on the team and they needed to start chipping away at that advantage.

A few preliminary interviews had been conducted the previous night as they'd tried to establish the victim's identity, but now a team from headquarters in Welwyn Garden City had joined them and the interviewing could start in earnest. The landlord of the Merchants' Arms had been shocked to hear of the death of one of his regulars and had furnished Tony Sutton with a comprehensive list of the locals who drank with Reggie, as he was known.

Whilst Sutton and DS Hutchinson organised interviews with the man's two dozen or so drinking partners, Warren and Detective Constable Karen Hardwick visited Reggie Williamson's grieving niece.

Tabitha Williamson was a young-looking thirty-something

who lived alone in a small flat only a few hundred metres from Hardwick's own apartment. A teaching assistant at the local primary school, the door of her fridge-freezer was covered in crudely hand-painted artwork, most with some variation on "Get Well Soon, Miss Williamson". Tabitha Williamson's pronounced limp and the crutches leaning against the kitchen table hinted at the cause of their concern. The diversity of spellings for "Williamson" brought a slight smile to Warren's lips as he and Hardwick waited patiently for Tabitha Williamson to finish fussing over the kettle and coffee pot.

Truth be told, the last thing Warren needed was more coffee and if her bloodshot eyes and shaking hands were anything to go by, Tabitha Williamson had consumed more than she should have as well. The old stereotype of the British, "Whatever the crisis, boil the kettle", was based on solid, empirical evidence in Warren's experience.

"Why don't you tell me about your relationship with Mr Williamson?" started Warren gently, when the three were finally seated around the cramped table.

"Please, call him Reggie. He hated formality of any sort; he was just a gardener, he always said."

"Of course. Tell us about Reggie."

"He was my dad's big brother. The two of them were best friends, although you'd never have known they were related." She smiled sadly. "I didn't get my red hair from my mother's side.

"Anyway, Dad taught French at a secondary school in Cambridge and Mum used to be a special needs teacher at the same school, but Uncle Reggie always preferred to work outside and he used to be a landscape gardener until he retired a few years ago to look after Aunty Una, when she got too ill to care for herself.

"He refused to let her go into a home and he ended up as her full-time carer until she passed away about three years ago."

"Were you and Mr… sorry, Reggie, close?"

She nodded, her eyes filling with tears again. "Uncle Reggie and Aunty Una never had kids of their own and I was an only child." She laughed quietly. "I was so spoilt! Two sets of parents doing my every bidding!

"Anyway, Mum and Dad died when I was at college. A car accident in France…" Her voice broke off and she took a fortifying gulp of coffee. "I'm sorry." She placed the mug down with a thump, her hands shaking.

Warren and Hardwick waited patiently until she regained control.

"I guess I'm lucky really. Nobody could ever replace Mum and Dad but Uncle Reggie and Aunty Una did their best. Anyway, Uncle Reggie had a job with the council as their senior gardener and landscaper, but about six or seven years ago Aunty Una started getting forgetful. They tried to shrug it off at first—people always do, don't they?—but pretty soon she was losing her keys, getting on the wrong bus and leaving the gas on.

"One afternoon we got a call from the police, who said that she had been found distressed outside their old house, wanting to know why she could see strangers through the living room windows and why her keys wouldn't work in the front door. They hadn't lived there for nearly thirty years.

"Anyway, pretty soon she wasn't really safe to leave on her own—she had always been a fit woman who loved to go for long walks and you never knew where she'd end up—so he gave up full-time work for the council and took his pension early. He used to do a bit of handyman work and the odd gardening job when he could find someone to sit with her for a few hours, but in the end even that was too much.

"I finally persuaded him to consider moving her into a care home and we were in the process of choosing one when she died suddenly in her sleep."

She drained her coffee and sighed deeply. "It was a mercy, I suppose. We were all very upset of course, but I think in the end we were mostly relieved."

"That was three years ago. What did do Reggie afterwards?" asked Karen Hardwick.

"He went back to gardening. Aside from Aunty Una it was his true love. I was a bit worried at first about how he'd cope, but he told me one day that he'd been grieving the loss of his wife for years before she died and she wouldn't want to see him moping around. Anyway, he didn't go back to work full-time—he said he was too old for that—but he has a few regulars in the local area and he does a couple of days most weeks.

"He missed her terribly of course, but he was generally pretty happy." She turned to Warren and her tone became pleading. "Why would anyone kill him? He was a lovely man. Nobody had a bad word for him."

"We don't know yet. That's what we hope to find out." He paused delicately. "Do you have a list of his clients? What about friends and family who didn't drink with him down the Merchants' Arms?"

"I don't know all of his clients, but he was pretty scrupulous about his accounts. I imagine he has a list somewhere. As to his friends, I'm not really sure. He's lived here pretty much all of his life and most of his friends are regulars at the pub. I suppose he may have kept in touch with people he worked with at the council, but when he was self-employed he worked alone."

"What about family?"

"Nobody close. My dad was his only immediate family and

like I said he didn't have any kids of his own. We have a few other aunts and uncles that we see at Christmas and New Year, but we don't really keep in touch." The tears were back. "He was all I had."

The young woman put her head in her hands, mumbling apologies as her shoulders shook.

Warren glanced at Karen Hardwick, who got up and placed an arm around the distraught woman's shoulders.

"Do you have anyone we can call? A friend perhaps, a partner maybe?"

She shook her head and laughed bitterly. "No boyfriend if that's what you're asking. That boat sailed long ago and Uncle Reggie would never forgive me if I called him up. I don't even have a cat." She suddenly looked up. "What about Smiths? Has anyone fed her?"

"Smiths?"

"Uncle Reggie's Border collie. He always calls his dogs after his favourite pint at the time they were born. Unfortunately, she was a bitch and he couldn't really call her John, could he?"

Warren shifted uncomfortably. Clearly nobody had told her the full story of how her uncle had been found. "I'm very sorry, but Reggie was found with the body of a dog. It looks as though he was walking it when he was attacked."

It's funny how it's sometimes the smaller things that are the trigger. Tabitha Williamson let out a low moan, before slumping forward. This time there were no apologies for her perceived weakness as the tears finally flowed freely, sobs shaking her slight frame.

It was several minutes before the young woman was able to regain control long enough to select the number of a girlfriend from her phone's contacts and pass it over to Karen Hardwick to arrange for her to come over.

Whilst they waited, Warren boiled the kettle again. He didn't want to leave the young woman alone until he was certain that somebody else could take over. However, on the face of it, handholding wasn't really the best use of a senior detective's time. Fortunately, he still had more questions he wanted to ask.

"Tell me about this boyfriend," he said once the coffee had started to perform its magic.

She snorted. "Not one of my better decisions. I should have ended it long before I did—God knows Uncle Reggie didn't mince his words." She stared into space. "What can I say? I was in love—or at least I thought I was. I know now, looking back on it, I was just afraid of being alone." She smiled tightly. "It's a funny birthday, thirty—makes you think about life and the future."

The speech was smooth, well-thought-out; no doubt the relationship had been dissected thoroughly in the past few months, probably in this very kitchen with the help of friends and wine.

"So Reggie didn't like him? Why?"

"No big mystery. He was a bit of an arsehole." She shrugged. "We met in a club in town about two years ago. It was lust at first sight as they say." She sighed. "Dark hair, Spanish, looked great in a tight T-shirt. He even had the right sort of name: 'Mateo Menendez'— what can I say?" She looked over at Karen Hardwick who smiled sympathetically.

"Anyway, it was your classic whirlwind romance. Expensive meals, presents, weekends away; I thought I'd really found the one. I guess I should have listened to Uncle Reggie."

"He didn't approve?"

She shook her head. "No. It wasn't that he didn't want to see me happy—quite the opposite—but he didn't trust him. Said he was too flashy. I just assumed that he was being over-protective."

"What went wrong?"

"Uncle Reggie was right. He was too flashy. All style and no substance—or as Reggie put it in the end, 'all flash and no cash.'"

"He took advantage?" Warren could see where this was leading.

She nodded. "After about six months, he said that the lease was up on his flat and so he moved in here. The funny thing was, although he was no longer paying rent on his own place he never really contributed here. When I brought it up, he offered to pay the bills, you know, gas, electricity, council tax and all of that. It was probably about equivalent to half the rent, so I agreed.

"Everything seemed fine for about six months until one day the broadband stopped working. Mateo said he'd deal with it, but a few weeks later it went off again. It was the school holidays and I was at home during the day whilst Mateo was out. I picked up the post. There was a red demand from TalkTalk and another from the electricity company.

"I asked Mateo about it again and he said it was a bank error." She shook her head. "I actually took him at his word; can you believe that?"

"He wasn't paying the bills?"

"Oh, it was worse than that. When he did pay off a bill, he was using one of those payday loans companies—you know those loan sharks that lend you money, no questions asked, then charge you thousands of per cent interest? Want to guess whose name was on the account? And of course, I hadn't been making the minimum payments because I didn't know about it. When the bailiffs turned up I had to use pretty much my entire life savings to stop them repossessing the flat and everything in it."

Her grief had turned to a palpable anger. "It's not just the money; it's the stain on my record. My credit file is an absolute mess; nine months on and I'm still writing letters every week trying to sort it all out."

"Where is this Mateo now?"

"The bastard is back with the mother of his two kids—two kids I knew nothing about. It turns out that when I thought he was out at work, he was around there playing happy families, trying to get back with her." Her voice quietened. "I don't know if I should be angry with her or sorry for her. I'm sure he's fleecing her just like he did me."

"And Reggie knew about this?"

"Yes, he helped me move all of Mateo's belongings out. In fact, it was his idea to give all of the stuff to the bailiffs when they turned up." She smiled grimly. "A small victory I suppose, but you take them where you can."

It was another ten minutes before Tabitha Williamson's best friend arrived and Warren and Hardwick were able to make their excuses and leave.

"Well, at least we have one name for the whiteboard," Karen Hardwick said as they left the flat and headed back to the car.

Warren was thoughtful. "Maybe. The question is: if this Mateo Menendez was the killer, what made him snap nine months after he split up with Reggie Williamson's niece?"

Chapter 4

Mateo Menendez was much the way that Tabitha Williamson had described him—dark, tightly built and rather too flash for Warren's taste. Despite his supposed Spanish upbringing, he spoke with a local accent. What she hadn't mentioned was how small his head was. It was all that Warren could do not to stare openly at him. Karen Hardwick fussed with the tape recorder, studiously not looking his way.

Warren knew that the science of phrenology—the diagnosing of a person's intelligence by the shape of their skull—had long since been discredited. Similarly, within reason a person's hat size had no bearing on their intelligence. Still, Warren found himself wondering how a full-size human brain could fit inside such a small skull. Up close the man's mass of tight, black, curly hair did little to hide it.

"Do you know this man?" Warren slid a recent photograph of Reggie Williamson across the desk. Tabitha Williamson had described an arrogant man, self-assured and full of self-confidence. True to form, he'd declined a solicitor for the interview, claiming he had nothing to hide. Therefore, Warren had decided against arresting the man. He would do so if he was unsatisfied with the man's answers, but until now Menendez was merely helping with inquiries. Just as importantly, the twenty-four-hour time limit for charging a suspect didn't start until he was formally arrested and read his rights.

Menendez barely glanced at the photograph. "Sure, Reggie Williamson. I dated his niece for a while." The answer was smooth, unhurried. Warren's hope that he might catch the man out in an easy lie had yet to bear fruit.

"And would you say that you and Mr Williamson had a good relationship? How did he react when you and his niece broke up?"

Menendez shrugged. "Reggie's a nice enough bloke. He wasn't very happy when Tabby and I split up, but that's to be expected, I suppose."

Assuming that Tabitha Williamson was to be believed, that was a significant understatement of how Reggie Williamson had felt about Menendez. However, it wasn't an overt lie. The jury was still out on the man's honesty.

"Can you tell us why you and Ms Williamson split up?"

For the first time, Menendez's cocky façade cracked. "Is this about Tabby? Is she OK? Has something happened to her?"

Warren ignored Menendez's question and repeated his own.

"We weren't getting along for a while. I got back with the mother of my kids—we decided to make a go of it again."

Again, something of a deviation from Tabitha Williamson's version of events, but he wasn't really lying, just downplaying some of the more unpleasant details to show himself in a better light—hardly an indication of guilt.

Warren decided to change tack.

"Tell me, what state were your finances in when you left Ms Williamson?"

"I don't see that's any of your business, Detective."

"No, you're right. I apologise." Warren smiled briefly. "What

28

I meant was, are you employed at the moment or were you back when you dated Ms Williamson?"

"I'm unemployed at the moment; I've been out of full-time work for about two and a half years. I'm signed up to an employment agency, but there's bugger all around here. I work when I can."

Still no obvious lies.

"Did Ms Williamson know about this when you started dating?"

Menendez licked his lips. "Sure, I guess so. We never really spoke about it."

"Seems strange that you dated all of that time and it never came up in conversation."

Menendez squirmed slightly. "Well, we had a very passionate relationship." He turned his gaze on Hardwick and smiled, showing a suspiciously white set of teeth. "You know how it is, everything's exciting and you're in love. You don't talk about the little details."

"Like paying the bills or taking out payday loans in somebody else's name?"

Menendez returned his attention to Warren. "Is that what this is all about? We had an agreement and now she's trying to claim that I set it all up in her name without her consent." His voice dropped. "I feel really bad about hurting her." He turned his attention back to Hardwick. "I loved her and didn't want to upset her, but I also love my kids and when I got a chance to become a part of their lives again, well, I had to take it. I'm sure you can understand."

"No, not really." Hardwick's tone was unyielding.

Menendez turned his attention back to Warren, giving up on Hardwick for the time being. "Look, we were short of cash at the end of the month. The bills were all in my name, so when we arranged the loan, we transferred it directly into my account so that it could be paid out immediately, rather than having to wait for Tabby to transfer it from her account."

"So why didn't you just arrange the loan in your name?"

He snorted. "I'm unemployed. Even payday loan companies have some standards."

Warren doubted that the man's story would stand up to serious scrutiny. He was sure that there would be a voice recording somewhere with Menendez's voice making all of the arrangements. It was interesting how a male caller had managed to set up the deal on behalf of a female client. However, that wasn't what he and Hardwick were here for.

"Tell me, Mateo. Where were you Thursday evening?"

The man thought for a moment. "I took the kids out to Maccy D's then they played in the park until it got dark, then we went home. Candy—that's my girlfriend, Candice—was out doing her Zumba class, so I put the kids to bed and watched TV."

"Which park was that?"

"The kiddie play park up on the common."

"And can either of the children vouch for your whereabouts?"

Menendez stared at him. "Tyson is three and a half. He can just about string a sentence together. Jayden is two. She still sleeps in nappies. What do you think they're going to tell you?"

Despite the man's protestations, Warren felt a slight thrill. Menendez had been on Middlesbury Common on the night that Reggie Williamson had been killed and so far had no alibi.

* * *

Questioning of Reggie Williamson's drinking partners had revealed nothing of interest. He and Smiths had been regulars at the Merchants' Arms for as long as anyone could remember, popping by most nights for a pint after a brisk walk. Few people like to speak ill of the dead, but it truly seemed nobody had a bad word to say about Reggie. Sociable, but not too loud; generous enough to get his round in and pop a quid in the charity box, but not flashy; willing to chat about current events and engage in a bit of bar-room philosophy, but with fairly mainstream views and not too opinionated. A useful darts player who'd won more than his fair share of pub quizzes, he was usually gracious enough to share his winnings—a round of drinks—with the runners-up.

A few of the regulars had known him as he'd nursed his wife, when his trips to the pub had dwindled to once week. When she finally passed away, everyone had given a few pounds to Alzheimer's Research in her memory, at his request. Since then there had been nobody special that anybody knew of.

His conversation and demeanour in the past few weeks had been apparently unchanged. The only source of concern he'd mentioned was Smiths' advancing years—she'd been slowing down lately and had a couple of accidents.

"All in all, a pretty normal bloke who it seemed got on with his life and didn't rub people up the wrong way," summarised Tony Sutton.

"Thanks, Tony. Pete, what have you got for us?" Detective Sergeant Kent was the unit's resident expert on the use of the various databases that the force had access to. A squat man in his mid-fifties with thinning hair that was more than compensated for by a full beard, he was edging close to retirement and had been helping train Detective Constable Gary Hastings in recent months. He was the officer in charge of coordinating information that came into the major incident desk that he'd help set up the previous night.

"Not a lot. He was basically unknown to us. Our only contact was a naughty drivers' course after being flashed by a speed camera on Hills Road in Cambridge—but then haven't we all had that?" There were a few smiles, some sheepish, around the room. The stretch of road alongside Homerton College and the sixth form was notorious for its rigorously enforced thirty miles per hour limit—a necessary precaution given the number of darkly dressed, drink-addled student cyclists without lights wobbling up the road at all hours.

"I contacted the council who confirmed that he worked for them for many years until taking early retirement to care for his wife, when he drew a reduced pension. A fair few in the Estates department remembered him and they've given us a list of people he worked with regularly.

"On a similar note, forensics are still searching his house. Nothing of interest yet, but they have found the box file that he used to keep track of his part-time gardening jobs. Documents analysis are going through it and compiling a list of customer contacts."

"Good, pass them on to Tony when you have them to set up interviews. Anything else?"

"The remainder of the mobile phone data from the cell dump is being collated as we speak, but there's not a lot we can do with it until we get a more precise time of death. Those cell towers serve hundreds of houses each. We're looking at over a million individual network access requests for the twenty-four hours between Thursday afternoon and Friday alone. Bloody smartphones, pinging Twitter every ten seconds to check if Beyoncé's changed her hair."

Warren thanked him quickly, knowing that if he didn't cut him off now they could be in for a lengthy grumble about the frivolous use of modern technology and its impact on modern policing.

So far nothing. Were they looking at a random stabbing after all? Warren hoped not. With no extrinsic motive or apparent link to the victim, such a killer would be hard to find. The explanation gnawed at him, however. The careful hiding of the body and the fact that no witnesses had come forward suggested that if the killer was mentally disturbed, they were still in possession of at least some of their faculties. It seemed a fair degree of planning and forethought had gone into the attack.

They needed a motive.

"Then it looks as if our best bet so far is Mateo Menendez—an unemployed love rat and small-time fraudster who did the dirty on Reggie Williamson's niece, Tabitha, and saddled her with large debts before going back to the mother of his two kids. A real charmer." He smiled slightly. "He made quite an impression on DC Hardwick."

"Not a good one. I need a shower."

"Any reason to suspect him, other than possible conflict with her uncle?" asked DS Hutchinson after the chuckles had died down.

"By his own admission, he was with the kids up the common Thursday afternoon. Unfortunately, he claims to have gone home when it got dark, which is a good hour before Reggie Williamson's mobile phone lost contact with the network. He says he was in McDonald's before he went to the park, feeding his two toddlers something appropriately healthy and nutritious. We're waiting for the restaurant's CCTV footage to see if he was there when he said he was."

"Where is he now?" asked DS Margaret Richardson, a mother of two, her expression clearly conveying what she thought of Menendez's dietary choices for his young offspring.

"Downstairs. I'm going to bail him for further questioning. He's cooperating so we haven't arrested him yet and he still hasn't asked for a lawyer, despite being advised of his rights. Either he's as arrogant as Tabitha Williamson says, he's incredibly naïve or he's innocent. Maybe all three. As soon as we get a time of death, we'll start picking away at his alibi."

* * *

A cause and time of death became available late that evening. Professor Ryan Jordan was one of a number of Home Office Certified Pathologists used by Beds and Herts Major Crime Unit and Warren was pleased to see that he'd picked up the case. Not only was the middle-aged American highly competent and easy to work with, he didn't insist on holding meetings in the morgue.

It wasn't that Warren was particularly squeamish—he wouldn't have been staring at the A4 colour photographs spread across his desk otherwise, he told himself—however, he'd rarely seen the need to see the victim's dissected remains up close and personal. He'd much rather have high-resolution photographs, pre-interpreted by experts far more qualified than he.

"The cause of death was fairly straightforward—single stab wound to the heart. Dead before he hit the ground. There would have been lots of blood, so the attacker's clothes would have been soaked, although the heart will have stopped pumping pretty much instantly so once he dropped there shouldn't have been a huge puddle."

Warren remembered the blood smears on the grass and the relatively small patch on the tarmac pathway. "Given the lack of blood spatter on the path away from the pool where we think he fell, would that be consistent with his attacker standing in front of him?"

"I'd say so. If he'd been attacked from behind—" Jordan mimed a stabbing action towards his own body "—he'd have sprayed at

34

least some blood forward, leaving marks on the sidewalk. It looks as though his killer caught the brunt of it."

Warren made a note on his pad. A search was already underway to comb bins and possible hiding places for discarded garments. There might also be spots of blood leading away from the scene of the attack. There hadn't been any rain and so they might still be visible. He made a note to request a fingertip search to find any such trace.

Assuming they found a suspect, perhaps they had been seen trying to clean clothes or dispose of rubbish unexpectedly.

"What about defensive marks?"

"None that we can find."

"So his killer took him by surprise. Do we have any information about the murder weapon?"

"From the size of the laceration, we're talking about something sharp with a five-to-six-inch blade. Not too wide, but pointed. No serrations. We've not found any traces of rust in the wound and, unfortunately, the nature of the attack means that it missed any bones or ribs, so there aren't any metal fragments that would allow us to identify the knife more precisely." Jordan shrugged. "I suspect that we're looking at a run-of-the-mill stainless steel kitchen knife, unused, or at least well cleaned before the attack. Assuming there was any premeditation, it may have been bought anywhere from a supermarket chain to a hardware store. Find me the weapon and I might be able tell you more, but until then I'm speculating."

Warren sighed. They'd found the victim's wallet, but nothing else. "So it could still be a bog-standard mugging gone wrong?"

Jordan shook his head. "I'm not so sure." He picked up the folder that he'd brought the photographs in. "Leaving aside all the inconsistencies, the precision of the killing worries me—a single stab wound to the heart. It's very clean. Straight into the diaphragm, missing the sternum and ribs, but angled upward directly into the heart. Ordinarily, I'd be happy to dismiss that as good luck. But there's also the dog."

"How was it killed? I didn't see any blood."

Jordan pulled out another sheet of paper. "According to the vet, its neck was broken. A shattered jaw suggests a single kick, snapping its head back with such force the cervical vertebrae were fractured."

Warren felt a chill go down his back. "What are you suggesting, Professor?"

"A perfectly targeted, instantly fatal single stab wound to the heart with no opportunity for the victim to defend himself and a precisely killed dog, both concealed quickly with little trace evidence left behind—I think we're dealing with a trained killer."

TUESDAY 27TH MARCH

Chapter 5

Warren was back at his desk well before 7 a.m. on Tuesday morning. The proverbial ticking of the clock had weighed heavily on his mind the previous night, resulting in broken and restless sleep. By late afternoon Menendez had been getting impatient and making noises about getting a lawyer so Warren had authorised his release, knowing that if Menendez was innocent, the suspect column would soon be empty. Before he left, Warren broke the news of Reggie Williamson's murder to him. The man's look of incredulity, then horror as he realised that he had been a suspect, strengthened Warren's suspicion that he was not who he was looking for. Regardless, he had been unable to resist one last dig at the man who had caused Tabitha Williamson so much misery and was probably fleecing the hapless Candice even now.

"I have my eye on you, Menendez. If your name comes across my desk in future, I'll remember. And I'll be happy to pass on the details of anyone else you've been ripping off."

It was an empty threat. Low-level identity theft and fraud never came anywhere near Warren's desk—but Menendez didn't know that. He'd looked suitably shaken as he left.

It was a small victory, but at the moment, Warren was taking them where he could.

By 6 a.m., Warren had finally given up on sleep and slipped out early, taking care not to wake Susan.

Professor Jordan had calculated a preliminary time of death roughly sixty to seventy hours before the body was found, which, allowing for the weekend's clock change, made it between about eight o'clock on the Thursday evening and four o'clock on the Friday morning. The range fitted with Williamson's mobile phone leaving the network at eight-thirty on the Thursday.

It had got dark at approximately six-fifteen that evening, which if Menendez was to be believed was the time at which he had left the park and returned home. Candice, his partner, had returned from her Zumba class just after nine-thirty and confirmed that Menendez had been sprawled across the sofa watching TV.

Warren had passed on the details of Menendez's mobile phone to the team working their way through the cell dump and was waiting to see if it would confirm his movements. Fortunately, the man was an avid social networker and his phone regularly connected itself to the network to look for new content. The team had already confirmed that the common and the flat Menendez shared with his partner were far enough apart for the phone to use different cell towers at the different locations.

The search of the common by the forensic team had not found any more clues within a two-hundred-metre radius of the body's dumping spot, and DSI Grayson had authorised the cost of emptying all of the bins within a kilometre radius. It was almost a certainty that the killer would have had to dispose of heavily bloodied clothes and possibly even the murder weapon. Unless he'd covered himself up, he was unlikely to have walked too far before doing so; even in the dark, the chances of being seen would have been too great for any sane person to have risked it, Warren decided. Warren just hoped that the killer was at least partly sane. Otherwise all bets were off.

He sighed and ran his hand through his hair. It was getting long; it probably needed a cut. Too late for that now. The press conference was scheduled for the late morning. Grayson, as usual, had mysteriously disappeared the previous afternoon and Warren was willing to bet good money that he'd be immaculately groomed for the cameras later.

There had been little to report overnight and he didn't expect anything until after the morning briefing, so Warren poured himself another coffee and settled down to do some paperwork. He chafed at the forced inaction but took solace in the fact that if he could shrink his inbox to a more manageable size now, he would be able to focus more clearly on the days and weeks ahead. That was the theory at least.

DSI Grayson still hadn't appeared by the time that Warren needed to leave Middlesbury to travel down to Welwyn Garden City for the press conference and Grayson's mobile was going straight to voicemail. This suited Warren fine, as he could drive himself down to the County's Headquarters. The cost of petrol was well worth it to avoid the terror of the high-speed jaunt down the A1 that Grayson favoured. The superintendent had the unsettling habit of finding the most reckless drivers in the pool, authorising use of blues and twos, then settling back and calmly playing with his Blackberry, whilst Warren—not a happy passenger at the best of times—would find himself stamping on an imaginary brake pedal all the way.

Tabitha Williamson and Karen Hardwick were waiting for him when he arrived. The young DC had insisted on driving around to pick Tabitha up, despite technically being off duty.

Grayson was apparently somewhere in the building in a meeting.

Warren knew nothing about it, which suggested it was unlikely to be connected to the day-to-day workings of Middlesbury CID. Laying the groundwork for that next promotion, Warren thought sourly, before mentally pinching himself for his uncharitable thoughts—the meeting could be about anything from budget setting to a statistical analysis of their latest performance figures. If that was the case, Grayson was welcome to it.

Tabitha Williamson was nervous and pale, but nonetheless adamant that she wanted to make an appeal for information. The Force's press officer therefore took her away to familiarise her with the set-up of the briefing room and explain to her what to expect. Karen Hardwick went with her.

"She's turning into a fine young officer, that Karen Hardwick." Grayson had pulled his uncanny trick of managing to appear, ghost-like and without Warren noticing. He was glad that the unit's commander had noticed her.

"She is. She's got good instincts. Having said that, she's doing the role of a family liaison officer, which isn't her job. I know Reggie Williamson wasn't Tabitha Williamson's father and he didn't bring her up, but she's pretty vulnerable. Any chance that we can get an FLO authorised to support her?"

Grayson pursed his lips; the money didn't come out of Middlesbury CID's budget, but it had to come from somewhere and Grayson was the one who'd have to ask for it.

"I'll look into it." No sort of answer really, but at least it wasn't a flat no.

By the time the press arrived, Tabitha Williamson had been prepared as much as possible and they took their seats. Warren had a feeling that information from the public could be what would turn the case and so they needed to make the story as newsworthy as possible. The inclusion of a photograph of Smiths and images of the grieving Tabitha Williamson would hopefully gain the story a few more column inches in the newspapers and a few more seconds on the local news.

They needed all the help they could get; Warren couldn't help comparing the half-filled room of bored journalists in front of him, waiting to hear about the death of a retired gardener in his sixties, to the packed and jostling crowd that had demanded information about the pretty, young, blonde women who had started disappearing before Christmas.

The press conference was over in time for the early evening news bulletins and first editions of the next day's papers and, finally, Warren was free to return to CID. It was hardly worth it. A cursory read of his team's summaries of the interviews conducted with Reggie Williamson's former acquaintances revealed nothing of any interest. The office was depressingly quiet. He stifled a yawn and glanced at his watch; the local news was due to start in twenty minutes or so. Time to go home, he decided, fighting down a brief twinge of guilt. His team had his number if anything important turned up and there was no point sitting there twiddling his thumbs. Perhaps he'd be able to sleep a bit better this evening? Turning off his computer and grabbing his jacket, Warren felt a familiar sensation of frustration. Day three of the investigation was nearly over and almost nothing was happening. Not a good sign. *Let's hope for something from the public appeal*, he prayed as he turned his office light off.

* * *

Despite his best intentions, Warren had been unable to resist accessing his email, reading the various reports as they entered his inbox and before he knew it, it was late again. He rubbed his eyes. They were at the slightly stinging stage. From experience he knew that the next stage was grittiness, then bloodshot eyes, then blurred vision. He had a suspicion that this would be one of those times. On the way home, he'd stopped off at the garage and bought some paracetamol. Headaches were almost guaranteed over the next few weeks and he wanted to be prepared. What a job. At least he could look forward to a quiet time at home—or at least that's what he'd expected.

"Mum and Dad are coming down for a few days, at the end of the Easter holidays to celebrate their wedding anniversary," Susan had announced as they prepared for bed. "They're going to spend a few days with us before spending some time with Felicity."

Warren had managed not to groan out loud, but his expression had given him away. Susan had pouted—she found her domineering mother to be as hard work as Warren did, but that didn't mean he was allowed to criticise her.

"Sorry sweetheart, it's just bad timing. I'd hate for this thing to get in the way of the celebrations."

Susan had been somewhat mollified, but she had done the sums the same as Warren; the school Easter holidays started at the end of the week, with the long weekend a week later.

"Is this going to be a big one, do you think?" she'd asked after the press conference had been aired on *Look East* earlier that evening.

Warren had only been able to nod. His gut was telling him that it was going to be a protracted investigation. The lack of progress so far had deflated him somewhat. Their plans for the Easter vacation would be on hold; at least they hadn't booked to go away anywhere.

Susan had picked up on his mood. "You looked handsome

tonight—I can't understand why they don't give you more screen time," she'd teased lightly.

"I can never compete with a Border collie, you know that."

Just as he'd predicted, Smiths had received almost as much screen time as Reggie Williamson—more if you counted the fact that she was also in the photograph of Reggie. Still, if it jogged a few more memories or made a few more people look in their bins or gardens for discarded items of bloodied clothing, Reggie Williamson's mobile phone or the murder weapon then it had done its job. As usual, Warren had found himself relegated to the background, behind John Grayson, who was resplendent in a freshly starched dress uniform. That suited him fine, he mused as he lay back on the pillow, willing sleep to take him.

WEDNESDAY 28ᵀᴴ MARCH

Chapter 6

The third dawn briefing since the discovery of Reggie Williamson's body was a low-key affair. If, as they believed, he had been killed Thursday evening it was coming up on six days since his murder. Aside from the increasingly unlikely Mateo Menendez, there were still no suspects. CCTV from McDonald's had shown Menendez with his two young children tucking into their fast food at about 4 p.m., verifying that part of his story. The confirmation said nothing about his whereabouts at the critical time surrounding the murder, but catching him out in a lie at this stage would have made Warren immediately suspicious.

The search area had been widened; they still hadn't found his mobile phone or the murder weapon. Teams of uniformed officers were still knocking on doors, but nobody seemed to remember anything. As always, the press conference had generated a flurry of calls which were being sifted through, but aside from a confession, nothing of immediate note had been offered.

As for the admission of guilt, the call taker had wryly noted that it had been logged alongside the caller's previous claims. If the more "eccentric" members of the community ever thought to use a different phone, then the call taker's job would be more difficult, since they'd be forced to actually investigate the call rather than simply cross-referencing the caller ID against the "Loony List".

As Warren left the briefing room, Tony Sutton came alongside him.

"Can I have a private word?"

The older man looked tired; in his left hand he carried a white envelope.

Warren motioned him into his office and sat down behind his desk. Sutton took the visitor's chair directly opposite. The man's hands were trembling slightly.

"Sounds serious," Warren offered after a few seconds of uncomfortable silence.

"This arrived in the post this morning."

Sutton pushed the envelope across the table. Now face up, the scales of justice logo of the Crown Prosecution Service was clearly visible. Warren slipped out the single sheet of A4 typed paper and read the contents quickly. It was a summons ordering Sutton to appear as a witness for the prosecution in the trial of Detective Chief Inspector Gavin Sheehy on charges of corruption and misconduct in a public office.

"Damn. We always knew it was a possibility. What do you think they want with you?"

Sutton took a deep breath. "They're going to hang him out to dry, make an example of him. Rumour has it they want me to testify that in the months leading up to his arrest he was secretive and non-communicative. That he received phone calls at odd times and kept on disappearing."

Warren sat back and eyed the detective inspector with concern. He knew how much his predecessor—Sutton's mentor—had meant to him. Warren had never met the man; rather, he had been parachuted in, newly promoted, the previous summer after DCI Sheehy had been arrested and removed from his post.

The arrest had come as a massive shock to the small, close-knit CID unit operating out of Middlesbury police station. Sheehy's friend and subordinate Tony Sutton had been arrested also, before being released without charge after a brief investigation. Sutton had felt betrayed and hurt after the man he admired so greatly—who had in fact persuaded him to apply to join CID years before—had been accused of corruption.

The repercussions from Sheehy's arrest cut deep, Warren soon found out after his arrival, threatening the very existence of the unit he had headed.

Middlesbury CID was something of an anomaly. Some years previously, the police forces of Hertfordshire and the adjacent county, Bedfordshire, had decided to pool their resources and formed a new, single Major Crime Unit, operating out of Welwyn Garden City. Faced with the closure of what he believed to be a unique and essential service in the very north of the county, DCI Gavin Sheehy had successfully fought against the closure of the small, but effective CID unit housed at Middlesbury police station. The result had been a highly focused, local team able to respond rapidly to major crimes in Middlesbury and the many little villages that surrounded the area.

With its extensive local knowledge and close ties to the community, the squad proved highly effective in reducing and solving crime. Nevertheless, it was expensive and Sheehy's uncompromising style had won him many enemies—enemies who were now circling, using Sheehy's recent disgrace as evidence that the team should be disbanded and absorbed into the main major crime unit. The result was that the unit was effectively "on probation", having to prove its worth. Detective Superintendent John Grayson was assigned to oversee the unit. If his job was to be impartial about the role of the unit, then he was a good choice—nobody could divine if he was in favour or against the continued existence of the team. Many suspected that the survival of the unit was linked directly to Grayson's perception of its usefulness to his own career goals.

None of this had been explained to Warren of course, who had been promoted to DCI the previous summer, moving from the West Midlands Police to fill the role vacated by Sheehy. It had been presented as a golden opportunity to gain command experience for the ambitious young officer; he had been ill-prepared for the maelstrom of local politics that awaited him upon his arrival.

Tony Sutton, smarting from the betrayal by Sheehy and the humiliation of his own, brief arrest, had been suspicious of Warren, assuming that he was there to covertly make recommendations about the future of the unit. The two men had butted heads over Warren's management of his first major crime, resulting in an explosive encounter between them. Since then, the two officers had grown to respect and like one another and, to his surprise, Warren had found himself warming to his new command and was starting to regard it as more than just a stepping stone to bigger things.

"So the court case starts next month? How do you feel about it?"

Sutton sighed. "I'm torn. The bastard deserves to go down—but I still can't quite believe it."

"What do you think they'll ask you about? The investigation cleared you of any involvement."

"Yeah, but it's still going to look bad for me. I was his friend and his immediate subordinate—people are going to question why I didn't suspect anything. You know how mud sticks—people will think either I was in on it or I'm a fool."

Sutton shook his head. "Maybe I was. I didn't spot the signs—or rather I chose to ignore them. The sudden phone calls, the unexplained absences…" He snorted derisively. "I thought he was having a bloody affair." He shrugged. "I didn't approve, but then who am I to lecture?"

Warren nodded in sympathy. Sutton was right. He had a chequered history when it came to extra-marital affairs. His first marriage had imploded after Sutton had indulged in a drunken one-night stand. Years later he was still rebuilding the pieces of that relationship and Warren knew that he felt ashamed and guilty, even as he and his former wife forged new relationships and cooperated to bring up their teenage son.

"Well, Tony, you know that you have my support."

Sutton nodded. "Thanks, Boss. I guess I'll just have to tell the truth, answer their questions and let the cards fall where they may."

* * *

His conversation with Tony Sutton had left Warren feeling downbeat. As much to clear his head and stretch his legs as to fulfil his caffeine and sugar needs, Warren decided to treat himself to a decent coffee and Danish pastry from the canteen, rather than simply adding another fifty-pence piece to the honesty jar next to the communal coffee urn. At last count, there had been twelve pounds fifty in the jar—all of it Warren's.

There was a copy of the Middlesbury edition of the *Cambridge News* lying on a table. Reggie Williamson's picture—the one with Smiths naturally—took up over half of the front page, along with a suitably lurid headline. The story was continued on page three, where another picture—this one a long-lens shot of white-suited CSIs working the scene up on the common—dominated.

The story was essentially a report of the press conference, along with a few tributes from various drinkers in the Merchants' Arms.

The shrill ringing of Warren's mobile phone made him jump.

"It's Tony, Boss. Where are you?" The DI's voice was excited, with no hint of the depression he had been exhibiting barely minutes ago.

"Downstairs in the canteen." Warren felt a thrill go through him; he hadn't been away from his desk for five minutes. Sutton wouldn't have called him on his mobile unless it was extremely urgent.

"It looks like we were too hasty releasing Mateo Menendez yesterday."

* * *

Mateo Menendez was extremely unhappy about being picked up for a second time. This time he refused to come voluntarily and Warren was given no choice but to serve the arrest warrant that Grayson had signed. He immediately requested a lawyer.

By the time a police solicitor had been arranged, a search of the flat that Menendez shared with his partner and their two young children was well underway and the life and background of the Spanish national was under the spotlight, with records requested from Spanish sources as well as UK authorities. His girlfriend was currently being questioned and specialist officers were assessing whether the older of the two children, three-and-a-half-year-old Tyson, would be any use as a witness.

The paper-suited man in front of Warren and Sutton was a lot less confident now. His clothes had been collected for evidence and his mobile phone, which had been so helpful up to this point, had now been formally confiscated and was undergoing rigorous forensic examination at the computer crime division in Welwyn Garden

City. Twenty-four hours previously, the young man had been unpleasantly arrogant, even trying to flirt with Karen Hardwick. Now he just looked scared.

"Before we start, I would like to know why my client has been called in again. In his last interview—which he gave without counsel present, I might add—it was established that Mr Menendez was at home at the time of the attack on the unfortunate Mr Williamson."

Warren ignored the implied rebuke concerning the previous interview. The recording on the PACE tape recorder would clearly show that Warren had advised Menendez of his rights; furthermore, he had not been under arrest at the time.

"Mr Menendez, I would be grateful if you could describe again your movements on the night of Thursday the twenty-second."

Menendez licked his lips nervously. "No comment."

"Are you sure about that, Mateo? We have you on tape already. I just want to clarify a few details."

He glanced over at his solicitor, who nodded almost imperceptibly.

"It's like I said, I took the kids to McDonald's then to the park up on the common. Then when it got dark, I took the kids back to Candy's and put them to bed."

"And are there any witnesses who can corroborate this?" It was the first thing that Tony Sutton had said after identifying himself for the tape.

Menendez hissed in frustration. "We've already been through this. The kids are too young, but Candy saw me when she came in about half nine."

Warren watched the man closely. On the face of it, his reaction was appropriate, but it seemed forced. As if he knew what reaction was expected of him and didn't want to disappoint.

He decided to give the man a bit more rope to hang himself with.

"Just to be clear; the sun goes down about quarter past six this time of the year. Are you saying that you left Middlesbury Common and returned to your partner's flat, number 27b Eastcotes Terrace, at that time? It's not very far; did you go home directly?"

The man's eye twitched slightly. "Yes, straight home."

"So you would have been in from about what, six-thirtyish until your partner returned from Zumba a bit after nine-thirty?" Sutton again.

"About that."

"Did you stay in for the rest of the night?"

"Yes, we watched a bit of telly and then went to bed."

"And again, can your partner corroborate this."

"Absolutely." The man's voice was confident again.

Warren nodded and scribbled on the notepad in front of him. "OK, you've been very helpful, Mr Menendez."

The man blinked in surprise.

"Am I free to go?"

His solicitor, an experienced-looking middle-aged woman, narrowed her eyes slightly, but said nothing.

"Just one more thing," Sutton spoke up. "Do you carry your mobile phone with you at all times?"

Before his solicitor could interject, the man nodded his head.

"Yeah, 'course. Who doesn't?"

"And you had it with you on Thursday evening?"

"May I ask where this is going, DCI Jones?" Menendez's solicitor was looking decidedly anxious now and was directing her question to the senior officer in the room. She had clearly worked out what was happening, even if her client hadn't.

"Just clarifying something," responded Sutton. Warren said nothing.

"Like I said, yeah I carry it everywhere. I definitely had it Thursday."

Now it was Warren's turn to speak up. "Given everything that you've told us, could you explain why cell-tower triangulation places your smartphone at Middlesbury Common from ten past five until almost twenty past nine, and why your partner thinks that you lied about bathing the children that evening?"

THURSDAY 29TH MARCH

Chapter 7

Warren and Sutton's elation lasted barely twelve hours. Nine o'clock the following morning found them perched between piles of unironed clothes on the edge of a suspiciously grubby sofa. Every surface in the flat, the two detectives included, was covered by hairs from the numerous cats wandering around the dwelling. The smell of cat's pee and old food was poorly masked by cheap air freshener and cigarette smoke.

Exactly what Mateo Menendez saw in Nicky Goven, was something of a mystery to Warren and Sutton. Perhaps it was her phlegmy cough, the hard-to-discern tattoo that covered pretty much her entire right calf or maybe he just liked the smell of incontinent domestic pets. At least four of the animals had wandered through in the few minutes that the two police officers had been there.

Her apartment on the edge of the common shared the same cell tower and this, Menendez claimed, was the reason why his smartphone was registered as at or near the common—rather than at home as he'd first claimed—for the hours either side of Reggie Williamson's murder.

"When did you last see Mr Menendez?"

Nicky Goven squinted at Warren from behind a peroxide-blonde fringe.

"Thursday evening. He always comes around then. He has Thursday evenings off work."

Warren glanced at Sutton.

"Where does Mr Menendez work?"

"He works in a call centre for the emergency services." There was a palpable pride in her voice. "He helps give advice for people whilst they wait for an ambulance."

Warren said nothing; there were no operational control centres within fifty miles of Middlesbury. It looked as though Menendez's habit of lying to women was not limited to Tabitha Williamson.

"What time was Mr Menendez around here?"

The young woman paused for a moment. "He turned up a bit after five, I guess, and stayed for a few hours."

"Could you be a bit more precise? When exactly did he leave you?"

For the first time since they arrived, Nicky Goven looked worried.

"Why? What's he done? Is he in trouble? Is this anything to do with that bloke who was killed on the common last week? I already spoke to a policewoman who knocked on the door Monday night."

"It's just part of a routine inquiry," soothed Warren.

She shrugged. "A bit after nine I guess." She thought for a moment. "Yeah that's right. There was a film starting and he said he'd like to stay and watch it but he had to leave because he was working the early shift."

The times certainly added up. However, Warren wouldn't be entirely satisfied until he got another independent confirmation. It was always possible that the fragrant Ms Goven was helping Menendez.

"Was there anyone around who may have seen Mr Menendez arrive or leave your flat?"

She thought for a moment, before scowling. "That old bitch—'scuse my French—who lives in the flat next along is always complaining that we make too much noise, 'cause the walls are so thin." She grinned wickedly. "I hadn't seen him all week. We gave her plenty to moan about."

Assuming the neighbour was in, and confirmed Nicky Goven's story—and by extension Mateo Menendez's new, more seedy alibi—then Menendez was no longer a suspect.

However, before he left Warren had a bit more business. Strictly speaking, it was nothing to do with him, but Warren felt sorry for the young woman—yet another victim of Middlesbury's self-styled Cassanova.

"Do you work, Ms Goven?"

She shrugged. "Yeah, I'm a hairdresser. I do a few shifts each week down the 'Clip Joint', on the High Street."

"And have you ever used any of those payday loan companies?"

If she thought the question strange, she didn't let it bother her. "Sure, once or twice." She smiled. "Actually, I let Mateo sort that out for me. I'm not very good with numbers."

Warren and Sutton swapped glances. It was stepping over the line, but a barely perceptible nod from Sutton erased any nagging doubts that Warren had.

"Don't. I can't say any more, but don't let him anywhere near your finances."

She looked shocked.

Sutton spoke up. "And whilst you're at it, I'd ask for a bit more information about his job. Perhaps he could show you his ID card. Does he drive?"

She shook her head.

"Then ask him which call centre he works at and have a little look on the web to see how far away it is."

The woman's bottom lip trembled slightly and Warren felt a rush of sympathy for her. It was now clear what Menendez had seen in her—a young woman, living on her own with her cats. She had a job and was clearly quite naïve.

The two detectives rose to leave, but before they did, Sutton took one last look around the grubby living room.

"If you don't mind me asking, what did you do with the kids whilst you and Mr Menendez were, umm, busy?"

Nicky Goven frowned in confusion. "What kids?"

* * *

Three hours later, Mateo Menendez was a free man. But his troubles were far from over. The older lady in the apartment next door to Nicky Goven had been very clear that Menendez and Goven were in that evening at the time when Reggie Williamson was being stabbed to death on the opposite side of the common. She'd been somewhat disgruntled when it transpired that Sutton and Warren weren't from the council to deal with her complaints about the noise, not to mention the smell, from the flat next door.

However, social services were now in the process of questioning his eldest child about how often Daddy left them on their own whilst Mummy was out. Interestingly, Menendez's partner did two other classes each week, again leaving the children in the care of their father.

"The bloke's a complete Fanny-Rat," opined Sutton. "I wonder how many other women he's milking for money. I just wish there was something we could do about it."

Warren agreed. The whole affair had left a nasty taste in his mouth.

More importantly, Warren had just crossed his name off the wheeled whiteboard in the main office. The suspect column was now blank.

SATURDAY 31ST MARCH

Chapter 8

The note had been pushed through the letter box sometime during the previous night. It was printed with an inkjet printer, on plain paper. Susan had found it when she went downstairs to put the kettle on.

I have information about Reggie Williamson. Meet me in the car park of the Feathers 4 p.m. Come alone.

Warren had been sitting waiting since a quarter to four. Despite the lingering warmth from a sunny afternoon, he wore a heavy coat in an attempt to conceal the stab vest Tony Sutton and the rest of the team had insisted that he wear.

Arguments had raged all morning over what should be done about the mysterious note. It could just be the work of a crank, of course; however, the fact that the author of the note knew where Warren lived was disquieting. At Grayson's insistence, both marked and unmarked patrol cars were stationed in the Joneses' street, keeping an eye out for any unusual visitors. Susan had agreed—reluctantly—to stay in and do some schoolwork, rather than meeting up with friends in town on the first day of the school Easter holidays. Unfortunately, a rush job from the document analysis department had reported that the paper and envelope were widely available commercially and that the printer used was a popular home model. Even if a suspect were identified, simply discarding the ink cartridge and printhead would make linking the note with an individual printer all but impossible. Needless to say, the writer hadn't left fingerprints or licked the envelope. None of Warren's neighbours had seen or heard anything.

In the end, it was decided that the note couldn't just be ignored. The case had all but ground to a halt over the previous thirty-six hours and the empty suspect column on the whiteboard continued to taunt Warren. A leafleting campaign on the common and the surrounding areas on Thursday evening, the one-week anniversary of the murder, had produced nothing and forensics had been unable to produce any concrete leads. Even the flurry of crank calls and confessions that had followed the press conference had now dried up – the nutters and the fantasists no doubt moving on to pastures new.

Background checks on anyone who had conceivably come into contact with the retired gardener in the past couple of years had proven similarly fruitless. The handful of historic convictions for teenage shoplifting, Friday night fisticuffs and driving offences that his circle of acquaintances had amassed over the past fifty-odd years were of no interest to the team and were about as numerous as one would expect for a similar-sized group of people who had spent most of their life in a small, North Hertfordshire market town.

It was starting to look more and more like a stranger killing, or a random mugging gone wrong. But it didn't feel like it to Warren; the killing was too efficient, the lack of forensic evidence unusual to say the least.

With all that in mind, Warren had decided to meet the author of the note and see what they had to say.

Of course, he had no intention of meeting them alone. Reggie

Williamson had been stabbed to death—it was entirely possible that his killer had written the note and Warren was uncomfortably aware that he was potentially placing himself directly in danger.

At the very least, it would be helpful to identify the person who claimed to know about the attack. So, in the hours preceding the rendezvous, various officers had stationed themselves in and around the pub. By the time Warren arrived, a nondescript Transit van containing a team of concealed, uniformed officers wearing stab vests and batons had been parked three spaces over for two hours. Small holes drilled in the side panels allowed the video surveillance team a clear view. At both ends of the road unmarked cars sat ready to form roadblocks if needed; more officers were on standby if necessary.

The clock on the dashboard of Warren's Ford Mondeo clicked over to two minutes to four. Across the car park, drinkers sat in small groups around wooden trestle tables, enjoying the warm weather. A waitress in her late teens cleared dishes for a young couple who appeared absorbed in one another and oblivious to the world around them. Warren just hoped that Detective Constables Karen Hardwick and Gary Hastings were paying as much attention to their concealed earpieces as they were to one another. You never could be sure with those two.

Four o'clock came and went. Warren shifted uncomfortably in his seat. His mouth was dry and he wished he was inside the pub, enjoying a pint of something frothy.

Suddenly a voice crackled in his earpiece, "Possible target approaching, on foot from main road. White IC1 male, average height, wearing a grey, hooded jacket and a baseball cap. His head's down. We can't make out his features."

Warren tensed, all thoughts of a drink vanishing.

A few seconds later the man emerged. Keeping his head low, he crossed the car park without glancing in either direction, heading straight for Warren's car. Warren opened the door and stepped out, ready to greet the man.

The visitor barely looked up; all Warren could make out was the grey of a beard beneath the shadow of the cap's brim.

"It's not safe to be seen. Get back in the car."

The man's voice was harsh, quiet. An older man, late-middle-aged, Warren surmised. He looked the visitor up and down. In response, the man pulled out the pockets of the hoody, showing them to be empty. He could still be concealing a knife elsewhere on his person, but Warren had to take the chance. Besides which, he already had a suspicion who it was and he was burning with curiosity.

Nodding, Warren slipped back behind the wheel of the car. The hooded man opened the passenger door and climbed in. Closing the door behind him, he turned in his seat.

"Hello DCI Jones, my name's Gavin Sheehy and I need your help."

Chapter 9

Warren stared at the man, taking in his dishevelled appearance; his scruffy grey beard and unkempt hair were both in desperate need of a good trim and the man's face was lined, with dark smudges beneath his eyes. Eyes that were slightly bloodshot, Warren noted. Up close the man's cologne was almost overwhelming and he smelled as if he'd just eaten two whole packets of extra-strong mints.

"I thought you said that you had information about Reggie Williamson?" Warren ignored the man's proffered hand. He was surprised at the intense feelings of anger he felt towards the man. Police corruption was something that Warren had felt strongly about ever since he'd joined the force; the betrayal of the public trust was a slap in the face to the thousands of dedicated officers who risked their lives day in, day out in an often-thankless job. Since moving to Middlesbury, the feelings had intensified as he saw firsthand the devastating effects that such betrayal had on those officers closest to the traitor.

Sheehy dropped his hand. It shook slightly, Warren observed. Clearing his throat, the older man unzipped his coat slightly, revealing the edge of a manila folder. "I have. But first we need to take a drive."

The car park was full of Warren's colleagues, all of whom were tensed and ready to rush in at the nearest hint of any trouble. To leave with Sheehy would be a breach of protocol and absolute madness, although Warren felt it unlikely that he was in any physical danger.

"Not a chance. If you have information on the murder then you can share it here."

Sheehy shook his head. "No. What I have is for your ears only."

"If that's your attitude, how about I run you down the station and charge you with obstruction and help myself to the information?"

Sheehy snorted derisively. "Investigation going well, is it? Lots of suspects all lined up?"

The man was right. They had drawn a complete blank; whatever information Sheehy possessed about the old man's murder, Warren needed to know it.

Warren looked at him long and hard.

"How do I know you didn't kill Reggie Williamson? That you're not some deranged killer who's going to stab me as soon as we move on?"

"If you thought that, you wouldn't be sitting here with me, even with a van full of rugby players three spaces along and Gary staring all gooey-eyed at that new detective constable over in the beer garden."

Warren's mind raced through the possibilities, but he'd already made his mind up. He slipped the car into gear.

"Where are we going?"

"I'll point; you drive." Sheehy wasn't silly enough to announce their destination to whoever may be listening. He raised his voice.

"And if that's you on the other end of DCI Jones's open radio link, Grayson, tell the officers parked at either end of the road to stay where they are. And it's a clear day with good visibility. I'll see the chopper a mile off and you can kiss goodbye any information that I'm going to give him."

Sheehy put a hand out. "Remove the earpiece. Save yourself an earbashing."

"Do as he says," instructed Warren to the surveillance team, a small part of him enjoying the sudden silencing of DSI Grayson's squawking as he pulled his hidden earpiece out and Sheehy tossed it out the window. He'd get it in the neck when he returned to the station, but he'd deal with that then. Hopefully the information Sheehy claimed to have would be worth it.

* * *

Sheehy's directions had been by hand gesture only; he was too experienced to think that Warren's earpiece was the only open communication channel from the vehicle. After passing the unmarked cars at the top end of the street—the officers glared openly, but made no immediate move to follow them—they were soon heading towards the north end of town. It didn't take Warren long to work out where they were headed.

"It's a lovely evening, Warren. You won't need your coat."

Warren sighed, tossing the heavy jacket with its hidden microphone onto the rear seat. He pointedly didn't remove the blue stab vest, but as they left the Mondeo in the small car park on the edge of Middlesbury Common he was uncomfortably aware that he was leaving behind his last means of communication with the surveillance team. He was going to have a lot of explaining to do when he got back.

"Is that where Reggie Williamson was killed?"

It was a rhetorical question—blue-and-white police tape still fluttered in the breeze.

Aside from a few young boys kicking a football at a makeshift goal made from rolled-up jumpers at the other end of the open field, the two men were now alone in the middle of the common. Nobody could possibly overhear them and Sheehy would have plenty of warning if anyone tried to approach.

"Well, I'm here. What have you got?"

Warren's tone was testy. So far Sheehy had been in charge and Warren was determined to regain the initiative.

"I can point you towards the killer, but first I need a promise from you. I need your word."

Warren stared at him for several seconds, searching the man's face.

"What sort of promise?"

"I need your help."

Warren thought for a long moment. It didn't take a detective to work out what the man was after. But what did he think Warren could do?

"What's in it for me? How do I know that you even have the information you claim?"

"A show of good faith. I can identify the person who ordered Reggie Williamson's death and another killing you aren't even aware of. Then, after you help me, I have other information. Information that you don't even know that you want yet."

"What sort of information?"

Sheehy shook his head. "First you have to help me clear my name."

It was exactly what Warren had been expecting but he was confused. "I don't see what I can do to help. I have no influence on the outcome of the investigation. It's in the hands of Professional Standards; in fact, I'd even question whether it is appropriate for us to be having this conversation."

"You're the only one I can turn to, Warren. This whole thing is not about whether or not I took a bribe. It goes much, much deeper than that. It's not even about clearing my name. It's about righting an injustice and making sure that evil men are put away for a long time."

Warren ignored the man's familiar use of his first name and his attempt at stirring rhetoric; he wasn't naïve enough to be persuaded by that old trick.

"Again, I don't see what I can do to help you; Standards are investigating the case and I have no access to their files or even their officers—by definition they have to be free from outside influence. I doubt they'd even grant me an audience. I didn't arrive until months after your arrest—this is the first time I've met you. Why the hell would they listen to me?"

He was starting to lose patience with the man. He was clearly a drinker and obviously clutching at straws. This afternoon's operation had cost the force a considerable amount of manpower and resources; if Sheehy had nothing to contribute to the Williamson case, then Warren was strongly contemplating arresting him for wasting police time. He said as much.

"Warren, I can help with the Williamson case and others, but it has to benefit both of us. I need you to help me fight these charges."

Warren shook his head in exasperation. "Haven't you listened to anything I've said? I can't intervene on your behalf. I have no influence here. You must know this. I don't understand why you want me to become involved."

Sheehy looked at him for several long, hard seconds. When he spoke again, his voice was low, almost gentle. "Warren, you are already involved. You've been a part of this since the moment you walked into that garage and found your dad dead in his car."

* * *

It was as if Warren had been punched in the stomach. All of the air left his lungs and he felt a wave of nausea pass over him. Immediately, the memories flooded back. He could taste the coppery tang of fear, feel the painful pounding of his heart, smell the choking exhaust fumes as they filled his nose and mouth. It was a smell that to this day Warren hated. As a teenager out clubbing in Coventry, he'd always make sure he was upwind of the taxi rank, the smell of their idling engines making him feel sick. He'd loathed the old Pool Meadow bus station, with its lines of chugging buses filling the air with smoky pollution.

Somehow, he found a voice, forcing it past the tightness of his throat. "You have ten seconds to explain yourself before I arrest you for wasting police time."

Sheehy ignored him. "What do you know about your father and his death?"

The voice that answered sounded like Warren's but it seemed to come from a long way away. "He killed himself after stealing money from a drugs bust." The voice dripped with bitterness and resentment.

"What if I told you that he didn't kill himself? That he never stole that money."

If Warren hadn't felt so weak and disoriented he'd have punched the man in the face as hard as he could. Could the man stoop any lower, invoking the name of Warren's father in a crude attempt to manipulate Warren into helping him? It was nearly a quarter of a century ago and Warren had suppressed his feelings for much of that time, but they never went away. And they hadn't softened. The hurt, the betrayal, then finally the anger and, yes, even hatred towards his father. The man he'd admired and looked up to, even wanted to be when he was older—that man had torn Warren's world apart. To know that his father had chosen to leave them had hurt so hard—that he had been unable to save him had hurt even more.

And then came the revelations. Thousands of pounds seized in a drugs bust, half of it going missing between the crime scene and the evidence room at the police station. His father's gym bag, housing sweaty towels, stained T-shirts—and wads of fifty-pound notes wrapped in elastic bands.

Quite why his father had decided not to collect the bag from his locker—he would probably have gotten away with it—instead choosing to kill himself, was never satisfactorily answered. Perhaps he had stolen the money on a whim, then felt guilt at what he had done? Unable to face the shame, he'd taken his life that early summer evening.

That was what his mother had clung onto, even as she saw her husband's memory destroyed, as friends from the force stopped calling or avoided talking to her when they bumped into her in the street. The name Niall MacNamara was toxic and Warren wanted nothing to do with it.

"Leave now, before I make you." It was all Warren could do to force the words past his clenched teeth. He no longer cared about Reggie Williamson, he just wanted this man out of his life; he could feel the sweat on his brow. It was as if Sheehy had slammed a wrecking ball into Warren's carefully constructed defences, bringing down the walls. Warren needed time to rebuild them, to reconstruct the ancient structure.

Sheehy ignored him. "Warren, your father was a good man; he was an honest man. He wasn't a thief… and he didn't kill himself. I know this. I've known it for twenty years. And everything that's happened recently—it all stems back to what happened that night."

Warren closed his eyes, concentrating on breathing. He wanted nothing more than to race back to his car, to leave in a cloud of burning rubber and run and hide. But he couldn't. The memories from that horrific evening had left their mark, but now another scar was itching. One he'd ignored but which was now shouting for attention. Why? Why had it happened? He had to know. He was trapped. If he left now, refusing to let Sheehy talk, he could never have peace. A long-dormant seed had started to germinate and he had to know the truth.

"I knew your father back in the late Eighties. We met about two years before… you know. I was a young DC, with only a couple of years' experience."

Sheehy stared at his feet. "I was working in North Herts, but I was seconded to West Midlands as part of a small team working as liaisons on the investigation into a huge, cross-county crime ring. Your father was a senior detective sergeant on that team and we worked closely together." Sheehy raised his head, looking Warren directly in the eye. "He was a good man. And I liked him a lot."

Warren didn't trust himself to speak.

"It was a massive enterprise. Basically, it was modelled on the Italian Mafia: drugs, prostitution, stolen goods—you name it; these guys did it. And they were ruthless, anyone who crossed them ended up dead.

"But they were also clever. All of the action was taking place in the West Midlands—Birmingham, Coventry, Nuneaton. But the guy who headed it lived in North Herts and was ostensibly a legitimate businessman. He owned a string of restaurants, fast-food places, leisure centres, B&Bs, minicab firms—you name it. He partnered local tradesmen. All cash businesses. All built from scratch or bought legitimately, with no links to the Midlands and no evidence of any wrongdoing. They even had a charitable foundation, helping unemployed kids learn skills and trades. Local politicians loved him and he was on the front page of the local newspaper at least once a week.

"But we knew the bastard was a crook. The Hertfordshire businesses were just a front and a way of laundering money. Back in those days you could move money around a hell of a lot more easily than now and a secret Swiss bank account really was a secret. He was worth millions. And he was a murderer. We knew of cases going back to the 1970s—drug dealers mostly but the odd prostitute as well.

"The problem was we couldn't prove it. He covered his tracks too well. And he rarely got his own hands dirty. We busted a few dealers here and there, but there was never any direct link to him. Witnesses had a tendency to suddenly develop amnesia or even to disappear. We were going nowhere fast. We needed a break."

Sheehy paused. "You have to realise, Warren, that we knew this guy was filthy. In fact, we had tons of evidence that placed him right in the centre of his little ring. Most of the grunt work was carried out by his right-hand man, but it was him that we wanted. What we didn't have though was the one remaining piece that would open up everything else. He was too high-profile for us just to go on a fishing expedition—we'd never get a warrant to search his house or business premises. And that was what we needed. With a warrant we would be able to raid him and that would be enough to open a bridge between the evidence we had and him. But without that information, we didn't have enough to get a warrant. Catch-22."

Warren didn't like the sound of this. Where was it leading? He also had a suspicion about who Sheehy was talking about—and the implications were massive.

"What did you do?" His voice was slow, steady.

Sheehy licked his lips nervously. "Although he kept his hands clean most of the time, it wasn't always that way. Back in the early Eighties, he was dabbling in the club scene—supplying drugs to clubbers. The problem was that if you really wanted to make money, you needed the clubs—or at least the door staff—on your side. And most of the clubs that were willing to take part were already under the control of a guy named Frankie Cruise.

"He approached him about a partnership, but Cruise was an arrogant bastard and wouldn't play ball. In the end, he shot Cruise dead. The mess was all cleaned up, of course, but everyone knew what had happened. In fact, he encouraged the rumours to enhance his own reputation. But obviously, that wasn't good enough for court and no judge was going to grant us a warrant based on that. Especially not for someone so high-profile and well connected; he knew where all the skeletons were buried.

"However, ballistics recovered a nearly intact bullet from Cruise after his body floated back to the surface in Coventry Canal. It was no good to us without a gun though.

"Then in mid-1987, we got word that he had been boasting at a party he was hosting at that Hertfordshire mansion of his, about how he had killed a man. He must have really wanted to impress his guests because he eventually went up to his bedroom and fetched the handgun that he claimed to have used to kill Cruise. He was brandishing it like some sort of trophy."

Sheehy paused. "Your father and I knew that was the weapon he had used, and that it was the final piece of evidence that could blow the whole case open. But we still couldn't get a warrant. We were told it was just hearsay. The PACE regulations were still fairly new and nobody wanted to be seen to be harassing such a prominent local figure.

"So we made contact with his handyman, who was unhappy with the way he was being treated. We persuaded him to steal the gun, which was kept in his bedroom."

Sheehy, looked away, unable to meet Warren's eye.

"You have to realise, we knew that he was guilty. We had so much evidence. That all came out at his trial. It just needed a catalyst to start everything working."

"So you planted the gun and framed him for murder." Warren's voice was bitter. He felt sick.

But Sheehy was shaking his head vehemently. "No! We didn't frame him for anything he hadn't done. We just left the gun at the scene of a drugs raid. It was collected along with a load of other weapons. Routine ballistic testing linked the gun to the Cruise murder. There were fingerprints all over the gun. Luckily for us, he's had a few run-ins with the police over the years. Usually all the charges were dropped when the witnesses mysteriously changed their minds, but his fingerprints were still on file.

"All it did was give us the excuse to raise a warrant. As soon as that happened, we were able to build that link between him and the case we'd built. The case was sitting there, ready to go. It just needed that link."

"Vinny Delmarno."

It wasn't a question. The man had been released whilst he was still with West Midlands Police and there had been anger about the things that had been said in the press. Allegations of corruption and fabricated crime scenes—allegations that Sheehy now claimed were true.

Sheehy nodded but said nothing as if speaking the man's name out loud was a curse.

"So why are you telling me all of this now?" Warren's voice was bitter, the anger now simmering just below the surface, "It can't just be an attack of conscience. You've had over twenty years to come clean. Delmarno's been out how long now?"

Warren was confused; it made no sense. By all reports, Sheehy was in deep trouble already. What benefit was there to adding this long-forgotten miscarriage to his litany of sins? It was clear from his tone that he felt that what he and Niall MacNamara had done all those years ago was still right. Noble-cause corruption they called it.

Sheehy looked at his hands and Warren noticed they were trembling. "Reggie Williamson was the gardener who supplied us with the gun."

"That's what this is all about?" Warren couldn't hide the scepticism in his voice. For sure it was a hell of a coincidence, but surely that was all it was?

He said as much.

"When Vinny Delmarno was released, he swore blind that he would find out who put him away and would get his revenge."

Warren still wasn't convinced.

"There's more."

Sheehy opened the coat, revealing the concealed file folder, and removed a newspaper article, handing it over. A cutting from a local Hertfordshire paper from February, page one but not the lead. Stapled to the back was a narrow column from page four, continuing the story—a black-and-white headshot, formal-looking and probably taken from an official website, took up barely two inches.

Retired coroner and wife killed in
drink-driving smash: Verdict

A former coroner, killed in the early hours of 31st December 2011, was driving too fast and was under the influence of alcohol, an inquest ruled today. The crash, which killed Dr Anton Liebig, 67, and his wife Rosemary, 66, instantly, happened after a sharp bend on the A5062, on the way back from an awards dinner at The Allingham Golf Club in Hertfordshire, where Dr Liebig—captain of the senior men's team—had presented several trophies.

A police spokesperson said that skid marks at the scene of the accident revealed that Dr Liebig had rounded the blind bend at a speed in excess of fifty miles per hour, before apparently losing control and leaving the road, where he hit a tree. A post-mortem revealed a blood alcohol level of 85 milligrams per 100 ml. The legal limit is 80mg.

The coroner, Dr Lila Schiff, called upon North Hertfordshire District Council to look into the safety of that stretch of road, which has been the scene of numerous serious accidents in recent years, resulting in three fatalities.

Dr Liebig worked as a coroner throughout Warwickshire, before retiring. Rosemary Liebig was a keen painter. They are survived by a son and two grandchildren.

Warren finished reading the report and looked up at Sheehy. "So?"

The story meant nothing to him. He worked in Middlesbury CID. The incident would have been dealt with by traffic down in Welwyn. Besides which, Warren had had enough on his plate over the new year to worry about the ins and outs of some drink-driver.

Sheehy took a deep breath. "Anton Liebig was the coroner who oversaw your father's inquest, Warren."

Sheehy's voice was fading out, replaced by the sound of blood rushing through Warren's ears. His father's inquest.

He still remembered that day. The courtroom had been nothing like he'd expected it to be from the TV. A small, wood-panelled room with a row of tables for the "interested parties" to sit—interested parties such as Warren, his mother and his grandparents. A chair sat empty for his brother who hadn't come home the previous night. Behind them several lines of blue plastic chairs constituting the "public gallery" were mostly filled with journalists, representatives from the Police Federation and a few family friends. Nobody from the station that Niall MacNamara had worked at for more than half his career were present. None of his police "friends". He'd been dropped; nobody wanted to be associated with him now, the thief who'd stolen drugs money then taken the coward's way out.

The formal hearing had been a short, almost anti-climactic affair, delivered by the coroner sitting at his slightly raised dais, a much younger version of the man in the newspaper photograph. The family already knew the verdict, having been told quietly beforehand.

Suicide. Carbon monoxide poisoning from his own car engine, administered by a hosepipe attached to the exhaust, an empty bottle of whisky by his side. Found by his teenage son. No suspicious circumstances.

No mention was made of why he did it; that was beyond the purview of the court. But everyone in that room knew the rumours, were aware of the investigation underway. And you can't libel the dead.

Sheehy's voice pulled Warren back to the present. "Your father didn't commit suicide; he was killed. Revenge for what he did? I don't know. But I knew the moment I got the call about your dad's death it wasn't a suicide. I've known for over twenty years."

He continued to avoid Warren's eyes, having the sense not to try and apologise. He couldn't; the words didn't exist that could in any way lessen his guilt, to begin to atone for the literally decades of hurt that he'd help cause.

"Why?" That one word was all Warren could manage. A half-dozen questions were all rolled into that one word.

"Fear. I was scared, Warren. Shit-scared. They'd killed your father and covered it up. Somehow, they hadn't fingered me as his

86

accomplice—too junior, I guess. My name didn't appear on any paperwork. So I kept quiet."

He still wouldn't meet Warren's eyes.

"He was supposed to die in prison, kidney failure. He'd been on dialysis for years. They even put it forward in mitigation, tried to get him a shorter sentence. Perhaps it worked. With the case we had he could have gotten life with thirty years. He got twenty-two. I forgot about him. Got on with my life.

"And then he got a new kidney. God love the NH fucking S. His name came up on the transplant list as the best match and before you know it some poor donor's kidney is inside that bastard's body.

"The kidney took, he served the rest of his sentence and now he's free."

Sheehy's voice was a mixture of bitterness and fear. "And now he's clearing the decks. Settling scores and cleaning up his mess. Reggie Williamson for his betrayal and Anton Liebig because he was a loose end who could link him back to his first act of revenge—the death of your father.

"And that just leaves me. I'm the only one left."

Warren found his voice. "I still don't understand. What has this got to do with the current investigation into your misconduct?"

"It's a set-up; it's all fake. Delmarno wants his payback but killing me would be too easy. He's had two decades to dream about what he wants to do to me and he wants to do it slowly. He wants to ruin me, send me to prison and make me suffer like he did. And then, when I'm finished and due for parole, that's when he'll probably make his final move. I'll be dead before I walk out that prison."

Chapter 10

Warren received a less than rapturous welcome when he returned to the station.

"My office, now."

The roasting from Grayson was pretty much what he'd been expecting; the man had been unable to decide which of Warren's misdemeanours should be addressed first and in the end had simply settled on a chronological listing: getting in a car with a potential killer, removing his earpiece so he could no longer receive instructions, leaving a contained area with a suspect, circumventing surveillance and ignoring procedures for the collection of a witness statement.

However, Grayson had reserved most of his vitriol for Warren's apparent agreement to help his predecessor fight the charges against his name. Sheehy had said nothing about it where they could be overheard, but Grayson wasn't a fool. It was obvious that was what Sheehy was after.

"It's not your job to help some bent copper fight Professional Standards. The Federation and his lawyers can do that. You've got enough on your plate solving this murder; besides, we can do without the negative publicity. We're going to have enough shit flying at us when this comes to court next month without the press getting wind of your escapades."

Warren stood and took the flak, mostly allowing the shouting to wash over him. It was to be expected and he was too emotionally tired to care about a bollocking that would ultimately lead nowhere. Regardless, he was struck by two remarks all-but buried within the verbiage; the first, a cynical observation that Grayson had never concerned himself before with the amount of work piled on Warren's "plate"—he usually loaded it as gleefully as a glutton at an all-you-can-eat buffet. Secondly, it was the first time that Warren could recall the man referring to Middlesbury as "we" or "us".

After the obligatory threat that he was contemplating suspending Warren, Grayson finally asked what Sheehy had to offer.

"That's it?" he responded when Warren had finished. "This Reggie Williamson offered a gun to Sheehy back in the 1980s, which Sheehy then planted at the scene of a crime to frame him and now this Vinny Delmarno character wants his revenge? Sheehy really is a dirty bastard. It sounds like it's all coming back to bite him on the arse."

"Well, it's not as if Delmarno is an innocent in all of this," Warren found himself defending Sheehy—a position he was not exactly comfortable with.

Grayson was dismissive. "Who gives a shit about Delmarno? He got what he deserved. Besides, it's clear that Sheehy has form when it comes to corruption." He sighed. "Regardless, it's something. See where it takes you. Is there anything else?"

"No, sir." The lie came more smoothly than Warren was comfortable with.

"Well let's hope this leads us somewhere. This afternoon's little jaunt cost us an arm and a leg."

The dismissal was clear and Warren wasted no time turning for the door.

"Oh, and Warren, take that bloody stab vest off or everybody will see through this carefully cultivated, cuddly facade."

* * *

Warren's first stop on leaving Grayson's office was DS Peter Kent's desk. The veteran detective looked up.

"You survived, I see. Those vests are worth every penny."

Warren smiled tightly. "Apparently coming out of the Super's office wearing one ruins his cuddly image."

Kent snorted in amusement. "His bark's worse than his bite. Although he can certainly bark loud enough."

Warren winced. Kent was at the far end of the room from Grayson's office. "You heard that then?"

He smiled. "Why do you think half the office has gone for a coffee break?" Kent's smile faded. "How was he?"

No need to ask who "he" was.

Warren shrugged, replying cagily, "I never met him before today, so I can't say if he was any different to when he worked here."

Kent said nothing, waiting.

"But unless he was unkempt and a daytime drinker when you knew him, he's probably not doing as well as you hope."

Warren's sympathy for his predecessor was close to non-existent; however, he had been a much-loved boss and people like Pete Kent had known him for years. Warren would have to be careful not to be too dismissive of their feelings.

"What can I do for you anyhow, Chief?"

Although all officers in CID could use HOLMES 2, the

service-wide computer database that was used to store records and reports on major incidents, Warren had a feeling he'd need specialist help.

"I need details on a cold case from the Eighties. Will they be available electronically?"

DS Kent looked at him warily. "They might be. The original HOLMES went live in 1986 for major incidents, but it's a bit patchy. It hasn't got half the functionality of HOLMES 2 and some forces still did a lot of their record keeping manually, scanning them in after the fact. The cross-referencing can be pretty poor. What do you need?"

"I need the records for a joint Hertfordshire–West Midlands Police operation concluded in 1988. I don't have an operation name, but it resulted in the conviction of a Vinny Delmarno. If you could get me his records as well, that would be great." Warren glanced at the clock above Kent's head; the man's shift finished in half an hour. "Actually, get Gary on it when he returns from his break."

"I'll do it, Chief. I'm not in a rush. Gary's finishing himself in a few hours then he and Karen are off on that dirty get-away they think nobody knows about. I'll only end up reinventing the wheel if he starts the job and then hands it over."

Warren thanked the man and turned to head back to his office, before another idea struck him. "Could you also get onto Revenue and Customs and check the tax and National Insurance returns for Reggie Williamson during the same time period? I'd like to know what he was doing and who he was working for back then."

"I'll see what I can do," the older man promised, "but it may take a while. HMRC deal with most requests during office hours."

"Well, do what you can. I'll be in my office. Print it out when you're done."

One last thought occurred to him; he glanced over at Grayson's office before leaning in to Kent. "Do me a favour and keep this between us for the time being."

Kent glanced over at Grayson's office and smirked slightly, as Warren had known he would. "Of course."

* * *

Tony Sutton was a lot politer than Detective Superintendent Grayson. Nevertheless, he made it quite clear how reckless he thought his DCI had been and was similarly disapproving of Warren's tacit agreement to help clear Sheehy's name as a reward for more information.

Warren had wrestled with the revelations that Sheehy had made all the way back to CID. He'd been standing in front of Grayson, absorbing the man's anger before he'd eventually decided that he wasn't ready to share everything Sheehy had revealed to him or broach the subject of his father's death with the man.

The wound that Sheehy had so brutally reopened on Middlesbury Common was gaping wide and Warren was confused and bewildered; however, his instincts were telling him that he couldn't trust the man until he knew more.

To somebody of Warren's age, those events in the mid-Eighties seemed a lifetime ago, but he was uncomfortably aware that officers such as Gavin Sheehy and John Grayson had started their careers back then and were still in the force today, working in positions of influence and responsibility.

Sheehy's account had almost made it sound as if he and MacNamara had planned the whole stitch-up single-handedly, but even back in the Eighties the police didn't work that way. The two officers would have been part of a much larger team and it was almost inconceivable that they worked alone or were even the masterminds of the subterfuge. Until Warren read the report on the case, he wasn't sharing the contents of the manila folder, sandwiched between his stab vest and shirt, with anybody.

Chapter 11

"Is that all we've got?"

The pile of printouts was surprisingly small for such a major incident.

"For the moment. West Mids were charged with entering the paperwork into HOLMES, but they prioritised the key documents." Kent looked apologetic. "I'm still tracking down everything as it's been filed a bit sloppily. I guess once they'd secured his conviction they expected him to die in prison and so they didn't bust a gut scanning everything in. These are the records for Vinny Delmarno. I'll get the rest to you when I've collected it all together."

"Well, I'm sure that if it's in there you'll find it, Pete. Thanks."

The documents had been divided into two piles and joined together with oversize paperclips. The first was the record for Vincent (Vinny) Delmarno. Warren recognised the formatting from the Police National Computer. The second was other associated paperwork, such as reports from the National Probation Service.

Like all prisoners released from a life sentence, Delmarno had to serve out the rest of his sentence "on licence". According to the NPS, he lived with his wife on the easternmost fringes of Middlesbury, reporting to his probation officer fortnightly. The latest account was dated the beginning of the month and reported that he was meeting the terms of his parole satisfactorily.

A biography of Delmarno had attached photographs showing him after his arrest and more recently on release. Warren stared at them. Was this the man who had killed his father? He felt a cold shiver run down his spine. Over two decades in prison had changed the man almost beyond recognition.

According to his date of birth, Delmarno had been just shy of thirty-five years old when he'd been convicted, a little younger than Warren was now, but his hair was already snow white. His face was swollen and darkened, a symptom of his end-stage-renal failure.

By contrast, the photograph taken upon release showed a fit-looking man in his late fifties. Although lined and hardened, the face had lost its swelling and the skin tone had returned to the natural, olive complexion that spoke of his Italian heritage. His hair, though white, was as full as the day he went in.

The one feature that had not changed was his eyes. Warren had seen thousands of mugshots over the years, but rarely had he seen such hatred staring out of a photograph at him.

The biographical details were terse and factual, but Warren found himself filling in the missing details with his own knowledge both from his upbringing in Coventry and the time he served with the police.

Delmarno had been born in July 1953, the son of an Italian father and an Irish Catholic mother who'd met in Coventry shortly after the war. Both parents died whilst he was in prison. Schooled at one of the city's three Roman Catholic secondary schools—not the one he'd been to, Warren was strangely relieved to see, even though they would have attended twenty years apart—he'd been expelled at age fifteen for fighting. After a few minor skirmishes with the law as a youth, he apparently avoided arrest until 1988.

The list of crimes of which he was suspected filled three pages. Drug dealing, living off immoral earnings, assault and attempted murder. In almost all cases, charges either weren't filed or were dropped.

As Sheehy had explained, it was the shooting of Frankie Cruise in 1984 that was his undoing and the search warrant obtained after the handgun was "found" at the scene of a drugs bust in Coventry had led to his trial on a dozen further charges, including two counts of conspiracy to murder, money laundering and possession with intent to supply. As in the past, he was cleared of many of the charges when witnesses failed to attend or his lawyers successfully had them thrown out on a technicality. Nevertheless, he received life with a minimum sentence of twenty-two years and eight months for the murder of Frankie Cruise.

He was released on the sixth of September 2010.

The final page contained a list of Delmarno's known associates. Most were either behind bars themselves or dead, either of natural causes or murdered. It also listed his wife, Jocelyn, and his son, born five years before his father's incarceration.

If Warren had expected some remarkable insight into the events of the past week or even twenty-four years previously, he was to be disappointed.

"Anything you want me to do before I go home, Boss?"

The question was as much a peace offering as anything else and so Warren felt even more guilty as he dismissed Tony Sutton for the evening. The older man had looked at him for a few, long seconds before nodding and saying good evening. Sutton was no fool; he knew that Warren was hiding something from him. The two men had barely spoken over the last few hours; for want of a better word, Sutton seemed to have been sulking.

That suited Warren fine. He hadn't yet decided how much to share with Tony Sutton. The man had been investigated immediately after Sheehy's arrest and cleared of any wrongdoing, but Warren couldn't dismiss the possibility that he was helping his former DCI and friend to play him, manipulating him to help clear the man's name. Warren hoped that wasn't the case. He'd come to value Sutton's counsel—and friendship, he realised. Until he could be sure, though, he was on his own.

Chapter 12

It was late by the time that Warren arrived back home. Susan's expression suggested that he was in for another earbashing—it was definitely today's theme.

"You did what?"

"I already knew who he was. I was certain that I wasn't in any danger. Besides, I had my stab vest on."

"Covers your neck does it?" Even when angry, his wife could be logical to a fault. "So what did this Gavin Sheehy want? Did he actually have any evidence to help you work out who murdered that poor man?"

"I'm not sure. The folder he gave me was just the write-up of a fatal collision over the New Year. Nothing jumped out at me."

The two of them had moved into the lounge and the red wine Susan had poured herself seemed to cool her temper somewhat. Nevertheless, Warren was reminded that Susan's temperament probably owed more to her fiery mother than her decidedly docile father.

Warren had been thinking about what to tell his wife ever since he'd left the office. The fact was, he needed a sounding board; his decision not to tell Tony Sutton the full details of his conversation with Sheehy had left Warren feeling isolated and he valued his wife's insights. And he needed her support. He closed his eyes.

They had been dating for more than two years before Warren had told Susan the full story of his father's suicide. They'd been on holiday in Prague, lying in bed after a romantic meal down by the Charles Bridge. Warren had never shared his true feelings about his father's death and how it had affected him.

He'd been scared that people would see him differently, and he was ashamed. He knew he shouldn't be—that his father's sins were not his own—but he couldn't help it.

Susan had listened without saying anything, her tight embrace easing his halting speech until it was flowing like a tap—years of hurt and resentment finally getting its release. When he was eventually finished, she'd whispered into his ear, "Thank you."

The next day, standing on top of Petřín Hill, Warren had asked her to marry him.

The touch of Susan's hand brought Warren back to the present.

"For most of my life, I've thought my father abandoned me and my mum and brother, that he was corrupt and a thief. Today I found out that I may have been wrong all of these years."

Warren felt Susan stiffen. She said nothing. And it was as if he'd been transported back in time to that evening in Prague as he again unburdened himself to the woman he loved so much.

"What are you going to do?" asked Susan when he finally finished.

"I don't know. Gavin Sheehy has admitted that he and my father helped secure an unsafe conviction all of those years ago, he's not an honest man. But what if he is telling the truth?"

"You can't ignore it."

She was right—he had to check the truth of what Sheehy was saying for himself. But how? Events had been successfully concealed for nearly a quarter of a century.

"Sheehy claimed to have more information. You have to get it from him. Whatever it takes."

"But how can I know if I can trust him?"

"Does it matter?"

"What do you mean?"

"Look at what Sheehy's asking you to do. He's basically asking you to investigate the allegations made against him. Furthermore, he's given you potential clues that could help you solve one confirmed murder and another possible killing. Treat it like any other case. Take what he's given you and add it into the mix. As for the allegations against him—surely it can't hurt to do a bit of digging around, to see if he really is being framed?"

"Grayson has banned me from looking into Sheehy's case."

"So when has that stopped you before?" She placed her hand on his chest and kissed him lightly on the forehead. "Follow your gut, Warren. You need to see this through. If there is any truth at all to what Sheehy is saying, then you need to know."

She kissed him again. "We need to know. You can't let it lie; you know that."

Warren nodded wearily. He was exhausted. Not just from the long hours he'd worked, but also the constant adrenaline.

"You're right," he admitted. "I'll get Mags Richardson to look over the report into Dr Liebig's accident. She worked Traffic before joining CID. She'll spot any inconsistencies. If it looks as though there are suspicious circumstances, I'll go back to Sheehy and see what else he has."

"What about Tony Sutton?"

"Not yet. He was investigated alongside Sheehy when he was first arrested. I need to satisfy myself that he is completely clean before I bring him in on this."

Susan squeezed his hand again. "Well, do it quickly. You can't work this alone. You need help."

Susan was right as usual. The logical science teacher had cut through the confusion and suggested a course of action. Marrying her was still the best decision he had ever made.

Chapter 13

He's walking down the garden path again, the coffee cups balanced in his hands. He tries to stop, the feeling of dread mounting in him, but it's useless. His legs, ignoring his desperate commands, carry him relentlessly towards the garage door. Towards what he knows lies on the other side.

No, not again, he cries out silently. He knows it's a dream, of course—the same dream that visited him every night for years. Almost a quarter of a century on, the dream comes less often now. But when it does, it's lost none of its power.

The rusty hasp needs a tug, and the spilled coffee scalds him. As always, he tries to turn back, but try as he might, he's committed, the same story playing out again and again. His ears are filled with the chugging of the car's engine. His nose is clogged with exhaust fumes.

And then he's at the car door, swinging the hammer with all of his strength. Please let it be different this time, he pleads, just this once.

But it's not. The whisky bottle clatters to the floor as he reaches in to turn off the engine. But he's too late again. The last thing he sees before he jerks awake, sobbing, is his father's white, bloodless face…

"Warren, it's OK. Warren, I'm here." Susan's voice was soothing, the warmth of her arms around his chest. Gradually his heart rate slowed, calmed by her gentle caresses.

"The dream?"

Nothing more was required. They've been together for eight years and she recognised its symptoms—the crying and the tears, the way he cradled his hand as if scalded by hot coffee. The dream comes to him just a few times a year now, usually around the anniversary or his father's birthday. It doesn't take a genius to work out why it's chosen to come back tonight.

Warren nodded. Reached out for the glass of water on the bedside table and took a long swig.

"I'm OK now. It only ever comes once." Despite the fluid his voice was croaky.

The bedside clock read three-thirty.

"Go back to sleep." He kissed her on the forehead.

It's true, the dream does only come once in a night and afterwards, Warren would sleep a deep and dreamless sleep and would awake in the morning fully refreshed. It's as if it's been purged from his system and won't need to return again for at least a few more nights.

But tonight was different. In a few minutes, Susan's breathing changed as she drifted back to sleep. But sleep didn't come to Warren. Try as he might he couldn't stop thinking about that night, reliving it again. Why? Why wouldn't his subconscious let it go?

He started to obsess about small details. The way the hasp squeaked as he forced it open. The clatter of the whisky bottle as it hit the floor. His father's pale, bloodless lips.

The hasp. It squeaked as he forced it open.

As he forced it open.

Suddenly Warren sat bolt upright in bed, realising that what Sheehy had told him must at least be partly true. If his father was inside the garage, who had closed the rusty hasp on the outside of the door?

SUNDAY 1ST APRIL

Chapter 14

Warren finished leafing through the report describing the road traffic collision that had killed the late coroner Dr Anton Liebig and his wife, Rosemary, three months before. Putting it down on his desk he turned to the inquest findings, skimming the legalese before skipping to the narrative verdict. Something wasn't right; he was sure of it. The deaths and their timing were too coincidental, but to his untrained eye everything seemed normal. Despite his reluctance to involve too many people at this stage, he needed help.

Leaning out of his office door, he summoned DS Margaret Richardson from her desk in the far corner. Richardson was a heavy-set woman in her mid-forties. A mother of two, she had worked traffic for a number of years before switching to CID.

Warren pushed the printouts across the desk to her. "I need your expertise. I want you to read these reports and tell me what you see."

Placing her ever-present bottle of mineral water down next to Warren's laptop, she fished out a pair of small reading glasses, picked up the pile of papers and started reading.

It took her barely five minutes to finish both of the documents—five minutes that Warren spent trying to appear unconcerned and busy.

"Well, it seems fairly straightforward at first glance. I can see why the inquest drew their conclusions." She raised a hand, ticking off each point. ".Dr Liebig was driving late at night, on a narrow country road in poor weather with a blood alcohol level above the legal limit. The car was in good repair, but he was driving too fast for the conditions around a deceptively sharp bend with a reputation as an accident black spot. Best estimates put the car's speed at over fifty miles per hour prior to it leaving the road shortly after the bend."

"And the conclusion from the inquest?"

"Pretty much what I'd expect. The car plunged down a steep embankment and impacted a tree, which impaled Dr Liebig through the windshield, killing him instantly. His wife died from massive internal bleeding at the scene as the emergency services attempted to cut her out. Death by dangerous driving, namely excess speed and impairment by alcohol."

Warren nodded. "Is there anything in the report that doesn't fit that explanation?"

Richardson's tone was cagey. "Well, sir, you have to realise that RTCs are complex, especially when there are no witnesses or survivors. There are always unanswered questions; the best we can do is come up with a sequence of events that fits the evidence and decide if an offence has been committed. In the case of a fatal accident, it's up to the coroner presiding over the inquest to determine if there was anyone at fault, or if steps should be taken to reduce the likelihood of a similar accident. In this case she recommended safety barriers to prevent cars leaving the road, and improved signage."

Warren leant back in his chair. "OK, I understand that, Mags, but I have reason to suspect that this accident might not be as clear-cut as the report suggests. Are there any inconsistencies here or unanswered questions?"

"Let me have another look." Picking up the papers again, she took a pen out of a coffee cup masquerading as a pencil pot and raised an eyebrow. Warren signalled his agreement. The originals were safely locked away.

This time, she took longer. Warren forced himself to turn back to his bulging inbox, resisting the urge to try and interpret the officer's upside-down handwriting. However, he was rereading a missive about next year's budget predictions for the third time, and still not comprehending it, when Richardson finally put down the papers and cleared her throat.

"Anything?"

"Well, if you want to turn over every stone, there are a few discrepancies, I suppose." She sounded a little uncomfortable, clearly concerned that she might be overstating her observations.

"I'm all ears," responded Warren, trying not to sound too eager as he picked up his own pen and turned over a new page in the spiral-bound scribble pad next to the phone.

"First off, his blood alcohol level was 85 milligrams per 100 millilitres. That's only just above the legal limit. That doesn't mean he was safe to drive, but he wasn't pissed. Eyewitness reports state that he drank two small glasses of red wine with a three-course meal, about three hours prior to leaving the golf club. After the wine, witnesses say he switched to soft drinks. An analysis of his stomach contents is consistent with a large meal, traces of red wine and a substantial amount of what appears to be Coca Cola. The pathologist thought there might have been traces of spirits in there, but the blood alcohol results were back so he didn't pursue it further."

"What about his blood-glucose levels? The report noted that he was diabetic, but I don't know enough to tell if they were too low. Could he have become hypoglycaemic and lost control of the car?"

Richardson shook her head. "Unlikely. His blood glucose was 14.2 millimoles per litre. If anything that's too high. It may have contributed to fatigue or confusion, especially if he was tired late at night and under the influence of alcohol."

Warren studied her intently. "Your expression tells me you aren't convinced."

Richardson sighed. "It may be nothing, but I'm not happy about the skid marks on the road." She flicked the folder open to reveal flood-lit photographs of the road surface. Two thick, black tyre marks were clearly visible after the apex of the left-hand bend, heading straight on, before veering sharply to the right and off the road. The rear of the Liebig's Jaguar was just visible at the edge of the image. Its wheels were hanging well clear of the road, hinting at the sharp downward angle that it had come to rest at. Blue smears across its shiny paintwork advertised the presence of emergency vehicles, their flashing lights just off camera.

"It looks to me as though he had made it safely around the bend; although he was travelling very fast, he was in a performance car with good tyres. For some reason though, he slammed on the brakes and swerved violently as he exited the bend, losing control."

"An obstruction? A deer in the road perhaps?" Warren had had his own rather uncomfortable encounter with just such a creature the previous winter.

Richardson shook her head slightly. "I don't think so. There aren't many deer in that area and he was an experienced driver. I doubt he'd have over-reacted for something like a rabbit."

"Anything else?"

"Well, there is a report of two cars travelling at high speed, very close to one another about a mile prior to the accident; however, the witness herself admits it was very dark and it was hard to judge distances and speed."

Warren leant back in his chair and tapped his pen against his lip thoughtfully. The evidence pointed towards a tired driver under the influence of alcohol, possibly a little confused from high blood sugar, taking a bend too fast then losing control. But the inconsistencies gnawed at him like a dog with its favourite stick. Were they just the inevitable loose ends from a perfunctory investigation into an apparently clear-cut case, or were they more significant?

Chapter 15

They were meeting in a car park again. As before, Sheehy insisted that they drive to a secluded area where they couldn't be overheard. It wasn't necessary. Warren had told nobody about this visit.

"So, you're convinced I'm telling the truth?"

Convinced was too strong a word, Warren decided. However, everything that Sheehy had told him so far had been borne out. Warren admitted as much.

"You said that you had more information for me."

Sheehy shook his head. "You know the agreement. I've given you a show of good faith; now you need to do the same. You need to help me."

Warren sighed. He still didn't see what he could do to help the man.

Sheehy had brought another file folder with him. He removed another newspaper clipping and handed it over wordlessly. The clipping was dated the eighth of April the previous year—roughly four weeks before Sheehy's suspension.

Police sting closes Herts-based
drug distribution network

Hertfordshire and Bedfordshire Major Crime Unit, working with colleagues across East Anglia, announced today the results of a series of dawn raids conducted at the weekend. Twelve arrests were made as a result of the months-long investigation, Operation Fahrenheit, into drug production and distribution, mostly centred in North Hertfordshire. The majority of the arrests were for dealing, however, three individuals were charged with production of Class B drugs, including cannabis and ecstasy. Several kilos of crack-cocaine were also retrieved from one of the properties in Middlesbury, along with firearms and an undisclosed quantity of money. A spokesperson for Herts and Beds Major Crime Unit said that the raids had netted a number of known and unknown dealers, as well as the man that they believe is behind the operation.

"Drugs are a scourge in our communities. Illegal drug use is a major contributor to violent assaults, robbery, theft and antisocial behaviour. Hertfordshire prides itself on its comparatively low crime rate and this sends a strong message that the production, distribution and use of illegal drugs in our county will not be tolerated."

He said that the operation was ongoing and that more details would be revealed in due course.

Warren handed back the piece of paper. "So what has this got to do with you?"

"The man at the centre of the operation was one Billy Obsanjo, a Middlesbury-based gangster wannabe. We'd been watching his operation for about a year, working with the drug squad down in Welwyn. He had big ambitions, but at the time he was still mostly active in this area, hence our involvement. His 'crew', as he called it, all went to school together and they operated cannabis factories out of terraced houses up on the Westfield estate. We'd closed a few of them down over the past few months and made a couple of arrests, but they were all low-level dealers and it was clear to us that even though the operation was pretty small-scale at the moment, it was well organised. Our biggest worry was that it would gain a real foothold and it'd expand, bringing in undesirables from outside the county. Our aim was to shut it down whilst it was still small."

"So what went wrong?"

"We'd had an eye on Obsanjo for some time, but we couldn't ever link him with the operation. Most of the dealers that we arrested were too far down the totem pole to give us a name and those that were more connected wouldn't say anything. Obsanjo might be small-time but he had convictions for assault and there were unconfirmed rumours that he wasn't above threatening families and loved ones to ensure people kept quiet."

"So you had nothing? Why not just fit him up? It's not like you haven't done it before."

Sheehy opened his mouth, before closing it again. After a brief pause, he continued, "He was a slippery bugger. Every time we thought we had him, he'd get away before we could arrest him at the scene. We'd be left with a few pot plants, a couple of wraps of heroin and if we were lucky, some dumb idiot who was too stoned to run away when we bashed the door down.

"Anyhow, it was his own arrogance that got him in the end. He hit his girlfriend one time too many and she reported him for assault. She knew that if he found out she'd been to the police he'd probably kill her, so she gave us details of where and when we could find him with some of his product. This time, when we made the raid we hit seven properties simultaneously. We caught him with his pants down—literally, he was in the back room getting favours off some junkie."

"OK, so where do you come into all of this?"

Warren had his suspicions, but he wanted Sheehy to spell them out for him.

"I was DCI here in Middlesbury, as you know, and I helped coordinate the investigation and organise the raids in this area. The thing with Obsanjo though was that although he was running this operation, he was a dumb shit. We couldn't figure out how he kept one step ahead of us. Seriously, he was mean and violent and ambitious, but he wasn't at all bright. He simply shouldn't have been able to avoid us like he did.

"Anyhow, we'd finally got him and we charged him with intent to supply, unlawful production, the whole works. Good enough to get him twenty years if the judge and jury saw it our way. We just put his avoidance down to luck—his good luck, our bad luck.

"Anyway, a few weeks after the operation was concluded, we'd all moved on and suddenly Professional Standards arrive at my house at 6 a.m. on a Sunday morning, mob-handed, brandishing warrants. I'd come off a night shift and so Judith answered. It frightened the hell out of her. By 7 a.m. I was in custody suite one, waiting for my lawyer. I still didn't know what it was all about."

Sheehy had stopped pacing and was now grinding his teeth.

"They said that Obsanjo had claimed he was able to avoid arrest for so long because he was getting regular tip-offs about when raids were about to occur. He was bribing a member of Middlesbury police to tell him what our plans were."

Warren contemplated the man before him.

"And he named you?"

"Not in so many words, but he gave a description that could have been me. He claimed his source would disguise himself or conceal his identity whenever they met. He'd phone him on a Pay-As-You-Go mobile phone."

"Well, they must have had more to go on than that. Trying to get a more lenient sentence by cooperation is hardly a new ploy and claiming to have been helped by some bent copper is old hat."

"He had copies of internal memos about the operation that he claimed had been passed to him by his source. In return, he handed over bundles of cash. Used notes mostly, wrapped in elastic bands and stuffed in envelopes." Sheehy paused. "Somebody was dirty, make no mistake about that. But it wasn't me."

He continued his story. "Anyway, they interviewed me all day. By mid-afternoon, I wasn't really that concerned any more. Allegations are made all the time. You know that. I figured that Professional Standards were under pressure to put on the whole cart-and-pony show because of the politics—you know that they have been looking for an excuse to close us down ever since we survived the merger. But the fact was I hadn't done anything wrong and I was confident that there was nothing to worry about. I've grown a pretty thick skin over the past few years and I figured it would all be over in a couple of weeks: 'nothing to see here, move along.'"

He went quiet. "But I was wrong. About four o'clock in the afternoon the investigator in charge, some DCI Lowry, came back in, brandishing a fistful of photographs like a trophy. They'd found a shoebox hidden in the loft, with about eight grand in used notes all rolled up neatly in elastic bands, just like Obsanjo claimed.

"Forensics found traces of drugs on the notes above the usual background levels and Obsanjo's thumbprint on one of the envelopes. They also found a Pay-As-You-Go SIM card in my desk at work that matched the number Obsanjo claimed had been used to call him."

The man went silent, waiting.

Warren thought hard. What the man was saying was incredible; the evidence as he'd laid it out was compelling and he could see why

Professional Standards had arrested and charged him. The man in front of him was desperate, of that there was no denying and there was no reason to accept what he was saying as the truth. Except that the evidence he had given Warren so far had been largely true. And what did he have to gain by lying? The chances that Warren would find evidence to exonerate him were slim—even more so if he wasn't actually innocent.

"So why do you think Delmarno is behind this?"

Sheehy sighed. "It's the only thing that makes sense. Vinny Delmarno made it clear that he wanted revenge, that he wanted those responsible for sending him to prison to suffer. This happened barely six months after he was released. Then in December, Anton Liebig is killed in a supposed car accident and finally Reggie Williamson is stabbed to death on Middlesbury Common. It's too much of a coincidence."

It wasn't enough. Warren knew, but he couldn't dismiss it. "So who was feeding the information to Obsanjo? You said that you thought it was authentic, that somebody had been passing material on."

Sheehy shrugged. "I don't know. You know how big these sorts of operations are. Middlesbury was taking point because of our local knowledge and connections but there was a huge team behind this down at Welwyn. It could have been any one of them. Vinny Delmarno's got deep pockets; he could definitely afford to pay somebody."

Warren chewed his lip, thinking hard. The idea that there were other corrupt officers beyond Sheehy—maybe even officers he knew and worked with—left a sour taste in his mouth. "What about Tony?"

Sheehy grimaced. "What they did to him was spite, pure and simple. There was no reason to suspect him, other than his friendship with me. They humiliated him, dragging him into this. Poor bloke didn't even know what it was about."

"You know that he's been summonsed?"

Sheehy nodded and sighed. "I'm innocent, but I'm a detective—I can put myself in their shoes. I can see why they arrested me and why they are confident of a conviction. But there's no need to drag Tony into this. What's he going to say? That I sometimes used my mobile phone or that I wasn't always available?

"These trumped-up charges have been a godsend for some. I freely admit that I've been a pain in the arse and that fighting to keep Middlesbury CID open made me more enemies than friends, but so be it. Frankly I'm proud of it and I'll take the flak on the chin, but it's hurt people I care about. I pretty much guaranteed I'd never make it above DCI, and that's fine. Heading that unit was the best job I ever had and I'd happily do it until retirement—but I always regretted that it probably scuppered Tony's chances as well. He's too good to stay as a DI—you know that—and it's not right that standing next to me for a cause he believed in should kill his future ambitions."

Warren said nothing, but Sheehy's words rang true. Before Sheehy's disgrace, many assumed that Tony Sutton would one day head up the unit. The police service was not a monarchy. Jobs were given on merit, but Sutton's experience and local knowledge would ordinarily have stood him in good stead, if and when the vacancy became available.

And that was perhaps why Warren decided, there and then, that he would investigate Sheehy's claims. Tony Sutton had shown himself to be a good and loyal officer and his passion for policing in the small area that Warren was starting to call home was second to none. Warren thought back to the massive row that he and Sutton had shortly after his arrival at Middlesbury. Sutton had claimed that he had no desire to be promoted further—that may be true, but it offended Warren's sense of right and wrong that politics should deny the man the chance.

And then there was the future of Middlesbury CID. If Sheehy was convicted of corruption, it could very well be just the lever needed to close the unit for good. And Warren knew that he couldn't let that happen without a fight.

It had been a steadily growing feeling over the past few months. At first Warren had seen command of the unit as a valuable stepping stone in his career. The closure of Middlesbury would not impact him directly—how could it? He had no association with Sheehy and the events before him, and under his direction the unit had achieved many notable successes in a relatively short space of time. John Grayson might be the one to take the public plaudits, but Warren was the senior investigating officer and those who mattered knew exactly who had done the legwork. Warren could move on from Middlesbury with plenty of commendations in his file for a job well done.

But he didn't want that—not yet anyway. He liked Middlesbury CID. The officers under his command were fine detectives and getting better. And besides, he and Susan were settled. Their first house was turning into the home that they had dreamed of; Susan's job was proving to be challenging beyond her expectations, but the school was predicting a modest rise in exam results for the first time in several years.

Both of them were settled and neither wanted the upheaval of moving across the country or the stress of a long daily commute—and of course, if everything went to plan, within the next couple of years the spare bedroom would be turned into a nursery.

"What do you want me to do?" Warren listened; it wouldn't be easy and he'd need help.

Walking back to the car, leaving Sheehy to find his own way home, he pulled out his phone. It was answered on the second ring.

"Tony, we need a chat. Fancy a pint?"

* * *

"So this is the man that Gavin claims is responsible for his recent spell of bad luck." Sutton had been grinding his teeth for the past few minutes; he clearly still resented the fact that Warren appeared to be taking the man's assertions seriously.

"So he says," Warren responded neutrally, too tired to get into another argument.

The men's meeting an hour earlier in the back room of the Rose and Crown had been a tense affair. Sutton had been extremely unhappy when he heard that Warren had spoken again to Sheehy.

"Why do you trust him? We've still got no evidence that this Delmarno character has anything to do with Reggie Williamson's death. We can't even prove that Williamson ever worked for Delmarno—Inland Revenue, or whatever they're calling themselves these days, got back to us. Williamson was basically self-employed throughout the Eighties, mostly cash in hand. He declared whatever he could get away with and paid flat-rate National Insurance. There are no details of who paid him or who he worked for. For all we know Gavin's just yanking our chain. We should drop it; let Professional Standards sort it out."

Despite his reticence, Sutton had agreed to accompany Warren back to the station.

"Well, I suppose the first thing we need to do is find out what this Vinny Delmarno has been up to over the past couple of years." He held up the sheet from the probation service. "I'll see if we can get anything from his probation officer. Maybe he can tell us if Delmarno was around when Reggie Williamson was stabbed."

Warren shook his head. If Delmarno was still connected enough to arrange for Gavin Sheehy to be framed for corruption, then who knew where else he might have influence. Sutton voiced his scepticism.

"Look, Tony, even if we find out that Delmarno had a cast-iron alibi for the time of Williamson's murder, Sheehy said that he ordered his killing, not that he did it himself. Let's keep this to ourselves for the time being."

Sutton looked at him suspiciously. "Why do I get the impression that you are keeping a lot more to yourself?" His eyes bored into Warren's. "What else did Gavin say to you during your walk in the park? You were up there over half an hour and you were as pale as a ghost when you came back down."

Warren felt his ears burn. He shook his head. "We argued before he told me what he knew about Williamson."

Sutton continued to stare at him for a few more seconds, before finally looking away. "If you say so, Boss."

Warren pulled over the latest pile of papers left on his desk by DS Kent. "Operation Leitmotif—catchy moniker."

Sutton said nothing, still brooding.

Kent had been right. The available documentation was patchy. An operation the size of Leitmotif, spanning two counties and involving officers from two forces, would have generated tens of thousands of individual records, most of which would be sitting in brown cardboard boxes in an archive somewhere. Modern protocol called for every piece of evidence, witness statement or scrap of paper to be recorded, annotated and scanned into the massive

HOLMES2 database before being divided into physical evidence, which had to be kept so that it could be produced in court, and non-physical evidence, which could be securely destroyed, the electronic version being sufficient. Back in the early days of computerisation, such a job would have been a mammoth undertaking and so whoever had been in charge of archiving the case had clearly been selective. Many of the documents had also been scanned only retrospectively, Warren noted, with accession dates several years after the case's conclusion.

Most of the material was of no interest to Warren, concerning the ins and outs of Delmarno's empire. Much of it was in the form of witness statements from informants, often listed only by code name.

"I wonder how many of these characters actually showed up to testify?" sniffed Sutton who had finally become interested in the case, despite himself.

"Not many, by the sounds of it. Delmarno was acquitted of most of the charges laid against him. There isn't a lot of forensic evidence backing up the claims, so his lawyers managed to tear them apart. We need a list of who these code names refer to; some of them might still be alive."

"I wouldn't bank on it. I'll bet a fair few of them ended up the same way Frankie Cruise did."

"Speaking of which, here it is." Warren held up a sheaf of papers. "The reports surrounding Cruise's murder." He fanned them out on the table. "Let's see: ballistics report on the bullet retrieved from the scene, autopsy report, no witness statements obviously—" he moved to another page "—another ballistic report, this time for a handgun retrieved at the scene of a drugs bust up in Hillfields, Coventry." He scanned the page. "Tests show it was the same gun that fired the bullet that killed Cruise." He picked up another sheet. "Fingerprints were retrieved from the gun: a clear thumbprint on the grip and an index finger and thumb on the top-slide, and a partial print on the trigger. Lots of others, but none clear enough to identify." He lifted a final page. "Confirmed match to Vinny Delmarno."

"So Delmarno's handgun definitely killed Cruise then?"

"It certainly looks that way. The question is: how did a gun that Vinny Delmarno supposedly kept in his house in Hertfordshire end up in the neck-end of a Coventry housing estate?"

"Any explanation?"

Warren scanned through the rest of the papers. "None here. It's definitely a mystery and it must have been something the defence asked in court. However, according to this account—" he pushed another sheet across the table "—the drugs bust didn't net anybody. They scarpered before the raid team could catch them. The gun was left behind with a few packets of cocaine and heroin."

"So nobody could explain where the gun came from or contradict the team's account of how they found it. Bloody convenient." Sutton's eyes had taken on a familiar glow; despite everything, he was clearly intrigued. "I wonder what the officers in question had to say about it."

Warren shuffled through the papers again. "Nothing. I can't find the officers' statements."

Sutton frowned. "Well, that can't be right. They'd have been cross-examined in court and their statements read out."

"It looks as though they were never scanned into HOLMES." Warren scowled. "What do you think the chances are that the paperwork is still sitting in a box in the West Midlands Police archives twenty years on?"

Sutton snorted. "I wouldn't bet my pension on it. I'm pretty sure that if it was assumed to have been scanned into HOLMES the original would have been destroyed long ago. It would be good practice. If the information is captured, the original paper statement wouldn't be considered physical evidence so there's no need to retain it."

"So, what Sheehy claims could be correct? He could have left the gun at the scene?"

"Assuming he was there. I haven't seen anything naming officers involved in the raid yet."

Sutton was right. Warren quickly rifled through the papers one more time. "Nothing relating to the raid at all. We have no idea who was present or who else was working with Sheehy."

Sutton looked at him curiously. "You think Sheehy had an accomplice?"

Warren had skirted over the mention of his father in the affair. Why had he done that? Was he trying to protect his father's memory—such that it was—or was he just not ready to bring up the subject yet? Warren's head was still in turmoil over the rest of Sheehy's revelations and he needed some time to clear it before deciding who to share the information with. Unbidden, his eyes flicked towards his briefcase where he'd stowed the documents and the newspaper clipping about Anton Liebig's fatal car accident.

"Well, it stands to reason," Warren hedged. "I find it hard to imagine that Sheehy was able to get hold of the gun from Reggie Williamson and plant it in that raid without anyone else helping him. He was only a rookie DC after all."

Sutton nodded, apparently taking Warren's dodging of the question at face value. "You're probably right, which raises an even more intriguing question—if Sheehy was a junior officer, then who was the senior officer orchestrating everything?" He inclined his head towards the paper strewn across the desk. "I don't know about you, but I'd love to know who authorised that drugs raid."

MONDAY 2ND APRIL

Chapter 16

Billy Obsanjo was awaiting trial at the Mount Prison on the out-skirts of Bovingdon Village. Gaining access to him had been easier than Warren expected. He'd simply contacted the prison and asked for permission to visit him. Obsanjo, through his lawyer, had agreed immediately. When asked for the reason for his visit, Warren had been vague, saying that he wanted clarification of a few points and the solicitor had immediately stressed how Obsanjo was willing to help the police in any way necessary. Warren found himself wondering just what sort of incentives had already been offered to the man for his cooperation.

After activating the car's door locks remotely, Warren crossed the car park, heading for the squat, nondescript building. Now that he was here, his gut was tight with nerves. Warren knew that what he was doing could potentially result in his suspension, or even worse. On the face of it, there was no legitimate reason for him to be here and Professional Standards would take a very dim view of his visit at the very least. They would probably regard it as potential interference with an ongoing investigation. For that reason, Warren had spent the previous night agonising about his approach. Having Obsanjo's solicitor present and making certain that everything was recorded would hopefully show that he hadn't acted improperly, but he still felt sick.

Tony Sutton knew nothing of Warren's trip. The man already had a cloud hanging over him and the last thing Warren wanted was for his name to be drawn to the attention of Professional Standards again. Besides, he was due to appear at Sheehy's trial and any attempt on his behalf to speak to Obsanjo would at best invalidate his testimony and at worst could well be regarded as an attempt to interfere with a witness. Warren's visit would be logged—he just hoped that nobody in Professional Standards would think to check that log in the immediate future. He'd deal with Sutton's disapproval later.

Visitor hours for inmates were not due to start for a few hours and so processing Warren was quick and straightforward. Although a police officer, no special courtesy was afforded him and he was searched before his belongings were taken off him and locked away just like any other visitor; prisons were rife with drugs, mobile phones and other contraband and it all had to get in there somehow. Finally, with only a digital voice recorder and a notepad, he was escorted to an interview room.

The prison was surprisingly quiet. The inmates had already had their breakfast and showers that morning and were now back in their cells watching TV or staring at the four concrete walls that defined their daily existence, waiting for their lunch to appear. For Warren, the crushing, lonely boredom was probably the biggest disincentive for getting locked up, he had long ago decided.

Billy Obsanjo was much as Warren had expected from his file. A slightly built man, verging on gaunt, his dark skin had an unhealthy pallor, his jowls darkened with several days' stubble. His plain, red T-shirt revealed detailed tattoos that were more pornographic than artistic.

The file had been a case study in a life gone wrong. Born twenty-six years ago to a second-generation Nigerian mother still in her teens and an unknown father, he'd been a persistent absentee from his third year of junior school. By the time he started secondary school, he was bouncing between his maternal grandmother and, when she was sober enough, his mother. His first brush with the law came before his fourteenth birthday for criminal damage to a boarded-up shop. By the time he was seventeen he had multiple convictions for shoplifting, joyriding and drug possession.

His first conviction for assault came in his early twenties after he resolved a disagreement in a nightclub using a headbutt. By this point, he had been unemployed since finally leaving school at sixteen with no qualifications to speak of—his only legitimate work experience had been from his court-ordered community service and a failed attempt at a work scheme.

Despite this, he never seemed short of cash and pretty soon his unaccountable financial solvency drew the attention of the authorities and he became a person of interest to the police.

"So what can we help you with, Detective Chief Inspector?" Obsanjo's solicitor was a slightly portly, middle-aged man with a squint and a receding hairline that he kept on running his hand through, as if checking that it hadn't shrunk any more. Despite the man's apparent openness, his body language clearly telegraphed his reluctance to be there.

"I wondered if you could help clarify a few details about the alleged tip-offs you received."

"Ain't nothing alleged about it. I given all of the stuff to you already." Despite being brought up in Hertfordshire and not even owning a passport, Obsanjo's inflection was a bad pastiche of US movie gangster speak. The TV series *The Wire* had a lot to answer for, Warren decided.

He smiled tightly. "Of course, as I said, though, I need to clarify a few details. First, can you tell me who your contacts were within the police?"

Obsanjo puffed his cheeks out. "For fuck's sake, how many times you going to go over this?"

"Indulge me." Warren kept his smile in place, but his tone was stony.

"OK. No, I can't tell you who my contact was. He forgot to leave his business card behind."

Warren ignored the sarcasm. "So there was just the one person?"

"Far as I know."

"And who came up with the idea for your little… arrangement? Who approached whom?"

"He approached me."

"So you met him. Can you describe him?"

Obsanjo shrugged. "It was in a pub car park. I didn't see him clearly; he just stepped out of the shadows. There was a streetlight behind him and he wore a hoody, so I couldn't see his face." Obsanjo snorted. "I thought he was trying to mug me. Nearly put a blade in him." Obsanjo's solicitor cleared his throat loudly.

"Or I would of if I'd had one," Obsanjo finished lamely.

"So a total stranger approaches you in a pub car park and asks for money for information. And you went along with it?" Warren was sceptical.

Obsanjo shrugged. "I didn't believe him either, but he knew stuff about me. Stuff that only the pigs know. He offered me a 'show of good faith', to prove he was legit. Told me that there was a raid due on one of my factories, 5 a.m. the next morning. That if he was right, I should call this number and we should talk."

"I didn't believe him, but I figured it best to move stuff out and not be around. Next morning a whole vanload turned up, just like he said, and kicked the door in."

"So you rang the number?"

"What do you think?"

Sheehy had been right. The man really wasn't that smart. He'd accepted the man's corruption at face value. It had never occurred to him that Sheehy might have been working undercover, gaining his trust, to make it easier to arrest him. Obsanjo had just assumed that his contact was bent—in this case he'd been correct, but that was more luck than judgement.

"So how did it work? Did you pay him directly? Was it a monthly arrangement? What?"

"He gave me his bank details and I set up a standing order—how do you think I fucking paid him?" Obsanjo was clearly sick of repeatedly answering the same questions; no doubt Professional Standards had gone over his story several times, checking for inconsistencies.

His solicitor was also clearly bored. Nevertheless, he touched his client's arm gently. "Just answer his questions, William. You know that they have to check everything out fully."

Obsanjo settled into a brooding silence, his arms folded.

Warren tried again.

"How much did you pay him?"

"Two grand. Every time he sent me information."

"And how many times did that happen?"

Obsanjo shrugged. "I dunno. Ten or twelve times."

Twenty thousand pounds or more paid in bribes. A large sum of money, but it meant that Obsanjo could keep on earning many times that. It was the cost of business and a pretty small cost at that.

If Obsanjo had been a legitimate businessman, the taxman would have taken a far bigger slice of his earnings than he'd paid in bribes.

"So you met him a dozen times—can you describe him?"

Obsanjo kissed his teeth. Warren ignored the insult, pretending he didn't recognise the gesture.

"No, I only met him once. We used disposable phones. He would call me when he had more information. I would stick the money in an envelope and leave it somewhere. When I dropped the money off, I'd pick up whatever he had left."

"And what sort of information did he leave you?"

"You seen it. I gave it to you all the first time."

"Remind me."

"Memos, lists of times and dates that they were going to raid, places to avoid."

"And in all that time, you never saw him clearly?"

"No, like I said. He had his back to a streetlight."

"Was he tall, short? Old, young? What did you notice about him?"

Obsanjo huffed and again his solicitor told him to cooperate.

"He was normal height. Not too fat, but his hoody was baggy. He was white; I saw his hands."

"What about his age?"

Obsanjo screwed his eyes up. "Not young—his voice was a bit raspy." Suddenly his voice picked up. "I remember now, he had a beard. I could just see the shadow."

Warren's heart beat faster. "What sort of beard? A goatee? Was it dark or light?"

"A full beard, I think. Scruffy, grey or white."

Sheehy had a beard.

Chapter 17

Warren and Sutton were meeting in the back of a different pub this time.

"I just don't know what to think." Warren had concluded his summing up of his meeting with Obsanjo. "On the one hand, the only real description that they had to go on was that of a middle-aged white man. But once they zeroed in on Sheehy, there's so much more to go on. The money, the SIM card and the information that Obsanjo handed over."

Sutton glared at his pint. The room they were meeting in may have been tucked out of the way, but Warren had worried that the landlord might come in to see what all the shouting was about. Sutton hadn't taken the news that Warren had gone behind his back to meet Obsanjo very well.

Still, true to form, once he'd said—or rather yelled—his piece, Sutton had gone back to moody contemplation of the matter at hand.

"It does add up. It's like Gavin said, we just could not catch a break with this guy. I lost count of the number of times the door-kickers went in, all fired up, and returned empty-handed. Somebody must have been feeding him information. You've met the guy; did he strike you as some great criminal strategist?"

Warren shook his head. "No, quite the opposite in fact. I see a chancer who fell and landed with his bum in the butter and ran with it until it all went wrong. Hell, he's probably amazed it lasted as long as it did."

"So we're left with several possibilities." Sutton spread his fingers. "First, Gavin is being framed. Somebody else was feeding Obsanjo that information and when it all came crashing down, they stitched up Gavin by planting the evidence. Obsanjo never did see his contact and so it wasn't too difficult to point the finger Gavin's way and have it stick."

"That implies that Obsanjo wasn't in on the stitch-up and that he's just been used."

"Not impossible. The second possibility is that the whole thing is a complete fabrication—that somebody saw Obsanjo's arrest and decided to use it to their advantage. They contacted Obsanjo and worked with him to plant the evidence to frame Gavin."

Warren frowned. "I don't like that one. It implies that the whole thing was done retrospectively; there's too much chance involved. As soon as Obsanjo was arrested—which they probably couldn't predict ahead of time—they'd have had to go and plant the money in Gavin's house. Then they would have to somehow collate convincing leaked evidence and put it somewhere that Obsanjo could send Professional Standards to so they could discover it. Then somehow produce a SIM card, which contacted Obsanjo's phone on a regular basis. And all of this would have to be coordinated with Obsanjo as he waits in prison—which realistically would require it to be done via privileged conversation between Obsanjo and the most corrupt brief in the profession."

"I agree. Which leaves only the third possibility—that Gavin is guilty as charged and this whole thing is a last, desperate attempt to save his own skin."

It was clear where Sutton's suspicions lay. He drained his pint and stared moodily into the empty glass.

"Well, for the time being, I have to operate on the assumption that Gavin was framed, which realistically only leaves the first possibility. The question is how can I prove it, one way or the other?"

The two men were silent for several minutes, before Sutton spoke up again.

"Something has just occurred to me, but I'm not sure how or if it helps us."

"At this stage, Tony, I'm all ears."

"What if Obsanjo's arrest wasn't entirely an accident? Presumably Obsanjo was caught because he wasn't tipped off in time, or the information he was given wasn't correct. What if that was deliberate—that all of the pieces were in place to bring Gavin down and it was decided that next time we planned a raid there'd be no warning. Obsanjo ends up inside, facing a long stretch, and he gets thinking—it wouldn't take long for a genius like Obsanjo to figure out that he might get some leniency if he squealed."

Warren thought about it. "It's certainly a possibility. And it could be useful to us. If we tell Obsanjo that his contact failed him deliberately, he's going to be pretty pissed off. If he is in on a conspiracy to frame Sheehy, then it might be enough to make him give up who was really behind it all. And if it was Sheehy, or he genuinely doesn't know, then what have we lost?" Warren's enthusiasm was infectious and even Sutton was smiling.

"You might just have come up with a way out of the conundrum."

"Let's not get too carried away; this might not work. Besides which, it means visiting him again and lying to him on tape."

Sutton's face fell. "Good point. It'll be hard for this not to come back on you when he tells Professional Standards. You're already batting on a sticky wicket after visiting him today without telling them—or me," he added pointedly.

Warren sighed. The elation he'd felt a few moments ago had gone completely. Another thought occurred to him. "It's quite possible that he's being fed information on the inside."

"What do you mean? How can you know that?"

"Well, up until now his description of his contact has been frustratingly vague, a middle-aged white man, of average build and height, his face not visible."

"Yeah, so?"

"Well suddenly today he remembers more details and what a surprise they match Sheehy. Either somebody has been feeding him information, perhaps showed him a photograph, or Sheehy is guilty and Obsanjo really did suddenly remember what his mysterious contact looked like."

Sutton breathed out, a frustrated hiss. They were going around in circles.

"We need more."

Warren nodded his agreement. The question was: what was the next step? It was time to follow Susan's advice. "There's something I haven't told you. That I haven't told anyone."

Warren suddenly felt nervous; he'd been rehearsing what he was going to say for the past hour and he still didn't know how he was going to do it.

Sutton's face remained carefully neutral until Warren finished, before taking a deep breath and puffing out his cheeks.

"Shit." Sutton shook his head. "I'm not sure what to say."

Warren waited expectantly, his fingers toying nervously with the beer glass in front of him.

"I knew the story about your father—it's all in the records and

136

when you were confirmed in post, I did a bit of research." Sutton was unapologetic. He'd already been quite open in the past about how he'd made it his business to investigate his new commander.

"I admit I was curious to meet you—I guess I wanted to see if it had any effect on you as a copper—none that I can see."

"Glad I passed the test."

Sutton ignored the forced flippancy. "The thing is, even if Sheehy is telling the truth, when he says he planted that gun to stitch up Delmarno, is there any evidence that he even knew your father? I haven't seen anything."

Warren shook his head. "No, but it's a hell of a story."

"That's exactly my point. No offence, Chief, but it doesn't take Sigmund Freud to work out that your father's suicide is your Achilles' heel. Gavin is in deep shit—he's desperate and he's on the outside now. If he wants somebody on the force to do his dirty work, he's going to need to give them a hell of a bloody incentive. I think he's playing you."

Sutton sat back. His expression was resolute, his arms folded.

Warren didn't like the implication that he was being taken for a fool and said so.

Sutton remained adamant. "I'm sorry, sir, but I don't see anything here to convince me. You said that he gave you information as a show of good faith, but so far it's just words. Sure, the records surrounding Delmarno's conviction are patchy, but I'm seeing cock-up not conspiracy at the moment. I want more."

Warren opened his briefcase. "This is what he gave me when we met." He passed over the results of the investigation into Anton Liebig's death, annotated with Mag Richardson's notes.

"You kept these close to your chest," remarked Sutton, clearly somewhat offended that Warren hadn't shared them sooner.

"You could say that. Why do you think I kept my stab vest on so long?" The attempt at levity fell flat, eliciting little more than a grunt as Sutton scanned the sheets.

"So who are this Mr and Mrs Liebig?"

"Read the reports, first. Keep an open mind."

Warren knew that he was biased; he wanted Sutton's honest opinion before he complicated matters by revealing more. Sutton shrugged and carried on reading.

"OK, the crash investigation was pretty cursory, I can see that, but it was New Year's Eve. Mags knows her stuff, but I'm not seeing anything that screams conspiracy. I don't see the relevance here."

"Dr Liebig was the coroner who presided over my father's inquest and declared it a suicide." Warren passed over the newspaper clippings. "It's legitimate. I went and checked the court records online."

Sutton looked thoughtful. "You know that I have to point out that if you could access the court records, so could Gavin?"

Warren fought to keep the frustration from his voice. "It's a pretty big coincidence though, don't you think? Vinny Delmarno is released from prison swearing revenge. Gavin Sheehy, the man who stitched him up, gets charged with corruption. Reggie Williamson, who provided the gun used in the stitch-up, is stabbed to death. The third person involved in the conspiracy, my father, died in a mysterious suicide whilst Delmarno was trying to avoid conviction. And the man who pronounced that death as a suicide dies in a suspicious traffic accident some months after Delmarno's release."

"I agree that it's a hell of a coincidence—but it's also bloody convenient." Sutton raised a hand to stop Warren's argument. "Gavin's had a year cooling his heels to come up with this. Taken individually, these are all interesting but otherwise unrelated incidents. The only glue that binds them together is Gavin's story. We need real evidence linking Delmarno to these events, more than just suspicion and the word of a self-confessed corrupt copper."

It was the use of the word "we" that convinced Warren that despite his bluster, Sutton was willing to investigate further.

"So what do you suggest we do next then, Inspector." Sutton grimaced; he still wasn't happy.

"We need to find out what we can about Dr Liebig."

"My thoughts exactly."

Chapter 18

Warren and Sutton pulled into the small village of Risby to the west of Bury St Edmunds. It had taken the two men the better part of an hour to negotiate the ever-congested A14 eastwards into Suffolk.

David Liebig, the only son of the late Dr Anton Liebig and his wife Rosemary, lived in a smart, one-storey cottage near the river. Before setting out, Warren had called the forty-year-old and arranged for him to meet them at his home.

David Liebig was clearly his father's son. Tall and spare, with a receding hairline, he possessed the same sharp features and generous nose. However, the hollowness of his eyes, with their dark smudges beneath, spoke of sleeplessness and recent weight loss.

"I don't understand why you are here," he started after inviting the two officers into the airy, well-lit living room that overlooked the tree-lined waterway only a few paces beyond his garden wall.

"The inquest was concluded last month. Case closed." His mouth twisted into a grimace.

"There are a few details surrounding that night we would like to clarify," said Warren, trying to be vague; everything so far was little more than speculation and the last thing he wanted to do was to pique the man's interest. If his suspicions were correct, they would need to proceed with caution. Discretion at this stage was essential if they were to investigate any foul play without alerting any guilty parties. But it would be a difficult balancing act—the man in front of them was the son of a former coroner. He could very well know that the presence of two such senior detectives was irregular. With the benefit of hindsight, perhaps it would have been better not to have brought Tony Sutton along with him; however, now that Warren had finally brought him in to his full confidence, he wanted the man's impressions and insights.

Liebig regarded them for a few seconds, before shrugging wearily. "Go ahead."

"What do you know of the events of the thirtieth of December?"

"Just what I was told. I was woken at 6 a.m. by two uniformed police officers on the Saturday morning—the thirty-first—who told me that my parents had been killed in a car accident shortly before midnight. They left the road at high speed on a winding country lane and hit a tree."

The man closed his eyes in pain, but his voice remained steady. "No other vehicles were involved. Both died at the scene. A few days later the autopsy revealed that Dad had been over the drink-drive limit."

Warren watched him carefully. "According to our records, your parents lived near Huntingdon in Cambridgeshire, but the accident took place in central Hertfordshire, about fifty miles away. Why were they so far away from home?"

"They had been to the annual awards dinner at Dad's golf club. He was team captain for the seniors and was making a presentation and a speech. Mum didn't play, but she was friendly with a lot of the other wives and women players and it's a pretty big shindig: formal dress, silver service and live music. They went every year. It was a really big deal."

"So your father was familiar with the route he was driving?" asked Sutton.

"Very. He'd played a couple of times a week for the past twenty-odd years. Obviously, he usually drove home earlier in the day, rather than at midnight, but the accident occurred on his usual route. He knew those roads like the back of his hand."

"According to the golf club's website, the clubhouse is actually a hotel and guests can stay over after such an evening for a modest fee. Why did your parents decide to drive home that night?"

Liebig sighed and rubbed his eyes. "Ordinarily they would have stayed, but this year they needed to be back home." He paused, his voice turning bitter. "My wife and I split up last year. It's been a bit… unpleasant. She took the kids with her. Mum and Dad didn't get to see them at Christmas, but Rebecca—my wife—agreed to let us have them for the day on New Year's Eve. Mum and Dad were going to come over and give them their Christmas presents—spoil them a bit."

He bit his lip. "Telling them that Nanny and Granddad wouldn't be coming and trying to explain to a four- and a seven-year-old that they wouldn't see them again was almost as bad as the knock on the door that morning."

Warren waited respectfully for a few moments as the other man composed himself.

"Forgive me, but it seems quite a drive to play a game of golf. There are plenty of good clubs nearer to home, surely?"

Liebig snorted. "Yeah, that's what Mum used to say. In fact, part of the reason they moved down to Huntingdon when he retired was to be closer to the club. Dad used to be a coroner in Warwickshire and it must have been a four-hour round trip. I spent my teens living in the village of Kenilworth near Coventry—your accent sounds familiar. Do you know the area at all, DCI Jones?"

"Yes, I'm familiar with it." Warren didn't elaborate. It was getting a little too close to home. "So how did he come to join a club down here?" he pressed.

Liebig frowned. "I'm not really sure. I know that one or two of his colleagues were members. I think some of his friends from his Cambridge University days also played at the club." He smiled slightly. "That was the only reason Mum agreed to move back to Cambridgeshire, I think. They met at Cambridge when they were students and they still have lots of friends around here. Whilst he was off playing golf, Mum would catch the bus or the train into Cambridge or Ely and spend the day with them. I don't think she really enjoyed living up in the Midlands. I don't know what she'd have done with herself if they'd stayed there after retirement."

"Did your Mum not drive then?"

"No not really. She had a licence and occasionally she'd take the car to the shops but she never enjoyed it and never had her own car. Dad deliberately bought an automatic with all of the driver's aids you can think of to persuade her, but she wouldn't drive at night or anywhere she wasn't familiar with."

That explained why Dr Liebig had driven that night, even if he'd had a drink. But so far, they'd uncovered more questions than answers. Exactly why Dr Liebig had joined a golf club several counties away remained a mystery in Warren's mind. Was it significant?

Warren decided to change tack. "The circumstances surrounding the accident—what do you make of them?"

Liebig's face hardened slightly. "I have trouble believing them, to be honest." His right eye twitched slightly and his voice tightened.

"Dad was a coroner for years. He presided over thousands of inquests, including those caused by drink-driving. He was evangelical about it. He made me and my friends attend an inquest when we started driving lessons to scare us into not drink-driving." His mouth twitched. "It worked. Anyway, eyewitnesses said that he had two small glasses of red wine with his meal and then socialised for several hours before they left. There would have been pretty much no alcohol in his blood when he drove home."

"The pathologist stated that he was over the limit. He also said that he thought there were traces of spirits in his stomach."

Liebig shook his head in frustration. "That's what doesn't make any sense—Dad didn't even like spirits. The autopsy also said there was lots of what appeared to be Coke in his stomach. That makes more sense. Dad used to drink Diet Coke when he was out. He was diabetic, so he didn't drink anything with sugar in it."

"That brings us onto another finding—your father's blood glucose levels were rather high. How well did he control his diabetes?"

"Again, that's weird. Dad had been diabetic for years. He was pretty careful with his diet; he made sure that his levels were stable. I was really surprised to find out that his blood sugar was so high."

"Did he take medication to control it? For example, did he inject insulin?"

Again, Liebig shook his head. "Dad was a type II diabetic. They call it 'insulin-resistant' these days. Insulin had no effect. For the most part he just made sure that he ate a low-sugar diet. He'd been going to the club for years and he wasn't the only person with special dietary needs. The chefs would prepare him low-carb dishes. And like I said, he didn't drink sugary drinks. He did take a drug before eating sometimes to help keep him on an even keel. Glinide, I think it was called, but he didn't like to use it if he was driving, since it can sometimes lead to hypoglycaemia—low blood sugar." He snorted again. "Ironic really—maybe if he had taken it he wouldn't have been hyper and maybe he wouldn't have crashed."

The questions were continuing to stack up. He could see from Sutton's face that he too was struggling to process the information. With nothing else to ask, Warren rose to his feet and thanked the grieving son for his time, apologising again for the intrusion.

As he led them to the door, Liebig was quietly contemplative. "I guess you coming here wasn't a bad thing. Maybe it'll spur me on to finally deal with their affairs. I've only been back to their house once since the accident. And I couldn't stay in there after I saw the place."

Sutton nodded sympathetically. "I guess it holds a lot of memories for you."

"Some, although it wasn't my childhood home. I think it was the desecration and the damage that had been done that really upset me. I'd barely had time to accept Mum and Dad's death and tell the kids when the neighbours rang to tell me about the break-in."

Warren stopped so fast that Sutton bumped into his back. "What do you mean, break-in?"

Liebig looked at him curiously. "Didn't you know? The night they died, they were burgled. The bastards tore the place apart, stole all of Mum's jewellery and set fire to the living room."

Chapter 19

The crash site looked very different to the photographs taken at New Year. For a start, somebody had taken heed of the inquest's recommendation and put up crash barriers on the bend and for the twenty or so metres either side. Secondly, the trees and shrubbery lining the route were now in full bloom, in stark contrast to the leafless, wintery scene in the pictures.

Nonetheless, it wasn't difficult to orient the photographs correctly and identify where the car had swerved off the road. Tony Sutton and Warren had parked in a lay-by a couple of hundred metres past the bend and were now standing on the side of the road dressed in high-visibility jackets. Dusk was a couple of hours away, but the dense canopy overhead cast dark shadows.

"You know that we should probably close the carriageway off for this."

Warren said nothing.

"But that would require permission and we'd have to file a report." Sutton looked at Warren. "I don't think you're ready to file a report about this yet, are you?"

"Is that a problem?" It was a genuine question; he was relying entirely on Sutton's goodwill.

"Just try not to get run over. The paperwork's a bitch."

Warren smiled.

Even with the newly grown foliage, it was easy to see where the car had come off the road. The trunk of the oak tree that it had impacted was heavily scarred, fresh wood easily visible where the bark had been smashed off. The large branch that had shattered the windscreen and all but decapitated the two occupants was still broken at the end and split. In contrast to the rest of the tree, it remained leafless.

Sutton was comparing the tree's position to the diagram of the crash scene. "He was well past the apex of the bend and would have been travelling in a straight line for thirty-three metres, before the skid marks start and the car swerves to the right." He paused as he did some quick mental arithmetic. "At fifty miles per hour, that's about a second and a half. Whatever caused him to swerve happened after he had exited the bend."

"A sudden obstruction? Something ran out into the road?"

"That seems most likely. But what? There are no deer reported around here. I wouldn't have thought he'd have panicked too much for a rabbit or a hare. A badger maybe, they're pretty big I suppose."

"A late-night reveller wandering home? They cause the car to swerve off the road and they're so panicked they leave and keep quiet?"

"Well, it wouldn't be the first time, but we're several miles from anywhere—hell of a walk home, even after a skinful."

Warren stared up the road thoughtfully. "Let me read that report again." He took the sheet off Sutton and scanned it quickly. "This eyewitness report. She claims to have seen two cars at about that time, travelling fast and close together a mile or so before the accident scene." He pointed to a sentence in the interview.

"She says that she couldn't make out any detail, in part because the car behind had its main beams on and dazzled her." He paused. "A few years ago, I read a thriller about the death of Princess Diana. The book claimed that her driver was blinded by somebody using a flash gun from a camera, which caused the crash."

"But they were travelling in the wrong direction. I can see that an aggressive driver flashing his lights and sitting on his bumper may have forced Liebig to take the bend faster than he should have, but why would he swerve?"

"What if it was a team effort?" Warren pointed up the road to the lay-by. "How do you think you would react if you exited a sharp bend at high speed, with some arsehole right up your backside, before suddenly being confronted with a pair of main-beam headlamps sitting in the middle of the road, especially if you're a little the worse for wear from booze, fatigue and too much blood sugar?"

Sutton grimaced. "Impossible to say, but probably not well."

* * *

"We should have worn plus fours and signed out the unmarked Aston," commented Tony Sutton as Warren's eight-year-old Ford Mondeo turned into the long, sweeping driveway that led towards the Allingham Golf Course and Hotel. The club of the late Dr Liebig was certainly a step up from Allesley Park Pitch and Putt where Warren had spent his childhood summers. A sprawling stately home, Grade-I listed according to the website that Tony Sutton was currently navigating on his phone, it looked more like one of the National Trust houses that his grandparents had used to drag him around as a child.

"What I'd like to know is how a retired coroner could afford to play at a place like this on a government pension." Sutton carried on reading. "The green fees alone are thousands a year. It doesn't even say how much membership costs. You have to ask."

"That's certainly something I've been wondering," admitted Warren. Their earlier visit to the late coroner's son had failed to answer questions about why Liebig had chosen to join a club so far away from his home; the inflated membership costs just added to the mystery.

"Staff parking is around the back." Sutton pointed out the discreet sign.

"We aren't staff," said Warren firmly. The slight smile on his colleague's face suggested that he approved of Warren's decision to park his decidedly middle-class family car alongside two Bentleys, a Porsche and a vintage Jaguar.

By the time the two detectives had exited the car, a smartly suited man in his mid-forties with a thin moustache and a slightly dubious French accent was pacing towards them.

"I'm sorry, gentlemen. That parking is reserved for members."

Warren ignored him and flashed his warrant card. "We have an appointment with Mr Molinie."

To his credit, the valet's faux smile hardly faltered as he ushered the two men through the hotel's ornate doors. Warren barely had time to take in the wood-panelled splendour of the beautifully appointed reception before another, older man appeared through a partially hidden door next to the main desk.

"Mr Jones, I am Mr Molinie, the hotel manager." The man's manner was polite but brusque, his handshake brisk. He didn't wait for Warren to introduce Sutton, instead gesturing the two men to follow him through the doorway. The two police officers exchanged glances; it was clear that he wanted them out of sight as quickly as possible.

Crossing the threshold, they found themselves in a small, claustrophobic space that had been converted into an office. On the other side of the hidden cubbyhole another door, this one unconcealed and slightly ajar, exited into what appeared to be a service corridor. The smell of cooking and muffled shouting over a noisy radio suggested that the kitchen of the hotel's five-star restaurant lay nearby.

Safely out of the view of any well-heeled guests, the manager turned to face them. "So what can I help you with, officers? My understanding is that the inquest into the tragic death of Dr Liebig has been concluded. An unfortunate accident, I believe. My staff fully cooperated with the investigation."

"As with any such death, there are always a few loose ends that need tying up. We're just here to do that," lied Warren smoothly.

The manager looked at him for a few long seconds, before shrugging. "Of course. I have copies of the information that you requested."

Picking up a foolscap folder stuffed with loose sheets, he plucked a printed list out. "For large parties, guests pre-order their meals. Our head chef has been here many years and she knew that Dr Liebig and three other diners had special dietary requirements, and she prepared dishes with a low glycaemic index." He pointed to a row on the list. "For starter, he had a hearty winter broth with wholegrain bread. For main course, a steamed salmon with fresh, seasonal vegetables and a creamy sauce—no potatoes or other starchy foods—then instead of a sweet dessert a cheese board with wholegrain crackers."

Assuming that the menu records were accurate, it would seem that the meal consumed by the unfortunate diner was not the cause of his unusually high blood sugar readings. Warren decided to return to that question later. "What about alcohol? As you are no doubt aware, Dr Liebig was found to be above the legal limit for driving."

The manager's smile stiffened slightly. "I'm afraid that we have no information about what he drank, and of course, it would be up to the guest to ensure that they were fit to drive." He licked his lips nervously, clearly worried that the two detectives might be assisting relatives to prepare some sort of civil suit against the hotel. "Of course, we take our responsibilities very seriously and if a guest feels that they are not in a suitable condition to drive home we will help make arrangements for a taxi or even offer them a very reasonable overnight rate if they decide to stay."

"So you can't tell us anything about what Dr Liebig drank that evening?" Sutton was staring at the man hard, his instincts telling him that the man wasn't being entirely forthcoming.

"Well, I know how many bottles of wine were ordered for the group as a whole during the meal, but of course, there were carafes of iced water and there is no record of who drank what." He spoke quickly. "I believe that an acquaintance sitting near to Dr Liebig testified that he drank two small glasses of red wine with the meal and that he didn't think that he was served anything else alcoholic."

"So they were able to order drinks throughout the evening? How did they pay for their drinks? Was there a tab or did they pay cash at the bar?"

Molinie sighed slightly. "It was an open bar with silver service. Guests simply asked one of the waiting staff, who then fetched the drink from the bar."

Warren's interest piqued. "So perhaps one of the waiting staff might remember serving Dr Liebig?"

"Well, it was a few months ago. I doubt they could remember that long ago."

"You'd be amazed what the human brain can recall," interjected Sutton flatly.

"We tend to use outside agency staff for such large functions. I don't personally know each waiter or waitress."

"I'm sure that a hotel as smoothly run as this—which is able to print off the exact dining history of a past guest—maintains impeccable employment records," stated Warren, without breaking the manager's gaze.

"Well, we do try to use the same agency for all of our functions," the man admitted weakly.

Sutton cocked his chin towards the reception area behind the wall. "I notice there's a pretty big party this evening—would I be correct in assuming that you'll be bringing in agency staff tonight?"

The manager closed his eyes briefly. "Yes. We're bussing in about a dozen serving staff from Middlesbury Catering Services to serve guests this evening. They're mostly college kids from Middlesbury Tech."

"Are they likely to be the same staff who worked the thirtieth of December?"

Defeated, the manager nodded. "We usually ask for the same staff so that we don't have to waste time giving them a tour of the hotel before their shift starts." Clearly deciding that cooperation would be the quickest way to get the two police officers out from under his feet, he motioned to the phone.

"Why don't I give the company a ring and ask for a list of those working that night and see if they are coming tonight."

"That's very kind of you, Mr Molinie," said Warren sincerely. "Just one more thing…"

"Yes, you can use my office." The manager sighed.

According to the emailed list from Middlesbury Catering Services, a dozen serving staff had been supplied for the awards dinner, nine of whom were amongst the minibus-full due to arrive within the next half hour.

The two detectives decided to speak to each member of staff individually.

"My gut tells me that something weird happened that night," Warren confided to Sutton as they waited for the minibus to arrive.

"Mine feels the same way. But what?"

"I'm not sure, but I think we'll know it when we see it. Let's just play it by ear and listen to what they have to say. But I'd like to make sure that we don't spook them too much. We'll ask them to keep it discreet."

The minibus arrived on the hour. All of the fourteen young people on board had obviously worked at the hotel before as they each grabbed their bags and headed towards the kitchens without being shown.

By now, the hotel manager was clearly feeling under pressure and wanted the two detectives out of his way. Therefore, he didn't waste any time in sending the nine staff to his office, one at a time, to be interviewed by Warren and Sutton.

The staff, a mixture of women and men mostly in their late teens or early twenties, seemed quite happy to help. Three of them looked at the photograph of Dr Liebig before shaking their heads apologetically, unable to recall him. Two agreed that he looked familiar but were certain that they hadn't served him.

The sixth waitress looked at the picture for several long seconds, before screwing up her eyes in concentration. "I definitely saw him.

I didn't serve him, but I was responsible for the other end of his table. I'm trying to remember who worked that half of the table."

Warren felt his heart rate start to increase. "Zack," she proclaimed triumphantly.

"Zachary Eddleston?" asked Sutton, as he looked at the names on the list. If she was correct, then the server in question had been on this evening's minibus.

"I don't know his surname, but he's here tonight. Dark hair, pale."

Thanking her for her time, Warren saw the young woman out of the door, before beckoning to Molinie. "Can we skip to the last name on the list: Zachary Eddleston?"

Molinie nodded, disappearing into the bowels of the hotel. A few seconds later he returned, with a skinny, dark-haired young man in tow.

"What's this about?"

The young man appeared nervous. Warren smiled.

"Nothing to worry about, I'm Detective Chief Inspector Warren Jones and this is Detective Inspector Tony Sutton…" He'd barely finished his introduction before the young man turned on the spot and bolted through the door.

* * *

Tony Sutton was closest to the door and it took him only a few quick paces to catch up with the fleeing youth. The burly officer's years on the forces' rugby team served him well as he tackled the young man. By the time Warren had made his way around the desk and joined the DI, Sutton had the waiter in an armlock.

After frogmarching him back into the office he shoved him against the desk and kicked his feet apart.

"I'm going to search you. Do you have anything on you that you shouldn't or any sharp objects that could harm me or my colleague?"

Grounds for an arrest were pretty shaky but running away from a police officer was suspicious and gave reasonable justification for a search, Warren decided.

Eddleston shook his head, saying nothing. Aside from a few scuffs on his smart black trousers and messy hair, he appeared unharmed. Good. The paperwork if the lad tried to claim assault was time-consuming and tedious.

Sutton expertly patted the youth down before turning his pockets inside out. Finally, he reached inside his jacket and retrieved a battered packet of cigarettes. Eddleston's eyes closed briefly, a look of pain on his face. Opening the box, Sutton pulled out a cheap Bic lighter, two cigarettes and—with a look of satisfaction—an inexpertly rolled joint. A quick sniff by both officers confirmed their suspicions.

Eddleston was clearly defeated and simply nodded wearily when Warren instructed him to sit behind the desk and not to even think about running out the other door. The two detectives stepped into the deserted corridor and bent their heads together.

"Well, the weed would explain why he tried to do a runner," Sutton suggested.

"Maybe, but it's bugger all. It's a single joint so he can't be done for intent to supply and he probably knows that we have the leeway to just warn him and confiscate." Warren paused thoughtfully. "It could be a useful lever though."

Sutton nodded his agreement as he fished a plastic evidence bag out of his jacket pocket and dropped the joint into it. "Do we play the usual roles?"

Warren nodded. "Yep. Unleash your inner arsehole, Tony."

Sutton smiled. "A pleasure…"

* * *

The evidence bag slid across the table as Sutton marched back into the room. He leant over the nervous youth who appeared to have developed a twitch under his right eye. Warren sat down wordlessly.

"Unless my nose deceives me, this appears to be cannabis. A class-B drug. I'll bet you've been supplying this shit to half the staff in this hotel. Or is it just the kids from the catering agency? Perhaps a bit of puff before the shift starts, you know, to mellow you out and relieve the boredom?"

Eddleston shook his head vehemently. "No, sir. Nothing like that. It's just the one joint. I got it off a mate this morning. I was going to have it when I got home tonight."

His shaky voice and politeness was encouraging—an otherwise good kid experiencing his first brush with the law. Warren suspected that when he ran Eddleston's name through the PNC later nothing would come up. That should make things a little easier.

Sutton snorted. "Really, you expect me to believe that? I'll bet if I speak to the manager of this hotel or ring up the catering college they'll be very interested in what we've found. Druggies like you bring them all sorts of problems. They'll be happy to get rid of you."

The kid was buying it, Warren could see. There was fear in his eyes as he digested the implications for his future. The hotel would certainly fire him, as would the catering agency. He might even lose his place at college.

"No, it's not like that, I swear. It's just the one joint. I'm not even a regular user. I just have the odd toke at a party. I've been a bit stressed lately and my mate had a spare one. He gave it to me to

156

help me sleep. I didn't even pay him for it." The kid was starting to babble now, the twitch under his right eye almost constant.

Warren placed his hand on Sutton's shoulder, as if to restrain him, then leant forward. "I'm sure a bright lad like you knows the consequences of being caught with drugs in the workplace—" Eddleston nodded "—and I'm sure that you also know that we have the option to either arrest you and charge you with possession, issue you with an on-the-spot-fine or let you off with a warning."

Eddleston stared at his hands. Warren reached across the table to an A4 folder and removed a full-colour headshot of Dr Liebig. "Did you serve this man on the night of the thirtieth of December?"

"Shit," Eddleston whispered quietly before looking away.

His indecision was palpable. After a few seconds, Sutton slid the evidence bag closer to the young man. He bit his lip.

"Your decision, Zachary. We just want information."

Warren's voice was low, almost soothing, in stark contrast to his racing heart. Finally, it looked as though at least some questions were going to be answered.

"I didn't think I was doing any harm. These rich guys, they make all sorts of weird requests. I figured if he wants a drink but doesn't want his missus to nag him, then who am I to say no? I didn't know he was driving."

The explanation seemed weak, as if he was trying to convince himself as much as Warren.

"Take it from the top, Zachary. Tell us what happened."

Breathing deeply, Eddleston sat up. "I was in charge of serving his end of the table. I knew who he was as I had to serve him a specific dish. During the meal, I poured him two glasses of red wine." He paused. Warren and Sutton said nothing.

"After we cleared the meal, they had all the speeches and stuff.

I went to serve him more wine, but he turned me away. I just topped up his water glass and moved on." Eddleston looked at both officers.

"He never actually said he was driving, so later in the evening when I got told he wanted another drink I just assumed that he was staying over but his wife didn't like him drinking."

Warren felt confused. "So Dr Liebig asked you for another drink later?"

"Well, sort of. At least I thought he did." Eddleston could see that he wasn't making sense. "After the speeches, there was live music and an open bar. As part of the service, waiting staff are encouraged to keep an eye on the guests they've already served and fetch them drinks and stuff. Dr Liebig asked me for a Diet Coke, so I went to prepare it. Then one of the managers approached me and said that Dr Liebig wanted something with a little more kick, but that his wife mustn't know. He gave me a twenty-quid note and said there was more if I kept on serving him."

"Who was the manager?"

Eddleston shook his head. "I honestly don't know. I've seen him around once or twice but I don't know his name."

Warren motioned for him to continue.

"Anyway, apparently he liked his Diet Coke to be prepared in a special way. Half a shot of vodka, then fill up a tall glass half and half with Diet Coke and regular Coke, lots of ice and a slice of lime. Make sure it's well mixed."

Sutton stared at him. "And you didn't think this was at all weird? He asks for a Diet Coke and you practically prepare a bloody cocktail for him."

The look on Eddleston's face suggested that he probably had found it weird, but the liberal application of twenty-pound notes had quelled his doubts.

"These rich folks make all sorts of weird requests." His tone turned defensive. "I mean that's nothing. That night there were three new girls serving—the minibus picked them up on the way. All very pretty—Eastern Europeans. None of them spoke proper English and they didn't have a clue what they were doing. None of them came back with us on the minibus. Draw your own conclusions." He folded his arms.

"OK, so how many of these drinks did you serve Dr Liebig?"

Eddleston's brief show of defiance faded. "Probably five or six over the night. He was pretty thirsty."

Warren glanced over at Sutton. With only half a shot of vodka in each glass the total amount of alcohol consumed was probably just enough to tip him over the limit. And diluted with plenty of Coke, ice and lime it was probably tasteless. But why the strange mixture of regular and Diet Coke? And who was the manager who bribed Eddleston, allegedly on Liebig's behalf? It seemed that for every question they answered another two replaced them.

* * *

"We should arrest him and charge him with manslaughter," Sutton voiced as the two detectives held another quiet conference outside the door to the office.

"I agree, but I'm worried about the rumours if we march him out of here in cuffs and stick him in the back of the car. Even if we could do it with nobody noticing, it won't take long for the other staff to figure out why he's disappeared before his shift even starts. If Eddleston is telling the truth, he's the monkey not the organ grinder."

Sutton nodded. "The last thing we want is for this mysterious manager who supposedly bribed him to get spooked and disappear. Let's bring him in tomorrow and sit him down with a sketch artist. We can always arrest him down the station if we want to. He's scared enough not to do a runner."

After securing a relieved Eddleston's agreement that he'd attend the station voluntarily the next day, the two detectives thanked Molinie for his assistance, implying that they'd concluded their investigation and it was now closed. The hotel manager clearly couldn't care less and was glad to get them out of his way before the evening guests started arriving. The two men left by the same door that they'd arrived by, deep in their own thoughts.

Chapter 20

"OK, so Eddleston was bribed to spike Liebig's drink, which may have led to him crashing the car. But it's not a particularly effective method of murder, is it? The amount of alcohol only took him slightly over the limit. He could have driven home easily without incident." Sutton was playing with his lower lip as he mulled over the revelations of the past hour.

"Maybe they didn't intend him to crash? We should check the call logs for anonymous phone calls reporting a drunk driver. Somebody might just have wanted to cause trouble for him."

"Possible, I suppose. Maybe Liebig pissed somebody off at the club. My old man plays skittles for an over-sixties league. You wouldn't believe the backstabbing and politics that a bunch of pensioners with nothing else to occupy them can conjure up to pass the time."

The two men lapsed into silence.

"What puzzles me is why this mysterious manager was so insistent on the way that Eddleston prepared the drink. Surely a long glass of Diet Coke with ice and lime would be enough to hide the taste of half a shot of vodka? Why mix it with regular Coke as well?"

"I've had a thought about that, Tony. What are your plans for this evening? Would you like to take part in a scientific experiment?"

"I'll get my lab coat and safety goggles."

* * *

Susan answered the door to the two men, offering Sutton a peck on the cheek in greeting.

"She never welcomes me that way, Tony," joked Warren as he carried the carrier bag full of bottles and ice into the kitchen.

"Seeing Tony's a special treat. I have to put up with you every day," retorted his wife as she led the smirking DI into the living room.

By the time Warren reappeared the other two were sitting at the coffee table, with Sutton leafing through one of the A level Biology textbooks that Susan had piled on the coffee table.

Carefully placing the tray of drinks on the table, Warren handed out pens and paper.

Susan eyed the full tray. "I hope you're doing the washing up. You must have used every glass in the kitchen. And that better not be permanent marker you've used to write on them."

"I don't think so. Either way there's plenty of vodka left. I'll use it to wipe off the ink afterwards."

"No you won't. I've seen what brand you bought and you aren't wasting that on marker pen. You can use some of that revolting stuff we brought back from Tenerife."

Warren lined the glasses up on the table, using coasters to stop the condensation marking the expensive, polished wood.

"OK, eight different drinks. I want you to tell me what's in them. Keep it fair. Just write down on the paper what you think they are without saying anything and I'll tell you if you're right at the end."

Sitting back, he waited as Sutton and Susan carefully took

a mouthful from each of the sweating glasses before recording their thoughts on the paper. Eventually they were finished.

Warren lifted the first glass from the tray.

"Regular Coke," said Sutton firmly.

"I agree. You can feel the sugar on your teeth."

Warren replaced the glass and pointed to the second.

"Diet Coke. It has that slight aftertaste from the artificial sweetener."

"Me as well, Guv. I drink enough of the stuff to tell the difference."

"Number three is Diet Coke, maybe with a splash of vodka," stated Susan.

Sutton shook his head. "I don't think so. You're right about the Diet Coke but I couldn't taste any vodka."

"Number four definitely had vodka in it," said Susan confidently.

"Yeah, I'll give you that. Probably full-sugar Coke as well."

They both agreed that glass five was Diet Coke and vodka, but again disagreed about number six.

"Diet Coke with vodka," claimed Susan.

"Diet Coke, but with all of that ice and lime I'm on the fence about the vodka."

Glasses seven and eight were both marked down as Diet Coke only.

"Well, unless you've pulled a fast one, Boss, you've successfully hidden the Diet Coke and full-sugar Coke mixture."

"No fast one. The last two were a fifty-fifty mix. Number seven had half a shot of vodka in it as well. I also hid half a shot in glass three and slightly more in glass six."

"Well, Susan spotted the vodka in those two but I was pretty fooled. Do you think the mix of Diet and regular Coke was to hide the taste better?"

"Maybe, but I think Susan may have another explanation."

Susan picked up one of the textbooks and opened it at a marked page.

"After Warren called me earlier, I dug out the textbooks and did a bit of research online. Apparently, Dr Liebig was a diabetic suffering from type II diabetes. What do you know about diabetes, Tony?"

"Not a lot beyond what they teach us on the first aid courses and what his son said when we interviewed him. They have to control their blood sugar or they get really lethargic and pass out. Some use insulin but apparently that didn't work with Liebig."

"That's correct. Basically, when you eat food that has sugar in it, or lots of starchy carbohydrates that are broken down into sugar, that sugar, called glucose, is absorbed into the bloodstream. This then causes the concentration of glucose in the blood to rise."

Picking up a pen, she sketched a graph with a curving line rising.

"In non-diabetics, the pancreas releases the hormone insulin, which takes the excess glucose from the blood and stores it away inside the liver until it's needed, reducing the concentration again." The line on the graph dropped back down again to the same height it had started from.

"The body tries to keep the concentration of glucose in the blood between four and seven millimoles per litre." At Sutton's questioning look, she waved her hand. "Don't worry about what that means; it isn't important. Anyhow, everybody knows that if a diabetic's blood glucose concentration gets too low, they get ill. Non-diabetics tap into those stores of glucose in the liver to replace what the body has used up. Diabetics don't have those stores so they need to eat more sugar. With me so far?"

Sutton nodded.

"What people don't always realise is that too high a concentration of blood glucose is also dangerous. Really high levels can cause ketoacidosis, which can lead to coma or even death. But over time, even slightly raised levels can cause long-term complications such as blindness or nerve problems or even organ damage, with few or no immediate symptoms."

"Dr Liebig's concentration was fourteen point two. What effect would that have?"

"That's not enough to cause him to pass out or anything but it's still unhealthily high. His body would probably have been trying to get rid of the excess glucose from the blood as best it could."

"How could it do that if insulin doesn't work?" asked Sutton.

"Urination. The classic test for diabetes used to be sweet-tasting urine."

"Piss off!" choked Sutton.

"Exactly," remarked Susan, who'd heard pretty much every joke imaginable from her A level students over the years. "Non-diabetics don't normally release glucose in their pee unless they've eaten a ridiculous amount of sugar. Diabetics can release enough that you can taste it. Of course, these days there's a blood test."

"Glad to hear it," muttered Sutton. "Hang on. Didn't Eddleston say that Liebig was thirsty? That he had five or six drinks over the evening. That's a lot of Coke."

"Exactly," said Warren. "It was a vicious circle. The more sugar he drank, especially on top of a full meal, the more he needed to pee. The more he peed, the more thirsty he felt, so he drank more."

"And every time he asked for a glass of Diet Coke, he got a load more sugar and half a shot of vodka." Sutton shook his head. "Devious."

The three sat in silence for a few moments, contemplating what they had discovered.

"We need to find out who owns that damn golf club and get a list of its members," decided Warren.

"I agree, but I think that's a job for tomorrow, Boss. In the meantime, what are we going to do with all this Coke?"

Warren picked up glass five. "I don't know about you two, but I intend to conceal some evidence."

TUESDAY 3RD APRIL

Chapter 21

Vinny Delmarno glanced at his watch impatiently. They'd agreed upon 7.30 a.m.; the man was already almost ten minutes late and Delmarno hated waiting.

"Relax, sweetheart, he'll be here soon enough. He's probably stuck in traffic." Jocelyn kissed him lightly on the forehead. Delmarno forced himself not to say anything; he knew that if he did it would just start an argument and he wasn't in the mood. She just didn't understand.

It was something that nobody had warned him about when he'd left prison—the impatience. In prison you had to be patient. Time passed slowly behind bars; locked in a cell for anything up to twenty-two hours a day, you learnt to let time pass at its own pace. There were only two ways to make the time pass faster he had found; however, he'd sworn off drugs and alcohol when he got the new kidney and there were only so many hours a man could sleep each day.

Even when you were allowed to leave your cell (and the number of hours each day varied with the prison, the number of staff and the whim of the current Home Secretary), much of that precious time was spent patiently queuing: for food, showers, even to use the library. Those who didn't learn to be patient were the ones who broke. The ones who spiralled down and either didn't survive or emerged from prison destroyed in soul and spirit.

Delmarno hadn't broken.

But now he was out and he was impatient all the time. Twenty-two years he'd wasted. Twenty-two years waiting as the world spun on oblivious to him. He'd been reduced to a spectator in his own life, fed titbits of information from the outside world by his lawyer, his family and the few friends who'd remained in contact. He'd watched impotently as the empire he'd created—and he did think of it as his empire—was dismantled, piece by piece. Some of the parts were broken by the police, others swallowed up by rivals and former allies alike. Other bits just ground to a halt from a lack of leadership and energy; like a steam engine without its engineer, there was no one to stoke the fires and keep the boilers going and eventually it lost its momentum.

He supposed he should feel fortunate that his accountant knew what he was doing, otherwise he'd have nothing. They'd known each other since their school days, remaining friends even as Delmarno was forced to leave the school at fifteen. Paul Rubens had stayed on at school, excelling at maths and heading off to university to study accountancy. By the time Rubens had qualified, Delmarno was already making serious money and wondering what the hell to do with it.

It had been Rubens who had suggested that he go legitimate. The 1970s were turning into the 1980s and Delmarno was a very wealthy man. The problem was that he couldn't spend it. The police weren't stupid and neither was the taxman. "Living beyond his means" was the phrase they used. Everybody knew that they got Al Capone on tax evasion and Delmarno wanted to avoid that fate.

So up sprung Vinny Delmarno the businessman. He moved

south, leaving the Midlands behind, and opened a string of cafés, bought himself a fleet of second-hand minicabs from an old boy looking to retire and started "legitimising his cash flow". The excess cash that he was unable to launder—his income from drugs and prostitution alone still outgrossed his legitimate businesses by a factor of three to one and even the best accountant in the world can't bury that discrepancy—was salted away into numbered bank accounts: Switzerland mainly but the British Virgin Islands, Gibraltar and the Cayman Islands also provided a home for his ill-gotten gains. He also stepped back from the "hands-on" side of the business, leaving others to collect money from the willing, change the minds of the unwilling and bury the no-longer willing.

Everything was going wonderfully, right up until the beginning of 1987. Shortly after his thirty-third birthday he'd started to notice the first annoying symptoms—fatigue and constant peeing. After ignoring it for some months, he'd finally visited his GP. The diagnosis of kidney failure was delivered less than twenty-four hours before the police arrived, warrants in hand, to start turning his comfortable existence inside out.

Where had it all gone wrong?

He'd been stitched up. There was no way that his handgun could have found its way from the safe at the back of his wardrobe in Hertfordshire to a squalid bedsit in Hillfields, Coventry.

That he'd actually used the gun to kill Frankie Cruise was a technicality in Delmarno's mind; the fact was somebody had taken his gun and planted it for the police to find in a part of Coventry that Delmarno had thought he'd never set foot in again.

His lawyers had challenged the legality of the search warrant raised, but by that time the evidence collected was connecting Delmarno to a case meticulously prepared from years of investigation by two police forces. It was a complete ambush and no judge was ever going to throw all of that out on a technicality.

And so Delmarno went down—a life sentence for the killing of Frankie Cruise with a minimum tariff of twenty-two years and eight months. Given everything, he supposed he could have been looking at thirty years plus, but his lawyers had used his declining health in mitigation.

Big deal. By sentencing him to twenty-two years instead of thirty, the judge knew he was still sentencing him to death in prison. Even with the renal experts who cared for him in jail, the odds were against him surviving even half that time.

The doorbell rang, interrupting his thoughts. Finally. Plastering a smile on his face, he greeted his old friend Rubens with a hug, shaking off the other man's apologies for his tardiness and escorting him into the kitchen with the offer of a drink.

The two men had been meeting each other once a month since Delmarno had been released. The accountant was technically retired—his copper-toned skin and open-necked shirt evidence of that, but he'd been more than willing to clamber back into the saddle when Delmarno had come calling.

It was his only chance of getting his hands on the man's money. Along with everyone else, Rubens had expected Delmarno to die in prison and had made plans accordingly. Despite his natural cunning and streetwise business acumen, Delmarno had never fully understood the technicalities of accountancy and it had been easy for Rubens to set up his old friend's business affairs so that he would be the beneficiary when he eventually died. Of course, he didn't die and now he was back out and demanding access to the cash that Rubens had so carefully hidden away.

Rubens was nothing if not a pragmatist and a patient one at

that. The odds that Delmarno would keep himself out of trouble and out of harm's way for long on the outside weren't in his favour and Rubens was confident that he'd eventually have unimpeded access to those prudently invested stockpiles. In the meantime, he'd just bide his time and enjoy the generous retainer that Delmarno passed his way.

Rubens' leather briefcase was the same one that he'd bought with his first pay packet in his first job and for that reason alone he'd never bought a new one. After manipulating the stiff, metal hasp, he took out his little notebook computer and a stack of legal documents. Placing a pair of small, rimless glasses on his nose he squinted at the device's tiny ten-inch screen. At home he used a larger, seventeen-inch machine, much kinder on his aging eyes, but there was no way he could fit it into his beloved briefcase. Delmarno watched on with amusement.

"First I'll give you the financial report for this quarter." Rubens pointed to the spreadsheet displaying a summary of all of Delmarno's holdings. "We're still losing cash from pretty much everything. It's not that your businesses aren't turning a profit day to day—they are—it's that their overheads are increasing." He highlighted a column in the table. "Take the minicab firm in Hitchen. Two of the cars have been in the garage this month with major repairs needed to get them back on the road. At least two others are heading that way. They should have been sold and replaced eighteen months ago, but there wasn't enough money. The banks aren't lending at the moment to small businesses, so they've been run into the ground. When they finally give up the ghost you'll be lucky to get scrappage, let alone part exchange against new ones."

The story was the same across his portfolio; the truth was that Delmarno's legitimate chain of companies—signed over to his wife

Jocelyn on the day he divorced her—were running on empty. Lack of investment over the past few years, exacerbated by the economy's woes, had left them in a parlous state. Like the minicab firm, some of them were one stroke of bad luck away from insolvency.

Outwardly they were keeping up appearances. The cash kept flowing in. The house still looked like a show home; Jocelyn was still a member of all the right gyms and spas and remained a "lady-wot-lunched" with her vacuous friends three times a week. But the wheels were coming off.

"My biggest concern is the apartment block in Hertford." Rubens face was serious. "The shell is built, the lifts are working but the electricians and plumbers and decorators are refusing to do the interior work without cash up front. And with investors still wary after the house price crash you can't even sell them off to a developer willing to finish them without losing money. They need to be completed and either sold off as ready to live in or rented out to recoup your capital." He smiled humourlessly. "I don't think I can blame Jocelyn and that idiot firm of advisors she employed for the housing market collapse, but they can certainly take responsibility for a lack of forward planning and investment in the rest of your businesses."

"Can I make them pay for their negligence?" Delmarno fought to remain calm; losing his cool wouldn't help matters.

"I doubt it. They'll have a top-drawer legal team and they can afford to drag the case out until we go bust."

Delmarno hadn't been suggesting that he took them to court to air his grievances, but he didn't bother to correct Rubens, deciding instead to let the matter drop. For the time being at least.

"So we need capital?" It wasn't really a question.

To her credit, Jocelyn had woken up to the problem some time ago and after greeting her ex—soon-to-be-current again—husband on his release from prison had tearfully laid out the problems that they were facing. Delmarno had been angry, naturally, but in the end he'd known who to call. And today their problems would be solved.

"About half a million will do it."

Delmarno nodded his agreement. The sum would barely make a dent in his vast reserves hidden around the world. Unfortunately, they were beyond his grasp. Simply transferring that money from a numbered account overseas would trip alarms across the globe. September eleventh had a lot to answer for, he mused. In the past such a transaction may have incurred scrutiny from the tax authorities. These days the security services would also be interested—and he really didn't want MI5 breathing down his neck.

But now that problem was solved.

"Entrepreneurial Investments International—EII, they even have their own logo." Rubens produced a piece of letter-headed notepaper with a flourish. The logo looked like it had been done by a child learning to using Microsoft Paint and EII sounded like a scream from a Bruce Lee film, but Delmarno didn't care.

"They are a shell company registered in the British Virgin Islands, all legitimate as far as their tax and regulatory authorities are concerned." Rubens grinned. "Not a very high bar to meet, it has to be said. According to their website—" he switched windows to a rather crude webpage adorned with the even cruder logo "—they are an international investment firm looking for new opportunities in Europe. Somehow they stumbled across your modest little empire and have decided to infuse some much-needed capital to allow you to realise your full potential. Get Jocelyn to sign here as soon as the two of you are remarried."

The CEO of EII had signed the contract, with a blank space above Jocelyn's name. It grated with Delmarno intensely that until he and Jocelyn became husband and wife again, he had no legal control over the companies he had founded. That would be fixed soon.

Delmarno looked at the signature of EII's CEO. "Who's this Pieter Van Dirke?"

"Dunno, I picked it out of the local telephone directory."

"So whose signature is this?"

"Mine. I used my left hand."

Chapter 22

The call came as Warren was making his lunch for the day ahead. He glanced at his watch and sighed in irritation. His head was fuzzy after the late night and the consumption of rather more vodka and Coke than was sensible on a weeknight. With Susan on holiday, he'd somehow forgotten to set the alarm and he was going to be pushing it to make it in time for the morning briefing.

"We've reports of an unexplained death in Carlton Way," the despatcher informed him.

"What do we know?" Warren asked, cradling the phone between his shoulder and ear as he sliced his cheese sandwich down the middle with a bread knife. Wrapping it in cling film, he tossed it into a carrier bag that already held several pieces of fruit and a fat-free yoghurt.

"Few details yet, sir. Victim is a white male, found at the bottom of a flight of stairs. Nothing else. Paramedics are in attendance and the scene is being sealed off by uniform."

"I'm on my way. I'll be about fifteen minutes," Warren promised, looking at his watch. After hanging up he gulped one last mouthful of coffee, wincing as he burnt his tongue. After a moment of indecision ,he grabbed a bag of cashew nuts and a chocolate bar from the snacks cupboard. To hell with the diet, he decided. He had a feeling it was going to be a long, tiring day.

Carlton Way was just a few miles down the road and the morning rush hour had yet to hit its stride. A rather shabby street, most of the houses had been converted into low-cost rental units, inhabited primarily by students from the University of Middle England. Warren arrived in about twelve minutes, feeling rather pleased with himself. He'd worked hard since the summer to learn the layout of his adopted town and had calculated a successful shortcut without the aid of his satnav. Flashing his badge at the middle-aged constable manning the entrance to the road, he parked and stepped into the early morning sunshine.

The front door to number fifty-three was slightly ajar, but the large, well-built sergeant guarding it would easily block the view of any rubberneckers. Although at this early hour, none of the neighbours were in evidence.

"The body's just inside the hallway, at the bottom of the stairs, sir. Paramedics confirmed he was dead then left the scene to us."

"Who found the body?" asked Warren as he pulled on a pair of rubber gloves and knee-length plastic booties. Until he was sure that it wasn't a crime scene, he had no intention of leaving any contaminating evidence. Chances were it was an accident and Warren had only been phoned as he was on rota as the senior police officer on call for any unexplained or suspicious deaths, but he wasn't going to make SOCO's job any harder, should he decide to call them in.

"His girlfriend, we think. She's in the back of the ambulance in hysterics. She looked through the letter box and saw him."

"Do we have a name yet?"

"Not that I've heard. The paramedics are trying to calm her down."

"Seems a bit strange that his girlfriend would be calling around at this hour," mused Warren as he took his notepad out and prepared to step over the threshold.

"I reckon she was picking him up for work," opined the uniformed police officer. "She's dressed in a smart blouse with a name badge—she could be a waitress."

Warren nodded. It was possible he supposed. They'd find out soon enough. After pushing the door open with a gloved fingertip, he stepped in.

The body was that of a dark-haired white male, wearing nothing but a pair of grey boxer shorts and white sports socks. A sprinkling of acne across the pasty, white skin of his shoulders hinted at relative youth. He lay sprawled face first on the tiled floor, his feet still resting on the second and third steps. It was immediately obvious from the angle of the man's head that his neck was broken. Stepping closer, Warren could smell the strong, acrid smell of super-strength lager, the sort favoured by people with serious alcohol problems.

A binge drinker making a wrong turn in the middle of the night and falling headfirst down the stairs? It was a familiar and tragic tale.

Don't jump to conclusions, the rational voice at the back of his mind cautioned. He looked up at the staircase. Uncarpeted, it was made of hard, polished wood, the steps angular and sharp-edged. There was no bannister on either side. Warren winced. A header down those steps would be nasty even if you didn't break your neck.

Squatting on his haunches, Warren angled his head down to get a look at the victim's face. He was reluctant to turn the body over, lest he mess up any potential evidence. At the very least, they'd want a photograph of him *in situ*.

His breath caught in his throat. Seconds before, he'd been expecting to dismiss the scene as a tragic accident, but Warren didn't believe in coincidences. Staring sightlessly back at him were the glazed eyes of Zachary Eddleston, the young waiter he'd interviewed less than twenty-four hours earlier.

WEDNESDAY 4TH APRIL

Chapter 23

Early morning and the main briefing room was full to bursting, with most of Middlesbury CID's serious crime team in attendance. DS Kent was connecting a laptop to the overhead projector.

Warren took his place in front of a pair of wheeled whiteboards. Immediately the chatter amongst the assembled detectives died down.

"As you all know, yesterday officers were called to an unexplained death in a student property in Carlton Way." A picture of the dead young man lying at the bottom of the stairs was projected onto the white-painted wall that doubled as a screen. "After an investigation by SOCO, the death has been categorised as unexplained. However, because of circumstances surrounding the young man's death we will be giving this the full treatment." Warren paused and looked around the room. "Given potential sensitivities in this case we will not be releasing any details to the press at this time and will be referring to it as 'unexplained, pending further investigation'. Is everybody clear on that point?"

Murmurs and nods of assent rippled around the room, even if nobody knew the reason for the sensitivity.

The display changed to that of a headshot of a young man in his early twenties. Pale, with jet-black hair and dark eyes, he was smiling and laughing at something off camera.

"Zachary Eddleston, aged twenty-three. A catering student at Middlesbury College and part-time hospitality worker, he shared the flat with two other students, both studying at the university. Both of those students are away over the Easter holiday and weren't present at the time of the deceased's death.

"He was found at approximately 6.30 a.m. on Tuesday the third of April by his girlfriend, Donna Carter, who called to pick him up for the breakfast shift at the local Travelodge. He failed to answer the doorbell, and when he didn't pick up his mobile phone she looked through the letter box and saw his body at the bottom of the stairs. She called the police and paramedics, who forced the front door.

"I was the attending senior officer and at first glance, it seemed that Mr Eddleston had fallen, face first, down this flight of stairs, breaking his neck. He smelled strongly of alcohol."

The projection changed to one of the stairs. Several winces went around the room at the sight of the unforgiving, wooden steps.

Warren paused, and the guilt he had been feeling for the past twenty-four hours roiled in his gut. The young waiter had been nervous and scared when confronted at the golf club. Had they taken enough precautions to ensure the young man's safety? A glance at Tony Sutton's face showed that the older man shared his doubts.

"The apparent narrative is that the deceased had been drinking heavily Monday night, alone in the living area. We found the remains of four cans of Tennent's Super lager with his fingerprints on the coffee table, alongside an empty takeaway pizza box."

A photograph showed the scene.

"He then apparently went to bed. At about 3 a.m., he fell down the stairs, face first, breaking his neck. As you can see, he was wearing what we presume is his nightwear."

Nods went around the room; the story seemed plausible.

"However, there are too many inconsistencies to ignore." The scene switched to a top-down line drawing of the upper floor of the house.

"The deceased's room was here." Warren used a laser pointer to circle the front room of the house. "The stairs are here, next to the entrance to the bathroom. To get to the stairs from his room, you would pass his housemate's bedroom, then the bathroom door, turning back on yourself."

"Could he have taken a wrong turning on the way to the bath-room?" asked DS Hutchinson. "After four cans of Tennent's Super he could easily have gotten confused in the dark."

"That's what we assumed at first; however, it's almost a straight line from his room to the bathroom. He'd have had to double back on himself to fall face first down the stairs."

"What about when he left the bathroom?" persisted Hutchinson. "He'd have been facing the right way—a step to the right, rather than the left and he'd have been at the top of the stairs, rather than safely on the landing?"

"We don't believe he went to the toilet before he died. Preliminary results reveal that he had a half-full bladder when he died. It should have been empty when he exited the bathroom—and let's face it, after that much booze once he'd started peeing there was no way he could stop halfway." There were a few slight smiles at the gallows humour.

"Maybe he got up for a glass of water? He probably had a thick head from the lager," suggested Mags Richardson.

"There was a three-quarter full glass of water on the bedside table, so why would he have gone to get another?"

There was a pause whilst the team digested the information. Warren could see that they weren't convinced yet and he was pleased, he wanted his best officers to pick apart his theory, to show up any holes that needed patching.

"There are more inconsistencies. First of all, the choice of lager. His girlfriend and his housemates are adamant that Zachary didn't have a drink problem. He was a purely social drinker. His tipple of choice was either red wine with a meal or cheap, regular-strength lagers like Carling or Foster's. He'd even been heard to describe super-strength lagers as 'tramp juice'. They couldn't imagine him drinking it himself.

"We found a single can of Carling in the recycle bin and a receipt showing that he had bought a four-pack a week earlier with his weekly shop. The recycle bins were emptied on the Friday. Having a can of lager with a pizza in front of the TV would be consistent with his normal behaviour on a Monday evening. He knew that he had to get up for work the following morning. He probably drank the other three cans over the weekend. We have been unable to find a receipt for the four-pack of Tennent's. We're questioning local shops nearby but we've not found out where they were bought. Furthermore, he was pretty diligent about recycling. Why were the cans left on the coffee table, when he threw away the Carling?"

"Could he have drunk the Tennent's later? Then after getting pissed he didn't bother tidying up, he just left the cans on the table and went to bed?"

"It's possible, but there's more. SOCO have combed the bedroom and found what they believe to be traces of lager on the pillow and the headboard of his bed, consistent with that from a slightly shaken can being opened. They believe that at least some of the beer was consumed in the bedroom."

Warren waited a few seconds for the evidence to sink in.

DS Hutchinson was first. "So they are suggesting that the beer was drunk in the bedroom, then he went downstairs with the empty cans—but instead of throwing them in the recycling bin he neatly placed them on the coffee table?"

"And he'd have had to pretty much pass the recycling bin to get to the living room. From what we can tell he was a pretty tidy guy; it seems implausible." Warren concluded.

The circumstances were bizarre and the timing suspicious. It wasn't enough for court, yet, but he could tell by the excited mutterings from the team that he was right not to take it at face value. Now they were just awaiting the rest of results from the autopsy and the toxicology reports and maybe then they could find out what really happened that evening.

Chapter 24

Warren's hope for some quick answers about the Allingham Golf Club and Hotel, which seemed to play such an important role in these latest deaths, were soon dashed.

"I called that helpful hotel manager, Mr Molinie, yesterday only to find out that he has gone away for a few days and can't be contacted." Tony Sutton looked frustrated. The two men were meeting in Warren's office, away from the rest of the team. Eddleston's death was still unexplained, but Warren had deliberately not declared it suspicious yet, reluctant to draw the attention of senior officers until he had a clearer idea of the bigger picture.

"The relief manager finally returned my calls but refused to answer any of my questions without a warrant."

"So we have no idea who is on the club's member list?"

"That's right. I did a web search, but aside from the names of a couple of past tournament winners, the club keeps a pretty low internet profile."

"Do we know who the owner is?"

"No." Sutton shook his head. "Mr Molinie is listed as the licensee for the bar but I'm sure he's not the owner."

"What about Companies House?"

"It's not listed as a limited company, so they don't need to disclose the names of the directors and before you ask the tax office needs a RIPA request before they'll hand over any information."

Warren huffed a breath out in frustration. Applying for a warrant or requesting information under the Regulation of Investigatory Powers Act would leave a prominent paper trail and risk just the sort of interest he was trying to avoid. "OK, let's come back to that at a later date. What have Zachary Eddleston's friends and family said?"

"Nothing much that we didn't already have. His girlfriend confirms that he had done a couple of shifts previously at the golf club, but they only started dating a couple of months ago and he never mentioned anything strange."

"What about his flatmates?"

"Nothing from them either. Apparently they don't really know each other very well and Zachary worked a lot of odd shifts on top of his college work, so they didn't socialise very much."

"Parents?"

"Both pretty distraught as you'd expect, and I sensed a bit of tension."

"Oh?"

"Nothing significant. I just got the impression that his parents thought that he could do a bit better for himself than catering college—they were a bit snobby if you ask me. Suffice to say, they didn't know very much about his work life."

"OK, what else have we got?"

"The doorknockers have finished their rounds. None of the neighbours saw or heard anything suspicious. A lot of the other properties in the street are also student rentals, so the neighbours don't really know each other."

"No curtain twitchers?"

"'Fraid not."

"What about the serving staff from that list we had?"

"I've spoken again to the young lady who gave us Eddleston's name in the first place, but she had nothing else. She reckons that the only managers they ever deal with are Mr Molinie and the deputy, and she has no idea who owns the hotel. She also couldn't recall anyone fitting the rather vague description Eddleston gave us. I'll keep on plugging away at the list, but it'll take me some time. I'm assuming you don't want me to call in anyone else to split the load?"

"Sorry, Tony, I'd rather you didn't for the time being. But keep the questioning short and quick. Call me in if anyone has anything interesting."

Sutton sighed. "Why do I feel that we're going nowhere fast?"

Warren summoned up a tight smile, determined to at least sound upbeat. "You know what these things are like, Tony. Nothing for ages whilst the clues trickle in, then 'bang' it all comes together."

Sutton tried a smile of his own. "If you say so, sir."

* * *

"I wouldn't want to speculate above my pay grade, but I don't think the death was an accident," started Andy Harrison, the Senior Crime Scene Manager in charge of the Zachary Eddleston unexplained death investigation.

The slightly overweight Yorkshireman was spreading sheets of printed paper and photographs across Warren's desk.

"OK, take me through your findings," invited Warren as he and Tony Sutton left their chairs and leant over the table.

"First of all, we got the blood tox and stomach contents analysis back from the lab. The volume of strong lager in his gut was consistent with four cans of that Tennent's muck we found in the living room, but his blood alcohol level was not nearly as high as you would expect from that amount of drink. Enough to make him a bit lairy, but he wasn't rip-roaring drunk. He could have been a bit unsteady on his feet and tripped, but it wasn't a foregone conclusion."

"So he had consumed the lager fairly close to the time of death," suggested Sutton, "and it hadn't had time to be fully digested and absorbed?"

"Precisely. He'd consumed the cans quickly, probably within half an hour of his circulation stopping. However, the remains of the pizza he'd eaten for tea were pretty well digested. More like four to five hours."

"So he'd eaten his dinner around what, ten, eleven? Then several hours later guzzled four cans of super-strength lager in quick succession," suggested Warren.

"In his bedroom," interjected Sutton, "before taking the cans back downstairs, ignoring the recycle bin and leaving them on the coffee table in the living room. Then for some reason he took a header down the stairs."

"That doesn't make much sense," mused Warren, scratching his chin absently.

"Well, there's more, Chief. The pathologist performed a full autopsy to determine the cause of death." Harrison moved an X-ray film of the young man's head, neck and shoulders to the centre of the desk.

"Just as you'd expect, he died of a broken neck. Pretty much instantaneously." He pointed to a bright white line across the vertebra. "At first glance it's a classic fracture of the C2 vertebra. You see it in car accidents or sporting injuries where the victim hits

191

a surface chin first, snapping their head back. In this case it also tore the carotid arteries."

"So he went headfirst down the stairs—pretty much what I thought at first glance," said Warren, his hopes of proving it to be a suspicious death starting to evaporate.

"Well, Professor Jordan wasn't entirely happy and he had a closer look." Harrison pulled over a colour photograph of the victim's face. The thin, bloodless lips were visibly cut and the skin on the chin was split wide open. A second photo showed a mess of broken teeth in the mouth, which had been levered open with a wooden tongue depressor.

Warren stared at the photograph. "I don't see it. These injuries look consistent with him landing chin first on the hard, wooden flooring forcing his head back and fracturing his neck."

A sudden intake of breath from Tony Sutton suggested that the Detective Inspector had spotted what his boss hadn't. "No blood."

"Exactly. The poor bugger was dead before he took that dive."

Warren's head spun, the implication clear and ugly. "What else have you got?"

"The Prof did a full check of his body and found suspicious markings." Another colour photograph. "First off, look at his shoulders and arms."

The caterer's arms had the white, pasty cast of a bloodless corpse. A stark contrast, Warren noted, to the tops of his shoulders and his chest, which had a faint pinkish hue. The colour was clearly that of a freshly dead body, but there was a definite difference between the two patches of skin.

A close-up of the tops of the shoulder showed faint, circular impressions.

"There could be plenty of explanations for the discrepancy,

but try this on for size. The victim was lying in bed, on his back. Another person kneels on his shoulders, pinning him down so he can't move. He's there for some time, long enough for the blood to leave his arms. He probably had a major case of pins and needles at the very least."

"Long enough to force four cans of Tennent's lager down his neck?" asked Sutton.

"Quite possibly."

"What about the fingerprints on the can? That would suggest that he drank them himself?" Warren was now playing devil's advocate.

"We dusted the can and found only a single set of his prints on each can. Nothing else. He would have had to remove each can from the bag and chug it in one go—and that's going to be pretty hard going by the time you're on your second or third one—and then place it on the table downstairs, all without adding more prints."

"So you're suggesting that the cans were wiped before he drank from them—hence no prints from the retailor—then taken downstairs by somebody else careful enough not to leave their own prints?"

"It's certainly one interpretation."

"So how did he die? You said that he was dead before he fell down the stairs?" Warren's mouth was dry.

Harrison slid another photograph across the table, this time of the back of the young man's head. A faint, reddish mark was visible at the base of the skull where the pathologist had shaved the hair away.

"The Prof reckons he had his neck snapped." He stepped over to Sutton, facing him. Placing one forearm behind Sutton's skull, he placed the heel of his other palm under his chin.

"You need to know what you are doing and it takes a fair bit of strength, but get the angle right and enough leverage and it's possible."

Sutton swore quietly. "Who the hell would know how to do that?"

"Probably the same sort of person who could snap the neck of a Border collie with a single kick."

Warren felt a flush of light-headedness come over him and grabbed the desk for support. Murder. And he was to blame, at least in part. He should have arrested the young man the moment he had admitted to doctoring Liebig's drinks that night. Then he'd have been safely in custody, rather than at home and vulnerable. Instead, he'd told Eddleston to finish his shift and attend the station the next day, so as not to raise the suspicion of whoever the mysterious manager was who had bribed him that evening. But it was too late. They'd already alerted the suspect. He'd probably been tipped off the moment he and Tony Sutton had blundered into the hotel, bullying the manager into letting them interview the agency workers about the night Liebig had died.

"Thanks, Andy," he managed to mumble, before stumbling out of the room.

He was halfway to Detective Superintendent Grayson's office when he felt Tony Sutton's grip on his elbow.

"What are you doing?" he asked, turning towards the Detective Inspector.

"You don't think I'm letting you go in there on your own, do you?" the older man hissed as he pulled Warren into the alcove separating the suite of offices from the main open-plan workspace.

"What do you mean?" asked Warren.

"I'm not bloody stupid. I saw the look in your eyes. You're blaming yourself for Eddleston's death. You're about to march into that office and ask to be removed from the case and referred to Professional Standards."

Warren didn't try to argue. "It's my fault, Tony. What was I thinking? I should have arrested him there and then. Taken him into custody. He'd have been safe here."

"For one night maybe. Then he'd have been killed the next night. Or the night after that. He was as good as dead the moment he spiked Liebig's drink back in December."

Warren shook his head. "That's not the point, Tony. I didn't follow procedure." He leant wearily against the wall and closed his eyes. "I'm too close to this. It's clouding my judgement. I shouldn't be on the case."

"Bullshit. You made a valid operational decision and any tribunal would see that."

Warren smiled humourlessly. "Maybe I'll call you as a witness in my defence."

"No need, I'll be standing next to you."

Warren stared into the other man's eyes. "You're serious…"

"Damn right I am. I agreed fully with the decision at the time and I haven't changed my mind." He paused. "If you want to go down for this, I'm going to go down with you."

"Don't be bloody silly, Tony. I won't let you."

"You can't stop me. And ask yourself who's being silly here. Who the hell do you think is going to continue this investigation if you throw yourself on your sword? It'll be brushed under the carpet. Nobody is going to want to stir up the shit over some alleged miscarriage of justice from twenty-odd years ago. This isn't the Guildford Four. Vinny Delmarno was guilty of that murder and a lot more besides."

"You sound as if you approve of what they did."

Sutton's jaw tightened but he said nothing. After a long few seconds he turned on his heel and stalked back into the office.

Chapter 25

Warren had called Sheehy again. Despite the hour, the man sounded thick-tongued and slurred his speech slightly. However, he agreed to Warren's demand for a meeting.

This time the two men drove out to a small park on the outskirts of the town. The cloak-and-dagger stuff was getting rather old hat, although after what had happened to Zachary Eddleston, Warren couldn't help feel that perhaps Sheehy's paranoia wasn't as silly as it had first seemed.

Warren had asked if Tony Sutton wanted to join him for the meeting. The older man had declined, instead offering to follow them at a discreet distance as backup. Warren hadn't pushed; it was clear that he didn't know what to feel about his former mentor and friend.

"This is getting serious. I need everything that you have about this case and I need it now."

Sheehy's breath stank of mints and coffee again, but his eyes were focused and his speech had become clearer in the past hour or so. He ignored Warren's demand. "You first. Have you been to see Obsanjo?"

There was no point getting into an argument. Warren outlined his meeting with the incarcerated drug dealer.

"So you believe me?"

Warren wasn't ready to go that far and he said so.

Sheehy unzipped his windcheater, removing another folder. He handed it over. "Another show of good faith, Warren."

"What is it?"

But Sheehy was already walking away.

* * *

The A4 folder was stuffed with papers. Some of them freshly printed, others clearly photocopies of older documents or newspaper clippings. Warren spread them out across the briefing room table.

"Let's see what Sheehy's got to say for himself, shall we?" Warren's light tone belied the emotions he was feeling.

"Boss, what's wrong?"

Warren felt dizzy, the piece of paper he was holding in his hand suddenly seemed hot and he dropped it back on the table as if burnt, before pushing his chair back. He was going to be sick. He managed the half-dozen steps to the wastepaper basket next to the door before his knees gave way and he collapsed in front of it, retching.

Beside him Tony Sutton was opening the door, calling into the CID office for assistance.

"It's OK, Tony. I'm OK." Warren's voice was thick, as if his tongue was too large for his mouth. He sat back, his breathing steadying.

Sutton pressed a plastic cup of chilled water from the cooler into his hand and Warren drank gratefully, the cold liquid soothing the burning in his throat, washing the taste of bile and stale coffee from his mouth.

Sutton picked up the sheets of paper that Warren had dropped back onto the table.

"Oh shit," he muttered as he looked at the heading.

Autopsy report, Niall MacNamara. Conducted on the eleventh of May 1988.

"You shouldn't be reading this, Boss. It's not right." He thumped his hand down on the table. "What is wrong with that bastard Gavin? He can't do this…"

Warren waved weakly as he pulled himself to his feet.

"It's all right; just give me a moment."

"You don't need to read this," Sutton repeated more firmly. He was obviously appalled. Sheehy had practically ambushed Warren. That Warren had never really come to terms with his father's suicide and the issues surrounding it was clear to all who knew him. The man had changed his surname to his mother's maiden name when he'd joined the police. Obviously his birth name was listed in his official file and there had been no attempt at subterfuge, but it was clear that he wanted to dissociate himself from his father and his shameful past, that he didn't want that burden hanging over him as he forged his own way in the world.

"I have to do this, Tony. I've put it off too long." Taking a deep breath, he took the sheets of paper from the reluctant DI.

The autopsy was typed onto a standard proforma. The clunky typeface and the slightly skewed angle of some of the text indicated that it had been filled in using a typewriter. That wasn't really surprising. From what Warren could remember computers were still pretty primitive back then, printers even more so. The proforma had probably been filled in by hand then typewritten, likely by a secretary.

It was the first time that he had seen the report. He'd handled his father's death certificate. He'd come across it when dealing with his mother's estate after her death, but he'd buried it in a box file and locked it away with his and Susan's life insurance policies and wills.

Somehow reading the dry medical language served to distance him from the meaning of the document and as he read it out loud, his voice became stronger.

"Deceased is a white male, approximately five feet eleven inches in height, weighing twelve stones seven pounds, positively identified as Detective Sergeant Niall MacNamara, date of birth fourth of October 1942. He was found in the driving seat of his petrol car, with the windows rolled up, engine running and a hosepipe running between the exhaust system and the passenger compartment.

"Subject was in apparently good physical condition with weight and muscle tone within healthy parameters for a man of his age (forty-five years). A core body temperature of 35.1°C (95.2°F), and the degree of rigor mortis suggest a time of death within one hour of his body being discovered."

Warren's voice trembled. What if he'd found his father earlier? He'd been in his bedroom, on a pleasant summer's evening reading Isaac Asimov's *The Robots of Dawn*. He'd never finished it, unable to come back to it even as an adult. What if he'd decided to leave his room and get some fresh air? To take a walk down the garden to see what his dad was up to in the garage? To follow his dad's repeated suggestions, he realised with grim irony.

His father hadn't been a very bookish man; the only time Warren had ever seen him reading for pleasure was on the beach, on the family's summer holiday. Warren would stuff his rucksack with as many paperbacks as his junior library card would let him take out (six if he remembered correctly) and within a week would be spending his pocket money on whatever trashy novels he could find in the beachfront shops, buried amongst the saucy postcards and sticks of rock.

His father by contrast would take a single thriller with him, John le Carré usually, and read it in dribs and drabs over the fortnight. Warren wasn't even sure that he'd finish it. Because of that, Niall MacNamara couldn't understand why his younger son would rather spend a summer evening in his room absorbed in a good novel than outside, running around getting into trouble. Like James, Warren thought ruefully.

He continued reading, "Lividity is fixed in the buttocks, except where the body was in contact with the car seat, consistent with the deceased having died in the seated position." Under the pull of gravity and free from the pumping of the circulation, the blood settles to the lowest point, where it becomes fixed, staining the skin. Moving a body after death can result in a discrepancy between the position it is found in and the position it died in. Warren's father had been slumped in the driver's seat.

He turned the page over to the section entitled "Dissection of organs".

The weight and appearance of each of his father's internal organs had been recorded, with no abnormalities.

"Lungs are clear of vomitus and stomach contents, indicating the deceased did not choke from alcohol regurgitation."

His father had been a healthy man in his mid-forties. If he were alive today, he'd be looking forward to his seventieth birthday, probably in good health. Unbidden, his father-in-law sprang to mind and he pushed down the faint feeling of resentment. Susan's parents were about the same age as his parents would have been and were active and full of life. "Seventy is the new fifty," he'd read somewhere. His father hadn't even seen fifty.

The next section was titled "Cause of death".

"Physical examination of body reveals no trauma, puncture marks or injuries sufficient to cause death. Stomach contents

200

reveal a significant volume of alcohol, probably whisky, consistent with a bottle found at the scene, and food remains matching the description of the deceased's last meal. (Blood toxicology report to be completed.)

"Deceased's skin has red flushing indicative of raised levels of carboxyhaemoglobin, from carbon monoxide poisoning. (Blood sent for gas analysis—results to be appended.)"

Warren turned over the sheet to reveal photocopies of laboratory results. This time the sheets had been printed using a dot-matrix printer, the perforations from the tractor-feed paper showing as black circles on either side of the copies.

Skimming through the header, he saw that it had taken almost a week for the results to return from the laboratory. Warren remembered that week as a blur, a hideous limbo where the family couldn't even plan the funeral properly as they awaited the death certificate and for his father's body to be released. Of course, he now appreciated that the blood results had been returned in record time, no doubt due to pressure from above, either as a professional courtesy to the family or more likely a desire to clean up the mess they'd found themselves with.

First the routine toxicology screen had ruled out any illegal narcotics or prescription drugs.

The blood alcohol concentration was approximately 0.18%— equivalent to 180mg/100ml, more than twice the drink-drive limit and sufficient for significant inebriation but not fatal.

The main finding was in the blood analysis, which revealed a carboxyhaemoglobin concentration of 64%—well over the 50% plus required for victims to pass out and die.

Carbon monoxide poisoning. The autopsy confirmed what Warren had known for all those years. The report was signed by a Dr

Beno Richter, a barely legible scrawl with the full name typewritten below and appended by a number of post-nominal acronyms that attested to his training and certifications.

Warren pushed the form away. What had he expected? A piece of paper stating, "Whoops, we got it wrong. Your old man didn't kill himself after all."

Sutton pulled the report across and reread it himself.

"You OK, Boss?"

Warren nodded tightly. "Why did he give me this? What's the point? It just tells us what we already know."

Sutton let out a huff of air, now more exasperated than angry. "You're right. But he must have had a reason. Gavin's a lot of things but he isn't the sort of man just to fuck with your mind for no reason."

Warren stared at the sheet of paper. "What are you not telling me?" he murmured. Something wasn't right. He was sure of it but he didn't have the training or expertise to spot it. He pushed the sheets back into the folder. He didn't have the expertise, but he knew someone who did.

Chapter 26

It was the first time Warren had set foot inside Professor Jordan's office. The Home Office certified pathologist usually corresponded by telephone or email and occasionally liked to "stretch his legs" as he put it and visit Warren in Middlesbury. For his part, Warren rarely attended autopsies. Was that because of his father? Finding his body all those years ago had left an impression, that much was clear. Had it also left this subconscious aversion to death? Or was he reading too much into it? He'd hardly have chosen his present career if he had a phobia of death, would he?

Shaking himself out of his reverie, he looked around the office. It was pretty much what he'd expected of the man—a visiting professor at Cambridge University. The left wall was lined with bookcases filled with medical and legal texts. A few of them had his name on the spine.

The opposite wall had two full-size filing cabinets with sturdy-looking locks. In the space between the cabinets and the door was what Warren had once heard referred to as "a glory wall", a collection of certificates and photographs charting the occupant's distinguished career.

An impressive collection by any standard, they started with a bachelor of science from the University of California, Berkley, moved onto an MD from Johns Hopkins University (so the letter 's' in Johns wasn't a typo, Warren noted), followed by a PhD from the same institution. Next to that were certificates charting his membership of numerous professional organisations, both in the US and the UK.

Interspersed throughout were photographs of Ryan Jordan at a variety of ages, ranging from his university days (triumphantly grinning around a gumshield, forehead covered in lank, sweaty hair, his arms around two others still wearing their football helmets), to a more formal pose probably taken in his mid-thirties (white coat, serious expression, stethoscope carefully arranged around his neck) and finally a recent picture of him in front of one of the Cambridge colleges (formal gown and mortar board).

"I'm told it makes it easier for the bereaved to accept what I'm telling them." Jordan shrugged apologetically. "Not everyone who comes in here hears what they want to. Having those up there at least tells them I didn't fall off the back of a turnip truck."

Jordan was a tall man in his early fifties. Although he'd lost the brawn of his early, football-playing days he was still a trim figure, his hair still more black than grey.

"Is that your wife?" Warren asked, pointing at a picture of a handsome, blonde-haired woman of a similar age.

"Yes, that's Sarah. The reason I quit a cushy pathology residency in Baltimore and decided to join the NHS." He smiled. "I had a visiting fellowship at Cambridge. I'd been here eleven months. I was due to fly back to Maryland in three weeks, when Sarah walked into the bar where I was celebrating my mate's stag do." The American's use of the words "mate" and "stag do" sounded more natural than Warren would have expected.

"My first monthly phone bill when I got back was over three

hundred bucks—no Skype back then. The next month it was more than half what I paid in rent. The following month I persuaded the dean of the medical school to grant me two weeks' unpaid personal leave. He wasn't happy, but I guess he just hoped that I would get it out of my system. I know my parents did.

"Anyhow, to cut a long story short, it was only my visa expiring that made me return to the States. By that time I'd already made enquiries about what I would need to do to retrain in the UK and I handed my notice in the day I got back.

"My father went nuts. He's a paediatric surgeon and he'd done his own residency in Baltimore. But by the end of the year, I was learning the ropes as a junior doctor in Addenbrooke's."

Warren whistled. "Quite a change."

"Yeah, although it was only temporary, more a sort of crash course to make sure that the US medical system isn't as bad as you Brits think it is. I was up to speed and qualified inside twelve months, a married man in another six. Eighteen years this November."

It was clearly a tale that Jordan enjoyed telling. Now he'd finished though. He leant back, the leather in his chair creaking. "So why are you here, DCI Jones? You didn't come down here to listen to me wax lyrical about my love-struck past."

"Warren please, Professor."

The man's mouth twitched. "Ryan then," he insisted.

"I need you to do a favour for me," Warren started.

"You said as much on the phone." The pathologist's tone was light, but a slight wariness had entered his eyes.

"Nothing dodgy," Warren quickly reassured him. "I need someone to take a look at an autopsy report, to see if there's anything… unusual."

He passed the folder across the desk.

Jordan opened it, an eyebrow immediately rising.

"1988. A bit before my time. I would have been in school—sorry, university. I hadn't even started my MD. Hell, I still wanted to be a paediatrician like the old man. And the system in the US is completely different. I didn't start writing these things in the UK myself for another ten years."

Warren felt the hope seep out of him. It was precisely because Jordan hadn't been around in the late 1980s that he had thought to go to him. Something was rotten and he was starting to wonder just who it was safe to turn to.

Jordan obviously saw the disappointment in his eyes. "Hey don't worry, Warren. I didn't say I wouldn't look at it. I just want to be straight with you."

"Thanks, Ryan. I appreciate it."

Jordan looked at his watch. "I have a meeting in ten minutes with two parents whose son wrapped his car around a lamppost at sixty miles per hour, killing him and his younger sister." His mouth twitched into a grimace. "I have to tell them he was twice the alcohol limit and both were high on cocaine. They're in denial. That's why they're coming in here. Leave the report with me and I'll look at it this evening and call you as soon as I've read it."

Taking his cue, Warren stood up and stuck his hand out. Jordan met him, shaking firmly.

"I'd appreciate it if you keep this between us for the time being, Ryan."

Jordan nodded once, curtly. "I had a feeling that would be the case."

Warren turned towards the door, but Jordan called after him, "I don't know what this is about, Warren—no need to tell me yet—but take a bit of advice from a doctor. Go to bed. You look exhausted."

* * *

Despite himself, Warren followed Jordan's advice. He'd lost track of how long he'd been awake and a near miss on the A1 confirmed that he needed sleep before anything else.

The house was quiet when he got home. Susan had spoken about visiting a friend and so he took himself straight upstairs.

It was dark when he awoke and Warren felt a rush of disoriented panic. He looked at the bedside clock: nine-fifteen. He checked his phone. No messages or missed calls. He accessed his work email as he walked downstairs. A couple of dozen, none of them urgent judging from the subject headers.

His throat was dry and he stopped in the kitchen for a glass of water, before joining his wife in the living room.

"Why didn't you wake me?"

"Well, good evening to you too, my darling husband." Despite the lightness in her tone, Warren caught the rebuke.

"Sorry, I'm still a bit tired."

Susan pushed her laptop to one side and stood up, stretching on tiptoes to kiss him lightly on the forehead.

"How often do you take an afternoon nap? You must have been exhausted. You've been coming to bed after me and getting up before me for over a week and we both know you aren't sleeping properly even when you do make it to bed."

Warren grimaced an apology. "Sorry, sweetheart, you know how busy it is at work right now." An understatement if there ever was one.

Susan looked as though she wanted to say something, but thought better of it. She knew him so well, he thought.

"Anyway, you look so cute when you're sleeping that I couldn't bear to wake you." And just like that his clever wife cut through the tension. Warren returned her kiss.

"I got some sound medical advice today; I was told to go to bed. The doctor didn't say what I had to do when I was there."

Susan hugged him tightly. Things had been so busy, most recently with Warren and before that at school, that she'd missed her husband. It felt as though the two of them had been little more than flatmates, passing each other on the stairs, grabbing the occasional meal together. They had even spent much of the time in separate beds, following their rule that if one of them was working very late and the other had to get up they'd use the guest room to avoid disturbing each other. It was a sensible and pragmatic idea, but how she missed her husband.

Warren needed Susan. His emotions were worn thin, his nerves frazzled. He'd needed the sleep; he'd need even more before he started again the next day, but he needed his wife more. Nothing else mattered when he was with Susan. The world and all its stresses and strife melted away when they were together and he craved the respite, however temporary.

Taking her hand, he led her out of the living room, up the stairs. Already she'd kicked off her shoes and slung her thin cardigan over the banister. This was something that Susan loved to do, a guilty fantasy that stemmed from a brief teenage obsession with racy romance novels. She'd long since stopped reading them, but the image of a staircase leading to the bedroom strewn with clothes had lingered.

Warren didn't mind. It meant less time wasted.

His phone rang.

Ignoring it was an option.

It rang again.

He looked at his wife, at her now unbuttoned blouse, the bedroom less than half a dozen paces away. *That's what voicemail's for*, he told himself firmly.

A third ring.

He glanced at the Caller ID.

Ignoring it wasn't an option.

THURSDAY 5TH APRIL

Chapter 27

Eight a.m. in Jordan's office. Warren's eyes felt gritty from lack of sleep. Susan had been understanding as always, and he'd tried his best, but he'd been going through the motions; the call from Ryan Jordan had hung over Warren like a grey blanket and within thirty minutes they were back in the kitchen, Warren eating reheated spaghetti whilst Susan planned lessons for the upcoming term.

They'd gone to bed shortly before midnight, but Warren couldn't sleep. His head was filled with questions. Jordan's voice had been edgy, his tone urgent, and now Warren felt like a teenager on exam results day. Desperate to know how he'd done, but scared of what the answer might be.

"You were right. This report is… unusual."

Warren's pulse quickened.

Jordan had taken a photocopy of the document so he could mark it with red pen. He pointed to an underlined section on the first page.

"There are a few discrepancies, notably with the timings. First, the report states here that 'a core body temperature of 35.1°C (95.2°F), and degree of rigor mortis suggest a time of death within one hour of his body being discovered.' It's questionable whether rigor mortis would have set in within an hour of death, especially given that carbon monoxide poisoning tends to delay its onset. It could have been sloppy wording, I suppose. You could argue that the 'degree of rigor mortis' could equally mean 'lack of rigor mortis', but why not say that? The man was an experienced pathologist."

"What about the core temperature? Doesn't that sound about right?"

Jordan shrugged. "Core temperature was and still is a standard measure, but it isn't completely accurate, especially over the first few hours post-mortem. The temperature of a body actually remains constant for the first few hours—they call it the temperature plateau and it can be hard to predict how long it lasts. The temperature stated is about what you'd expect from somebody applying Camp's law rather than Henssge's nonogram, but it's of questionable accuracy."

Despite his fatigue, Warren noted the unusual phrasing of Jordan's answer. He'd implied that the temperature stated had been calculated from the time of death, rather than the other way around. Had he simply misspoken?

Jordan continued, "I'm also concerned that the temperature was taken at 10.46 p.m.; it says here that the body was discovered at approximately 8.30 p.m. That means the time between death and the temperature being taken is two and a quarter hours, plus that one hour. It doesn't seem to add up.

"On top of that he mentions livor mortis, staining of the skin due to pooled blood. It's consistent with the deceased being found in a seated position. First there are questions about whether the lividity would have become fixed in the short period of time between death and the deceased being found—I have my doubts but the science is not conclusive. However, the lab results show that the deceased died of carbon monoxide poisoning, resulting in that characteristic pink flushing of the skin from carboxyhaemoglobin. Even if livor

214

mortis had started, it would have been fairly pale at that stage and I'm not certain that it would have been distinguishable against the flushing from the carbon monoxide poisoning.

"Warren, either the person who conducted this autopsy is of questionable competency or the report has been altered or faked. I think that the deceased was dead for some time but the report was altered to make it seem as if he'd only been dead for an hour."

* * *

Warren was struggling to process what Jordan was saying. It was coming so thick and fast. Why? Why would anyone fake the time of his father's death? Did this mean Sheehy was right about his father's death not being a suicide?

For his part, Jordan was still talking. "The report is also interesting in terms of what it doesn't say, as well as what it does say. The cause of death is given as carbon monoxide poisoning from inhaling car fumes. To rule out strangulation or choking from inhaled vomit, Dr Richter looked inside the lungs. However, he makes no mention of particulate matter from the exhaust smoke. It's dirty stuff, car exhaust, and you'd expect to see at least some residue in the lungs."

Jordan continued, "And I'm not happy with this toxicology report."

He pushed the photocopy of the dot matrix printout towards Warren. Again, he'd used red pen to highlight his areas of concern.

"The report is what we'd expect from a person who gets drunk and gases himself. Plenty of people used to do it back then. You guys didn't make catalytic converters compulsory until the 1990s, so death from exhaust fumes, accidental or deliberate, was a lot more common. But here's the thing. According to the report the deceased drove a petrol 1985 Audi 90; on a whim I had a look on the internet and apparently some models of that car came with a catalyst. Unfortunately, there's no information on whether that model was the one used here."

Warren remembered the car—how could he not? It had been his father's pride and joy, bought in part with over-time pay from policing the miners' strike the year before. Top of the range, with a two point two litre engine, it could very well have had an expensive optional extra like a catalytic converter.

Warren was shaken out of his reverie by a direct address from Jordan.

"Take a look at the name and the date."

He passed over a magnifying glass.

The date was in the top left-hand corner of the sheet, the name on the right. Warren saw it immediately. "It's not the same typeface."

"Correct. The toxicology reports were printed off on a dot matrix printer. Probably one that came bundled with the computer in the lab that they used to process the results. Somebody's gone to the trouble of finding another dot matrix printer, blanking out the date and the name then overwriting it with a new one. But they couldn't find the exact same type of printer and so the font is slightly different to the rest of the printout.

"And whilst we're on the subject of typing, look at the main pro-forma." He pushed it back across the table. "It's far from conclusive, but these things were almost always typed up by secretaries. Getting a typewriter to line up perfectly with those little boxes is damned fiddly—I know, I've tried. If I had to make a guess, I'd say that this was typed up by somebody who didn't spend hours each day using a typewriter. The text is just slightly off-centre and isn't perfectly straight. The text in these two boxes actually overlaps the edge of the box, even though there is more than enough space. I think the good doctor typed this himself."

Jordan's words were starting to blur together in Warren's mind; something wasn't right. Something was nagging at the edge of his consciousness, demanding his attention.

"But why? Why go to all that trouble? What were they trying to conceal?"

"That's the sixty-four-thousand-dollar question, isn't it? If I were you, I'd try and track down this Dr Richter and see what he has to say for himself—although you may be lucky to find him still alive. It's been a long time. And I'd love to see the original report, before it was monkeyed around with."

The questions were mounting and Warren felt a wave of despair wash over him along with that nagging feeling. What was he missing? Unbidden, the dream came back, his father's pale face as he slumped forward in his seat.

"Warren, are you OK?"

Warren was aware of Jordan suddenly next to him, his cool hands taking his pulse.

"You've gone as white as a ghost. Sorry, poor choice of words." The doctor sounded flustered as he pushed a wastepaper basket in front of Warren. "Put your head between your legs and breathe deeply."

"He was pale," mumbled Warren.

"Say again?" asked Jordan as he poured water from a bottle on his desk into a coffee mug.

"He was pale," repeated Warren. "When I found him in the car, he was pale, not pink."

* * *

"Who was it, Warren? Who was this Niall MacNamara?"

Warren was feeling stronger, the mug of water replaced by a strong cup of black coffee. "Sorry I can't offer you anything stronger, but the days when a physician kept a bottle of medicinal brandy in the bottom drawer of his desk are gone, I'm afraid."

Warren's dizziness had passed, but he still felt wobbly. He took another calming swig, not yet able to speak.

"He was clearly someone important to you. Your reaction alone was evidence of that. And what you said, 'When I found him in the car he was pale not pink'. This case dates back to 1988. You aren't even forty yet. That makes you mid-teens at the time this happened."

Warren nodded. "My father."

Warren barely knew Ryan Jordan. They were professional colleagues whose paths crossed every few months. He was also a doctor, a pathologist used to dealing with the bereaved. Perhaps that's why Warren found him so easy to speak to, found himself talking about his father in a way that he hadn't even spoken to Susan about. That he'd never spoken to anybody about.

"Warren." Jordan's voice was gentle. "I'm not a counsellor and I don't pretend to be, but I have been dealing with the bereaved for most of my professional career. Yesterday, when I told you to go to bed—that still stands. You're running on empty. I can see it just by looking at you." He pointed towards Warren's hands, which were still shaking. "How much coffee have you had to drink already this morning?" Warren didn't answer.

"You're going to burn out from nervous exhaustion. In the past year, you've run several high-profile murder investigations, lost your grandmother and moved house and job. I'm amazed you've kept going so long. You have to take a break."

"How can I?" Warren looked at the man imploringly. "This isn't just any investigation. It isn't something that I can just pass on to somebody else to take over. I'm at the centre of it and I don't know who I can trust."

"You can trust me, Warren."

Warren knew that he was right, and that either way, he had no choice. He had to trust somebody. Jordan was an outsider—he had nothing to do with the politics of Middlesbury. But who else could he trust?

It was time to revisit his past.

Chapter 28

"Warren, great to see you. Come on in."

Warren hadn't seen his old mentor, Detective Chief Superintendent Bob Windermere, since his retirement party the previous Christmas and the man hadn't changed a bit. But then he'd barely changed in the thirteen years that Warren had known him.

Windermere was one of those men who forever appeared to be between the ages of thirty-five and sixty. Of average height, with a full white beard and thick, grey hair, photographs of him playing rugby for the force in his late thirties could have been taken yesterday. Up close, one could see that the lines on his forehead were etched a little deeper and those who had known him five years ago knew that the reading glasses poking out of his top pocket were a relatively recent addition, but beyond that little seemed to have changed.

"Well, retirement certainly seems to be agreeing with you." Warren took stock of Windermere as he was led into a large, stone-floored kitchen. The man's shoulders remained broad, his stomach rounded but hardly fat and the forearms, exposed by his habitually rolled-up cuffs, were thick and muscled.

His most striking feature as always was his voice. A deep basso profundo, its rich notes were made for public speaking. The gravitas that such a wonderful timbre lent his words gave him an authority that Warren envied. Whether reading some crook his rights or giving the eulogy at a colleague's funeral, when he spoke everybody listened. The closest comparison Warren could think of was the similarly deep-voiced Neil Nunes, the Jamaican-born Radio 4 continuity announcer—although Windermere had a strong Brummie accent, rather than Caribbean.

"Still a work in progress, I see," Warren said diplomatically.

Windermere's laugh as always was even louder and deeper than his voice. "You should have seen it when I moved in. I practically had to camp in the lounge."

The cottage had been up a winding road that Warren's satnav showed as an empty field. There was no excuse for the mapping software's inaccuracies really. The house had been there for two hundred and thirty-six years, Windermere proudly informed him.

"It's stage one of my grand retirement plan to move down by the sea and live out my days fishing and improving my handicap. I bought it with my lump sum. The aim is to live in it for a year or so whilst I do it up and then sell it for a profit so I can buy something down in Cornwall."

"Oh, I see. And is Nerys into fishing as well?" Warren was doing a bit of fishing himself—he couldn't see Windermere's rather prissy wife putting up with living in a building site.

Windermere smiled tightly. "Nerys doesn't get a say these days."

"Oh, I'm sorry to hear that," Warren said awkwardly.

"No you're not." Windermere's grin returned. "She was a stuck-up bitch. Everybody said so."

He slopped boiling water into two mugs without asking.

"Happened about six months after I retired," he responded to Warren's unspoken question. "She finished the same month as I did.

I guess we were both at fault—we just didn't plan our retirement." He led Warren into the living room.

"I mean we did our financial planning, of course; both of us are on damn good pensions and we'd had a chat with the bank manager and all of that, but we never actually planned what we'd do with our time."

He smiled humourlessly. "The thing about a two-month cruise is that it only lasts two months and then you've got thirty bloody years together, God willing. Take my advice—" he'd slipped back into mentor mode now "—make sure you've got hobbies and plans lined up for when you retire or within six months you'll be sick of the sight of each other."

Warren nodded, not entirely sure what to say. Fortunately, Windermere filled the void.

"Anyhow, everything was all very civil—we've no kids, thank God—and Nerys' pension is broadly similar to mine, so we just split everything fifty-fifty and went our separate ways."

"I'm pleased to hear that." And he was. Bob Windermere had been a DCI when Warren joined CID. He hadn't got on well with his first DCI, but when he'd retired, Warren had been transferred to Windermere's team and never looked back, eventually counting the older man as a friend as well as his boss. He'd worked with the man day in, day out for five years before Windermere's promotion to detective superintendent had pushed him up the ladder. Even then, Warren, by now a detective sergeant, still sought the man's advice and it was for this reason he'd travelled for over an hour to see him.

Sitting across from him, Warren was reminded what an easy man he was to underestimate. In fact, legend had it that it was just such a misjudgement that had landed him with the nickname "Santa" after a rival detective inspector, jockeying for position as the next DCI, had learnt that Windermere played Father Christmas at his church's Christmas fete each year. True to form, Windermere had taken the derogatory nickname, turned it around and wore it with pride. As for his rival… Well, it seemed that his new role as the force's home-security consultant didn't really suit him and he eventually returned to uniform. The message was clear—don't mess with Windermere.

It was a message that many a criminal lowlife had ignored and lived to regret. The scars on Windermere's outsized knuckles hinted at a man who wasn't afraid to get stuck in, back in the days when nobody questioned how a suspect could fall down a flight of stairs in a single-storey police station.

Now those knuckles were wrapped around a mug of steaming coffee; new cuts and scrapes had joined the old scars along with splashes of paint and plaster dust.

"Well, you're certainly keeping busy."

"Good, honest, hard work. My old man was a master builder: brickie, plasterer, joiner, plumber, even electrics. He didn't touch gas, but he'd do everything else. I used to go out with him on weekends and holidays—he wanted me to have a trade to fall back on in case the police didn't work out." Windermere chuckled. "I think I was a super before he accepted that I probably wasn't going to take over his business when he retired. I learnt some bloody useful skills though." He nodded at a pile of precariously perched books on the coffee table. "Mind you, a lot of it's changed and I'm a bit rusty, but it's good to work with my hands again."

He took a long swig of his coffee and his eyes narrowed. "But you didn't come all this way to hear me banging on about my idyllic lifestyle. What do you want?"

Warren took a deep breath. "Bob, do you remember my father?"

Windermere looked at him for a long second. "Yes. He was in CID—we never worked together on a case, but of course I knew him."

"Why didn't you ever say anything?"

Windermere got up and walked towards the window. He took another long swig from his coffee.

"There was a… debate when you applied to Coventry CID. We knew who you were, of course. It was all on the application form. One or two of the more… conservative members of the unit were uncomfortable." He snorted. "Funnily enough, it wasn't your father's actions that bothered them. It was your name change. They felt that you were trying to hide your past. Bloody nonsense. It was in the second box on the application form under 'previous names'. Anyhow, I figured it was exactly the opposite. That in fact you were trying to move on with your life, to prove that you were your own man."

He turned back. "In the end, you were highly qualified for the position and you really shone at interview. And as the old saying goes: 'The sins of the father shall not be visited upon his sons.'"

Warren was quiet for a few seconds. "What do you know about my father's death?"

Windermere pursed his lips and breathed out heavily. "Not a huge amount, to be honest. As soon as it became apparent that there was corruption involved, we were locked out of the investigation." He glanced over, saw Warren waiting expectantly. "What is this about, Warren? It was nearly twenty-five years ago. Why are you bringing this up now?"

"I need to know what happened."

Windermere shrugged. "OK. From what I heard, Niall had been involved in a drugs bust up in Wood End. Nothing out of the ordinary, just the usual smash and grab. We got a tip-off, watched the place for a bit and when we were sure of what we had, raised a warrant and went in. You know how it works. You shout, 'Police— open up,' as you smash the door off the hinges. Anyway, they found half-a-dozen dealers, a couple of junkies zoned out in the back room and a couple of prostitutes paying for their heroin in favours. When they searched the place they recovered a few grands' worth of drugs and about fifty thousand in cash, mixed notes."

"Then what?"

Windermere sighed. "The story goes that on the way back to the station, before the cash was counted, your old man filled a hold-all with about half the money. I guess he figured nobody would miss it. Sloppy procedures, but it happened all the time back then. Wood End was a pretty nasty part of town and sitting in the middle of a drug den counting cash was nobody's idea of a fun time—better to take it all back to Little Park Street and sort everything out there."

"So how was he caught?"

"One of the dealers reckoned he'd seen your old man doing it out the back window of the van. He told his lawyer, who put it forward as a bargaining chip."

"So this is all on tape then?"

Windermere shook his head. "Of course not. You know better than that. Deals like that are made under the table."

"Well, when did they arrest Dad?"

Windermere placed his cup back on the table. "They didn't. The day after the raid, he killed himself. The allegations didn't surface until a few days later. They found the money under a towel in a gym bag in his locker."

"So why did he kill himself? He thought he'd gotten away with it. It doesn't add up."

Windermere took his glasses out of his pocket, polished them on his shirt. "I don't know, Warren. I really don't. I like to think that he was a good man at heart, that he stole the money in a moment of weakness and that he changed his mind and regretted it."

"And killed himself," Warren said bitterly.

Windermere returned his glasses to his pocket. "What's brought this on, Warren? Why are you here?"

"Bob, I need your help." The pain in Warren's voice was clear.

"Anything, Warren, you know that."

"Dad didn't kill himself."

Windermere blinked. "Say again."

"Dad didn't commit suicide. He was murdered."

"Go on." Windermere's tone was neutral, his poker face impenetrable, the brief flicker of surprise now buried.

"I've seen the autopsy report. It doesn't add up. There are too many discrepancies. I think it's a fake."

"It was clearly good enough for the coroner at the time of the inquest. What makes you think you know better all these years later?"

Windermere wasn't being aggressive, Warren knew. It was what had made him such a good investigator. When you took something to Bob Windermere, you'd damn well better be able to justify it. On the other hand, convince him and he'd back you 100 per cent.

Warren took out a photocopy of the annotated autopsy and took Windermere through what he and Ryan Jordan had discovered. Windermere, as always, remained inscrutable throughout, saying nothing. The questions would come after.

"Rather circumstantial, don't you think?"

Before Warren could respond, Windermere continued, "It's twenty-odd years on and both the coroner and the pathologist are dead. All you have are rumours and hearsay to tell us that this Dr Richter was incompetent—unfortunate, but not unheard of—and that it looks like the report may have been altered." He pointed at the documents on the table.

"But that's pretty flimsy. All you've got is a photocopy of some typewritten forms. There could be a hundred reasons why they had to make alterations to them. The date could be wrong on the lab's computer or somebody could have entered it incorrectly. As for the sloppy typewriting, maybe he did do his own reports? Budgets were pretty tight back then; hell, it could have been his secretary's first day on the job." Windermere paused. "What spurred this on? What made you look at this all again?"

"Gavin Sheehy claimed to have been involved in a stitch-up with my father in the Eighties. He thinks he was murdered as revenge."

Windermere snorted. "Jesus, Warren! Sheehy? That's your source? He's a bloody crook; you know that. I thought you had more sense. Why do you think they appointed you to take over, why I encouraged you to take the job?"

The words stung more than Warren would have expected.

"And I bet he's claiming he's been set up to discredit him or some such nonsense."

Warren felt waves of frustration welling up in him. "They said that my father died of carbon monoxide poisoning. He should have been flushed bright pink. He was grey, his lips blue." Warren's voice trembled with the memory.

Windermere placed a hand on Warren's shoulder. "Warren, you know as well as I do how unreliable witnesses' memories are. You were a kid. Are sure your memory isn't playing tricks on you?"

Warren shook his head vehemently. "I saw that face every night for ten years. The dream never changes; I even remember scalding my hand when I spilt a mug of coffee trying to open the garage door—a garage door closed from the outside." He lay back, the soft leather sagging comfortingly.

Windermere picked up the coffee mugs and disappeared into the kitchen. By the time the kettle had re-boiled and the cups were replenished, Warren was fully back in control. He nodded gratefully, noting the faint smell of brandy as he inhaled the steam.

"Not enough to stop you driving home," Windermere reassured him, taking a sip of his own. "OK, let's assume Sheehy's not just taking the piss; what did he tell you?"

"He claims that he and my father were working together on an Operation Lietmotif, a cross-county initiative to bring down a major player in the Midlands' drug scene."

"Vinny Delmarno."

"Exactly. Anyway, after a couple of years they had uncovered enough details of Delmarno's sordid little empire to put him away and bring it all down but the problem was that Delmarno was too clever. He pulled the strings but no longer got his hands dirty. They needed the final pieces of evidence that would link him to the network. My father and Gavin Sheehy were convinced that the evidence existed but they needed a search warrant for his Hertfordshire home to uncover it."

"Go on." Windermere's face was inscrutable.

"Back before he got 'respectable', Delmarno was a lot more hands-on. In September 1984, a major dealer in Coventry, one of Delmarno's rivals, was found shot dead. The list of suspects was as long as your arm and the case remained unsolved. Anyway, my father and Sheehy received a tip-off from a source that a couple of years after the event Delmarno had been boasting about killing

Frankie Cruise and getting away with it. He produced a handgun that he claimed was the same one he'd used to shoot him."

"Do you know who the source was?"

"Sheehy didn't say."

Windermere said nothing.

"Anyway, Delmarno was known to be an unpleasant man to work for and so my father and Sheehy approached his gardener, Reggie Williamson. They persuaded him to steal the handgun."

"The same gun that appeared at the scene of a minor drugs bust three weeks later?"

"Exactly. Ballistics matched it to Cruise's murder and of course it had Delmarno's fingerprints all over it. More importantly it gave them enough to raise a search warrant and find the evidence that linked Delmarno with their case."

Windermere chewed his lip thoughtfully. "It's a compelling theory, but there are a lot of questions." He spread his fingers out, enumerating each point.

"First, why would Sheehy confess all of this to you? He's in enough trouble as it is. I'm assuming you recorded the conversation?"

Warren said nothing, his guilty expression enough.

"Bloody hell, Warren, that's basic procedure." Windermere let out a puff of breath. "OK, fair enough. It probably wouldn't have stood up in court anyway. Next point, you don't know who this informant is who supposedly tipped off your father and Sheehy. Is there any evidence that they even existed?"

Warren shook his head, his frustration mounting.

"Third point, Sheehy claims that your father was killed in revenge for the stitch-up. What about him? Surely he was just as guilty—why didn't Delmarno go after him also? Why wait all this time then suddenly decide to try and get him sent down?"

"My father was a fairly senior detective sergeant at the time; Sheehy was still a DC, part of a team. He probably escaped their attention."

"To be identified over twenty years later? How likely is that?"

"Delmarno has made it clear that he wants revenge for what had happened to him. He's probably been searching for the identity of those involved since he got out." It sounded feeble even to Warren.

"So let's move on to this Reggie Williamson. Is there evidence linking him to the case? You've said that he was Delmarno's gardener and general handyman—do you have proof of that?"

Warren sighed. "No. There are no employment records or National Insurance records. He was listed as self-employed at that time."

"So we don't even know that he knew Delmarno? Tell me about how he was killed."

Warren recounted the limited evidence that they had uncovered so far.

"So there's nothing to suggest that this was any more than a random stabbing?"

"But why? Williamson was a shabbily dressed man with no money to speak of. He didn't even have a mobile phone worth nicking."

"You and I know that, but that doesn't mean his attacker did."

"But what about the lack of forensic evidence? Stabbing somebody's a messy business. Surely they'd have left something behind?" He ploughed on before Windermere could interrupt, "And what about the single stab wound to the heart and the single kick to kill the dog?"

"A lack of evidence is not going to stand up in court. And as to the method of killing—it could have been good luck, or perhaps the person has been doing kung fu down the local sports centre. It doesn't mean they were a trained assassin."

Warren could see the scepticism in his former mentor's eyes and he felt a surge of anger. "Dammit, Bob, this whole thing stinks." He rose to his feet. "I'm sorry you can't see that."

"Don't shoot the messenger, Warren." Windermere's voice was calm, soothing. He placed a hand on the younger man's shoulder. "You know how this works. You have to have all of your ducks in a row."

Warren nodded, mumbling an apology, taking his seat again.

"OK, let's assume that Sheehy is telling the truth. What about this coroner business? If his theory is true, then why would Delmarno kill him after all of these years? After all, he helped Delmarno cover up your father's death. He did him a favour, after all."

"I don't know," Warren admitted. "It could have been a loose end that needed tidying up."

"So what evidence do we have that he was murdered, rather than killed in a drink-drive incident?"

"It's still all circumstantial," Warren admitted, as he outlined what they had discovered about the accident and the interview and subsequent death of Zachary Eddleston.

"It's a pretty big coincidence, I'll grant you that, but they do happen, you know." He raised a hand quickly. "I'm just playing devil's advocate here."

"I can't accept that. The day after Zachary Eddleston confesses to spiking Liebig's drinks and possibly causing his death, he's found at the bottom of the stairs in suspicious circumstances."

Windermere was silent, his eyes closed, thinking. Warren waited patiently. This was what he'd come for—the advice of his old friend and mentor.

"First, are you sure that you aren't seeing what you want to see?" He opened his eyes and looked squarely at Warren. Warren met his gaze, unflinching.

"Yes. Something isn't right here. There's too much for it to be a coincidence." He leant forward. "Bob, you always told me that a detective should trust his gut. That if something didn't feel right, he had to pursue it until it did feel right."

"Warren, I've always trusted your instincts, you know that, but I need you to be sure that you aren't grabbing at straws. Let me propose another interpretation." He took his glasses out of his pocket, as if they helped him think.

"Gavin Sheehy gets himself into trouble; he knows he is going to be investigated by Professional Standards and he becomes desperate. Then in comes his replacement—none other than the son of his former colleague whom he worked with years ago. Maybe they did plant evidence, I don't know, but the point is that he sees the opportunity to explain his problems away as a stitch-up, using you to help him.

"So he takes a calculated risk. He confesses to you his part in bringing about an unsafe conviction all those years ago. He's pretty certain that nothing can come of it; he makes sure that you aren't recording him and even if you are it'll never stand up in court. In the meantime, he sees a way to solve the problem of Vinny Delmarno once and for all. Maybe he has been looking over his shoulder since the man was released. He kills Reggie Williamson and points you in the direction of Delmarno. That way he implicates Delmarno in the man's killing and eliminates one of the few concrete links between him and Delmarno's false conviction."

Warren sat back, stunned. "You think Sheehy killed Reggie Williamson?"

"It's at least a possibility."

Warren was thoughtful. "What about Liebig?"

"Let's suppose that it did take place in the way that you've worked out, but what if the person orchestrating the whole thing was Sheehy? He sets up the clues so they all point towards Delmarno. Did you get a description of the man who approached Eddleston the night that Liebig was killed?"

"Not much, grey hair, middle-aged, small-to-average height and build. We were going to have him in to look at some mug shots of Delmarno to see if he recognised him."

"How would you describe Sheehy?"

Warren sighed. "Grey hair, middle-aged, small-to-average height and build."

"Warren, I don't know what happened here. I don't know if Gavin Sheehy is innocent or not—all I know is that you have to be careful who you trust. Keep this to yourself, Warren." He stuck out his hand. "You know that I am always here for you, and you can call me, day or night."

The conversation was over. Warren felt disappointed. He'd come here searching for answers, looking for clarity. All he had was more questions.

FRIDAY 6TH APRIL
GOOD FRIDAY

Chapter 29

The office was quiet on Good Friday. As far as most of the officers in the unit were concerned, both the Eddleston and Williamson cases were going nowhere fast and so those who had booked time off for the long Easter weekend had taken it.

Sutton and Warren knew otherwise, of course, and both men were in Warren's office. Sutton was taking his jacket off; he'd just returned from the Good Friday service at his local church. It was another thing for Warren to feel guilty about; the previous night he'd cancelled his plans to visit Susan's parents. When they'd asked if he would be joining them for Easter Sunday, he'd been non-committal and he'd fibbed when Bernice had asked if he had been to church on Thursday evening for the ritual washing of the feet. Truth be told, he wasn't sure that he wanted to spend the weekend with her parents. Even if he could afford the time, he didn't have the emotional energy to deal with them just now.

Nevertheless, he felt bad about not seeing Granddad Jack. The old man's mood had picked up with the weather after the death of Nana Betty the previous winter, but Warren was still worried about him. He resolved to at least phone and wish him a happy Easter. If Susan had suspected he was lying, she hadn't said anything before she'd driven herself up to Warwickshire, simply promising to call when she got there.

Sutton sat down heavily.

"I'd hoped for a bit of divine inspiration, but nothing came."

"Perhaps I should try," suggested Warren grimly. "We're going in circles here."

The two men sighed as one. Warren was beginning to ask himself why they were in. Perhaps a day off would bring new insight. He looked at his own coat. He should just leave—go home and sleep on it. Sutton should do the same. He said as much.

Two minutes later, neither man had moved.

"It keeps coming back to the same question," Warren started.

"Who authorised that raid?" Sutton finished again.

Windermere's warning came to mind unbidden: *be careful who you trust*. Was whoever signed that order still in the force nearly a quarter of a century on? The office was quiet; everyone who had leave was off enjoying the pleasant weather, even DSI Grayson, who was no doubt at his club playing eighteen holes in the spring sunshine.

Warren sat bolt upright. His sudden movement disturbed Sutton who had been staring into space. He opened his mouth, but Warren's raised finger kept him silent.

Fragments of ideas, half-thought-out notions, were slowly starting to coalesce.

"Tony," Warren started slowly, "you've known Detective Superintendent Grayson longer than I have. Where does he play golf?"

Sutton frowned at the apparent non sequitur, before his eyes widened. "I have no idea. You don't think…"

"It's just a thought, Tony," cautioned Warren, trying to dampen his own growing excitement. If Sutton had confidently named a different club to the Allingham Golf Club, then Warren would have dropped the idea immediately as absurd.

"Leave that question to one side. When did he join Middlesbury CID? He hasn't been here very long, has he?"

Sutton shook his head. "He was brought in a couple of weeks after Gavin was removed from post. His role was to run the unit and help clear up the mess whilst they looked for a new DCI to take over. When you were appointed, he stayed on to help settle you in—" his face twisted slightly "—and to take credit for all of our hard work."

Warren ignored the last comment—Sutton had made it clear many times what he thought of Grayson.

Before Warren could interject, Sutton continued, "But what motive would he have to kill Reggie Williamson after all of these years? It looks as though they got away with it." He shook his head. "Nah, I don't buy it."

But Warren was on a roll. The germ of an idea was now growing. He grabbed a piece of paper and a pen, writing "GRAYSON" in block capitals in the centre and circling it.

"Humour me," Warren instructed. "First question: was Grayson in the force back in 1988? And did he have any influence back then?"

Sutton nodded. "I think so, although I've no idea what rank he held."

Warren pulled over a separate piece of paper and wrote "Questions?" at the top of it and "Grayson's service record" underneath.

"Next, where does he play golf and is he a member of the Allingham Golf Club?"

Sutton shrugged again and Warren added a new line to the questions sheet.

"Now we start to look at motive."

Sutton still looked sceptical, but Warren could see that as always he was unable to resist the intellectual challenge. "If Grayson and Sheehy were involved in the original conspiracy, then when Delmarno started to make noises about tracking down the people that stitched him up, Gavin could have got scared and gone to Grayson."

"Who could have decided that Sheehy needed silencing and attention deflected away from him," finished Warren.

Sutton contemplated it for a few moments, before shaking his head slowly. "I'm not convinced. If he was the person in charge of the conspiracy, why would he frame Gavin? Why not kill him? Every day that Gavin was alive he could have spilled the beans on Grayson's involvement. He could even have used it as a bargaining chip with Delmarno—if Gavin is to be believed, he and your father were just foot soldiers. If Grayson was behind the conspiracy, then surely he was the bigger prize? Why not trade Grayson's name for protection?"

"Hell of a gamble. He probably didn't know for sure if he was even in Delmarno's sights. The last thing he'd want to do is draw attention to himself unnecessarily. And would you trust the word of a character like Vinny Delmarno?"

Sutton conceded the point with a nod.

Warren continued, "Perhaps he then went to Grayson and tried to convince him that they needed to do something?"

"But why would Grayson have turned on Gavin?"

"Maybe he threatened him? Do something about this Delmarno character or I'll do something about it myself." Said out loud, it sounded even weaker, and Sutton pounced.

"So again, why stitch up Gavin? Why not kill him? Or even better, why not do something about Delmarno? Bringing in Professional Standards is madness, surely? Those bastards are like a terrier with a freshly caught rat."

Warren scowled in frustration.

The two men lapsed back into silence.

"And another thing," started Sutton, "if he was going to all of that trouble and placing himself in so much danger, you'd have thought Grayson would have benefitted from Delmarno's conviction."

"And you don't think he did?"

Sutton shrugged. "I guess if he was on the serious crime squad he could have." He grimaced. "If he did get a promotion out of it, he didn't exactly capitalise on it. He was a DCI for decades as I understand it. He only got superintendent rank a few years back."

"And how long do you think he's got until retirement?"

Sutton joined the dots. "Just a few years. And it'll be a big hike in pension for him if he retires as a chief superintendent."

"Taking over and 'cleaning up' Middlesbury CID would certainly help him next time he goes up for promotion."

The two men mulled the theory over in silence, before Sutton restarted, doubt still in his voice. "It's a pretty big set of coincidences. And it suggests that he is behind at least three other murders: Reggie Williamson, Anton Liebig and Zachary Eddleston."

Warren's voice was now less certain. Nevertheless, he persevered, extending the fingers on his right hand. "Let's look at them one at a time: first, Reggie Williamson. Leave aside the trained killer theory; Bob's right, he could just have gotten lucky. Grayson's an experienced detective. He'd know how to dispose of evidence. What was he doing Thursday night?"

Sutton thought back. "No idea. I wasn't on duty. We'll have to check the shift logs. See if we can account for his whereabouts."

Warren moved to the second finger. "Anton Liebig. And we can probably do Zachary Eddleston at the same time." Sutton reluctantly nodded his agreement. "Eddleston reckons that the guy who bribed him was average height or slightly smaller, late middle-age with grey hair."

"Well, that describes Grayson, but it's hardly conclusive." Sutton crossed his arms.

Warren hissed in frustration. "If we'd brought Eddleston in to do an eFit, he'd probably have walked right past Grayson's office. That would have cleared things up mighty quick." His face darkened. "If only we'd brought him in that evening, instead of sending him home."

Sutton raised a hand to forestall his boss's self-recrimination bubbling to the surface again. "You can't know that. Besides, it was late evening. Grayson had probably buggered off hours ago."

Warren managed a faint smile of thanks, before turning to his laptop. "Let's see if we can at least answer a few of these questions."

The first thing he did was call up the shift-management program. "Reggie Williamson died on Thursday night. Presumably Grayson would have needed at least a couple of hours either side to prepare, then to clean himself up afterwards."

"He was on shift earlier in the day, but went off duty at six," observed Sutton, coming around the desk.

"And you don't recall if he was in the office for the late shift?"

Sutton shook his head, looking slightly embarrassed. "I was catching up on paperwork with my headphones on. He could have walked right past me and I'd never have noticed."

"OK, what about the thirtieth of December, the night Liebig was killed? I know he wasn't on leave, not with those murders going on." The new-year period had been a busy time for the unit. Warren keyed in the appropriate date. "He finished shift at six. Again, plenty of time to go home and get ready."

"OK, Zachary Eddleston, Monday the second."

"Off shift again. It's hardly conclusive. Grayson's a nine-to-six man most of the time." Warren shook his head.

"And even if he was on shift, it doesn't mean anything," agreed Sutton. "He spends half his time out of the office God only knows where. Unless he was sitting in front of us, this doesn't mean anything. And this assumes that he was working alone."

Warren decided not to pursue that angle for the time being. "Well, let's see what he was doing in the Eighties."

Warren opened up the force's personnel database. A biographical summary of Grayson's career immediately appeared, along with a recent photograph of him in uniform. "Richard John Grayson. I always wondered what the 'R' stood for," mused Warren. "I wonder why he doesn't use it?"

"Rumour has it, his nickname was 'The boy wonder'. I think if my parents had named me 'Dick Grayson' I'd have stopped using it in the Sixties as well."

Warren thought for a moment before making the connection. "Ouch. If I had to be named after a superhero sidekick, Robin wouldn't be my first choice." Despite the frustration and emotional stress of the past few days, Warren suddenly found himself laughing. "I wonder how he looks in spandex?"

"I'll bet his mum used to tell him his tea was ready by calling, 'Dinner, Dinner, Dinner, Dinner, Dinner…'" added Sutton, chuckling.

"To the Batmobile, Superintendent!" Warren managed, before losing control completely.

"When he makes an unwilling arrest, there are big coloured

speech bubbles saying 'Pow.'" Sutton was leaning against the desk, his eyes watering slightly.

Warren struggled to regain some control. "Oh, God, I'll never be able to hear the phone ring in his office again without thinking, 'Bat phone.'"

"I wonder if they call him down to Welwyn by projecting a bat symbol into the night sky?"

The two men roared with laughter, before Warren shushed them. The last thing he wanted was one of the support workers to overhear them and for word to get back to Grayson; the man wasn't famed for his sense of humour. However, it felt good to laugh.

Finally under control, Warren clicked on the next link.

Grayson's service history was disappointingly brief, with only key dates. A link at the top of the screen offered more detail. Warren moved the mouse pointer over it, but stopped before selecting it.

DSI Grayson was Warren's superior officer; as such Warren had no automatic right to see information about him beyond "public knowledge". Clicking the link would have triggered a request to personnel, who would have asked for justification. Warren could think of no satisfactory answer that he was prepared to give at this time and he was unwilling to lie unless he had to. He said as much to Sutton.

"Let's make do with what we've got."

"OK, most recent posting, DSI Hertfordshire Constabulary, Middlesbury CID. He took over a week or so after Gavin's removal," read Sutton.

"Before that he was based at Welwyn Garden City—it just says CID. Doesn't tell us what he was doing, or what unit he was working with. He was made DSI back in 2009."

"Look at that." Sutton pointed at the screen. "Before his

promotion in 2009, he worked out of Welwyn for eighteen years as a DCI. That's a hell of a long stretch at such a low rank—no offence, Boss—for someone as ambitious as Grayson."

"Especially since he was made DCI at thirty-three," agreed Warren. Was Grayson just average ability, or had he stepped on toes?

"And he was promoted to DI at thirty—that's someone on the fast track," opined Sutton.

But Warren was suddenly less interested in why John Grayson had gone from being "the boy wonder" to stalling in the middle ranks, than what he was actually doing around that time.

"Look at that," he muttered. "The promotion to DI came with a secondment—to West Midlands eighteen months before Delmarno's conviction."

"And his promotion to DCI came with his return to Herts, a year after," finished Sutton.

* * *

The realisation that John Grayson—the man who sat in the office across the corridor, the man who had tried to discourage Warren from pursuing the investigation into the decades-old conspiracy that seemed to be at the heart of the whole affair— might himself be involved, left Warren out of breath.

Sutton was more sanguine; nevertheless, he could see that his boss wouldn't be dissuaded. "OK, what do we do now then? Who do we take this to?"

Warren shrugged helplessly. The police by its very nature was a hierarchical organisation. But the logical place to take their concerns, the next level in the chain of command, was the very place they couldn't go. The whole affair must have been orchestrated by somebody of a senior rank back in the 1980s. John Grayson may or may not be the person they were looking for—but the same could be said of anybody else of similar rank. If they bypassed Grayson, they could very well end up taking what they knew to somebody else at least as involved. What a bitter irony, Warren thought, if Grayson was entirely innocent but the person they reported to was in fact the one who they were looking for.

"What about Professional Standards? They are looking into Gavin's case already and they are surely best placed to deal with this?"

Warren shook his head, the warning from Bob Windermere ringing in his ears.

"Can we trust them? It's been twenty-odd years. Those involved in the conspiracy could be working literally anywhere in the force. Hell, if we want to really go down that road, what better place for somebody that dirty to end up working? They are the most secretive unit in the whole force. They have the ability to go anywhere, speak to anyone. If something needs burying, who would be better placed?"

Sutton shifted in his seat. "I see what you're saying, but don't you think that's a bit paranoid?"

"No!" snapped Warren, before apologising. He rubbed the bridge of his nose wearily. "OK, maybe you're right. But what can I do? Who can I trust?"

* * *

An hour later, Warren sat alone in his office. Sutton had finally gone home. The older man had looked troubled. Maybe he was right; maybe Warren was paranoid. Ever since he'd got to know Tony

Sutton, the man had made it clear that he disliked John Grayson and was suspicious of the man's motives. The fact that he, of all people, hadn't immediately warmed to Warren's suspicions about Grayson's involvement gave Warren pause for thought.

His mobile rang. He looked at the caller ID.

"Professor Jordan," he mouthed, feeling a sudden surge of excitement.

It was short-lived.

"Warren, I've been doing some digging around into Beno Richter, the pathologist who conducted your father's autopsy." Jordan's voice was grim and Warren felt his heart sink.

"I'm afraid that he died in 1996 from alcoholic cirrhosis." Warren felt his hopes dashed; he'd known it was a long shot, but Warren had prayed that the man would still be alive, would perhaps be able to answer some of the many questions he needed answered.

"The man was dodgy though." Jordan's tone now switched to one of anger. "I started putting a few feelers out amongst some older colleagues, since West Midlands, London and the South East are under the same group practice. It seems that Richter had quite the reputation.

"He used to be some sort of surgeon but he'd turn up to theatre with shaking hands, smelling of mouthwash. After one near miss too many, they figured it was only a matter of time before he killed someone and so they stopped him practising.

"He should have been struck off, but you know how it is, he was a good old boy who went to all the right schools and knew the right people, so they brushed it under the carpet, and made him retrain as a pathologist. I guess they figured he couldn't do too much damage if the patient was already dead." Jordan clearly regarded that type of thinking as an insult to his profession and a personal affront.

"So they assigned my father's autopsy to the departmental drunk." Warren's tone was bitter. "That still doesn't explain why he changed the report and fiddled the time of death."

"There's more. Apparently there were rumours of sexual misconduct swirling around at the time. The details are a bit hazy, but it seems that he was accused of trying to force himself on one of the junior office workers when drunk. The police were involved, statements were taken and he was questioned, but the young woman dropped the charges then resigned."

"When was this?"

"Back end of 1986, beginning of 1987."

"That was over a year before Dad died," Warren mused. "They can't have been planning that far ahead, surely?"

Jordan sighed. "I don't know, but it's worrying."

It certainly was. The suggestion was that whoever orchestrated his father's killing had a tame pathologist in his pocket. How many other autopsies had been compromised? How many other murders covered up?

Warren felt a chill run through him as he realised that the implications went even further. How did the killers know about Dr Richter's predicament in the first place? An allegation of sexual misconduct was unlikely to have been public knowledge at that stage. It would have been whispered about perhaps on the grapevine but how would someone outside of the coroner's office have heard about it?

The only logical suggestion was that somebody in the police had tipped off Delmarno who'd then persuaded the young woman to drop the charges, ensuring that Dr Beno Richter was now beholden to him.

Warren wasn't naïve; he knew that corruption existed and the weekly revelations from the investigations into the *News of the World* phone-hacking scandal were uncovering more and more examples, but a pathologist and a police officer, in the pay of a serious criminal like Delmarno? It was like something out of 1920s' Chicago.

The chill turned to hopelessness. How could he possibly clear his father's name and work out what happened that awful night when the whole thing had been covered up so comprehensively and the only people who might have been able to tell Warren what happened were dead?

Warren felt helpless. Whoever orchestrated the conspiracy all of those years ago not only had senior enough rank to arrange the killing of his father, but had also been able to successfully bury it for decades by bribing senior public officials. What chance did Warren have of uncovering this person and seeing that justice was finally served for his father and those others? And yet again, the question that kept on haunting him: who could he trust?

SATURDAY 7TH APRIL
EASTER SATURDAY

Chapter 30

Warren had booked Easter Saturday off months ago. The plan had been to spend the long weekend with Susan's parents up in Warwickshire, but Warren had begged off a couple of days ago. He could still go. Perhaps he ought to. The excitement of Friday's insights had been swiftly followed by the realisation of what an impossible task he now faced.

Outwardly, the investigation into Reggie Williamson's murder appeared to be proceeding as expected. In contrast to the frenetic pace of Warren's most recent cases, most murder inquiries took months, even years to conclude. A small team could expect to spend weeks sifting through evidence. And whilst his team no doubt felt frustration at the clear suspect column and apparent lack of progress, they were experienced enough not to worry yet.

And as far as Zachary Eddleston was concerned, they were still awaiting final toxicology reports, and so the death remained unexplained for the time being. In fact, the only person in the team who knew the true state of affairs was Tony Sutton. He too had come in on his day off but had finally gone home after Warren had pulled rank and ordered him out.

The telephone made him jump and he almost dropped the handset.

"DCI Jones? It's David Liebig here."

He wondered what the man could want—and what he could tell him? At this stage in the investigation, the last thing Warren wanted was to let it be known that he thought the coroner's death was anything but ill fortune.

"Mr Liebig, what can I do for you?"

"I was right about your visit the other day being good for me. I finally decided to get my parents' affairs in order and move on."

"I'm glad to hear it. I hope you find peace." The words were trite, but he wasn't really sure what else to say.

"The thing is, my parents had a safety deposit box. Mostly full of the usual: deeds to the house, some stock certificates, a couple of pieces of expensive jewellery handed down from my grandparents. But there were also some papers from Dad's work. I don't really know what to do with them."

"What sort of papers?" Warren's voice caught in his throat.

"I'm not sure, but there's what appears to be an autopsy report from the 1980s. Why do you think he kept that?"

* * *

Warren arrived at Liebig's house in record time, his mind spinning. There was no doubt in his mind that the mysterious autopsy report was his father's, or that it had been the target of the break-in of the Liebigs' house the night they were killed. The unsuccessful break-in, it would appear. It had taken all of his self-control not to rip it open there and then, but his detective's instincts won over and he took care not to touch the brittle paper before he placed it in the plastic evidence bag. It was unlikely that there were any fingerprints on the document—getting ridge patterns off paper was a hit-and-miss affair at the best of times and he had no idea what effect twenty-plus years of gathering dust would have—but he was determined not to destroy any potential evidence.

Professor Jordan had been almost as excited as Warren and they agreed to meet at Middlesbury CID, rather than wait for Warren to drive the extra twenty miles to his office at the Lister Hospital in Stevenage. He was already waiting when Warren arrived.

Jordan eyed the plastic evidence wallet as Warren placed it carefully on his desk and put on a pair of gloves.

"You know there's unlikely to be any trace evidence on there, don't you," he reminded him.

"I know, but too much has gone missing or been buried. I'm not going to risk losing anything else."

Jordan pointed at Warren's signature in the chain-of-custody box. "And you know that it's unlikely that will stand up in court."

Warren ignored him and carefully opened the brown paper envelope and spread the typewritten sheets out across the table. Opening a desk drawer, he removed a digital camera.

"I'm not risking contamination by handling the papers or photocopying them. We'll look at photographs initially." Warren's voice was brittle; it was clear that he still hadn't slept properly since Jordan had last seen him. The stains on the coffee mug and the slight tremor in the detective's hands hinted at how the younger man was still functioning.

With the photography complete, Warren packed the sheets back into their envelope, sealed them in the evidence bag and signed it again. Jordan gave up protesting about the futility of trying to maintain the chain of custody and dutifully countersigned the bag. Warren had transferred the photos from the camera's memory card to his laptop, but at Jordan's suggestion copied them across to the professor's iPad, the tablet computer being an easier way to view the documents.

The differences between the original autopsy report and the faked report were immediately obvious, even before they started to compare them properly, with the typewritten text neatly aligned with the boxes on the proforma.

The fake report had copied much of the original report verbatim, making sense of the discrepancies that Jordan had noted before.

"I'm pretty sure that Dr Richter didn't write the fake report. I'm guessing somebody else with limited forensic knowledge rewrote it and he just signed it. That would explain these mistakes." Jordan pointed to a section on the fake document.

"The fake report states 'a core body temperature of 35.1°C (95.2°F), and degree of rigor mortis suggest a time of death within one hour of his body being discovered'. The original document records the core temperature as 34.9°C and states a time of death between four and six hours; rigor mortis would be in its early stages, which makes more sense given the wording. Lividity would be starting to be fixed." Temporarily switching away from the autopsy report Jordan opened an app. "This is what I use to estimate time of death. It's a bit more accurate than the method used here." He quickly entered the details from the report. "Six point five hours with 95 per cent confidence that death occurred between three point one and nine point three hours previously. How does that stack up with the events that night?"

Warren thought back. "The last I saw of Dad was about five-thirty. We had tea and then Dad went down the garden. Mum went out to see her friend up the road and I was upstairs in my room reading. My brother, James, was probably hanging around with his mates up the park. Mum must have got back about eight-ish and put the kettle on. I remember her calling down the garden to ask if Dad wanted a cup of coffee. He didn't reply." Warren paused. "Mum made him one anyway—Dad never turned down coffee—and sent me down to the garage with it… The rest, you know."

Jordan jotted a few numbers down. "That means five and a quarter hours between you last seeing him and his core temperature reading, which is within the range calculated by Richter and myself just now. Rigor would have started to set in and the lividity may have started to fix."

He pointed to the next line. "No mention of red flushing."

"What about the rest of the report?"

Jordan flicked to the next page. Both men saw it at the same time and Warren gasped quietly. The amendment was just a few words, but it changed the meaning of the report entirely.

"Lungs contain some vomitus and stomach contents. Larynx shows some swelling and bruising. Petechiae in both eyes are consistent with strangulation."

"Christ…" It was a whisper.

"I want to see the toxicology reports," stated Jordan and Warren could almost hear the cogs turning in the pathologist's brain as he flicked forward several pages.

"Carbon Monoxide 2.8%; Blood alcohol content less than 0.01%."

He flicked back again.

"Stomach contents reveal a significant volume of alcohol, probably whisky, consistent with bottle found at the scene and remains of food consistent with deceased's last meal. (Blood toxicology report to be completed.)

"Deceased's skin does not have flushing consistent with raised levels of carboxyhaemoglobin, counter-indicating carbon monoxide poisoning. (Blood sent for gas analysis—results to be appended.)"

The final paragraph was damning.

"Despite the apparent circumstances that the deceased was found in, it is my belief that he did not die from self-administered carbon monoxide poisoning whilst under the influence of alcohol but was killed by manual strangulation. Verdict: homicide."

SUNDAY 8TH APRIL
EASTER SUNDAY

Chapter 31

Easter Sunday. The holy day of obligation had been second only to Christmas in Warren's household as he'd grown up. Every year, unless his father was working, the family had gathered around the dining room table and enjoyed a roast with all of the trimmings. They'd never been one for Easter egg hunts, but Warren and his brother, James, would usually end up with their own body weight in chocolate. A small compensation for being forced to sit through the longest and dullest service in the liturgical calendar the day before.

He knew from Susan's anguished text message that she'd been dragged along by her parents. This year's marathon had lasted a record two and a half hours, with all seven old testament readings performed, each followed by a psalm then a truly epic homily that welcomed almost a dozen new converts to the church. This was then rounded off by the priest's traditional invitation to all of the children in the congregation to come up for a blessing and an Easter egg. Warren felt a sense of relief that he'd been spared the ordeal, followed by a slight pang of guilt. He hadn't been to any services at all this year.

He glanced at the clock in the kitchen where he'd been sitting in front of his laptop since 7 a.m., willing the appearance of an email with news of a breakthrough. Nothing. Not even the customary junk email.

Office or church? The question sprang unbidden. He was still on annual leave, under no obligation to go into the office. There were no pressing leads. It was just a case of sifting through data.

For the second day in a row, Warren felt helpless. The papers found by David Liebig had helped confirm what they already knew—that his father's death was a murder. But what help was it? The document was over twenty years old; those involved in its creation were dead. The original was locked in his office, but what use was it? There were unlikely to be retrievable fingerprints on it. Perhaps there were some DNA traces, but how could he get it tested? In order for it to be any use in court it had to be processed in an approved laboratory. It had to be entered into the computer system using the correct identifiers and had to be assigned to the correct case.

But what case? He could hardly assign it to his father's suicide. That was sealed and marked as solved. Any attempt to add further information to it would immediately be noted, and questions would be asked, if only to forestall what appeared to be human error. If he assigned it to another case then any halfway competent lawyer would claim a breach of the chain of evidence and demand it be declared inadmissible.

For the time being it would need to stay locked away.

He picked up his phone. Perhaps Sutton might have some ideas. His thumb hovered over the speed dial, before he placed it down again.

It was his DI's day off and he knew that he was likely to be celebrating Easter as well.

Sod it. Perhaps Sutton was right and he should try a bit of divine inspiration.

The church around the corner from Warren celebrated Sunday

services at 9 a.m. It was already nine-forty and he saw little point in turning up for the last few minutes, even if that was when the Eucharist was served. It took Google mere milliseconds to find the times of service at Saint Ignatius on the other side of town and within a few minutes Warren was on his way to the 10 a.m. mass.

If he'd thought that the gentle familiarity of the Catholic mass would provide inspiration, or at the very least some peace for his tortured soul, he was to be disappointed. By the time the congregation were invited to renew their baptismal vows, the emphasis on death and Christ's resurrection had left Warren weak-kneed and nauseous.

He had to leave. After clambering into his car, he pulled out of the car park. He didn't know where he was going or why, he just needed to drive.

The car radio was tuned to BBC Radio 4 but it was too depressing. He stabbed at the search button. Maybe he'd turn it back to the BBC when "Desert Island Discs" came on, but for now he craved something more upbeat. The radio found Heart and immediately his mood lifted. Somebody had requested "Take on Me" by A-ha and before he knew it he was singing along, transported back to the Eighties nights that he'd loved so much as a student.

Thank God Tony wasn't there. The DI was, in Warren's opinion, a bit of a musical snob and he'd taken to hiding his CD collection in the glovebox whenever he gave him a lift.

The song faded out, segueing into the next track without any irritating commercials or even more annoying chatter from the DJ. Immediately, Warren felt his mood dip. The opening bars were familiar. He knew them but couldn't place the song. For some reason, he felt overcome with melancholy. And then as the lyrics started he recognised it. It was a song he generally avoided, the words a little too close to home. Words that made him think a little too hard.

The car in front slowed suddenly, its brake lights glowing a bright cherry red, before it swung into the middle of the road to turn right without using any indicators. Warren swerved hard, giving the driver a long blast on the horn. The driver responded with a finger.

Just occasionally, Warren had fantasies about leaving CID and transferring to traffic so that he could do something about these sorts of drivers.

Turning his attention back to the road and the radio, Warren realised it was too late to turn off the radio. The song had got him now. Somehow, he manoeuvred the car to the side of the road, dimly remembering to hit the hazard warning lights.

The lyrics drilled into him, their simple poignancy finally releasing the emotions that had been so cruelly exposed and for the first time in years, Warren MacNamara cried, wishing, just like the singer to dance with his father again.

MONDAY 9TH APRIL

Chapter 32

Warren had finally made it home on Easter Sunday, feeling slightly foolish, but at the same time much lighter. The sudden release of emotion had had something of a cathartic effect and he'd immediately fallen into a deep, dreamless sleep.

"Sir, I've got an idea about how we might get hold of some of those missing documents that DS Kent was trying to track down for you. I'm surprised Pete didn't think of it."

Warren's interest perked up immediately as Gary Hastings entered his office. The young detective constable had returned from his short break in Devon with Karen Hardwick and his skin was lightly sun-kissed. Pete Kent had left his notes in his in tray and Warren had decided that in the absence of any other pressing leads, he may as well let Hastings continue Kent's work before the sergeant came back in after the Bank Holiday. So far the younger man hadn't questioned exactly why he was looking at such an old case and Warren hoped to avoid that discussion as long as possible.

"Go on."

"The operation was a joint one between Hertfordshire and West Midlands, right?"

"Yes, West Mids were responsible for scanning everything into HOLMES since most of the offences happened on their patch."

"Well, back then before computers were in full use, joint operations needed two sets of all documents."

It was true. Nobody had ever accused the police of being afraid to generate unnecessary paperwork, Warren thought cynically. It must have been even worse before the sharing of information was routine; the first generation of the HOLMES system was only just finding its feet by the mid-1980s.

Suddenly, he saw where Hastings was heading. "The archives in Welwyn."

"Yes, sir. All solved cases are filed. These days the paper documents are scanned then marked for destruction, but if West Mids were responsible for that happening, it's possible our copy of the paper documents weren't flagged as scanned and so were left un-shredded. They could still be on the shelf in Welwyn."

* * *

The paper archives in Welwyn took up a lot less space than they once did; nonetheless, the scanning and destruction of unnecessary paper documents from old cases was a slow business and the room resembled a warehouse, its metal shelves stretching to the ceiling and accessible only with assistance. Large signs warned against climbing the shelving to find what one needed. You couldn't even use the ladders unless you had a "ladder safety training certificate". (Tony Sutton, upon seeing the email inviting him to attend the course had politely declined, citing a clash with an "arse-elbow differentiation workshop".)

Entry to the archives was restricted to those holding the rank of inspector and above and officers needed to sign in with their warrant cards. All photocopying of documents had to be recorded and it went without saying that their removal was largely prohibited. In deference to the Bank Holiday the archives were only open for a couple of hours that day, unless specifically requested. Warren was still wary about raising that sort of interest and so he'd faced an agonising wait until he could just turn up unannounced.

For the most serious crimes, even when solved, the case was often regarded as unclosed since appeals could and did occur decades after conviction. It was therefore necessary to sift out the day-to-day chaff generated by any investigation that could simply be scanned, from those documents where a physical copy of the original document should be available for presentation in court.

For that reason, the two cardboard files containing Hertfordshire's copies of the paperwork from the Delmarno investigation, Operation Lietmotif, were still waiting to be processed, their order on the job priority list well towards the bottom.

Warren's mouth was dry; at last he was going to find out who had been responsible for the operation. The person who started the ball rolling, the person who Warren suspected was still calling the shots a quarter of a century on, the person who had almost certainly covered up the murder of his father. With trembling hands he opened the neatly ordered box file.

An hour later, he admitted defeat. The single document that he wanted was nowhere to be found. There had to have been one though. The drugs raid must have been authorised by somebody, with everybody involved listed, and that document would have been a necessary part of the prosecution's submission to the court.

But that was decades ago and those details simply hadn't been read out loud in court during the hearing, and so didn't appear on the court transcript. Warren felt a cloud of despondency come over him. Had the document been destroyed?

An idea slowly came to him. What if it hadn't been destroyed? What if it was too important to be destroyed? Twenty minutes later he had the answer—or at least the next step on the road to getting the answer he needed.

The signature was illegible, but the name in the access log was neatly printed and easily read. On the tenth of September 2010, barely three days after Delmarno's release from prison, DCI Gavin Sheehy, Middlesbury CID, had visited the archive.

Chapter 33

Warren and Tony Sutton walked up the garden path, legs brushing against the rose bushes lining both sides of the paving stones.

"Gavin's wife loves roses." Sutton was nervous, making small talk.

Warren said nothing, letting him continue. It would be the first time Sutton had met his former mentor since the whole affair had kicked off the previous year.

"For their silver wedding anniversary, he even had a variety named after her." He pointed to the centre of the lawn, where a small flower bed had been cut as a centrepiece. The neatly pruned shrub stood in contrast to the overgrown grass and unweeded flower beds that surrounded it.

The house was quiet this time in the evening, feeling empty. A small patch of light shone through a crack in the curtains.

Warren rang the doorbell. Beside him Sutton was tugging at the hem of his suit jacket, licking his lips nervously. Warren had told Sutton that he didn't have to come, that he didn't need to be here for this meeting. But Sutton had insisted. And Warren was grateful for his presence. Meeting the man who'd helped cover up his father's murder because he was too cowardly to do the right thing still made him feel sick; the sturdy presence of his friend and colleague lent him strength.

No answer.

Warren rang the bell again.

Still no answer.

"Where is the bastard?" Warren's voice was clipped, angry.

He pulled out his mobile phone again, dialled the number that Sheehy had given him, ready to leave another angry voicemail.

The ringing was faint but unmistakeable.

The two detectives exchanged glances. Either Sheehy had left his phone at home before going out or he was in the house.

"What's he playing at?" snapped Warren. He'd returned to Middlesbury from the archive in a despondent mood, although he'd tried to hide his disappointment from an eager Gary Hastings.

However, it hadn't taken long for Warren's dejection to turn to anger. It was now obvious that Sheehy had been playing with him all along. Whether the story he had told Warren was true or not, one thing was absolutely clear—he had been manipulating him for his own purposes since the moment they had met in the pub car park almost ten days before. The information that he'd given Warren had been trickled out a snippet at a time and Warren felt foolish for letting it go on as long as it had. It was true what Sutton and Bob Windermere had said; the death of Warren's father was his Achilles' heel, clouding his judgement. He'd never have allowed the likes of Sheehy to call the shots normally.

It was early evening before Warren finally got through to Sheehy. He hadn't said why he wanted to meet him again and had ignored the man's demands that they continue to meet discreetly. Warren had had enough of Gavin Sheehy's games. It was time Warren took control of proceedings and if that meant confronting him in his own home, then so be it.

Giving up on the doorbell, he rapped hard on the door.

After a few more seconds of silence, his knuckles now stinging, he moved across to the window, jamming his face against the glass, trying to see through the gap in the curtains.

Sutton moved behind him. "Open up, Gavin. It's Tony," he shouted through the letter box, before suddenly letting the spring-loaded brass plate snap back with a loud clattering noise.

"Shit. Get the door open, now!"

* * *

It had taken repeated blows from the shoulders of both men to force the solid front door open and Warren could feel the bruises forming as he watched the ambulance pull away, its blue lights flashing.

"Will he survive?" Grayson's mobile had rung out twice before he'd finally picked up. The raised voices in the background suggested that he was at his club.

"Too early to say, sir. Tony and I cut him down. He hung the rope around the top of the stairs but the drop wasn't enough to kill him. He was unconscious when we found him, but he'd managed to get his feet onto the overturned stool, supporting some of his weight."

"Changed his mind, then?" Grayson's tone was neutral and Warren couldn't tell if he was relieved or contemptuous.

"Maybe." Warren was similarly non-committal. With all that had happened lately, he wasn't prepared to take Sheehy's apparent suicide bid at face value.

"SOCO are on their way. Tony Sutton has gone in the ambulance."

"Probably for the best. Any sign of his wife, what's her name, Jess?"

"Judith." It figured that Grayson wouldn't know the name of Sheehy's wife. "Apparently she moved out some time ago. She's staying with her elderly mother."

"Get someone onto it. The last thing we need is some bastard from the local press connecting Sheehy's address with the ambulance and doorstepping her before we tell her ourselves." Despite what Sheehy was accused of the service still looked after its own. "Any idea why he did it?"

"Too early to say," Warren repeated. Too much was happening at once, and he needed time to think. He also needed time to search the house. He knew he'd get it in the neck from the scenes of crime team, but he had to see if he could find whatever Sheehy had removed from the archives. It stood to reason that it was in the house somewhere.

Hanging up, he glanced at his watch. An apparent suicide—attempted suicide, he corrected himself, Sheehy was still alive as they wheeled him into the ambulance—was necessarily playing second fiddle to a fatal stabbing in Stevenage town centre and the CSIs had asked him to secure the scene for a couple of hours before they could send a team.

Pulling on a pair of latex gloves, he decided to start in the living room. Fighting his instincts not to disturb a potential crime scene, he looked around the small room.

Why had he done it? Sheehy had eventually agreed, albeit reluctantly, to Warren's visit and knew nothing of Sutton's attendance. What had happened during the hour or so it had taken them to travel to his house? Had the shame finally got to him and he decided to finish it all? It didn't seem to fit with what Sutton had told him about the man, the gutsy fighter who'd risked his career to keep his beloved Middlesbury CID open. The man who'd risked even more than his career to plant the piece of evidence that would bring down a criminal enterprise. Misguided perhaps, and Warren couldn't condone what he'd done, but it didn't sound like a man who'd kill himself.

But then he'd been under intolerable pressure. Warren couldn't bring himself to feel sympathy for the man, but he'd seen that pressure himself when they'd first met: the bloodshot eyes, the shaking hands and the attempt to cover up the smell of the booze with breath mints. And now the empty whisky bottle on the table.

Famous Grouse. Warren took a deep breath as, unbidden, the image of the bottle with its distinctive logo, rolling out of his father's lap and onto the garage floor sprang to mind. To this day, he still felt uncomfortable at the blanket advertising of the spirit during the run-up to Christmas.

After determining that there was nothing of interest buried amongst the bills and legal documents sitting on the coffee table, he moved onto the kitchen. Open-plan and clearly an extension, the centrepiece of the room was a large breakfast bar with enough room to seat four people. Three tall stools sat around the table. The fourth was lying on its side in the hallway below the noose.

Warren measured the height of the stool by eye and mentally added Sheehy's height. Looking at the position of the crude noose hanging from the upstairs banisters he could see that the drop was nowhere near sufficient for a hangman's fracture. Assuming that the pressure on the carotid arteries didn't lead to unconsciousness in a few seconds, death, if it came, would be by slow strangulation, taking several minutes.

How long had Sheehy been hanging there desperately trying to support his weight on the overturned stool before Tony had spotted him through the letter box? He'd been limp by the time they'd smashed the door open, his face a grotesque purplish-red mask, the noose biting deeply into his throat.

Warren shuddered, then pushed the thought to one side, moving back into the kitchen. The room was untidy and smelt of stale food, the dishwasher loaded with several days' worth of dirty crockery, a multitude of different stains attesting to the broad variety of different food colourings used by the local takeaways. Lifting the lid of the overflowing bin, Warren found nothing of interest underneath the foil food containers and ready-meal packaging.

Off to the side of the kitchen was a small utility room housing a washer-dryer, a chest freezer and a plastic crate filled with empty beer cans and yet more whisky bottles. Still nothing of interest and Warren was starting to wonder if there was anything to be found in the house. Had Sheehy still got the information that Warren was convinced he'd taken from the archive? If he didn't have it, where was it?

Exactly why Warren suddenly felt the need to open the laundry hamper he didn't know. But the double bin bag containing a blood-covered shirt and trousers wrapped around a kitchen knife and dismantled mobile phone suddenly changed everything.

* * *

"Reggie Williamson."

It wasn't a question.

"Forensics will need to confirm, but it looks that way, sir."

Grayson breathed out heavily. He was still dressed in an expensive shirt and trousers. Sheehy's suicide bid wasn't enough to get him to leave his club, but the suggestion that the suspended DCI might be responsible for a murder certainly was. Warren caught the faint whiff of red wine and wondered if Grayson had driven himself over or caught a taxi. Now might be a good time to find out where the man played golf, but before he could formulate an innocuous-enough question, Grayson spoke again.

"Does Tony know yet?"

"He's on his way back from the hospital. I told him to stop by before he goes to see Judith."

"Any thoughts yet? Could this be why he tried to kill himself?"

"It looks that way."

Grayson stared at him hard for a few seconds. He'd clearly heard the uncertainty in Warren's voice.

"Find out," was all he said. Warren nodded. It was all he could do. The adrenaline from finding Sheehy then discovering the murder weapon in the hamper had worn off to be replaced by a bone-deep weariness.

Pulling himself to his feet, he headed out the door. First stop the coffee urn, he decided.

* * *

Sheehy was in a medically induced coma, Sutton had informed him. There was no telling how long his brain had been starved of oxygen or the long-term effects. He would almost certainly survive, but whether he would ever wake up was in the hands of God and medical science.

Sutton had been impatient to get on the road to Colchester to break the news to Judith Sheehy, insisting that he did it himself rather than family liaison. It had been an emotionally trying night for the man already and Warren had hated adding to his burden.

"I can't believe it. It doesn't make sense."

"What other explanation is there, Tony? I saw it myself. The forensics are just a formality."

Sutton was pacing around Warren's office, a tightly coiled ball of fury. "No, it doesn't make any sense."

"I know it's hard to believe…"

"No, I mean it doesn't make any sense. Why would he kill Reggie Williamson? What would his motive be?"

"To silence him maybe? Williamson was the one who stole the gun from Delmarno; if he could finger Sheehy for the planting of evidence then Sheehy's going down for a long time. Not to mention what would happen if Delmarno found out. What if Reggie Williamson was blackmailing Sheehy?"

"So why would Gavin come to you and confess to planting the evidence in Delmarno's original conviction? He's not stupid; he knows we had to be recording everything he said."

Warren got to his feet. Sutton's pacing was infectious. He counted the points off on his fingers.

"First, you're right he's not stupid. He took steps to ensure that we couldn't record him. And even if I had managed to smuggle a wire out there, he knows that any recording we made would be useless in court. Second, he was trying to pin the blame on Delmarno for Williamson's death. If he kills Williamson and successfully gets Delmarno sent back to prison he's killed two birds with one stone. He knows we won't do anything about his confession. Who gives a toss? Delmarno's been convicted of murder when on licence, nobody's going to open an investigation into an alleged miscarriage of justice from way back in the Eighties."

"So why was he hiding the murder weapon in his sodding laundry hamper? A bit difficult to explain if Judith decides to come home unexpectedly. Why not just get rid of it? He's a bloody detective. He knows all the tricks in the book when it comes to getting rid of evidence."

"Presumably he was waiting for an opportunity to plant it on Delmarno to secure his conviction. It's not like he hasn't done it before."

Sutton was silent for a few seconds, digesting. "So why try and kill himself?"

Warren couldn't answer. He admitted as much.

"Chief, there's more to this than meets the eye. Don't go for the easy explanation. Dig deeper."

Warren nodded, too tired to take umbrage at the suggestion that he might not fully investigate.

"And you, Tony. Don't make this personal. Gavin Sheehy might not be the man you thought you knew." Warren was acutely aware of how hypocritical he sounded. This case was as personal to him as it could be.

Sutton looked away, before nodding. "I have to go and see Judith," he mumbled grabbing his coat and draining his coffee. Warren groaned and looked at the clock—2 a.m. Grabbing his empty mug, he headed back to the urn.

TUESDAY 10TH APRIL

Chapter 34

"So let's go over what we have so far."

Tony Sutton looked as tired as Warren felt. The two men sat across from each other in the corner of an out-of-the-way greasy spoon that Sutton had recommended. It was 7 a.m. and neither man had enjoyed more than a couple of hours' sleep since the previous night. The full English breakfast weighed heavy in Warren's stomach, not helped by the three cups of coffee that he'd consumed already.

The two men's recap was less about what they knew, rather what they wanted to reveal to the rest of the team in an hour's time.

"Zachary Eddleston was murdered."

It was a statement more than a question, but Warren answered positively.

"And you think Gavin did it?"

This time Warren was less sure and he admitted as much. "Forensics have linked the knife and bloodstained hoody that I found in the laundry basket to Reggie Williamson's murder. They've also found a black jumper that matches the fibres left at Eddleston's flat."

"The knife is pretty damning, I'll give you that, but the fibres are weak. The jumper is pretty generic. Gavin didn't do brands. He was

283

completely indifferent to fashion." Sutton was still badly conflicted over his former friend and mentor. Warren noticed that he was starting to refer to him in the past tense, even though the man was still alive in hospital.

"Well, we've already got good motives for why he may have killed Reggie Williamson, so leaving aside Zachary Eddleston, my next question is: where does the bribery charge fit in?"

"Coincidence? He was dirty and got caught. Maybe that's what spurred Reggie Williamson to threaten him. Allegations that he planted evidence in the Eighties is hardly going to help his case is it? The jury will lap that up and the judge will throw the book at him."

Warren shook his head. "How would they know? There's no way the judge would let the prosecution admit it as evidence and it would be little more that hearsay."

Sutton shrugged, undeterred. "So they bring a separate case. It still isn't good for him." He speared a stray fried mushroom with his fork.

Warren pondered it for a minute. "If we take it to its logical conclusion, then Sheehy was responsible for Anton Liebig's car crash. Zachary Eddleston was a loose end remaining from that investigation. When we turned up, he figured that it was time to get rid of him, but he didn't want to raise suspicion."

"Well, that makes even less sense. Gavin highlighted that Liebig's death was suspicious. Until we started sniffing around that was all tied up neatly as a drink-driving accident and he's a copper; he knows we aren't going to accept Eddleston's accident as a tragic coincidence without a full investigation."

"Maybe it's all an elaborate ruse to frame Delmarno? I imagine that his being released from prison really screwed things up. It looks as though everyone expected him to die in there. Get rid of him and all of this goes away again."

Sutton disagreed. "That doesn't really add up. A few fibres from a ten-a-penny jumper is pretty flimsy. And why go to all the trouble of making it look as though his death was an accident if he wanted us to assume that Delmarno killed him?"

"Well, the accident didn't stand up to serious scrutiny. Maybe he was just being clever, pulling some sort of double bluff. We see the accident was actually a murder, so we look a bit harder and find a few fibres—then hey presto, we suddenly find the jumper in the back of Vinny Delmarno's car or he's wearing it when he gets arrested for some random offence."

Sutton shook his head. "Bloody hell, Boss. Do you think Gavin is that reckless? That whole premise rests on us matching a few fibres. Surely he could have come up with a more obvious link between Delmarno and the murder victims? Plus, it doesn't seem consistent. On the one hand he goes to all this trouble to stage murders and accidents to frame Delmarno, then he's quite happy to just stick a carving knife between Reggie Williamson's ribs?"

"I agree. It doesn't seem sensible. But let's assume for the moment that Sheehy was responsible, was he working alone? Was he the one who approached Eddleston and asked him to spike Liebig's drink?"

"That's a tricky one, all right. How would he have gained access to Eddleston? Surely he isn't a member of the same golf club as Liebig? That'd be a hell of a coincidence. Besides, wouldn't he be recognised by Delmarno?"

Warren rocked a hand side to side. "Maybe, maybe not. Delmarno may never have clapped eyes on him. Anyway, Eddleston said he was approached near the kitchens, that's probably away from where the guests were. Plus, the place was crawling with temporary staff. How difficult would it have been for a respectable-looking man in a suit to corner one of the waiting staff as he walked past? You know how it works, act like you own the place and a tired, busy, young lad with the promise of easy money isn't going to ask too many questions."

Sutton conceded the point. "And he could have been in disguise. A beard hides a lot of features."

"True. Although it's pretty strange that Eddleston didn't mention the beard. He said that the man who approached him was grey-haired, middle-aged and average build. His description was about as much use as Obsanjo's. Unless he recognised a photo of Sheehy down the station, he probably wasn't going to be much help. But if the man who approached him had a beard, you'd think he'd mention it."

"I guess we need to find out when Gavin grew his furry food-catcher, although it seems a bit daft that he would go to the trouble of disguising himself with a beard and then grow one in real life."

Warren blinked.

"Say that again, Tony," he said slowly.

"We need to find out when Gavin grew that scruffy beard of his. I was pretty shocked when I saw the state of him. He used to be quite fussy about his appearance."

"You mean he didn't used to have a beard?"

"No, he was always clean-shaven when we worked together."

The jolt of adrenaline that passed through Warren cut through the exhausted fog far more effectively that any amount of caffeine ever could. "Sheehy wasn't Obsanjo's contact." It was as if the voice wasn't Warren's.

"What do you mean?"

"Remember I said that Obsanjo suddenly remembered more details about his contact's appearance."

"Yeah, you said that he could have been describing Gavin."

Warren shook his head. "I got it wrong. He could have been describing his appearance *now*. He said that he was a middle-aged white man *with a beard*. Sheehy didn't have a beard when he was supposed to have been passing information."

Sutton looked stunned. "Gavin was telling the truth." He paused. "So what does that mean? That Obsanjo's contact was somebody else?"

"Or there was no contact and Obsanjo was shown a photograph of Sheehy and told to describe him to Professional Standards when asked."

Sutton was visibly shaken. "He could have mistaken you for one of them when you visited." He shook his head. "We've got to confront him. Let him know the game is up. If he is doing somebody's bidding we need to know who."

The two men lapsed into silence, both lost in their own thoughts.

"I'm going to have to go back in again. There's no other way."

"Shit."

Warren agreed with the other man's sentiment. Going back into the prison without the permission of Professional Standards was going to put him squarely in their sights again. They'd be furious. Warren's interference could destroy their case against Sheehy.

"You should go to Standards and tell them what you know."

Warren shook his head. "Even if they listen to me—and why would they?—how do we know they aren't involved? This whole thing runs too deep. Somebody wanted Sheehy framed and that someone has serious clout. They've probably been involved in this for almost a quarter of a century—they could be running Professional Standards by now, for all we know. Until we can be sure who to trust, this needs to be kept as quiet as possible."

And if he was wrong, by this time next week Warren might no longer be investigating anything.

Chapter 35

"Jones, my office, now."

Grayson was furious. Without waiting to see if Warren had heard him—although he'd have had to have been half deaf to miss the bellow—he stalked into his office, leaving the door open.

Warren felt a hard knot form in the pit of his stomach. He could only think of one reason the superintendent would be so angry. The dozen or so steps from the room where the team had been assembling for the morning briefing seemed to take for ever; for their part, the team suddenly seemed inordinately busy, their gazes firmly fixed on whatever they had in front of them. By the time he reached the threshold of Grayson's office, Warren's ears were burning red hot. As he closed the door behind him, he fancied he could feel the change in air pressure as the rest of the team exhaled as one.

"I've just been speaking to a DCI Lowry, from Professional Standards. He is going absolutely batshit and I can't say I blame him. Would you care to explain what the fuck you think you were doing tricking your way into the Mount Prison to have a chat with a witness in *their* investigation?"

Warren took a deep breath. Even to him, his excuses sounded poor. And he still couldn't be sure if he trusted the man standing in front of him.

"Billy Obsanjo is the person that Gavin Sheehy is alleged to have passed operational details onto in exchange for money. Sheehy claimed to know more details about the murder of Reggie Williamson and wanted me to investigate his case further in exchange for giving assistance."

Grayson looked as if he was going to have a stroke. "Are you taking the piss?" he managed to splutter. "Since when have we taken it upon ourselves to muscle in on another division's investigation without so much as a courtesy call? And a Professional Standards investigation at that!"

Warren opened his mouth to defend himself, but Grayson wasn't finished.

"And since when have we traded favours with bent coppers for information?"

Warren thought it best not to point out that Sheehy hadn't been convicted of any crime yet.

"If Gavin Sheehy knew something about Reggie Williamson's death—and I still think he's full of shit—then you should have hauled his fat arse down here and demanded he help us or face more charges for conspiracy and perverting the course of justice."

"Yes, sir."

Warren kept his gaze averted. He knew that he was skating on thin ice and if he wanted nothing more than a bollocking and a black mark on his record, he'd better keep his mouth shut.

Grayson stalked around his desk and dropped into his chair with so much force it almost toppled backward. "When I told you to pursue any leads that Sheehy offered, I did not mean for you to go into the Mount Prison, impersonate a member of Professional Standards, trample on their investigation and scupper their prosecution."

Warren started to defend himself. "I never…"

Grayson cut him off angrily. "It doesn't matter any more. Sheehy's in hospital, probably a vegetable, and Billy Obsanjo is no longer a problem."

The knot in his Warren's gut tightened further. "What do you mean?"

The look on Grayson's face was pure malice.

"Late last night, somebody used a sharpened toothbrush to make sure Billy Obsanjo's evening shower was his last. You were his final visitor and you've been cosying up to the man he was accusing of corruption. Professional Standards have got their hands full at the moment, but I strongly suggest you get an appointment with your Federation representative as soon as possible."

Chapter 36

Warren held things together until he made it to the gents' toilet where the fried breakfast and stomachful of coffee finally made a reappearance. Waves of exhaustion crashed over him as he leant his forehead against the cool porcelain cistern. It was all too much.

What was he going to do? The sensible thing was to go home and follow Grayson's advice. He had no doubt that a summons from Professional Standards would be forthcoming in the next couple of days. He should get himself a representative from the Police Federation and start planning what to say in his defence.

Should he just come clean, as Sutton had suggested? Professional Standards were best placed to take over this investigation. Insulated from the rest of the force, they could go wherever they pleased, talk to whomever they wanted to and demand whatever information they needed. All the questions that he had could be answered by Standards immediately.

But was it safe to do so? Bob Windermere's parting advice came back to him: *trust nobody*. Did that advice apply to Professional Standards as well?

And even if they were trustworthy, would he ever get the answers he wanted? Would he ever be told the truth? If the key players were too senior—and who knew what position they might hold twenty years on?—would the results of any investigation ever see the light of day?

The sudden ringing of his mobile awoke him from his reverie. He listened to the call carefully before making his mind up. Until Professional Standards decided otherwise, or DSI Grayson told him explicitly that he was no longer assigned to the case, DCI Warren Jones was still in charge and he was going to continue working it. The question was: how long did he have to produce the results he wanted?

* * *

The call from CSM Andy Harrison suggested that Warren's problems were not yet common knowledge and as far as everyone else was concerned, Warren remained Senior Investigating Officer.

"You know we'd have found the murder weapon eventually, don't you? There was no need for you to come traipsing in and contaminating the crime scene."

Andy Harrison's tone was more disappointed than angry and that made Warren feel even more guilty. He shrugged an apology.

"The team are still doing the rest of the house, so I'll keep it to the hanging for the time being."

The white paper suit was hot and Warren was already sweating. Quite how Harrison and his team could wear them all day was beyond him.

"The knot on the rope was fairly straightforward, your basic noose. It's easy enough to find out how to tie one on the internet. The rope itself was hemp, woven with a fifteen-millimetre diameter and brand new from what we can tell. No sign of the packaging. But that's not the most interesting thing we've found."

The two men walked up the stairs, rustling loudly. The carpet had been searched thoroughly for trace evidence already. Nonetheless plastic sheeting had been laid down to protect it from contamination.

Harrison pointed with a gloved finger at the banister that Sheehy had suspended himself from. "Look carefully at the rail," he instructed as he unhooked a powerful Maglite from his belt.

Warren bent closer. The wood had been stained a dark mahogany, and now that Harrison was shining his torch on it he could make out faint abrasions, where the lighter wood beneath was visible.

"There are brown residues on the rope extending from the point at which it was in contact with the rail to a point about a metre further along. I'd put good money on the marks on the rope matching the varnish and wood fragments from this bannister."

"What are you suggesting, Andy?" asked Warren, not wanting to put ideas in the CSM's head.

"We know that he didn't drop far enough to break his neck. Instead he underwent slow strangulation. But what if instead of dropping down he was hoisted up?"

Warren's breath caught in his throat. "How would that be possible?"

"Bring him underneath the bannister with the rope around his neck, throw the rope over the bannister and use it like a pulley to pull him up. All that weight on the rope would have caused enough friction for traces of the wooden bannister to become embedded in the rope's fibres."

"How many people would it have taken?"

Harrison shrugged. "In theory, as long as the person doing the hoisting was heavier than DCI Sheehy, it would only take one person to do the actual lifting. They'd just use their body weight and gravity. I suppose they could lift him up onto the stool whilst they tied off the rope, but in practice it would probably take two people."

"And then they kicked the stool away."

Harrison nodded. "The drop isn't enough to kill instantly. The only way you could get a standard drop is to tie the noose around the neck and drop the body over the bannister. That might do it."

Warren nodded. He'd seen that done before. "So why not do it that way? It looks as though they left him dangling and he was able to get his weight onto the overturned stool. That probably saved his life." Warren tried not to think how long the man had hung there, slowly throttling, before they'd forced the door. Despite his hatred at what the man had covered up all those years ago, nobody deserved that. "And why didn't he put up a fight?"

"I reckon he was already incapacitated when they strung him up. Was he drunk? Drugged?" asked Harrison.

Warren shook his head. "His blood alcohol level was high but not enough to knock him out. Preliminary tests have ruled out any drugs."

"I'd get the docs at the hospital to have a look at his neck. A fracture of the hyoid bone would indicate strangulation beforehand."

"Already done. They did an X-ray to check for spinal damage and they reported nothing. I'm sure they'd have spotted damage to the hyoid."

"Assuming the ligature hasn't covered them check for bruises around the carotids then. A basic chokehold or strangulation would have been enough to knock him out long enough to hoist him up. If they'd stuck around long enough after they'd kicked the stool away they'd have probably seen the strangling sensation wake him enough for him to try and support his weight on the stool."

The two men lapsed into silence.

"Seems a bit inefficient, don't you think? Why not just chuck him off the banister?"

"Trying to make it seem more like a real suicide is my guess. It goes against a hell of a lot of hardwired instincts to jump off the top of the stairs. I don't see it very often. Most folks just kick away the stool. I guess they don't realise how long it takes to die that way, probably ten minutes or more."

Warren felt a sudden cold chill. Whoever had tried to kill Sheehy had almost certainly been in the house just a few minutes before he and Sutton had turned up.

"Thanks, Andy," he called over his shoulder as he ran down the stairs as quickly as possible without sliding on the slick plastic sheeting.

He called over a uniformed sergeant blocking the doorway from prying eyes. "Get teams doorknocking. We need to find out if anybody saw anyone suspicious around in the hour or so before DI Sutton and I arrived at 8 p.m."

"DCI Jones?" It was Harrison again. "You know why else they might have chosen that method," he continued soberly. "They could just be sick bastards and wanted him to suffer."

Chapter 37

It's not difficult to get into a patient's room when the bored constable outside is under the impression that his role is to stop the comatose patient inside from escaping, rather than prevent somebody else from getting in. In this case an urgent call for assistance in the hospital's casualty department over his police radio was sufficient for the constable to leave his post, hoping that a bit of late-evening fisticuffs might liven up an otherwise dull shift. It would be several minutes before the bewildered officer returned.

A single desultory bunch of service-station daffodils sat in a vase on a bedside table not exactly covered in cards. News of what had happened hadn't been widely publicised and, besides, Gavin Sheehy wasn't top of anybody's "get well soon" list at the moment.

They say that when a person is in a coma they look relaxed, their faces unlined and composed. Not Sheehy—months of stress had formed creases across his forehead and the corners of his mouth. His complexion was greyish, the only splashes of colour the vivid rainbow of bruises across his throat and the tiny pinprick haemorrhages dotting his face and nose and, if anyone looked, his eyeballs.

The only sound in the room was the faint susurration from the oxygen mask—for all the good it was doing. The doctors said that he'd probably not wake up and if he did, he'd probably have brain damage and that he'd probably not remember anything.

Three "probablies". It wasn't enough for the man standing in front of the bed holding a plastic bag in his hand. It wasn't his intention to kill the man—at least not directly. He just needed to silence him. Turn "probably" into "definitely". And then, when Sheehy finally passed away and they conducted the autopsy, they'd find evidence of asphyxiation—but then they already knew that, didn't they? They'd found him hanging from a failed suicide attempt and they wouldn't see anything at the autopsy that they weren't expecting.

He opened the bag out then placed it across the man's face. No struggling this time. He was too far gone.

"Why did you do it, Pete?"

The voice was quiet, but DS Peter Kent nearly collapsed.

Warren Jones and Tony Sutton walked out of the tiny en-suite bathroom.

"You've known Gavin Sheehy since you joined CID." Sutton's voice was taut with anger. "He was at your wedding; he's your son's godfather."

Kent said nothing, his eyes darting wildly, even as he held the plastic bag over Sheehy's face.

"How far does it go back, Pete?" Warren's voice just sounded weary now. "Were you part of the original framing or were you brought in afterwards? How hands-on were you? You're trying to kill Sheehy now. I imagine you at least helped to hang him. What about Reggie Williamson?" Warren's voice started to rise as he moved towards him. "Zachary Eddleston?" Spittle flecked the sergeant's face as Warren shouted right at him. "What about my father?"

The heavy glass vase caught the edge of Warren's temple,

knocking him backwards into a portable ECG machine. As Warren floundered on the floor, Kent charged at Sutton like a bull. Although he'd been mostly deskbound for the past few years and was coming up to retirement, the DS still turned out most weekends for the force's senior rugby team and was quite capable of wading into a bar fight when necessary.

The two men skidded across the floor, crashing into the wall. Recovering his feet quickly, Kent charged for the open door and raced down the corridor.

Sutton reached the door first, followed a second later by Warren, but by this point Kent was already past the nurses' station, heading for the fire exit. Forcing their way past the wheeled medicine cart that suddenly blocked their path and ignoring the shouts from the nursing staff, the two officers pounded after him, Sutton pulling ahead as Warren fumbled with his radio for assistance.

The cool night air rushed in as Kent hit the crash bar, barely slowing as the door slammed open. By the time Sutton and Warren exited the building themselves, the fleeing detective was already halfway down the four flights of metal stairs, the clanging of their boots soon joining his in an echoing cacophony that rang across the quiet car park.

The emergency staircase opened onto a small patch of tarmac next to a footpath and service road, which curved towards the main entrance and exit. Follow that road to the left and it took you onto the main road; to the right and it headed towards the short-term parking bays in front of the A&E main entrance.

Kent headed to the right. Immediately a white Honda Accord pulled out of one of the bays, heading towards him. He raised his hand as if flagging a taxi.

Warren nearly fumbled his radio as he hit the bottom step.

Sutton, already a half-dozen paces ahead of him, was sprinting after Kent.

"Suspect is flagging down a White Honda, index number…" Warren's voice caught in his throat.

Ahead of them the white car accelerated towards Kent, its tyres squealing in protest. The racing detective dropped his arm, turning, but it was too late. With a crunch that could be heard clear across the car park, the Honda impacted Kent on his left hip, folding him like a pair of scissors. Even from several metres away, the explosion of blood as his head caved in the windscreen was shocking in its vividness, and then his body was in the air, spinning, arms and legs flapping loose like a marionette with its strings cut.

Sutton threw himself behind a parked ambulance, using its bulk to protect himself, but the driver lost interest, heading instead for the main road and escape.

* * *

"Looks as though it was stolen." Gary Hastings' face was pale. The shock of Kent's betrayal had been enough—his sudden death even worse.

"Registered keeper is a Mr Quint, lives in Basingstoke with his wife and twin three-year-olds. Hampshire Constabulary spoke to his neighbours who reckon they've gone camping in Spain for a fort-night, leaving their car in long-term parking at Stansted Airport."

It wasn't a big surprise. Warren hadn't expected the car to be linked to the driver. Now they just had to hope that forensics could retrieve something from the burnt-out wreck just reported in a remote field in rural Cambridgeshire.

"CCTV is on its way over from the hospital, but I doubt it'll be much use. The head of security reckons unless the driver got out of the car, you won't see him."

The air in the briefing room was a weighty mixture of shock, despondency, sadness and anger at what had just happened to a long-standing colleague and friend, tempered by what he'd done and tried to do.

Warren stood up abruptly. He needed to take charge, to reinvigorate his beleaguered team. "OK, everything DS Kent retrieved from HOLMES and the PNC is to be considered suspect. Gary, I want you to retrace Kent's footsteps. Everything he downloaded, you download. Everything he accessed, you access. Karen, I want you to work with him. Compare the documents that he gave us—" he pushed a bulging folder across the desk "—with the originals on the computer. I want to see what else he was hiding."

The two constables hurried out of the room, a renewed sense of purpose in their steps. Nobody in the CID office yet knew the full story aside from Tony Sutton, and the two men had yet to decide what to tell the rest of the team. Warren felt uncomfortable about keeping his colleagues in the dark, but he wasn't ready to reveal his own central role in the affair yet.

Furthermore, he worried about the flow of information out of the office. The betrayal by Pete Kent had been completely unexpected. What other surprises lay in store? They needed to take great care when deciding who to share information with. Gary Hastings had already appeared at Warren's door, grey-faced and sickened. As a courtesy, he'd emailed Pete Kent to tell him his idea about visiting the archives to look for duplicate copies of the missing documents. Hastings didn't know what was going on, but he'd put enough pieces together to realise that he may have had a small role in Pete Kent's decision to try and kill Sheehy.

"So where does this leave Grayson?" Sutton's voice was quiet, even though the two men were now alone.

Warren instinctively glanced at the door as if the superintendent was about to walk in. "Well, we know that he wasn't in the Honda. I checked the logs and he's been in his office on the phone all afternoon. He couldn't have been at the hospital."

"So if he is involved that makes three of them at least: Kent, Grayson and whoever was driving that Honda."

Warren pursed his lips in frustration. "Am I clutching at straws, Tony? Do I want Grayson to be involved, just because of who he is, or am I following the evidence?"

Sutton said nothing, just rubbed his eyes wearily.

WEDNESDAY 11TH APRIL

Chapter 38

Another day, another dawn briefing. The events of the previous day were still sinking in. CID was full of officers, many of whom were officially off duty that morning. The only notable absence was John Grayson, who was no doubt explaining the situation to the chief constable and working with the communications team on how to present it to the media. Warren felt a twinge of sympathy for the man, even as he filled his coffee cup yet again. He glanced at his watch. Four hours had elapsed since his last paracetamol and he swallowed the white caplets gratefully.

As before, he and Tony Sutton had held a discreet conference to decide how much information to share with their team and with Professional Standards. The call to meet them hadn't come through yet, but Warren expected it at any time.

His desk phone rang. It was his Federation representative.

"Tony, I need you to take briefing. I've got something I need to sort out."

* * *

"Please take a seat, DCI Jones."

The interview room was a nondescript affair. Equipped with

generic office furniture consisting of a cheap wooden table and a half-dozen padded, but still uncomfortable, metal-framed chairs, it resembled a score or more similar rooms that Warren had spent countless hours in during his career. However, this was the first time that he had found himself sitting on this side of the table.

"Please state your name, rank and current position for the record."

Warren's mouth was dry; however, he found enough moisture to answer confidently and clearly. "Detective Chief Inspector Warren Jones. CID Middlesbury, Hertfordshire Constabulary."

The man seated across from him nodded once and leant forward slightly, although he knew that the high-gain microphone on the PACE tape recorder would pick his voice up easily.

"Others present in the room consist of myself, Superintendent Stanley Markovich, Senior Investigating Officer, Professional Standards, Hertfordshire Constabulary."

The dark-skinned young man to his left spoke next. "DCI Mark Lowry, Investigating Officer, Professional Standards, Hertfordshire Constabulary."

"Sergeant Esme Fenchurch, Professional Standards, Hertfordshire Constabulary."

To Warren's left, the only other uniformed officer besides Markovich also spoke up. "Sergeant Anthea Crozier, Police Federation representative, acting on behalf of DCI Jones."

"Thank you for attending everybody." Markovich had a pleasant, cultured voice with just the slightest hint of an Irish burr. The polite smile that he directed at Warren didn't quite reach his steel-grey eyes.

"We're here today to discuss why DCI Jones met with one Billy Obsanjo at the Mount Prison on Monday the second of April."

Before Warren could say anything, his representative leant forward.

"May I ask what DCI Jones is being accused of and why he has been summoned to this meeting?"

Markovich didn't miss a beat. "DCI Jones is not being accused of anything at present. As I have said, we are just here to discuss why he decided to meet with Mr Obsanjo, a witness in a serious ongoing investigation, and why he chose to imply that he was a member of Professional Standards."

Again, the Federation representative beat Warren.

"With respect, at no point did DCI Jones represent himself as a member of Professional Standards. DCI Jones has a recording of the meeting—as I believe does Mr Obsanjo's solicitor—and it is clear that he does not falsely identify himself."

Markovich inclined his head, unwilling to entirely concede the point. "I think it is open to interpretation as to whether DCI Jones willingly allowed Mr Obsanjo and his solicitor to misinterpret his affiliation and intentions; however, we will be sure to include the recordings as evidence if necessary."

Before Warren could respond to the accusation, Lowry spoke up. "Perhaps you could explain to me why you were interviewing Mr Obsanjo."

The man's eyes bored into Warren's, making no attempt to conceal his contempt.

Warren licked his lips. "Mr Obsanjo was a potential witness in a complex investigation that I am currently pursuing."

"Which investigation would that be, sir?" asked Fenchurch. "According to our records you are currently investigating the murder of one Reginald Williamson on the twenty-second of March and the unexplained death of Zachary Eddleston on the third of

April. Mr Obsanjo has been in prison since the seventh of April last year. I fail to see the connection."

Warren had lain awake all night, trying to decide how to answer just such a question. He estimated that Lowry was no older than himself and Fenchurch probably a decade younger; neither of them would have been around at the time that the conspiracy had started. However, Markovich was probably in his late fifties, the same age as Gavin Sheehy, Pete Kent—and for that matter John Grayson; Warren knew nothing about the man's past—could he be implicated? Bob Windermere's warning rang in his ears.

"I have been looking into Mr Williamson's past and it would seem that the motives for his death may go back some years. Sources suggested that Mr Obsanjo may be peripherally linked to this investigation."

Warren was hedging, trying not to give away potentially damaging information, whilst at the same time avoiding falsehoods. Regardless of any future outcomes, lying to Professional Standards was a guaranteed career-ender.

"I see." Markovich stared at Warren for a few seconds, no doubt hoping that he would break the silence and give away more. Warren said nothing; he'd played that game himself enough times to know to keep his mouth shut.

"Could you perhaps tell me who this source is?"

"I'd rather not say at this time."

Markovich raised an eyebrow. "Are you sure about that, DCI Jones? Everything that is said in this room is treated with the utmost confidentiality, unless it impacts on our investigation. I would suggest that it may be in your interest to cooperate fully."

Warren said nothing.

Crozier cleared her throat. "I believe that DCI Jones has made his position quite clear."

"Would that source perhaps be Detective Chief Inspector Gavin Sheehy?"

Warren said nothing, fighting hard to maintain a neutral face.

"Could you tell us why you have met with DCI Sheehy on three separate occasions, not including the evening that you and DI Tony Sutton discovered him after his suicide attempt?"

Warren gave an involuntary start. How did they know about his meetings with Sheehy? Had Grayson told them? He thought for a moment, before deciding there wasn't enough evidence to decide. Grayson knew about a couple of his meetings, but surely not all three.

Markovich again. "Why did DCI Sheehy want to meet you? He was gone some months before you took up your current posting and nothing in either of your service records indicates that you knew each other before his arrest."

"I'd rather not say," Warren repeated.

Fenchurch held up a sheet of paper. "You and DCI Sheehy took quite elaborate precautions to ensure that nobody overheard what you had to say to one another."

Lowry again. "What was in the folder that DCI Sheehy handed you on Middlesbury Common?"

Warren suddenly felt foolish. It hadn't occurred to him that Professional Standards might have had Sheehy under surveillance.

"No comment," said Warren, uncomfortably aware that he sounded dangerously like a suspect in one of his own investigations.

Markovich leant forward. "I ask again if you are sure about that, DCI Jones?"

"My client has made it absolutely clear that he has nothing to say on that matter and you cannot compel him to do so, unless you arrest him."

Warren winced inwardly. The "discussion" was spinning wildly out of control in a direction that he was not at all comfortable with. "DCI Sheehy claims that he has been framed and he asked me to help clear his name."

Lowry made no attempt to cover his disbelief. "You expect us to believe that someone that naïve has made it all the way to the rank of chief inspector?"

"I don't think personal insults are necessary," interjected Crozier as she tried to regain some control of the interview.

Lowry ignored her, his voice rising. "We've been investigating Gavin Sheehy for over twelve months. Who the hell do you think you are? Crashing in here, trampling all over our investigation. If your meddling causes the CPS to drop the case, I'll personally see to it that you never set foot in CID again."

Markovich placed a hand on Lowry's shoulder. The younger man quietened down, but his face remained fixed in a scowl.

"I think we would all like to know why DCI Jones agreed to meet with DCI Sheehy in the first place and then chose not to discuss his concerns with Professional Standards." Markovich's voice remained calm, almost soothing.

Warren thought furiously, deciding what to say and what to omit. "I didn't know that it was DCI Sheehy who posted the note through my front door. I agreed to meet him, with the approval of Detective Superintendent Grayson, since he claimed to have knowledge of who killed Reginald Williamson."

Markovich glanced briefly towards Fenchurch, who nodded.

"OK, that much is on record. The question is why you agreed

to go alone with DCI Sheehy, breaking numerous protocols and procedures, including the maintenance of surveillance."

"DCI Sheehy refused to give me the evidence where he could be overheard."

"And that didn't strike you as odd?"

Warren shrugged helplessly. "Yes, of course. But we were desperate. We had no leads and no evidence." He paused. "I took a gamble."

Markovich's poker face remained in place. "So what happened next?"

"Sheehy said he had evidence concerning who was responsible for Mr Williamson's death, but that I would need to help him clear his name first."

"So just like that, you agreed? You decided to trick your way into the Mount Prison to see *our* witness, potentially scuppering *our* case? What are you, some sort of glory hound?" Lowry's voice was rising again. Either the man had a very short fuse or he and Markovich were playing their own version of good cop, bad cop.

Right on cue, Markovich spoke up. "Let's leave aside the circumstances surrounding DCI Jones's meeting with Mr Obsanjo for the time being." Lowry slumped back in his chair, his face a picture of disgust. "The question is why did DCI Jones decided to pursue this investigation on his own, knowing that DCI Sheehy was under investigation by Professional Standards?"

"DCI Sheehy made it clear that his cooperation was contingent on me helping him. I told him that I would assist him, in the hope that he would give us the information that he claimed to possess."

"So why didn't you come to us? You knew full well that he was under investigation. Why didn't you report that contact?"

"DCI Sheehy asked me to keep it quiet for the time being."

"And you went along with that?"

A glare from Markovich shut Lowry down again.

"I felt it likely that if you were to learn of my contact with DCI Sheehy, you wouldn't allow me to meet him again and that I would not get the information that I needed."

A glance from Markovich pre-empted Lowry's next outburst.

"So you unilaterally decided that your investigation was more important than our investigation? Is that it?"

The remark was deliberately provocative and Warren ignored it.

"It's rather unfortunate, don't you think, that the only person who can corroborate your version of events is lying in a hospital bed and isn't expected to recover."

"Or convenient, depending on how you look at it." This time it was Fenchurch who was trying to provoke him.

"Let's discuss that, shall we?" This time Lowry's tone was flat, businesslike. "According to statements from you and DI Sutton, you interrupted DS Peter Kent trying to kill DCI Sheehy in his hospital bed. Care to suggest why that was the case?"

CSM Andy Harrison's findings were already on record, so Warren had no choice but to take them through them.

"So DS Kent tried to kill DCI Sheehy, making it look like a suicide attempt. Then when that didn't work, he went back to finish off the job?"

Warren nodded.

"So what about the knife and the bloodstained clothes that you found in the laundry hamper? Do you think DS Kent placed them there? Did he kill Reginald Williamson or did DCI Sheehy do so? Could it have been a joint enterprise?"

"I don't have any evidence either way at the moment." It was weak, but the only thing that Warren could think to say.

"Well, again, we'll probably never know, since DS Kent isn't here either." Lowry's tone was accusatory, as if he held Warren responsible for the hit-and-run.

Markovich took over, as if summing up a case in court. "So the question, it would seem, is who is responsible for DS Kent's murder—I think we can call it that, can't we?—and did they have any link to the death in custody of our most important witness, Mr Obsanjo?"

"I guess that's the case, sir."

"And ultimately, we need to know what the motivation is behind all of this? Because at the moment, I'm not seeing how all of this fits together."

"Yes, sir."

"Do you have any thoughts that you would care to share with us, DCI Jones?"

"Not at this time, sir."

"I see." Markovich turned to the tape recorder. "I think now would be a good time for a break. Interview suspended, eleven forty-two."

The three Professional Standards officers rose as one.

"Let's reconvene in a few minutes, shall we? This old bladder's not what it used to be." Again, the smile didn't quite reach his eyes.

The door closed behind them. Warren turned to Anthea Crozier. "Tell me it's going better than it appears."

She shook her head.

A few moments later, the three officers reappeared and the tape was restarted.

This time, Markovich was blunt and matter-of-fact. Lowry and Fenchurch sat either side of him, Sphinx-like. The time for grandstanding was gone.

"DCI Warren Jones, your lack of a satisfactory response to

today's questions has left much unanswered. At this time there is not enough evidence to arrest you on charges of conspiracy to pervert the course of justice, nor is there enough evidence linking you to the deaths of Detective Sergeant Peter Kent, Reginald Williamson or the attempted murder of Detective Chief Inspector Gavin Sheehy for us to take you into custody."

Warren stifled a gasp. It was even worse than he feared. Were they seriously thinking that he was involved in their deaths? Even his Federation representative looked taken aback.

"However, I am not satisfied with the level of cooperation that you have shown in this interview and feel that you have made sufficient procedural breaches to damage the integrity of several different investigations and call into question the security of any criminal convictions arising from them. This, I feel, warrants your immediate suspension from duties whilst our investigation continues."

Chapter 39

The suspension of a British police officer from duty isn't quite as exciting as the suspension of an American officer, as portrayed in some US TV shows. Warren didn't have a gun and unless you counted his lanyard and ID card, didn't really have a badge. However, he handed over his warrant card, his computer privileges were revoked and he was escorted out of the building.

By mid-morning he found himself sitting at home, staring at the kitchen wall waiting for Susan to return from her parents' and wondering how the hell he was going to break the news of his suspension to her. And his in-laws. He groaned. If he'd been wondering how things could get any worse, he'd forgotten that Bernice and Dennis were coming down with Susan to celebrate their anniversary.

His phone rang. He glanced at the screen—an unrecognised mobile number. Should he just ignore it? He knew that his suspension from duty would have been kept quiet, with only those in his immediate circle informed, but it couldn't hope to remain that way for ever. Could the press have got wind of it already? The last thing he wanted was to appear in that evening's *Middlesbury Reporter*.

He looked at the clock. Barely two hours had passed since he'd left Welwyn. Could the news have spread that fast? If he answered the phone with his customary greeting, he'd be confirming to any journalists that the number they had got hold of was his personal number. He'd never get any peace again. His finger hovered over the reject call icon, before stopping in mid-air. Didn't his voicemail message confirm his identity? He couldn't remember.

He pressed answer.

"Hello." His voice was neutral. He'd let the caller identify themselves first.

"That you, Boss?"

Warren released a breath he didn't know he'd been holding. "Yes, Tony, it's me."

"Thank God. I wasn't sure if those bastards at Professional Standards had confiscated your phone."

"Tony, I appreciate the call but you know you shouldn't be speaking to me, even with a new SIM card."

Sutton ignored him. "We've got to meet."

"No, Tony. I'm suspended. You're skating on thin ice already and I'm not taking you down with me."

Sutton ignored him again. "Back room, Prince and Pauper, half an hour."

He hung up.

* * *

"We must stop meeting like this. People will think we are having an affair."

Warren smiled weakly at Sutton's attempt at levity.

Reaching into his jacket pocket Sutton produced a set of folded computer print-outs. "Gary Hastings and I went back and had a look at everything that Pete printed out for you about

Delmarno. The differences are marked with green highlighter pen."

There was a lot of green highlighter.

"Shit," Warren breathed. There were two new names under the list of known associates: Paul Rubens and Martin Bixby.

"Rubens is nothing. He's just a bent accountant. The most interesting person is next on the list."

"Martin Bixby. What do we know about him?"

Sutton produced another wad of papers. "Lots. Would you like the highlights?"

Warren nodded.

"Martin Bixby, born in Coventry on the sixth of July 1953—the day after Vinny Delmarno entered this world."

Both born in Coventry, they were probably both on the same ward in Walsgrave Hospital, Warren realised.

"They essentially grew up like brothers—same area of Coventry, same primary school and secondary school. Some minor offences, such as shoplifting, as kids, before they went their separate ways for a few years."

Sutton pushed another sheet of paper across to Warren. "This is where it gets scary."

Warren skimmed the page, a brief service record from the army. "There's not a lot here. Joined up 1970, aged sixteen and a half, followed by his service history until sergeant, but then nothing from 1976 until 1983 when he received a dishonourable discharge."

"The army refuse to give us any information about the reasons for his discharge, but we have a report that he was arrested several times in the preceding months for being drunk and disorderly. The last one was the week before Christmas when he put some poor sod in hospital with a fractured jaw and four busted ribs."

"What about this period between '76 and '83? There's no detail about what he was doing or where he was posted."

"That's the worrying bit. I phoned the MOD; the Military Police are usually pretty helpful, but they suddenly clammed up and claimed that they don't comment on former service personnel as a matter of policy—which is crap. So on a hunch I went down to see Lee Robson, he's ex-army."

Warren knew him, a late middle-aged sergeant who headed up a community support team. He worked out of Middlesbury.

"He reckons that looking at where he was posted and this policy about not commenting he was probably special forces."

"You mean like SAS?"

Sutton nodded. "Yeah, and it gets worse. As soon as he left the army, our intelligence suggests that he moved down to Herts and started hanging around with his old friend Vinny Delmarno."

"He's the hired muscle."

"Exactly. And it makes sense in a way. Delmarno was trying to go legitimate by this point, at least on the surface. He bought loads of small, cash businesses and was using them as a front to launder money. But he hadn't left his old life behind—it made him far too much money to do that."

"So he employed Martin Bixby to do his dirty work, whilst he was the smiling pillar of the community. And I guess this Paul Rubens was the one cooking the books."

"It looks that way. And a pretty good job he did too."

"Well, not that good. Delmarno got twenty-two years."

"Yeah, for *murder* not fraud. All the fraud charges were thrown out."

Warren shook his head. "How ironic. Sheehy claims that they only came up with this whole ruse to get enough evidence to take his business empire down, and it looks as though they didn't even manage that. So what happened next?"

"The fraud squad didn't immediately give up after Delmarno's conviction. He'd signed over all of his assets to his now-ex-wife when it became obvious that he was going down and so they carried on investigating. But in the end, Rubens had done such a good job at burying the money they eventually pulled the plug."

"So what's the current situation?"

"When Delmarno came back out the Offender Management Service did a little bit of background and it seems that his ex-wife Jocelyn—she kept her married name—is the sole director of a string of cash businesses. Some of them she got from Delmarno, others she bought or started herself in recent years. And according to a notice posted at Middlesbury Registry Office, the former Mrs Delmarno will become the current Mrs Delmarno in less than a fortnight."

"Presumably meaning that Vinny Delmarno gains control of his little empire again." Warren shook his head in disgust. "It's as if those two decades in prison never happened."

"Exactly. But before we finish, I have one little extra titbit."

"Don't be a tease, Tony."

"Any guesses what the maiden name of the ex-soon-to-be-current Mrs Delmarno used to be?"

"Not a clue."

"Allingham."

Warren paused for a second, before it hit him. "The Allingham Golf Club and Hotel."

"Exactly. As first wedding anniversary presents go, it sure beats paper."

Chapter 40

Exactly whom Jocelyn lunched with had never really interested Delmarno. He'd met "the girls" briefly a couple of times but hadn't been impressed; all fifty going on thirty (at least in their imaginations), they were frankly idle and lazy. All beneficiaries of large unearned incomes from husbands current, former or late, none of them actually seemed to do anything. He knew enough about them to "uh-huh" convincingly when Jocelyn filled him in on their pointless undertakings, but all he could remember was that one played golf three afternoons a week and another organised cake sales for a local church once a month. The rest of them seemed to lunch, have affairs and spend time pampering themselves.

What Jocelyn saw in them he would never understand; for all her faults she'd never been idle. Whilst she may enjoy her lunch dates, she had still run a half-dozen firms, raised a young child to adulthood on her own and regularly travelled the lengthy distance to whatever institution the prison service had decided he should reside in each year.

Regardless, the weekly lunch meet at the upmarket French Bistro in town was as regular and inviolable as the setting of the sun—so why wasn't Jocelyn there?

The rest of "the girls" were there. He could see them through the plate-glass window. He recognised the skinny, blonde one with the suspiciously perky breasts for a woman of her years. Next to her, stuffing her face with a cream cake was the chubby dark-haired one. Marcy? Apparently it wasn't her fault that she was fat; it was genetic, Jocelyn claimed—although the evidence of his own eyes suggested otherwise. Three others whom he recognised but could recall nothing about made up the party. But no Jocelyn.

He'd been sitting across the road for fifteen minutes, watching, and he hadn't seen her. Far too long for a loo break, surely? A sixth, empty place was laid at the table, but he could see now that it was waiting to be filled, its neatly concertinaed napkin still sitting upright, the cutlery undisturbed. Her erstwhile companions had clearly been there for some time when he arrived. Dirty plates had been removed and desserts delivered. Two bottles of wine on the table accounted for the raucous giggling that he could see, but not hear, through the window.

His visit from Rubens had reminded Delmarno of the importance of his upcoming remarriage. He needed to marry Jocelyn again to regain a say in his companies. Jocelyn, of course, needed his money to rescue their ailing empire and keep a roof over her head. They both needed each other; however, he figured it wouldn't hurt to make a few romantic gestures to keep her sweet and ward off any potential cold feet. And that was why he was sitting here across the road waiting to surprise her, a big bunch of flowers filling the car with their sickly perfume. Doing it in front of her friends would be an added bonus—he didn't trust them not to try and discourage her from remarrying her bad-boy ex, the bunch of gold-diggers. Such a publicly romantic act might at least convince them his heart was in the right place and quell the sniping.

So where the hell was she?

He'd rung her mobile phone several times but it had gone through to voicemail. Did that mean she wasn't picking up, had left it at home or it was switched off? He'd only bought his first mobile phone six months ago and to be honest, still didn't really understand how it worked.

He looked at his watch again. The flowers were making his nose twitch and he suddenly felt an overwhelming urge to sneeze. Sod it! She wasn't coming. After starting the engine and forcing the car into gear he pulled away from the kerb, tyres squeaking. He reached the end of the street just as the lights turned red and his mood darkened even further.

Glancing in his wing mirror, he noticed the white BMW parked on the side of the road. The blonde-haired passenger had her door half open but was still leaning across the driver's seat, giving him a long, lingering farewell kiss. He looked harder. Could it…

The impatient horn behind him told him that the light had turned to green. Assuming it was directed at her, the blonde straightened up, closing the door. The driver was obscured from view by the headrests, but the face of the woman was briefly visible in his mirror as she swung her bag over her shoulder and flicked her hair back, before darting across the road to the opposite pavement.

The increasing sound of blaring horns faded into the background as Delmarno sat unmoving, unable to tear his eyes from the departing woman.

Jocelyn.

* * *

It had taken half an hour of aimless, pointless driving before Delmarno was able to make sense of his emotions and decide what needed to be done. His shock had slowly morphed into grief, then into anger. Now it was a cold, hard fury that gripped the pit of his stomach.

He pulled over to the side of the road and pulled out his phone.

"It's me," was all he said when the person he was calling picked up on the second ring. These new mobile phones all had a screen that showed the caller's name; Jocelyn's even showed a picture of the person. However, Delmarno had started their phone conversations this way ever since they were still kids and they had to sneak into the hallway or wait until the house was empty if they wanted to make a call.

Briefly he outlined what he had seen. Not much. A white BMW with a partial number plate translated from the inverted image in his wing mirror.

"Wait until after the wedding, then I want his balls."

"And Jocelyn?" The voice on the phone was cold, emotionless, professional—no evidence that the man had a wicked sense of humour or that he would walk through fire for those he loved. He'd been that way ever since they'd first become friends; when it came to work it was as if a switch was flicked and he became a machine. A ruthless, heartless, killing machine.

The man's loyalty was unquestioning—that was why Delmarno had trusted him with everything. When his conviction had become inevitable, he was the one Delmarno turned to. Hidden in the shadows, he'd watched over Jocelyn, kept their son free from danger and now he was in charge of Delmarno's revenge—tracking down those who'd deprived him of his liberty. He was the person waiting in the blacked-out limousine that picked Delmarno up from outside the prison gates, hugging him tightly for the first time since he'd been convicted.

Jocelyn had visited him regularly as he'd waited for her in prison. Their reunion that night had been sweet release after so long—but of all the people he'd missed the most it had been his long-time friend and confidant.

Delmarno breathed deeply. The ache in his heart was almost as painful as the icy fury in his gut. Almost, but not quite.

"Wait until we're married again, then she needs to have an accident."

Chapter 41

Tony Sutton's revelations about Jocelyn Delmarno had turned a bleak day for Warren into one where the faintest of promise might be on the horizon. With Warren suspended, Sutton would need to be not only his eyes and ears but also his arms and legs.

"Now we know that Vinny Delmarno is the *de facto* owner of that golf club. I'd give anything for a look at its member list."

Sutton ground his teeth. "Well, we know that isn't going to happen without a warrant. I can't see any way to apply for one without raising red flags, especially now that the request will be coming from a lowly DI."

"And one that may well be under observation," finished Warren. "You need to be careful, Tony. The last thing we need is for you to be relieved of duty also. You have to keep your head down."

Sutton grunted his acknowledgement. "At least we can hazard a guess at who orchestrated the spiking of Anton Liebig's drinks."

"Pretty elaborate, don't you think though? Especially for a thug like Delmarno."

Sutton shrugged. "Who can tell? We know he left school at an early age, but who knows what he picked up elsewhere."

Warren tapped his teeth thoughtfully. Something was nagging him. Something that Susan had said the evening that the three of them had taste tested different combinations of vodka and Coke. He pulled the copies of Delmarno's records across the table towards them, leafing rapidly through them until he found what he needed.

He sat back in satisfaction. "One more question solved, Tony." He pointed at Delmarno's medical records.

"He had a kidney transplant whilst in prison after receiving dialysis for end-stage renal failure. We knew that," said Sutton.

"Read on. Why would a young man in his thirties end up so ill?"

Sutton scanned further, before quoting aloud, "Renal failure is believed to be a consequence of the patient's poorly managed type II diabetes."

"Who else would be in a better position to turn Dr Liebig's diabetes against him than somebody who has spent a lifetime dealing with the disease himself?"

Chapter 42

On the other side of town, the man in the white BMW hung up the phone. His icy demeanour crumpled. He felt sick. Delmarno knew about them. He hadn't put all of the pieces together yet, but it was only a matter of time. Either way, the moment that Jocelyn signed that marriage contract she was a dead woman.

His hands shook. Martin Bixby had loved Jocelyn Delmarno since the day his best friend, Vinny, had introduced him to his new girlfriend. Of course, it was nothing more than a harmless crush; she was Vinny's girl. End of. He'd been best man at their wedding, giving a heartfelt speech that teased his friend and expressed his happiness at her appearance in his life in equal measure. And if he'd drunk a bit much that night and been a touch emotional—well that's what best men did, wasn't it?

It had been after his return from the Falklands and his ignominious dismissal from the army that his true feelings for Jocelyn had surfaced. By now, Vinny was living the high life as a prominent local businessman down in Hertfordshire; Jocelyn, his beautiful wife, was the mother to his gorgeous little boy. Bixby's godson.

With a dishonourable discharge to his name, finding gainful employment for one with his talents would never be easy and so he'd jumped at the chance to work for his old friend, using the skills he'd acquired in his defence of Britain's overseas interests.

At first it had been just like old times. Vinny was the brains; he was the muscle. He thought back to the first time they'd killed a man together.

Vinny was a short-arse; his diminutive stature was something he'd always resented his parents for. Big apes like Angelo Constantino could impress with their brawn. Six feet five in his socks and a compulsive user of the steroids that his crew shipped around the booming gym scene of the early 1980s, he'd struggled to find the even larger bodyguards that his status demanded he have. It was his insistence on this single criterion above all else that had ultimately sealed his fate.

Vinny, on the other hand, had never liked being dwarfed by those around him and so Bixby, who stood barely three inches taller than him, yet possessed certain skills that most men did not, fitted the bill perfectly.

Any one of Constantino's thugs could have lifted him off the floor and twisted his head off. In fact, the first one to die had tried just that. Bixby had simply let the man lift him up before sliding the slim blade he wore strapped to his wrist between the man's ribs.

As the giant relaxed his grip, too dumb to realise that he was already technically dead, Bixby simply stepped backwards and then turned and kicked his defeated opponent's equally large sidekick in the kneecap. When you weigh over twenty stones, it doesn't matter if it's muscle or fat—gravity is already placing tremendous stress on your joints. The kneecap gave way with a sound rather like a champagne cork popping, followed quickly by a howl of pain from its owner.

As the brute crashed towards the floor, Bixby gracefully dodged the falling body before grabbing the man's head with his left arm and snaking his right arm across his chest. The bodyguard's huge downward momentum meant that Bixby need do little more than direct his head to turn the opposite way to the direction he was falling and let gravity do the rest. This time it was more of a crunch than a pop.

Constantino had been so transfixed watching the deceptively slight Bixby despatch his two men that the first he knew of Delmarno's presence was the warm breath on his cheek, followed by the stainless-steel glint of the carving knife as his throat was slit from side to side.

Three days later, Constantino's eight biggest customers all received a severed finger in the post. His two biggest suppliers also had the honour of a thumb each. The message was clear. *Constantino is gone. You work for Delmarno now.*

Thirty years on and times had changed. Those days were behind him. Or at least that's what Bixby had thought. Vinny should have died in prison, a victim of his lifelong refusal to follow the rules, whether they be legal or medical. As they'd waited for him to die, Bixby and Jocelyn had grown close. Together, they'd moved on. Delmarno's poisonous empire of drugs, prostitution and murder had crumbled to nothingness and they'd seized the opportunity to start a new life.

The string of legitimate businesses that Rubens had advocated Delmarno set up had thrived, surviving the turmoil of the Nineties recessions relatively unscathed. The income had been enough for the three of them—Jocelyn, Bixby and the godson he was now raising as his own—to have comfortable lives. They thought about Delmarno's money now and again, hidden away, gathering interest overseas, but they didn't really need it.

And Bixby found he enjoyed his new life as a legitimate, honest businessman. The challenge of running a string of businesses alongside Jocelyn stimulated him in a way he would never have thought possible back when he was a teenager, running around with Vinny and yearning to join the army.

Of course, now the dreams had stopped. Post-traumatic stress disorder was what they called it these days. Back when he had been a squaddie, they hadn't even acknowledged it existed. The nightmares had just been a part of the job that nobody spoke about. When they became too much you simply got drunk, started a bar brawl and purged the demons until the next time. However, under Jocelyn's gentle ministrations and—eventually—the support of a counsellor specialising in veterans, the dreams had largely gone.

Bixby stared out of the car windscreen. It had started to rain and with it he felt the despair that had been building since the moment Vinny had walked out of prison and back into his life. Jocelyn's life.

For the past twenty years he'd thought that he and Jocelyn would grow old together. Vinny was in prison, rotting away, no longer married to Jocelyn. She'd divorced him to save their assets—to stop the state from seizing their legitimate businesses. They could have walked away with everything, left Vinny to die in prison. But she hadn't wanted to. Appearances were everything to Jocelyn and whilst she had been forgiven for divorcing him to save their livelihoods, those around them still thought of her as "Vinny's wife", as the mother to Vinny's son.

And she still loved him. Bixby wasn't a fool. He knew that Jocelyn still loved Vinny and he accepted it. He still loved Vinny himself, despite everything. Neither of them wanted to cause him the pain or the shame that publicly revealing their relationship would bring. It was unnecessary. Vinny would die in prison and then, after a suitable period of mourning, the two would become public. They kept on believing it as he became sicker and sicker in prison. They carried on believing it when against the odds a matching kidney donor was found. They continued believing it until twenty years had passed and Vinny was starting to prepare for his release. And then it was too late. The world's economies were crashing; banks were refusing to lend money and suddenly the business advice that they had followed during the boom years was coming back to bite them.

Now they needed Vinny and his millions. But his last, desperate plan hatched years ago as he'd faced his death in prison was unexpectedly coming to fruition. Now Vinny Delmarno wanted his life back and with that he also wanted his wife.

"We should kill him."

It had hurt him to say it. It had hurt him even more when Jocelyn had said no. Without Vinny's millions, she had argued, they'd go bankrupt and he'd never give them to her unless they married again. But that hadn't been the real reason. She didn't love Vinny the way she loved Bixby—he was sure of that—but she still loved him. He was the father of her child.

Bixby snorted at the thought. Filipo had been five years old when his father had gone to prison. He'd met him twice a year at most until he'd turned eighteen and gone to university. Now he worked abroad and he'd only been back twice in the more-than eighteen months since his father had been released. He tried to time his phone calls to his mother for when he knew his father would be out.

The day before Vinny had been released, Jocelyn had raced around the house hiding the "family photographs" of Jocelyn, Filipo and Bixby. That had hurt the most, he'd found. As if to compensate, the mantelpiece in the flat he now rented on the other side of town was covered in those same photographs: first holy communion, birthdays, and graduations—"Uncle" Martin was the one with his arm around the boy. Unlike Vinny, Bixby spoke to Filipo every couple of weeks and had even spent a few days walking with him in the Swiss Alps the previous summer. Vinny didn't even have a passport.

"Then we should wait until he's signed over the money and then kill him."

Jocelyn had been unable to counter that argument and had changed the subject. They hadn't spoken of it again. But now things were coming to a head.

The wedding was days away. The moment that they became man and wife, Vinny would want her killed—and if Bixby didn't do it, he'd find someone else who would. The moment they were married, Vinny would arrange for his shell investment company to infuse the money they so desperately needed into their company. And it would be time to get rid of him, whether Jocelyn agreed or not.

Chapter 43

Warren's elation at finding the thread that linked Vinny Delmarno to so many killings was short-lived.

"We have no evidence." Once again Tony Sutton was the voice of reason.

Warren sighed, allowing his brief pleasure to evaporate under the weight of reality.

"I'm also struggling to find a coherent motive here."

Sutton had thought to bring along some pens and blank sheets of paper, which Warren pulled over. He wrote the names of all of Delmarno's victims in a list with spaces between them.

"Let's look at the way they were killed and the timings. For example, my father. That makes sense from a revenge point of view. It's also immediate. But what about these others?"

"Well, Anton Liebig was the coroner who declared that death a suicide, alongside that dodgy pathologist."

"But why wait all those years to kill him? And why give him membership of the golf club that you own?"

"An insurance policy? A tame coroner would be bloody useful to someone in Delmarno's line of work I'd have thought. And you've seen that club. There's no way Liebig could have afforded the green

333

fees. So rather than bribe him directly with cash, which is traceable, they just gave him a free membership."

Warren was unconvinced. "I get the whole membership thing. It makes a lot of sense, but Delmarno was already in prison by this point. His little empire was being wound up. I doubt he'd have had much use for a coroner. Surely he was a loose end who needed to be killed off? Why wait for so long?"

"Well, presumably his wife ran the golf club whilst he was in prison. Maybe she didn't know who Liebig was."

"But wasn't that sidekick of his, Martin Bixby, still on the scene? Couldn't he have dealt with him?"

The two men lapsed into silence for a few minutes, before Warren suggested that they move on. "What about Sheehy? Is that revenge again?"

Sutton looked troubled. "Again, why wait so long? Your father was killed back in the Eighties—why wait nearly a quarter of a century to do something about Gavin? And why go to such elaborate lengths? Especially when he was quite happy to have Reggie Williamson stabbed to death on Middlesbury Common."

"Well, Sheehy claimed it was because he was too junior to have been on his radar at the time."

"So what changed? If he wasn't visible back then, surely he'd have completely faded into obscurity by now?"

"Well, he found Reggie Williamson again."

Sutton was thoughtful. "Did he? Are we sure that Vinny Delmarno found him?"

Warren paused. "What are you suggesting, Tony? That Delmarno didn't have Williamson killed?"

"Somebody had to know who he was. But what are the odds that Vinny Delmarno would think to track down his old gardener years later and blame him for that handgun finding its way into the police's hands?"

"Pete Kent or Gavin Sheehy."

"Exactly. Or maybe even the two of them. Try this for size. Vinny Delmarno is released from prison—unexpectedly, remember; everyone thought he would die in there—and he's shouting about revenge. Kent and Sheehy are terrified that he's going to find out about their role in his downfall. There's one loose end that needs to be tied up and that's Reggie Williamson."

"So why did Pete Kent try to kill Sheehy?"

"Well, you know what they say about two people keeping a secret."

"It's only possible if one of them is dead."

"Precisely." Sutton sat back with his arms folded.

"So what about the whole bribery thing and Sheehy passing information to Billy Obsanjo?"

Sutton's face fell. "Coincidence?"

"And who killed Pete Kent?"

Sutton glared at the table. "Shit."

Chapter 44

Jocelyn Delmarno was scared: scared for herself, scared for Bixby and scared for her husband. Vinny knew about her and Martin—or at least he would figure it out soon enough. Martin's phone call had been uncharacteristically frantic, insisting that they meet up immediately. Vinny had seen her and Bixby that afternoon and called his right-hand man for help. The description of Martin's BMW had only been partial and he was certain that Vinny had yet to connect the car to him—he'd only owned the vehicle six months and as far as he could recall had never driven Vinny in it. Nonetheless, he would keep the car in the garage and use one of Vinny's fleet of Jaguars.

Using Vinny's Jags was more than an inconvenience for Bixby, she knew—he felt like he'd taken a step backward. Despite the change in circumstances over the past twenty-odd years, Delmarno still saw Bixby as his employee, little more than hired muscle. He had no idea that Bixby and Jocelyn had become equal partners—in deed, if not in name—over the past decades. That suited the couple just fine. As far as Vinny was concerned Bixby had simply looked after Jocelyn and his son, keeping them safe from both physical and legal harm. To do this, he had remained in the background, apparently nothing more than a driver, bodyguard and trusted help. Few knew that it was Bixby who had severed the connections between Jocelyn and Delmarno's murky past, ensuring that she remained free to start a new life. Even fewer knew that for the past decade, Bixby had been as involved in the day-to-day running of the businesses as Jocelyn.

The return to his former status had chafed at Bixby even more than he had thought it would and giving up his beloved BMW, bought with the fruits of his own hard labour, rubbed salt in the wound. Lying in bed, he and Jocelyn would discuss how they would return to the life that they had enjoyed for so many years. Vinny had wanted to remarry Jocelyn immediately upon his exit from prison, but she had demurred. Such a move would doubtless attract unwanted attention and so she convinced him to wait a while before holding a discreet ceremony in front of a few close family members and friends.

Delmarno had been reluctant, but in the end he had conceded that it was for the best. Bixby had hidden it well, but Jocelyn had known he had been heartbroken. The small flat that he had moved to was soulless. Aside from his treasured photographs, most of his possessions were still in boxes over a year later as if he regarded the move as nothing more than a temporary situation.

Jocelyn splashed water on her face and stared at her reflection in the mirrored medicine cabinet in the en-suite bathroom. What was she going to do? Running was the sensible course of action and Martin had begged her to do just that—to leave everything and just elope with him.

But she couldn't do it. Jocelyn had carved a new life out for herself and it was a life that she was proud of. For two decades she had run those companies and—present difficulties aside—she had made a damn good job of it. Vinny referred to them as his companies, as if she had merely been a caretaker in his absence. But to all intents and purposes they were hers. She'd nurtured them and grown them, increasing profits and taking on new challenges. And if anyone could claim an equal stake in their success, it was Martin.

But all that was hanging in the balance now. The simple fact was that she was days away from bankruptcy. Next month's wages and suppliers' invoices totalled far more than they had in the bank. Like it or not, she needed Vinny's money. Calling off the wedding or running away would be tantamount to signing the death warrant for her businesses and she couldn't do that.

Which made Martin's suggestion that they wait until after Vinny had signed the money over before killing him sound increasingly sensible. They could pay off their debts, then resume their former life. After all, they'd spent twenty years living as if Vinny was never going to leave prison, waiting for him to die—that was almost the same, in intention if not in deed, surely? But she couldn't do it.

The whole point of the past few years had been to move on from that sort of life. It had taken her years to realise it, but she now relished no longer having to look over her shoulder all of the time, wondering if the car that had just driven by unusually slowly was a police surveillance vehicle or was driven by a killer employed by one of Vinny's rivals. After the IRA bombing campaign of the early 1980s, Vinny had become briefly obsessed with the idea that one of his rivals might use a car bomb to take him out and had insisted that Bixby check under his and Jocelyn's cars with a mirror on a stick. The end of living with that constant fear and paranoia had been the single biggest improvement in her life.

Now that fear was back. Vinny had effectively asked Martin to kill her. And if Martin didn't, Vinny would almost certainly find someone else who would. Killing Vinny before he killed her would be the sensible thing to do, but she still couldn't do it.

The truth was that she still loved Delmarno and despite everything he was the father of their child. That Filipo wanted nothing to do with his father still pained her and she held out a hope, however slight, that the situation would change in time.

And then there was Martin. Jocelyn wasn't naïve. She knew that the nightmares that Martin had suffered were from more than his years in the army. The enemy combatants that soldiers killed were largely faceless and anonymous. Even members of elite units like the SAS rarely knew the names of those who they killed. So who was Martin apologising to as he thrashed in his sleep? His anguished cries were muffled, often slurred from the alcohol he'd regularly consumed before bed, but it was clear that he repeated the same litany of names each night.

She knew that Vinny had killed people to get where he was and that he had utilised Martin's unique skills to help him. The ghosts of those men had come back to haunt Martin in later years, even as he moved on from his violent ways. It had taken years for him to admit that he had a problem and still longer to seek help, and it was only in the last few years that he'd finally slain some of those demons.

But along with the return of Vinny had come the return of Martin's dreams. Jocelyn was rarely witness to them. Opportunities to share Martin's bed and fall asleep in his arms were scarce these days. Nevertheless, over the past eighteen months she and Vinny had spent nights apart; Vinny's transplanted kidney required an occasional overnight stay in the local hospital and Jocelyn had friends and relatives throughout the country that Vinny had no interest in visiting. On those all-too-rare occasions Martin and Jocelyn had conspired to meet up and spend the night together, rather than trying to snatch a couple of hours here and there when they could be certain that Vinny would be away.

Was Martin killing again? Vinny had been vocal in his intention to track down and punish those who had caused his downfall. Had he done so? And had he turned to his old friend and confidant to help him?

Jocelyn was terrified that Martin had returned to his old ways. It had taken him years to purge the guilt that had hung around his neck for so long and she was fearful of what a return to form would do to his mental state. And for that reason she couldn't let him kill Vinny. Bixby felt that he had betrayed Vinny; as his oldest friend had withered away in prison, Bixby had taken his wife, his home and his child. That Vinny didn't know this and still thought of Bixby as his friend made it all worse.

"Are you coming to bed or what?" The voice from the bedroom was slurred, impatient.

Jocelyn shuddered as she spat a mouthful of toothpaste into the sink before answering. The urge to stay in the bathroom until her fiancé passed out was almost overwhelming. Fiancée. She'd never really thought of herself in those terms, but she supposed that she must be.

Her knuckles turned white as they gripped the sink. There had to be some way of ending this relationship. It couldn't continue and she had been fooling herself if she thought otherwise. But how? One thing was certain—if Martin Bixby killed his friend, he'd be killing himself as well. And Jocelyn couldn't let that happen.

THURSDAY 12ᵀᴴ APRIL

Chapter 45

Jocelyn Delmarno stared at the glowing red digits of the digital alarm clock on the bedside table. It flicked over to 7 a.m. Swinging her legs out of the king-size bed that she shared with her ex-husband, Vinny, she placed her feet on the thick, shag-pile carpet. Beside her Delmarno grunted, before continuing his heavy, grumbling breathing. Getting up, she padded silently to the main bathroom, not wanting to risk waking the slumbering man by using the en-suite.

The face staring back from the mirror bore only a superficial resemblance to the woman who'd finally gone to bed six hours earlier. Bloodshot eyes and mussed hair spoke of a night without sleep, but those same eyes had a resolve and clarity that had been lacking in that earlier person.

She thought back to the events of the last few hours and was unable to repress a shudder. Despite showering before going to bed, she suddenly felt an overwhelming need to wash again, to stand beneath scalding hot water and scrub until she felt clean.

The sex—it could hardly be termed lovemaking—had been aggressive and angry. It was as if Vinny was staking his claim over her. She thought back to Vinny's release with a mixture of sadness and revulsion. It had been twenty-two years since the couple had shared a bed—twenty-two years since Vinny had felt the touch of a woman. The first time had been clumsy and brief. Disappointing, but understandable.

Yet Jocelyn needed more. She needed Martin. For years they had shared the same bed that she had just left. With Martin it truly was lovemaking. Over that time they had grown together, learning what the other needed, giving as well as receiving, offering not taking. The illicit thrill of those first encounters had given way to the gentle, caring embrace of a couple growing to know each other.

For Vinny though, time had stood still. His sexual desires were still that of a much younger man, but his aging, abused body was no longer what it once was. And so Jocelyn had resigned herself to a lifetime of perfunctory, poor sex with a man whom she loved, but was no longer in love with. Only her brief sojourns with Martin had brightened her life.

Now though, Vinny had changed. When she had finally joined him in bed, he hadn't even attempted to woo her, immediately clambering on top, pawing at her as if he owned her. She'd lain there and made all the right noises, but it had been over almost before it began. The look in his eyes as he rolled off her and reached for the light switch had been a mixture of anger and disgust. Unlike Martin, Vinny had never been one for cuddling. Tonight, however, he hadn't even offered her a goodnight kiss.

The clock had passed 5 a.m. before Jocelyn had finally come to her decision. She knew what she had to do. The next hours had been spent planning how to achieve her goal. By the time the clock hit seven, she could no longer bear to remain next to Vinny. She would shower, cook breakfast like she always did and then she had to go and meet someone.

Chapter 46

Warren stared at the ceiling. He'd been lying there since finally giving up on sleep in the early hours. If he'd hoped that the coming of the dawn would bring clarity with it, he'd been disappointed. The only decision he'd made in the past few hours had been to go to B&Q and get some more emulsion to apply a second coat to the plaster around the new light fittings.

Beside him Susan sighed in her sleep. The couple had stayed up late in bed, whispering whilst Susan's parents snored in the guest bedroom. By mutual consent, they had decided that sharing the news of Warren's suspension with Bernice and Dennis would not be a good idea or in any way helpful.

"What are you going to do?" It was the same question that Warren had been asking himself, and hearing Susan ask it as well hadn't led to any new flashes of inspiration.

"What do you think you should do?"

Warren sighed down the phone. This variation on the question wasn't what he'd hoped for when he'd finally got out of bed and rung Bob Windermere.

"I was kind of hoping you could tell me, Bob."

"I'm sorry, Warren. If you were hoping for a magic wand to get you out of this mess, I can't help. We'll have to go through it step by step and see what we can come up with."

Warren closed his eyes briefly. That was all he wanted. Despite himself he felt a slight lifting of his spirits. Bob Windermere was still the best detective he'd ever worked with; if he couldn't bring some ideas to the table nobody could.

"The first thing we'll talk about is what you are *not* going to do."

"What do you mean?"

"Trust those instincts of yours, Warren. You're right to keep your father's connection to this quiet. Say nothing to Professional Standards. They have nothing on you beyond potentially interfering with a witness. They can't arrest you and they've already suspended you, so that's all they've got. Suspension is a pain, but look at the positive: you can do what you need now without anyone breathing over your shoulder."

Warren hadn't really thought about it in those terms.

"You need to keep this between us. Trust no one. Least of all that Grayson character."

"You think he might be involved?"

"I don't know, but I think you're right to question his whereabouts in the Eighties. He's an opportunistic weasel. If this Gavin Sheehy was telling the truth—and I'm still not convinced—then he and that Pete Kent were at the bottom of the food chain. Somebody with rank needed to orchestrate that stitch-up."

"I need to know who ordered that drugs bust."

Windermere agreed. "Any ideas how you can find out?"

Warren described how the key documents had been removed from the archive.

"And you are sure that Sheehy didn't just destroy them?"

Warren shook his head vigorously, forgetting that Windermere couldn't see him. "Definitely not. They were his insurance policy."

"And you don't know where else they might be?"

"I searched his house and couldn't find them." A thought suddenly struck Warren. "Shit. Could that have been why they tried to kill Sheehy? What if he had the documents in the house and his attackers took them with them?"

"Then it's already too late. They'll be destroyed and it's all over. You've said yourself that there's no real evidence that'll stand up in court."

"It can't be." Warren shook his head again. "I can't let it go. Not now. Not when I am so close to the truth."

Windermere's voice was gentler than Warren had ever heard it. "Warren, you have to face facts. Even if this conspiracy was real and not just the desperate fabrication of a desperate man, it's been buried for twenty-odd years. People have died, others have moved on and still others may well be in positions of power. Any evidence that existed back then will have been destroyed long ago." He paused. "Let it go. It's hung over you for your whole adult life. Your dad wasn't corrupt. Isn't that enough?"

Warren's voice, when it came was cold. "No, it isn't, and I can't believe that the Bob Windermere I knew all those years ago would say such a thing. Forget about my father. What about the others? Anton Liebig and his innocent wife? Zachary Eddleston was twenty-three years old and guilty of nothing more than wanting a bit of easy cash. What about Reggie Williamson? He probably did what he did with the best of intentions and he's killed for it decades later. Do they not deserve justice?

"And what about Vinny Delmarno and this Martin Bixby? They should be behind bars for what they've done. You cannot tell me that the public is safer with those two psychopaths out there, killing anyone who stands in their way?"

The pause at the end of the line was so long that Warren almost hung up.

"You're right. I just wanted to protect you. Of course you have my full support. You know that. But promise me one thing."

"What?"

"If you get that piece of paper you come to me first. Don't do anything foolish. I still have connections. Get me that document and I'll make sure that the bastard whose name is on it gets what's coming to him."

Chapter 47

If sex with Vinny the previous night had been unpleasant, what Jocelyn had to do next was positively stomach-churning. A few deep breaths and one last squirt of her favourite perfume and Jocelyn climbed out of her car. Even though she was certain that nobody had seen her arrive, she injected a little more sway into her hips as she strode up the driveway.

When it came to business matters, Jocelyn was always careful to dress in a businesslike manner. Like so many women before her, she'd found that whilst the power that came from being the boss and having control of the money engendered a certain grudging respect from other, male colleagues, women were still largely judged by their appearance. Consequently, sensible blouses with trousers or conservative dresses with high necklines were her work clothes; minimal make-up and hair tied back into unfussy styles reinforced her seriousness.

Today though, she was wearing a tight dress that showed off a little too much cleverly supported cleavage and finished well above the knee. Her ash-blonde hair flowed freely around her shoulders; her lipstick was a shade of red that she reserved for special occasions with Martin—not even Vinny had seen her dressed like this in recent decades. Good genes, good diet and a tiny bit of surgical assistance meant that Jocelyn Delmarno didn't look a day over forty.

Forcing a smile—not that the target of all this preparation would be looking at her face—Jocelyn took one last breath and rang the doorbell.

* * *

Jocelyn Delmarno ignored the nausea bubbling up inside her and ran her fingers seductively through the chest hair of the man lying next to her; a faint sheen of sweat coated both of their bodies. The choking fumes from the cigar that he was smoking curled lazily above the bed and he sighed deeply.

Paul Rubens had lusted after Jocelyn for decades. He'd barely made a secret of it before Vinny was incarcerated and it had taken a firm word from Bixby to curb his unwanted advances after she became a "single woman". This was one of the reasons that Jocelyn had dropped the man's services as soon as she could—a decision that from a financial point of view had probably been a mistake. Say what you liked about the man, but he knew the ins and outs of Vinny Delmarno's crooked little empire better than anyone.

Cutting herself away her ex-husband's malign influence had given her the opportunity to drop the corrupt accountant's services and she had done it as soon as possible. Unfortunately, Vinny hadn't seen it that way and had retained the man's services even as he faced life in prison. As his empire quietly crumbled, its assets were squirreled safely away in a complex network of virtual companies and hidden bank accounts to wait for him, should he ever leave prison.

And Rubens held the keys.

Vinny was so naïve, Jocelyn thought. The loss of access to Vinny's money had been an essential price to pay for her dissociation from the life that she escaped and until recently, she had rarely mourned its passing. What Vinny didn't seem to realise was that whilst she had no direct control over the money, neither did he. The only person who did was Rubens.

She'd never been sure if it was childhood loyalty or the fear of Vinny's reaction that had stopped Rubens from simply disappearing with the money. That he wanted it was unquestionable—you didn't become a bent accountant out of a sense of charity. She suspected that just like she and Bixby, Rubens was merely waiting for the right opportunity. Friendship aside, he had probably been as disappointed as them when Vinny had been given a new kidney and made it out of prison alive.

Seducing Rubens had been as easy as she'd expected it to be. He'd probably fantasised about this for years, and just as she'd expected, his raw, animal lust had clouded his judgement. She'd worked quickly, not giving him time to think, practically throwing herself at him the moment the door had opened. The dress that she had so painstakingly chosen that morning was lying on the floor inside of ten minutes.

Rubens currently lived alone; wife number four had left some months previously and he had yet to replace her. Jocelyn grimaced at the thought; rumour had it that his wives and girlfriends were typically sourced from the grubbier corners of the internet in an arrangement more akin to a football-player signing than a Hollywood romance. Still, it was an agreement that both sides seemed to benefit from—Rubens enjoyed a few years' company with a young woman well out of his league; his companion enjoyed the sort of lifestyle impossible in her own country and, if the marriage lasted long enough, British citizenship to boot. Jocelyn had always viewed these young women with a degree of contempt, but given her own actions over the past few months—particularly the last few hours—could she really claim to be any different? She pushed the thoughts away. This wasn't the time to deal with them.

Rubens' initial lust and surprise was now wearing off. Jocelyn could see it in the slowly forming creases on his forehead. Rubens may be a predictable fool, who thought with his balls not his brains, but he wasn't a complete idiot. Now came the hard part.

"So what do you want?"

His voice was flat, emotionless. His eyes were closed, but Jocelyn felt as though he was somehow scrutinising her from behind his eyelids.

"Vinny's money. Or at least the half a million I need to save the business."

Rubens sucked contemplatively on the cigar.

"And what makes you think I can help you with that?"

"I'm not a fool, Rubens." Jocelyn's voice was hard. The seductive tone she'd been using for the past hour was gone. Jocelyn the businesswoman was back in charge now.

"I've seen the contracts. Vinny might not know anything about business law, but I do and I know that nothing moves in or out of those accounts without your say-so. If you wanted to, you could take the whole lot and disappear tomorrow."

"If that's true, then why haven't I done it already?"

Rubens opened his eyes and turned towards Jocelyn. The look was slightly quizzical, almost amused. *He's not taking me seriously*, she thought, the hot flash of anger immediately tempered by the realisation that his underestimation of her could only make things easier.

"You're scared of Vinny. You know that he'll track you down and kill you."

Male ego is so easy to manipulate, she thought with satisfaction as Rubens immediately denied the charge.

A few seconds later, Rubens started again, his voice triumphant as he seized upon the flaw in her logic.

"Assuming you're right and I'm worried about Vinny's reaction, then why would I give you the half mill? Stealing his money and giving it to his ex-wife so that she can use it to cut him off from his own businesses? I think it's fair to assume that he'd be even more pissed off with me than if I just nicked it all and took off. He'd at least understand that."

"You're right. He would understand it. And you're right, he would be angry. But imagine how angry he'll be when I actually explain what those contracts mean to him—how you drafted those contracts deliberately to give you sole control of his businesses."

"You'll never prove it." The tone belied the words.

Jocelyn laughed. "I don't have to prove it. I just need to say it. Vinny and I are getting married in a few days; I've got him wrapped around my little finger. He'll believe anything I tell him."

Rubens shook his head vehemently. "No way. Vinny won't believe you. The two of us grew up together, went to school together. Me, Martin and Vinny." His voice turned nasty. "We've had each other's backs since we were ten years old."

"It's funny you'd mention Martin." Jocelyn smiled wolfishly. "You see Vinny is a very jealous man. Very jealous. And Martin's a very good photographer. A real master with a zoom lens…"

Rubens paled. "You wouldn't dare." He rolled away from her, backing away as if she were a poisonous insect. "Vinny would be furious."

Jocelyn shrugged. "You're right. But he needs me as a co-signatory on his business. He doesn't need you; he'll just take the money that he wants. You know what he's like—" a pause "—you know what Martin's like. They can be very persuasive."

Rubens' jaw was working. Jocelyn could see his mind whirring furiously. There was doubt in his eyes—but also fear. Jocelyn fought hard to keep her own expression neutral. The plan that had seemed like a good idea at 5 a.m. now seemed like absolute folly. The whole thing was an elaborate house of cards built upon layers of lies, but it was all that she had left. If he called her bluff, it would all come crashing down around her. There was no way that she could go through with her threat. Vinny had already asked Martin to kill her after spotting them together. Claiming that her lover was Rubens wasn't going to change that fact.

And what about Martin? There were no photos of her entering Rubens' house; Martin didn't even know that she was here. He'd never have let her come.

"What do you want?" Rubens' voice was low, defeated. But his eyes still held anger. An anger that she would have to assuage; she couldn't afford it to fester. She needed to sweeten the deal, dampen down any resentment that might lead to him attempting revenge.

"Just the original proposed investment. That's all. Sign the money over to me, no need to even change the terms of the contract, just omit Vinny's name."

"And what's in it for me?"

"You get to keep the rest."

Rubens paused, his jaw working slightly. "Say again."

"Keep the rest. I don't want it." She stumbled over the words; she'd almost said "we"; she couldn't let Rubens know about her and Martin or her whole scheme would collapse. Rubens would go straight to Vinny and they'd both be dead within forty-eight hours.

Rubens' eyes widened. Jocelyn had no idea how much money

was actually in Vinny's myriad overseas accounts, but Rubens—the man who'd set them up and carefully husbanded them for the past two decades—knew the figures to the nearest penny, cent and centime.

Almost immediately, his face hardened again. "And so you think Vinny will just let you cut him off from his businesses and let me take his money from under his nose?"

Jocelyn smiled wolfishly. "Give me twenty-four hours and Vinny will no longer be a concern."

She could see that he was unsure—his natural greed conflicting with his sense of self-preservation. Steeling herself and forcing a seductive smile to her lips, Jocelyn decided to tip the balance. Burying her revulsion deep inside, she reached beneath the bed sheets again.

Chapter 48

The second part of Jocelyn's plan was even more repugnant than the first. And it needed to be done quickly. The longer she left Rubens to think about the situation that she had manoeuvred him into, the longer he had to see the flaws, to come up with a way to extricate himself from his dilemma.

Her hands shook as she drove back to the beautiful house that she had called home for the past twenty-five years. A blare of horns and an angry flash of lights interrupted her reverie. *Steady on*, she cautioned herself, as she waved apologetically at the lorry she'd blithely cut in front of—the plan would be for nothing if she killed herself in a silly road accident.

Of course, what she was about to do was at least as dangerous as driving without paying attention to other road users. Again, she thought about calling Martin; his reassuring presence would stop things from going too far. But she couldn't. Even if he let her go through with her foolhardy plan, things could quickly escalate out of control, and if Martin killed Vinny, he'd end up going to prison, or worse.

Pulling into the wide, sweeping drive, she saw that Vinny's car was parked in its usual place. Stopping next to it, she rested her hand on the ignition key. Last chance to call it all off, to turn around and run away. But where would she go—and could she really leave everything behind? Everything that she had worked for, for so long?

She turned the engine off and clambered out.

* * *

Vinny Delmarno was on life licence. He'd served twenty-two years in prison, but as a convicted murderer, his sentence would never be deemed spent. Once a week he attended a meeting with a case-worker from the local Offender Management Team and had to show that he was no longer a threat to society and was abiding by the law. Any breach and he would be recalled to prison, potentially to serve out the rest of his sentence. So far, he had given his probation officer no cause for concern.

Delmarno was reclining in the living room watching football on the large screen. A couple of empty cans of beer sat on the table in front of him. Good, thought Jocelyn, it would make the next part easier.

"Vinny, I'm leaving you. Pack your bags. I want you out."

The bluntness of the words surprised even Jocelyn. Until she'd walked through the door, she hadn't known what she was going to say. But, now that she'd started, there was no going back and the words poured forth.

"I've tried to love you but I can't. Twenty-two years I waited for you. I've changed. The world has changed. But you haven't. I can't go back in time. I can't return to the way things were."

The look of confused hurt on Vinny's face almost made her change her mind, to desperately try and swallow her words, claim it was all a big joke.

Then his expression changed, his face twisting in a manner she'd never seen directed at her before. A look of cold fury. The same expression she'd seen cross his face years ago when he thought she wasn't watching, that he'd hidden from her by carrying the telephone into the office and kicking the door closed. A few days later she'd seen him again, this time with a copy of the *Coventry Evening Telegraph* under his arm and a look of triumph on his face. The headlines recounted the suicide of a local police officer suspected of corruption. She'd known in her heart of hearts that the two events were somehow linked.

"Who is he?" Vinny's voice was low, dangerous. He unfolded himself from the couch.

"It doesn't matter."

"Of course it fucking matters!" His voice was a scream.

He rounded the chair in three paces and Jocelyn suddenly found herself stepping backwards. She stopped and, ignoring her instincts, stood her ground.

"You wouldn't know him anyway."

Vinny's breathing was ragged, his nostrils flaring. "Tell me!"

Vinny was a violent man; Jocelyn knew this. In addition to the man he had been convicted of killing, his hands were stained with the blood of countless others who had got in his way or tried to betray him. But in a quarter century of marriage, he had never lifted his hand against her. He was old-fashioned in that way, she supposed. But today had to be different.

His fists were clenching and unclenching, but somehow he maintained his self-control, remained beyond arm's length, as if by keeping that distance he could stop himself from stepping over that line in the sand.

Jocelyn stepped forward, forcing herself to keep her eyes open, to accept what she knew was coming.

"He's asked me to marry him and I've said yes." She placed her wedding ring and the engagement ring that Vinny had given her all of those years ago on the edge of the bar. And braced herself.

* * *

The split lip and swollen tongue made her voice thick and slurred; the tears were real enough. She'd driven for almost twenty minutes before finally pulling over and fumbling for her mobile phone.

The call was picked up on the second ring.

It took only a few moments for her to be put through.

"My name is Jocelyn Delmarno and I've been attacked by my husband. He says he's going to kill me. Please come quick…"

Chapter 49

The call to Sutton's office phone was the last thing he was expecting.

He was already in the stairwell next to the toilets, mobile phone in hand before the handset finished rattling in the cradle. Given the events of the last twenty-four hours, the last person Sutton should have been phoning was DCI Warren Jones, now that he was on suspension.

Warren's phone connected on the second ring.

"Jocelyn Delmarno's downstairs. It looks like her husband is on his way back to prison."

* * *

Jocelyn Delmarno was a victim of domestic violence. Therefore, there was no way that Sutton or anyone else in CID was getting face time with her any time soon, especially when he refused to give reasons for why he wanted to speak to her. After officers trained in dealing with vulnerable witnesses picked up the distraught woman from the roadside, she had been taken to hospital and assessed. Her injuries had then been photographed for evidence. Finally, she had been returned to Middlesbury police station to make a statement.

Again, Sutton hadn't been allowed access to the victim. However, interview room one had two-way glass and the sergeant interviewing Jocelyn Delmarno had decided that objecting to his silent, unseen presence as a point of principle wasn't worth the grief it would cause.

Jocelyn Delmarno was a handsome woman. Her date of birth claimed that she was fifty-one years old, but she could probably pass for forty on a good day, Sutton decided. However, today wasn't a good day.

The split lip and swelling to the left side of her mouth lent weight to her claim to have been the victim of a right cross. The bruising to her right temple spoke of where her face had impacted the kitchen counter as the punch had knocked her off her feet.

"So tell me again what happened, Ms Delmarno, in as much detail as you can remember. Take all the time you need."

Sutton quietly thanked the constable who had let him into the viewing booth and left. He didn't need to hear the story again. The most important thing in his mind was the warrant that had been drafted for Delmarno's arrest and return to prison for breaching his licence.

Ordinarily, the team would have twenty-four hours to question a suspect before they had to apply for an extension or release them. Because of that, teams often went in underprepared. That wouldn't be an issue this time. They could take their time in deciding how to question him. He wasn't going anywhere soon. Which was just as well. At the moment their investigation was still flying under the radar and Sutton wasn't going to draw attention to their interest in Vinny Delmarno until Warren gave the say-so.

* * *

Vinny Delmarno's rage had eventually evaporated to be replaced by a sense of shame and fear—shame at what he had just done and fear for the consequences. The Mafiaesque lifestyle that Delmarno had grown up idolising was a sanitised, Hollywood version where men were men and honour was the driving force behind what they did. As he grew older he soon came to understand that organised crime was a filthy, honourless profession. That the Mafia—be it Italian, Russian or even British—was populated by amoral scum, with no values. That even the Krays were ultimately nothing more than common thugs.

Regardless, Delmarno had always had one rule: never hit a woman. That he had arranged for the "disciplining" of prostitutes was not a contradiction—that was business, not anger. And besides he never actually did it himself. He had kept that rule his entire life. Until today.

And today's mistake just might be the end of him. He had no doubt that Jocelyn was on her way to the police. That within hours they would be there, warrant in hand, to take him back into custody. He swallowed hard. He was afraid, he realised. Twenty-two years had been stolen from him. How many more would he lose? He'd survived the last stretch on hate. Hatred for those who had betrayed him. But was that enough now? Martin had killed that treacherous gardener and the pigs who had framed him had all got what was coming to them. Did he have enough hate left to sustain him through another stretch? He feared the answer was no.

How long did he have now? An hour? More? He had no idea. Regardless, he wasn't going to be here when they arrived. He glanced at the clock. No time to get changed, he decided, as he grabbed a small rucksack from the hall cupboard.

Think. What did he need to take with him? What was necessary and what could he get Bixby to pick up for him at a later date?

Taking a deep breath, he tried to calm his racing mind. First stop: the medicine cabinet. He'd been a slave to its contents for almost half of his life. He thought back to those first warning signs. Could he have prevented it? The diabetes wasn't his fault, but his failure to control it and its ultimate effects were. He'd been arrogant. He accepted that now. Vinny Delmarno, king of all he surveyed, wasn't going to let bloody diabetes defeat him. He was young. He had his best years ahead of him. He had a wife, a kid and more money than he knew what to do with. Most importantly, he had respect.

He'd been a bloody fool. Decades staring at the same four walls gives a man a lot of time for introspection. He'd ignored the symptoms, the tiredness and peeing, for over a year before deciding reluctantly that maybe the doctors were right and it was time to start controlling his diabetes a bit better. When a change of diet and cutting back on the booze made no difference, he finally went to his GP. Protein in his urine, they said. *Well obviously, I'm diabetic*, he'd countered. No, the reply came, that's glucose. Protein is different. Protein is more serious.

Delmarno's formal science education had ended at fifteen, but pretty soon he was using terms like *glomerular filtration rate, proteinuria* and *haematuria* like a professional. But he'd left it too late. A lifetime of ignoring the rules—even those set by his doctors—was catching up with him, and by mid-1987 new words, like *dialysis* and most scarily of all *renal failure* were also part of his lexicon.

By the end of that year a lifetime of ignoring other rules meant that his newfound medical vocabulary was being supplemented by a new legal one: *remanded, living off immoral earnings* and finally *murder*. By the time he was formally charged in January of 1988 he was spending four days each week in hospital, surrounded by both nurses and lawyers.

He pulled out the packets of drugs. How many days' supply did he have left? Like all transplant patients he relied on a cocktail of immunosuppressive drugs to stop his body rejecting the replacement organ. Stop taking them and within days his immune system would reawaken, recognising the kidney as non-self, as foreign, and start attacking it as if it was a tumour or invading pathogen.

Six days' worth. He swore. He'd have to get Martin to pick up his repeat prescription within the next twenty-four hours. He doubted that the police would have the common sense to stake out his local pharmacist, but he wasn't going to take any chances and the sooner he got the next three months' supply the better.

Next stop: the master bedroom. Delmarno had learnt from his mistakes. He ignored the small safe in the wardrobe—the same safe that snake-in-the-grass gardener of his had stolen his gun from—that was just for show. (How had he got the combination? Delmarno had never received a satisfactory answer to that question.) Jocelyn kept her jewellery in it and a few hundred pounds in cash. Instead, he went straight to the king-size bed. With a grunt he slid it across the wooden floor, before dropping to his knees.

The floorboards had been replaced so expertly, that even when you knew what you were looking for the hairline gaps were all but invisible. A firm push on the edge of the correct board resulted in a muted click. Now the board could be slid to one side, revealing another, smaller safe. A quick spin of the reassuringly weighted dials (Delmarno didn't trust the newfangled digital ones) and the door opened to reveal what he euphemistically called his "life insurance policy". Except that this policy paid out to preserve his life, rather than at the ending of it. Five thousand pounds in cash—plus another five thousand euros—was useful, but the large, untraceable handgun and two dozen bullets would be even more helpful, he decided.

He glanced at the clock in the kitchen. Jocelyn had left forty-five minutes ago. If he assumed that the police would be here within the hour, it was time to leave. But where could he go? He entered the enclosed garage and stopped. Jocelyn would no doubt tell the police the registration numbers of all his cars. Wherever he chose to go had to be within walking distance. Bixby. It was his only choice. He pulled out his phone, before pausing again. Couldn't the police trace mobile phone calls? If he called his old friend, he'd be leading them right to him. Remembering a movie he'd once seen, he removed the phone's battery and placed it in the bin. The little gadgets were like tracking devices, he recalled.

Would Jocelyn tell the police that he was at Bixby's? He doubted it. She hadn't said five words to the man in all the time that Delmarno had been out of prison. He was just the hired help. He doubted that she even knew where he lived. Fortunately, Delmarno had always taken an interest in his old friends. It was one of the reasons they stayed loyal to him, he felt.

He took one more look around at the house that the Delmarnos had called home for so long. Was this the last time he'd see it? He remembered the time over twenty years ago when he'd done the same thing. That time he had been convinced that he would be coming back—and he had, twenty-two years later. Now he wasn't so sure.

Yet strangely, he didn't feel sad. It wasn't his home, he saw, with sudden clarity; it hadn't been for over twenty years. For the past few months, he had been little more than a house guest. Every room in the place had been redecorated at least once in the time that he had been gone. He hadn't chosen any of this wallpaper. He'd had no say in the pale cream gloss paint on the door frames. The chrome-and-glass kitchen was nothing to do with him. It was all Jocelyn. It was her home, the centre of a life that he was no longer a part of.

He curled his lip. Well, screw the bitch. She needed him more than he needed her. When all of this blew over, he'd start again. Rubens had already created that fictional investment company to channel his overseas earnings back into the country. He could just get him to invest the money in a new venture.

Delmarno smiled. This was just another temporary setback. In a few months' time it'd be back the way it used to be. A simpler time. Him, Bixby and Rubens against the world.

FRIDAY 13TH APRIL

Chapter 50

It was 8 a.m. and Bixby sat on the edge of the bed, wearing nothing but his underwear. He took another long swig from the bottle of whisky, having dispensed with the tumbler some hours ago. Shards of it mingled on the carpet with fragments from the broken picture frames that he'd smashed in an explosion of temper after the phone call. Blood from when he'd stood on the sharp splinters on his way back from the bathroom now stained the cream carpet. He should go and clean the cuts and bandage them, he thought distantly. Instead, he took another mouthful, the alcohol numbing the throbbing pain in his foot. How long until the booze numbed his brain enough for him to sleep without the dreams?

He squinted blurrily at the clock. Over twenty-four hours had passed since he'd last slept. If two hours of fitful tossing and turning could be called that.

It was all coming apart. The slow downward spiral that had started when Vinny left prison was now a terrifying plummet towards oblivion. Bixby felt as if he was being suffocated.

Barely twelve months ago, he and Jocelyn had been living their dream. Or so they had convinced themselves. Running clean, successful, legal businesses, Jocelyn had broken her links with the filth and corruption that had hung around Vinny like a stinking cloud.

They hadn't been rich—comfortable for sure, but not wealthy. And neither of them cared. Vinny had craved money; he'd driven himself to acquire material goods as a proxy for the respect that he'd been denied since childhood.

Bixby placed his head in his hands and thought about his old friend—a man whom he had once loved like a brother—whom he still loved. It was only that love that kept Delmarno alive, when all logic said that he should be killed.

Vinny was a disappointment to his family, to his father in particular. Short and weedy, he'd been an embarrassment on the football pitch. Nobody in his immediate family was remotely academic, so his failures at school were less of a source of dismay than his lack of athletic prowess. Perhaps if he had taken a more active interest in his parents' pizza business, he could have gained the approval that he so desired.

But his parents were conservative in matters of money. Years of hardship had lowered their expectations, had led them to favour security over risk-taking. When the shop next door to their pizza parlour had become vacant, a teenage Vinny had urged his father to take it over. To knock through and expand their business from an over-the-counter fast-food parlour into a proper restaurant and expand the menu to include some of the pasta dishes his mother was so expert at making. His father had refused, scornful of his young son's naiveté, and to this day, Vinny would speak disdainfully of a missed opportunity to capitalise on the growing popularity of Italian cuisine in the late Sixties and early Seventies.

But as an outsider, Bixby had seen what Vinny could not. That Delmarno senior was still scarred from his experiences during and after the war. The rise of fascism and the policies of Mussolini had led to the Delmarnos, like so many families, fleeing first to France, then after the war further afield. Settling initially in Birmingham, Delmarno's father, Ernesto, and his two older brothers had moved to Coventry to seek work during the post-war construction boom.

After marrying another member of this close-knit diaspora, Ernesto had spotted a gap in the market and started selling Italian-recipe ice cream and later pizza. These exotic foodstuffs had appealed to a niche market initially and times were hard. Added to that, casual and even overt racism had made fitting into this new society difficult at times. "Wop" or even the incorrect "spic" had been some of the milder racial abuse directed at the family in the early years. That the Delmarnos had fled Italy because of their opposition to fascism and the policies of Mussolini had cut little ice with some of the residents of a city still scarred by the devastating blitz of November 1940.

To outsiders, Vinny espoused a loyalty to his family that echoed the strongest of Italian traditions; yet Bixby had seen the real man. Vinny was contemptuous of his father's timidity, yet it didn't take a psychologist to see that everything he had done since was aimed at gaining his father's approval. Ernesto Delmarno had lived in near poverty, working sixteen hours a day six days a week and had still laboured to keep his ancient bicycle roadworthy. Vinny had bought his first new car before his twentieth birthday and had insisted on parking it outside his parents' run-down council house where all the neighbours could see it. When Vinny turned eighteen, his father had taken him to their local pub and bought him his first legal pint, but then suffered the ignominy of having to borrow money from a friend to purchase a second round; on the occasion of his twenty-first birthday, Vinny had hired the whole pub and paid for an open bar.

Yet despite his desire to prove himself a better man than his father, none of Vinny's fast-food outlets sold pizza…

Bixby took another swig and was surprised to find it empty. He looked blurrily towards the kitchenette, unable to remember if there was anything more to drink. The bottle dropped to the carpet and his head sank into his hands.

Everything was a mess; he just wanted to run and hide. But where to? And with who? He should be elated. In just a few days Jocelyn, the only woman he had ever loved, the woman who had finally given him a reason to grow old, had been due to become Mrs Delmarno for the second time, banging the final nail in the coffin of a relationship that started to implode the moment Vinny had left prison. For the second time he would have been forced to watch as Vinny took the woman that he didn't deserve away from him. And then what? Vinny was expecting him to kill her. To yet again make use of those special skills that made him so valuable.

But Jocelyn had solved that problem. Vinny was on his way back to prison, Rubens was due to arrange the money that would secure all of their hard work and they were free to resume the life that both of them wanted.

But he'd screwed it all up. Jocelyn hadn't been naïve enough to expect him to take the news of what she had done well—but neither had she expected the violence of his reaction. He hadn't hit her, like that bastard Vinny, but was that only because she'd fled before his rage had made him cross that line?

Why had he reacted the way he had? She'd done what she had done for them. He knew that she felt nothing for Rubens. She could barely stand the man. Yet the idea of him pawing at her body had sickened him. Somehow, he'd blotted out what she must be doing with Vinny each night, but now that too was running through his mind, on an endless loop.

The real question, the one he couldn't really answer, was what did he have to offer her? He knew that he'd been a good husband and father—yet what else could he give? To the world outside and to Vinny Delmarno in particular, he was just the hired help. Even those who knew him most closely thought he and Jocelyn were little more than business partners. His name wasn't even above the golf club that he had managed for the past twenty years. What would Vinny think if he knew that Jocelyn had been unable to set foot inside the club that still bore her maiden name, that instead she had left it to Bixby to nurture? Even worse, what would Vinny think if he knew that Bixby and Jocelyn had become more than business partners, that his only son called Bixby his stepdad?

To the world at large, Martin Bixby was just one thing—a thug for hire. A trained killer who could solve "problems" and make them go away. Who followed orders.

But he didn't always follow orders, did he?

"Kill Delmarno," the voice at the end of the phone had said, when Vinny was released. A voice he hadn't heard for over twenty years.

But Bixby didn't want to kill again. He hadn't killed since that warm, summer evening so many years ago. He still remembered the sensation, the way his victim had bucked wildly against the chokehold, chest heaving, a gasping, gargling noise getting quieter as the thrashing slowed. Finally, it had stopped, the body becoming limp in his arms. He'd maintained the hold for another thirty seconds, as he'd been trained to do, making certain that the man wasn't suddenly going to awaken. Then there had been the staging of the scene; to this day the smell of exhaust fumes could transport him without warning back to that night.

When he'd finished he'd locked the garage and walked briskly to the nearest pay phone, his head bowed, collar upturned in case anyone paid too much attention to a stranger in the quiet street.

"It's done," was all he'd said after the number had connected. The voice on the end of the phone had simply grunted in acknowledgement before hanging up.

After that, he'd dialled another number.

"It's done," he'd repeated.

The response of Vinny Delmarno's lawyer hadn't been much more verbose, "I'll tell him."

That evening Martin Bixby's life as a killer had ended.

Or so he'd thought. For years he'd done his best to forget what he had been, trying to blot out the faces of those he'd killed by burying their names and faces under a layer of booze, and when that didn't work he'd finally given in to Jocelyn's pleas and confronted his past. Endless sessions with therapists and psychologists, face-to-face or sitting in a large group, sharing feelings that a lifetime of training had told he should bury, hide away, lest he be seen as weak. Finally, he'd come to terms with what he'd done. For the first time in decades he'd been able to go to sleep without the help of alcohol, without feeling trepidation at what the night's dreams might bring.

And then Vinny had been released and Bixby found himself serving two masters.

To the voice on the phone, he promised he'd deal with Delmarno, but killing him wasn't the answer.

"You'd better. If I go down, you go down. Never forget that."

To Vinny, he'd promised to help him craft his revenge.

After a plausible wait he'd given Vinny the name of Gavin Sheehy, Niall MacNamara's partner in the planting of the gun. Killing Sheehy was the sensible thing to do; the disembodied voice on the end of the phone had said as much. Bixby's training told him that it was necessary. But Vinny had wanted his retribution. He'd wanted Sheehy to suffer the humiliation of false conviction and prison, followed by the knowledge that at some point in the future—at the moment when he least expected it—somebody would step out of the shadows and kill him.

Pete Kent had been furious to be contacted again. Decades had passed since he'd given in to the lure of easy cash and hints that what he was doing was ultimately for the greater good. Young DC Kent had convinced himself that his small part in the planting of evidence was morally the right thing to do and that he'd have played his role even without the money.

Had the man even thought about what he'd done over the past two decades? Had he and Gavin Sheehy ever talked about it? Surely it must have come up in conversation when Vinny was released. The men had worked together for most of that time, Sheehy receiving multiple promotions whilst Kent had ridden his coat-tails, ultimately landing a cushy desk job in the unit Sheehy commanded.

Yet that loyalty had counted for little in the long run. When Bixby had made it clear that he had no qualms about exposing Kent's role in the sordid enterprise, the man had changed his tune immediately. It had been Kent's idea to stitch up Sheehy by impersonating him in meetings with some lowlife drug dealer. He'd done it, he claimed, because it meant he wouldn't have to kill his old friend.

Bixby had successfully navigated the tightrope, appeasing both the voice on the phone and Vinny, all without any need to resort to killing.

Or so he'd thought.

The voice on the phone had thought differently.

Which meant that the first death was unavoidable. Anton Liebig knew what they had done. More importantly, he'd known who had ordered it done. Bixby had looked for another way, but the voice on the phone had been adamant. "If I go down, you go down."

He'd been wracked with guilt, in particular over the death of the man's wife—a complete innocent. But buried below that, in a part of his psyche that he'd tried hard to banish, he'd felt a rush of adrenaline that he'd not experienced in over twenty years—a job well done. Just like Niall MacNamara or countless terrorists before him, the death had been recorded as something other than homicide.

But it hadn't been enough. Liebig was just one loose end. There were plenty more that needed to be fixed.

He'd had no choice about killing Reggie Williamson either. It was Vinny's fault. Since he'd left prison he'd been like a dog with a bone. "How did the police get hold of that gun?" he'd asked.

Again and again. As always when he had a problem, he'd given it to his best man to solve.

He'd been somewhat appeased when Bixby had handed him the name of Gavin Sheehy and arranged for his downfall. But eventually he'd spotted the unfilled gap in the chain of events.

"How did Sheehy get hold of the gun to pass onto that shit MacNamara? It must have been somebody close to me. Somebody I trusted." He'd continued to obsess about it.

It had been as they sat around the table eating Sunday lunch that Bixby had realised that he would need to give Vinny someone else. Jocelyn had gone into the kitchen and Delmarno had leant over to him. After years of abstinence, spurning even the illicit hooch brewed up inside the various institutions that he'd spent the past decades in, Vinny had rediscovered the joys of alcohol. His breath smelt of a mixture of red wine and mild acidosis from elevated blood glucose.

"Keep an eye on her," he'd slurred. "I can't think of anybody else who could have stolen that gun."

An icy hand had gripped Bixby's insides. A week later, he'd finally given Delmarno the name of Reggie Williamson and some suggestions as to how he could exact revenge on the former handyman and gardener.

Delmarno had been contemptuous. "Don't waste your time on the fucking hired help," he'd snorted. "Just kill the bastard."

A few days later, when the police had announced the death of the former gardener, Delmarno hadn't even made the connection until Bixby reminded him. Delmarno had completely forgotten the man's name.

"Good job, Martin. Pity about the poor dog though. Did you really need to do that?"

Delmarno was now satisfied. As far as he was concerned, the chain had been completed. Reggie Williamson had stolen the gun. He'd then handed it on to Gavin Sheehy and Niall MacNamara, who'd planted it at the scene of some drugs bust in Coventry. MacNamara had been killed years ago, Gavin Sheehy was about to get what he deserved and Reggie Williamson had been dealt with. Honour was satisfied; Delmarno was about to get remarried and retake his place at the head of his empire and all was good with the world.

For a time, Bixby had thought that the killing was over. He'd retreated into himself, trying to repair the damage done to him by the recent killings. To lick his wounds and decide what he was going to do about Jocelyn.

And then DCI Warren Jones had turned up at the golf club.

Bixby had moved quickly and decisively. He had no idea if Zachary Eddleston had told the detective about how he'd been bribed to spike Anton Liebig's drinks that night; what he did know was that he could identify him. And so a college kid who was guilty of nothing more than naiveté and greed had to be killed. Problem solved.

The voice on the end of the phone had also thought that Bixby had solved their problems. He hadn't.

Bixby had been astounded when he was told who Jones was.

"Should I kill him?"

"No," the voice had instructed. "He's lead investigator on multiple murder investigations. Kill him and the whole thing will blow wide open. You need to cover your tracks. Remember, if I go down, you go down."

No more traces could be left. It was time to start cleaning up.

Reluctantly, Bixby had decided to kill Sheehy. Vinny's insistence on the humiliation of the man he thought had orchestrated his downfall now had to play second fiddle to Bixby's need to clear up the rapidly escalating mess. And then Pete Kent had called, panicking.

"Jones knows."

The veteran police officer, who knew all the secrets and had carefully delivered to the young DCI only the information that they'd wanted him to see, had got wind that Jones was making a trip to the archives. To find the information that he'd thought buried, safely deleted. Information that Gavin Sheehy had stolen and now held on to like a security blanket.

"Kill Sheehy and clear up any loose ends." This time the voice didn't need to remind him, *if I go down, you go down.*

Framing Sheehy for the murders of Reggie Williamson and Zachary Eddleston had come in a flash of inspiration. The bag containing the blood-soaked knife and the clothes that he'd worn that night up on the common was in a lock-up garage, paid for by cash, on the outskirts of town. Getting rid of the clothes would be nigh-on impossible for at least a few weeks, whilst the police investigation was at full strength. Besides which, he'd made sure that on the night of Reggie Williamson's murder, Vinny had no alibi. A return to prison for the former gangster would bring Jocelyn back to Bixby without the need to kill his old friend.

Pete Kent had put up only a token resistance when he'd told him his plan. The detective knew that if it all fell apart, he'd be spending the rest of his life in prison. And so it had been Pete Kent who'd turned up on his old friend's doorstep with a bottle of whisky, making certain that the front door didn't quite close properly. It had been Pete Kent who'd prepared the noose, throwing the rope over the bannister whilst Bixby had sat in the front room with a terrified Sheehy.

By the time Kent had finished setting the scene for his former friend's suicide, Bixby had determined that the single sheet of paper that could bring the whole conspiracy crashing down was no longer in Sheehy's possession. A simple chokehold, no different to the one that had killed Niall MacNamara so many years ago, was enough to render Sheehy unconscious, the faint bruising around his carotids easily covered by the chafing that would come from the rough hemp of the rope.

It had been logical for the heavier Kent to hoist Sheehy's limp form up whilst Bixby raced around the house, planting the blood-soaked clothes and weapon in the laundry hamper and putting the hoody that he'd worn whilst killing Zachary Eddleston in the man's wardrobe.

Finally, Kent had kicked the stool over, leaving his former friend to dangle, his face turning a hideous purple. The two men had exited via the rear of the house. Bixby had relocked the kitchen door behind them with a set of lock picks, managing the feat in half the time it had taken him to complete the same action on Zachary Eddleston's flat; it was as if the past thirty years had never happened. He was back with his boys in Northern Ireland. Breaking and entering, planting evidence and faking suicides or constructing crime scenes had been his bread and butter during his days with the regiment.

But he wasn't back with the regiment and Pete Kent wasn't one of his boys. He should have checked the man's handiwork, not trusted him the way he would have trusted his fellow soldiers to complete the job. Sheehy had survived. Just.

The voice at the end of the phone was furious. "Complete the job, soldier. Do it properly and don't leave any loose ends."

And so here he was. Yet another death on his hands. The look of terror on Pete Kent's face had lasted only a second but it had seared itself into Bixby's mind. The sound of the impact still echoed in his ears. It haunted his sleep, forcing him to seek oblivion in the bottle of whisky that Vinny had given him last Christmas.

But, as the saying goes, the night is always darkest before the dawn and the dawn was on the horizon. Jocelyn had effectively removed Vinny from the equation. That huge loose end had been neutralised without the need to kill him. Suddenly, all that remained now was to deal with that piece of paper.

Where was it? He couldn't imagine Sheehy destroying such a valuable piece of evidence. But he'd looked all over the house for it. He was a bit rusty, but they'd taught him to conduct searches in the regiment. If it had been there, he'd have found it.

So what would he have done with it? Sheehy had known his life was in danger. He must have arranged for it to be kept somewhere safe. He thought back to the man's last few moments, before his stranglehold had finally silenced him.

"Kill me and it all comes out. Every last detail."

He'd taken the words as those of a desperate man, a man who

would say anything to save his life. But what if he hadn't been bluffing? What if he had been telling the truth? Had he arranged for his story to be published after his death? A letter to be sent to the local newspapers?

Bixby dismissed the idea. Without real evidence, the man would be dismissed as a crank. A twenty-four-year-old conspiracy, with no corroborating testimonies, from a man under investigation for corruption. No serious news editor in the land would touch it. He must have known that.

And then it came to him. There was one person who would know what to do with the information if he received it. Bixby climbed to his feet, and headed for the kitchen. He needed caffeine and lots of it.

Chapter 51

Warren was bone-weary as he clambered up the garden path. He'd spent the morning with Tony Sutton, followed by the afternoon with his Federation representative, opting to meet her in a pub, rather than having her come to his house. He'd been bitterly disappointed—although not surprised—when Sutton had called to tell him that Delmarno had already disappeared by the time uniform had finally got around to visiting his house to arrest him. He was now listed as wanted for questioning, but as far as the police were concerned, he was just another name on their ever-growing list of violent former partners who they'd like to arrest, but didn't have the resources to actively search for. Unless he did something stupid and got himself picked up, or otherwise called attention to himself, he could stay out of sight indefinitely.

Warren still hadn't told his in-laws about his suspension and didn't feel ready to address that issue just yet, so he forced a smile as he fumbled for his house keys. Tonight was supposed to be a special evening. Dennis had insisted he and Bernice would take care of dinner since Warren had been unable to join them for Easter and Warren was determined to enjoy Dennis's magnificent cooking. The bottle of red wine he'd picked up from the Costcutter was from the more expensive end of the shelf and he had found some nice-looking bottled beers.

The door swung open freely as he inserted his key into the lock. The bottles smashed on the doorstep as he saw the devastation inside.

* * *

"Where's Susan?" Warren's voice was almost a shout as he tore the tape from Bernice's mouth. The side of her face was reddened, already starting to swell; the tears running down her face had caused her normally immaculate make-up to smear. True to form though, her voice was more angry than afraid.

"He took her. The man with the gun." Angry or not, she was babbling, clearly in shock.

Dennis, tied back-to-back with Bernice, sported a bloody nose, nevertheless his voice was more controlled as Warren ripped the tape off.

"He burst in through the back door when we were in the kitchen, he had a handgun and he grabbed Susan by the hair." Dennis coughed and spat blood. It looked as though he'd taken a hit to the mouth as well.

Warren didn't need to ask who the intruder was. Delmarno was almost certainly in hiding and that left Bixby.

"What happened? Where's Susan?" Warren repeated.

"He kept on shouting, 'Where did he put it?'" Dennis put his arm around his wife as Warren cut the tape binding the couple together.

"Susan didn't know what he was looking for, but he didn't believe her." Bernice had taken over the story, as was usual for the couple, her voice still shaking. "He kept on waving the gun around and shouting. When she carried on saying she didn't know what he was talking about, he started searching the living room."

The evidence of Bixby's hunt was all around them and Warren felt a chill at its obvious ferocity. It wasn't the cool, collected, methodical examination of a police forensic team, rather the madness of somebody desperate.

"That was when Dennis hit him with that vase." Bernice's tone was reproving, nonetheless she took her husband's hand and squeezed it.

"For all the good it did us," Dennis muttered thickly, his tongue exploring his swollen mouth.

"Did he say where he was taking her? When did they leave?" The couple were clearly disoriented and Warren needed them focused. Seconds could matter now.

"They've been gone about fifteen minutes, I think." Dennis had been facing the clock.

"After he tied us up he pulled her upstairs." Bernice's voice shook. "We could hear them crashing about and he kept on shouting at Susan. When he came back down he took her out the front door."

"Did you see which way he went?" Warren had his mobile phone out, navigating through the contacts to find the station's main switchboard, figuring it would be quicker than trying to work his way through 999. His hands shook and he hit the wrong contact, why didn't he put the station on speed dial?

The middle-aged couple both shook their heads. "I can't see out the window from down here," responded Bernice.

The phone rang in Warren's hand and he nearly dropped it in surprise. The Caller ID flashed up on the screen. The photograph had been automatically updated from Facebook. Susan.

* * *

The noises on the line had been muffled and it took a few seconds for Warren to realise that the phone had dialled him accidentally. No, not accidentally he soon realised, as he heard Susan's voice distorted by whatever material lay between her and the phone that she had somehow used to call him. She probably has me on speed dial, he thought with a brief flash of shame.

Why hadn't Bixby checked her for her phone, Warren asked himself even as he sprinted for the car? The answer was probably more worrying than reassuring. It suggested that Bixby wasn't thinking clearly—and that made him even more dangerous.

After realising that Susan had triggered the phone covertly, Warren had immediately muted his own handset, worried that any noise from his end of the line would alert her kidnapper. He prayed that her screen had already darkened to save the battery. Who knew what Bixby might do if he discovered the subterfuge? Not for the first time, Warren marvelled at his wife's presence of mind.

The three of them had stood gathered around the smartphone, listening for clues to Susan's whereabouts. The sounds in the background suggested that they were in a car, travelling quickly judging by the wind noise. But where were they going? Fifteen minutes had passed. At high speed that could put them ten or even twenty miles away from Middlesbury in at least a half-dozen directions.

"Why are we going to Hertford?" Susan's voice was muffled but clear.

"So we won't be disturbed. Now shut it. I'm thinking." The man's voice still retained some of his Coventry upbringing. Definitely Bixby.

"Good girl," Warren had breathed as he comprehended what Susan was doing.

Spinning on his heel, he'd started issuing orders, trying to cut through the dazed fog that still blanketed the older couple. "Dennis, I need you to phone Middlesbury CID and tell them what has happened. Give them Susan's number and tell them to get onto the phone company to track the handset and tap into the call." He'd scribbled the main switchboard number on a piece of paper.

"Ask for a DI Tony Sutton if you can. I can't remember Susan's number off the top of my head, so you need to look it up, Bernice. I daren't risk breaking the contact."

"Where are you going?" Bernice had asked, clearly afraid of being left alone in the house again.

"Hertford. They're heading in that direction."

"But where in Hertford?" she'd called out as he raced out the door.

"I don't know. I'll figure that out on the way."

* * *

The A10 was relatively quiet, but Warren spent a frightening amount of time on the wrong side of the road, overtaking slower-moving vehicles. Without blue lights and sirens to aid his passage he had to rely on his horn, hazard lights and flashing the headlamps to clear a path.

The final stretch of road towards Hertford was dual carriageway and Warren eased the car to over a hundred, undertaking where necessary. His fear for Susan was greater than his fear of crashing.

Why had Bixby taken her? As a bargaining chip? Bixby wanted something from him. Something that he thought Warren was keeping in his house. When he hadn't found it and Susan hadn't been able to tell him where it was, he'd taken her to force him to comply.

But what could he be after? What could Warren have that Bixby

386

wanted so badly? His father's autopsy report? It was almost certainly Bixby who had staged the break-in at the Liebig's house, not realising that the late coroner had kept his papers in a safety deposit box. Was that what this was all about? A murder committed twenty-four years ago and made to look like a suicide? But the autopsy report contained nothing that gave any clues to who had committed the murder. Why such a panic about suppressing it? The case was cold. The odds of it being solved even if it was reopened were slim to negligible. Warren had seen the evidence that had been collected from the scene, read the witness reports. The autopsy might be enough to overturn the original inquest verdict, but it wasn't going to point the spotlight at Bixby. And Warren was convinced it was Bixby who had killed his father. Whatever skills he had learnt during those six years in the SAS—doing who knew what, who knew where—had been used to kill his father and successfully hide it for almost a quarter of a century. Those same skills had been employed to kill Zachary Eddleston, Anton Liebig and Reggie Williamson. There must be something else that he was after. Warren didn't believe that Bixby was doing all this just to tie off a few loose ends.

A green road sign flashed past. The exit for Hertford was in three miles. He needed to figure out where they we_e going pretty soon. The junction for Hertford led to a large roundabout that could be used to access Hertford, Ware and any one of a dozen different towns and villages—and that was assuming Bixby had used that exit because it was the closest to his final destination.

Warren felt the despair wash over him. There had been no more clues from Susan, the phone sitting in its dashboard cradle, speakerphone on, was transmitting nothing more than the sound of a moving car. It had changed pitch recently and he'd heard the repeated sounds of gear changing. Wherever Bixby was, he was now off the main road, probably driving in an urban environment.

But where? It seemed logical that Bixby was taking Susan somewhere quiet where he wouldn't be disturbed. Warren wracked his brain. Delmarno's house? The wrong direction. If he wanted to take her there he should have turned off some time ago, well before the junction for Hertford. The same was true for the golf club. Assuming that Bixby hadn't noticed Susan's phone was switched on, it seemed unlikely that he would be driving aimlessly around to confuse any followers. Quite the opposite in fact. He'd want Susan tucked away out of sight as quickly as possible; the longer they were exposed, the more likely it was that they would be tracked down and captured.

A deserted lock-up? The back room of one of the many businesses Delmarno's little empire ran? Warren struggled to remember the list that Gary Hastings had printed out. Most of the cafés and cab firms that Delmarno owned were to the north of the county, in small towns like Middlesbury, Baldock, Letchworth or Bishop's Stortford where there was less local competition and business rates were cheaper. He'd steered clear of the bigger towns and cities such as Hertford and Stevenage.

The engine noise from the mobile phone stopped. There was a ratcheting noise that Warren identified as a handbrake being applied. They'd stopped moving.

"Why are we stopping here? It's a building site," Susan was still trying to give Warren clues. *Don't be too obvious; don't raise his suspicions*, he prayed silently as took the turn-off at high speed. The blare of horns behind him reminded him that his indicators didn't work if the hazard lights were already flashing.

"Quiet. Try and run and I'll have the gun out and a bullet in your back before you make two steps." Bixby's voice was low, hissing.

A building site. That narrowed it down a bit, but not much. Even in the depths of the recession there was still plenty of construction taking place around the county. Warren steered one handed up the slip road, fiddling with the satnav as he jumped the red lights. Even if he didn't know where he was going, he could at least use the map function to identify his location.

From the phone came the sound of a car door slamming and then the scrunch of gravel. A building site in the Hertford area. He needed to call it in, but he couldn't use his phone for fear of losing the connection with Susan. He should have taken Dennis or Bernice's as well as his own, he realised belatedly. Speaking of which, had they managed to get through to CID? Were the mobile phone companies playing ball, tracking Susan's phone? Were there armed response units on the way or was he still on his own? Warren felt as if he was in a bubble, sealed off from the outside world.

And then he remembered the last item on Gary's list. Of course, Delmarno owned a block of flats in Hertford. Warren wracked his brain, trying to recall the details. Weren't they still being built—still a building site? The perfect place—empty, quiet and deserted. But where were they?

He tried to remember the address.

South Street. Was that it? The roundabout had a BP filling station and a McDonald's takeaway and he swung across two lanes of traffic, entering the complex at high speed. Ignoring the shouts of an angry van driver queuing patiently for the pumps he cut in front of the line, bringing the car to a juddering halt in front of the cash machine outside the kiosk. The satnav had now booted up and had found enough orbiting satellites to locate itself. Warren held his breath. The mapping software was last year's update but if the flats were on a newly built estate the street name might not be on the system yet. The gadget thought for a second before announcing that no match had been found, delivering a list of similar-named streets. The postcodes were almost identical he noted, only the last letter changing. Did that mean that they were all close together? Close enough that if he just headed that way he could hope to spot the building site? He selected one at random.

A white Transit van had moved behind him, blocking his exit. The same van he'd cut in front of, he saw. The driver was brawny and tattooed and clearly in the mood for a fight as he clambered out of the seat and walked around to Warren's window. He hammered on the glass.

Susan's voice was coming from the phone again. Now it sounded hollow, echoey. "What are we doing here?"

The van driver continued banging on the window.

"If you want me to go upstairs, you'll have to carry me. You hurt my ankle." Susan's voice was shaky but clear. Bixby's response was drowned out by the van driver, who had now opened the door.

"What's your problem, mate? Think you're too fucking important to queue?"

Warren spun in his seat.

"Detective Chief Inspector Warren Jones. Shut the fuck up and move your van before I arrest you for obstruction," he screamed at the startled man.

The driver stepped back, but it was too late. The phone was silent again.

Warren strained his ears to catch any sounds, any more clues.

The line crackled, distorted. Please don't lose the signal, he prayed.

A faint ding, then a sliding noise and the signal became clearer again.

390

The delivery driver had clambered back into his cab and was reversing backwards.

Warren crunched the car into gear and pealed out of the garage, one eye on the satnav screen. The driver waved a finger at him as he passed. He should have commandeered his phone, but it was too late to go back as he entered the fast-moving traffic again.

There was a forty miles per hour limit on the main road into Hertford, but Warren ignored it as he navigated the roundabouts at closer to sixty. The satnav pinged repeatedly, warning him of mobile speed cameras but a speeding ticket was the last thing on his mind as he followed the flashing arrow.

Scratching noises were coming from the phone. A key in a lock?

Warren concentrated hard on the sounds even as he navigated the unfamiliar roads. He'd visited Hertford a few times but mostly to go to the theatre or visit the local police station. His lack of local knowledge gnawed at him.

"Sit down." Bixby's voice was rough and there was a scraping noise—a chair on a bare floor? Without more clues, he was guessing.

"What do you want me to do?" Susan's voice was more scared now and Warren felt his gut tighten even more. Four minutes to destination, the satnav predicted. Warren was travelling well above the speed limit and ignoring red lights, which would shorten that time considerably—assuming that he had the right address. He swerved to avoid a slow-moving bus. And assuming that he survived that long.

* * *

Susan could feel what little control she had over the situation slipping away. In the car she had felt safer, since Bixby couldn't do

391

much with her whilst he was driving. The last person she had called on her phone had been Warren and so he was top of the call log. The problem was that the phone had a touchscreen, making it impossible to navigate blindly.

Mobile phones were the scourge of teachers and Susan's school had a zero-tolerance approach to students using them in class. Nevertheless, some children persisted in trying to text their friends under the desk, risking confiscation and detention. The trick was not to look at the screen too much or sit with both hands in your lap. That was like a red flag to an eagle-eyed teacher.

With that in mind, Susan had fished the phone out of her back pocket and held it down by her side, between her leg and the car door. One quick glance had told her that she'd oriented it correctly in her palm and so she'd raised her right hand to her head, rubbing her aching cheek where Bixby had slapped her, whilst she swiped her left thumb in the unlock pattern. It had taken three attempts, before a peek told her that she'd succeeded. She'd thanked her stars that she routinely set the phone's ringtone to silent, before remembering to reduce the call volume as well. The last thing she wanted was Warren's tinny voice coming over the phone's speakers.

Bixby continued concentrating on his driving, using his indicators correctly, staying within the speed limit and trying not to attract attention. Should she try to attract attention? She'd dismissed the idea as soon as it formed, a dozen reasons that it would be a bad idea springing immediately to mind, not least the handgun sitting on the dashboard, hidden from casual viewers by a newspaper.

Briefly looking down again, she'd moved her thumb to the phone icon, before closing her eyes and trying to recall the layout of the screen. The default was the past call log and Warren's number would be at the top of the list. Pressing where she thought it was, she'd risked another quick glance to see if she'd succeeded.

Moving her thumb to the dial icon on the contact screen, she'd pressed again.

* * *

The map on the satnav showed a maze of streets with names similar to the half-remembered address. Warren was right in the middle of them, the satnav proudly announcing that he'd reached his destination. He hadn't. The street he was on was a tidy, well-maintained collection of terraced and semi-detached houses, clearly not a partially built block of flats.

A young woman walking her dog eyed him suspiciously and stopped to cross the road. Warren pulled alongside her and climbed out of the car. "Excuse me," he started. The woman pulled on the dog's lead as if encouraging it to move closer for protection. Hardly surprising, Warren thought. A wild-eyed, slightly dishevelled stranger pulls over and tries to engage you in conversation on a deserted street—he'd encourage Susan to do the same.

"Madam, I am a police officer and I need your assistance." The woman stopped tugging at the dog's lead and squinted at him. Somewhat appeased, she inclined her head slightly.

"Is there a construction site near here? A block of flats, perhaps?" The twist of her lip told him she knew of them.

"Two streets over, South Close at the end of the cul-de-sac. They're a bloody eyesore; they've been standing empty for months. If they're going to rip up the only piece of green space for miles around, they could at least finish them." It looked like she was only just getting started and so Warren made his thanks and climbed quickly back into the car.

There were voices coming from the phone.

Warren's blood ran cold.

* * *

"Ring your husband."

Susan was sitting on a wooden chair, the only piece of furniture in the bare and undecorated room. The lifts had worked, so the building clearly had electricity, but there were no plug sockets above the non-existent skirting boards and the hole in the ceiling didn't even have wires poking out for the light fittings.

The man with the gun was pacing around, a ball of tension and nervous energy. Susan watched him warily, her mind racing. The connection to Warren was still open and she didn't dare let him see that she had been transmitting the details of their flight to him.

"I don't have his number." It was all she could think of.

The man brought his face close up; his breath smelt of stale coffee and his sweat had soaked through the thin shirt he was wearing.

"Then look it up." His voice was tight, clipped. How far could she push him before he snapped? The man placed the gun against her right temple.

"I don't have my phone with me." Susan's mouth was dry, her voice scratchy.

The man snorted, his words and tone of voice more amused than his eyes. "Just my luck to get the only person in the western hemisphere under the age of forty without a mobile phone on them." A metallic click told her that the safety had been released. "Why don't you have another think about that?"

Susan couldn't let him have the phone.

Please Warren, please save me. Tears started to sting her eyes.

"I don't have my phone with me, I left it at home."

The gun moved from her temple, slowly scraping across her forehead, coming to rest in the space between her eyebrows. She wanted to close her eyes, but couldn't, her gaze fixed on the trigger guard, her eyes aching as they struggled to focus at such close distance.

The man said nothing for a few seconds, staring at her.

"I don't believe you."

Warren will save me. The thought arrived unbidden, but she was suddenly filled with an absolute certainty. Warren would save her. Her wonderful, brave husband who had chased after knife-wielding maniacs, pursued deranged serial killers through woods late at night and risked his life without thinking countless times would burst through that door and rescue her.

"Well, that's unfortunate. You see, if you can't put me in contact with your husband, then I really can't think of any good reason to keep you around. Now are you sure you can't help me?"

"No." Barely a whisper.

Warren will save me, Warren will save me, Warren will save me… The thought had become a mantra, filling her consciousness. Her certainty was absolute, her faith unwavering. *Warren will save me,* the thought continued to echo in her mind even as the man pulled the trigger.

* * *

Warren spun the wheel to the right, entering the cul-de-sac. It had taken another couple of wrong turns, before he'd finally caught

395

a glimpse of his goal through a gap in the houses in the neighbouring road. The street was large, closed at one end in the shape of a long key. Tall, narrow, three-storey houses, the lowest floor partly below street level, lined either side. None of them had front gardens, so it was no wonder the locals were annoyed that what appeared to have once been a piece of open land at the end of the road now sported an almost-finished block of flats. The head of the key opened out into a wide turning circle, with a small grass centrepiece surrounded by borders of brightly coloured flowers.

Parking was clearly in short supply, as witnessed by the lines of cars parked nose to tail the entire length of both sides of the road, blue-and-white signs threatening dire consequences for those without a parking permit. The metal gates that blocked off the far end of the road to allow access to construction vehicles visiting the apartment complex hardly helped matters.

There was one remaining space on the outer edge of the turning circle and Warren abandoned the car in it, barely taking the time to pull the handbrake and snatch the phone from the dashboard cradle.

He should wait for backup. He knew that. Every training course he had ever attended, every manual he had ever read said that the right thing to do when approaching a hostage scene—especially when the hostage-taker was armed—was to call in an armed-response unit and trained negotiators. Don't go blundering in, making matters worse. Wait.

That wasn't an option.

Bixby had found the phone. His cry of inarticulate fury had been only half as scary as his quiet tones when he spoke into the handset. It was as if he could switch off his emotions in the same way one would turn off an electrical appliance. Such control was the sign of a dangerously compartmentalised mind—the sort of mind that could commit the most horrendous acts then neatly lock them away and get on with living as if nothing had happened. The owner of such a mind was not the sort of man you wanted anywhere near your wife.

Warren had no idea what sort of vehicle Bixby had been driving, so had no way of knowing if he was even in the right place. Unable to contact Sutton without risking the connection with Susan's phone, Warren was reduced to gut instinct. And his gut was telling him that he had to get there within the next minute or he would lose Bixby and with him Susan. There was little chance that he would leave her behind; she was too valuable a bargaining chip. On the other hand, if he decided that she was slowing him down or impeding his escape, then he wasn't going to leave her alive to tell her rescuers which way he went and describe the car that he was driving.

"Jones, you know what I want. I don't know what you've done with it but I'll be coming to collect it. Don't call me, I'll call you." The tone was almost jovial.

Warren's phone was still on mute and he wasted valuable seconds trying to re-establish the sound to ask what he wanted. But he didn't get the chance. The last sound he heard was a crunching noise and the line went dead. The phone went straight to voicemail when he redialled.

* * *

Entry to the site was by a metal gate attached to the temporary security fences that surrounded it, metal grills set in concrete breeze blocks and sporting the usual health and safety notices about hard hats. The flats appeared to be largely complete, but the site felt empty, abandoned. It didn't look as though anyone had been working there for some time. Even the sign with its artist's rendering looked tatty, graffiti that would normally have been cleaned off accumulating in overlapping layers. The advertised opening date had passed some weeks ago—leaving such a blatant admission of failure there for all to see spoke volumes.

It was the open padlock and swinging gate that finally confirmed that Warren was in the right place. Taking a deep breath, he stepped through. Immediately inside an open drain was surrounded by high-visibility orange plastic mesh fencing attached to rusting metal poles. Three feet long with a tapering point, they were better than nothing.

The windows above were all empty, no curtains or lights, the silence eerie. The question was: where was Susan? The block had two floors and according to the advertising hoarding there were sixteen units for sale or rent.

Upstairs. Susan had let him know that through the phone. Opening the heavy front door—also unlocked—Warren recalled the ding he'd heard and the way that the connection had temporarily become crackly. They'd taken the elevator.

Warren ignored it and headed for the stairs at the far end of the hallway, peeking through the narrow windows in the double doors before opening them and slipping through. He was breaking every other rule in the book, but he wasn't silly enough to get in an elevator and announce his arrival to a waiting gunman with a ding and slowly opening doors.

Despite his fear it was all he could do not to sprint up the stairs; every beat of his pounding heart was like the ticking of a giant clock. He clutched the metal fence pole tightly and proceeded a step at a time, straining his ears for the slightest sound.

There was another set of double doors at the top of the stairs and again he peered carefully through the windows before emerging onto the deserted corridor. Four unmarked doors lined each side of the passageway and Warren felt a brief moment of panic. Which unit were they in? There was no way he could go through them all one at a time. Even assuming that Susan was still alive, the moment he started kicking doors down, Bixby would panic and the odds were good that he'd put a bullet in Susan's head and make his escape.

Warren pushed aside the negative thoughts that threatened to paralyse him. Of course Susan was still alive. Looking around he noted that plaster dust coated the uncarpeted floors; closer inspection revealed fresh footprints leading from the elevator to the nearest door.

Should he call it in? Bixby had ended the call and Warren could use his phone again without worrying about losing the connection. But what would be the point? Time was evaporating like a puddle in the sunshine; every second he wasted was another second closer to Bixby escaping and doing who knew what with Susan.

Warren clutched the metal fence pole tightly and lined himself up with the door. Saying a silent prayer, he lowered his shoulder then charged.

* * *

Warren felt his knees sag. Susan had been here moments before, he was certain. Small fragments of plastic that could have been from her smashed phone lay on the floor. He crossed the empty room, passed the lone wooden chair set in the centre and looked out the window.

Outside, the turning circle was filled with cars, double parked, turning the circular centrepiece with its neatly trimmed grass, well-maintained flower beds and wooden park bench into a de facto roundabout, the road narrowed so that two-way traffic was now an impossibility.

Warren had snagged the final parking space, his Mondeo abandoned haphazardly on the outside of the circle. Helplessness rose within him. In his mind he kept replaying the phone call with Susan, the terror in her voice that she was trying so hard to keep in check. And in the background the rough-edged voice of Bixby, a man who'd already killed and had no qualms about doing so again. He'd threatened to put a bullet in Susan's head and Warren believed him, the edge of hysteria in his voice making Warren question how in touch with reality he still was.

And now that man had Susan, an innocent in all of this. Caught up in an ancient tale of greed, hatred and revenge that she had nothing to do with, beyond having the misfortune to marry the man at the centre of it. Warren leant his head against the window. He should call it in he knew, do it by the book. The time for solving the problem by himself was gone. She was the wife of a police officer—she was one of them. No stone would be unturned. Every police officer in the county, the country even, would be on the lookout for Bixby and Susan. He took his phone out and navigated to the contacts.

And then he saw her.

And Bixby, dragging her across the road like a parent with a naughty child. Sunlight glinted off something metallic in his left hand. Warren's breath caught in his throat and then he was running.

Through the open doorway, back into the hallway, the stairwell and through the fire exit. The irony wasn't lost on him as he passed the lift. The lift now waiting patiently in the ground floor lobby.

The lift that he had ignored—as protocol demanded—in favour of the more open and controllable stairs. The lift that, even as he'd inched up the stairs, had been carrying his wife and her demented kidnapper down towards the road. Towards escape.

Hurling himself down the stairs three, even four at a time, he slid on the polished linoleum then crashed through the double doors into the entry hall.

* * *

Across the road, on the opposite side of the turning circle, Susan wasn't making life easy for Bixby, fighting and resisting him as he hauled her across the road to his waiting car.

"It'll do you no good," he snapped as he fumbled for the key fob with his free hand, trying not to drop the gun. "You're getting in this car and I'm getting what I want."

His voice was confident, self-assured. But Susan had spotted his flaw, his weakness. He needed her alive. As a bargaining chip. And whilst he still needed her, she had a chance.

"I'll say one thing, you're bloody brave. I admire that. I've seen hard men turn into absolute wrecks with a gun pointed at their head. They usually shit themselves—literally—when I pull the trigger and it just clicks."

Finally, the door unlocked, the hazard lights flashing. A tiny distraction, but enough for Susan to yank her arm free, at the same time kicking her abductor in the shins. It was a small victory, she made barely three paces before she felt her head snapped back, an excruciating pain setting her scalp on fire as Bixby grabbed a handful of her loose, flowing hair, stopping her flight almost as soon as it had started.

"Stop fucking around." His voice was angry now and Susan knew instinctively that she'd pushed as far as she could. Even though the handgun was unloaded, he could still club her senseless with it.

It had been a distraction, perhaps bought her a few more seconds. She hoped it had been enough. She slumped as if defeated and climbed into the rear of the car.

"Put your seat belt on. Safety first."

Like a switch the angry Bixby was gone, his voice almost jovial. That switch was what scared her most. Susan had spent much of her adult life teaching teenagers—wonderful, mercurial human beings whose emotions could flip one hundred and eighty degrees with almost no warning, but Bixby was ten times more volatile than even the most hormone-charged fourteen-year-old. He really could do anything.

Still, whilst he was focused on her he wasn't focused on his surroundings. She had no idea if Bixby knew what sort of car her husband drove, but it was clear that he hadn't noticed it parked across the turning circle.

And whilst his attention was on her, he wasn't looking back at where they had just come from. He hadn't seen Warren as he emerged from the apartment building. *It's up to you now, sweetheart*, she prayed silently. *Come and get me.*

* * *

Susan was putting up a bloody good fight, Warren saw, his feelings a complex mixture of pride and concern. *Just don't push him too far, darling*, he thought silently.

The white BMW that Bixby was pushing his wife into was diametrically opposite his own car. For a moment, Warren was paralysed with indecision. Could he get across the turning circle before Bixby drove off? The BMW was squeezed tightly between a Transit van and a Nissan, and Bixby would have to manoeuvre it forward and back to release it. But what if Warren didn't make it and Bixby pulled away before he could get there? By the time he made it back to his own car, Bixby would be out of the housing estate, travelling who knew where. Besides which he had a gun and even if he hadn't, Warren was under no illusions about his ability to tackle the man hand to hand. If he lasted five seconds, he'd be lucky. The only remaining option was to follow him in the car and call in assistance.

Whether it was the flashing of his lights or the thunk as the doors unlocked that finally alerted Bixby, Warren was unsure. The former soldier suddenly turned towards him, his face a mask of hate through the driver-side window.

Any chance of discreetly following Bixby whilst he awaited an armed response unit was now gone. And he knew that he couldn't risk a car chase, not through the crowded rush hour with his wife in the car.

He already had the Mondeo in gear before he realised what he was doing, the primitive, instinctive part of his brain racing ahead of the conscious part. Pushing hard on the accelerator, he spun the wheel to full lock and felt the bone-jarring thump as he mounted the kerb. The engine whined as the wheels spun for a second in the soft mud of the flower bed and then momentum carried the car onto the firmer grass and it continued to accelerate.

Across the turning circle, Bixby abandoned his attempts to free his car from its temporary prison and his head disappeared briefly as he reached across the passenger seat. Warren continued to press the accelerator, even as he belatedly scrambled for his seat belt.

In the rear of the BMW, Susan scooted across the back seat, towards the passenger side, bracing herself for the inevitable.

Bixby's head re-emerged and to his horror, Warren saw the gun rising in the driver's window. Bixby's right hand was holding the pistol as his left slotted a magazine into the base of the grip. Warren abandoned his seat belt, throwing himself across the passenger seat.

Safety glass rained down on him as the windscreen shattered, the driver's seat kicking as bullets thumped into the headrest where Warren had been less than a second before.

And then blackness.

* * *

Warren tasted blood, his ears ringing. He groaned as he tried to scramble back to reality. The gear stick dug painfully into his ribs and he coughed as he inhaled the acrid smoke from the airbag detonators. Warm liquid trickled down his chin from a bloodied if not broken nose.

A sudden jolt of adrenaline brought him back to full alertness. Susan!

He raised his head slightly, cringing with the expectation of a bullet. Nothing.

The heavy Ford had slammed into the driver's side of the BMW, pushing the lighter car across the road, sandwiching it between the Mondeo and a Citroen people carrier. Judging from the way the car was jammed between the two vehicles, it would take the fire brigade to get them out and Warren felt a stab of fear. What if his attempt to rescue Susan had killed her?

Bixby clearly hadn't been wearing his seat belt either and he was lying half in, half out of the driver's side window. Whether it had been rolled down or Bixby had shot it out, wasn't clear. Warren's breath caught as he saw Susan's still form slumped in the back seat.

The percussive blows from the twin airbags had done something to his balance and Warren fell rather than climbed out of the door. Scrambling back to his feet he limped around the crumpled bonnet of his car. Suddenly Bixby's eyes snapped open. Realising his hands were empty, he started looking around wildly before diving across the passenger seat.

He was going for his gun. Without thinking Warren threw himself forward, ignoring the jabbing edges of the car's bonnet, and forced his head and shoulders through the open window.

The gun was in the passenger footwell and Bixby was struggling to reach it with his left arm. Warren knew with absolute certainty that if he got hold of that gun he was going to kill Warren and Susan right there and then.

The time for elaborate plots and careful misdirections was over. Bixby was like a trapped animal, desperate to survive. Trained by the world's finest special forces, he would kill first then clean up the mess afterwards.

Ignoring the pain, Warren pushed himself even further into the car, clamping both of his hands around Bixby's left wrist, desperate to stop him from getting a firm grip on the gun.

Jammed in the tight confines of the driver's seat, Bixby had almost no leverage. Nonetheless, he managed to use his right hand to jab Warren repeatedly in his already abused ribs. Warren gasped with the pain, but kept up his pressure on Bixby's wrist.

The ringing in Warren's ears was fading but all he could hear now were the grunts of the two men as they struggled for control over the gun. It was a stalemate and Warren had absolutely no idea who would hold out the longest. And what was he going to do if he did win the tug of war?

It was probably the distant sound of a siren that spurred Bixby into breaking the impasse. Leaning his head back, he then snapped it forward. With little room to manoeuvre, it wasn't much of a head-butt; however, it landed square on Warren's damaged nose.

The sudden pain and fresh spurt of blood and tears was enough for Warren to loosen his grip. With an animal-like howl of triumph, Bixby snatched the gun up and started to bring it around. Half blinded, Warren ignored his nose and grabbed the killer's hand again in desperation. But Bixby now had the advantage and slowly he brought the gun around, inching the barrel upwards. It was only a matter of time, Warren realised, and the panic and adrenaline and pain started to give way to a feeling of helplessness.

Bixby bellowed in pain. Warren couldn't understand what his wife was screaming in the killer's ear but her fingernails, torn and bloody from her ordeal, were jammed into his eyes, digging in, and then she stopped screaming and Bixby bellowed even louder as Susan's teeth found his left ear.

The distraction was enough. Warren gave up on the battle of strengths, instead forcing his index finger into the gap between Bixby's trigger finger and the gun's trigger guard. The sheer force of the gun discharging was almost enough to cause Warren to lose his grip, but he'd been expecting it and he closed his eyes against the shower of plastic fragments from the glovebox. Unfortunately, the recoil had worked in Bixby's favour and the gun had been forced upwards a few more degrees.

Warren pulled the trigger again and once more the gun recoiled, forcing it upwards a few more degrees. Another explosion and now the entire central console was missing. How many bullets did the gun have? Warren knew next to nothing about the capacity of this model of handgun, and even if he did he'd lost count of how many bullets had already been fired.

Warren squeezed again and the remains of the dashboard disappeared. Again and a hole was punched in the windscreen. Again and another hole appeared.

Then nothing.

A click.

Another click.

Over the sudden silence the sirens were obviously nearer. And it was this sudden relief from the disappearance of the threat and the prospect of an imminent rescue that caused Warren and Susan to relax fractionally.

Bixby relaxed too and his sudden lack of resistance was enough to catch the Jones off guard. Letting go of the useless gun, he swung his left hand around in a sweeping haymaker, aimed directly at Warren's battered nose. At the same time he jabbed his right hand up and over his own shoulder, fingers extended towards Susan's face.

With both of his attackers temporarily disabled he lifted his feet over the shattered dashboard and kicked the remains of the windscreen out. Then, before they knew it he was out, headfirst, sliding down the BMW's bonnet to land awkwardly on the road.

And then he was gone.

Chapter 52

It was late evening before Warren was discharged from accident and emergency. His whole body ached, but the ringing in his ears from the airbags had subsided and aside from a swollen nose and an assortment of cuts, bruises and sprains he had been pronounced fit and well by the doctors.

To his relief, Susan and her parents were also largely unscathed, with Dennis having borne the worst of it, sporting a chipped tooth and a couple of nasty cuts to his mouth. Bernice may or may not have had a slight black eye, but true to form she had reapplied her make-up before leaving the cubicle.

Tony Sutton had already talked his way in to see his chief inspector whilst the doctors were assessing him and so Warren already knew that the immediate search of the surrounding streets had failed to locate Bixby. The DI was now back at the Joneses' house, working with Crime Scene Manager Andy Harrison and his SOCO team. Karen Hardwick and Mags Richardson were en route to the site of another abandoned vehicle north of Hertford, whilst Gary Hastings continued to work the computers back at Middlesbury CID, trying to determine if Pete Kent had concealed any more information about Martin Bixby.

By all reports, the CID office was filled to bursting as off-duty colleagues came in to help out and others stayed past the end of their shift. At times like this, the Police were like a family, and the close-knit nature of Middlesbury CID made it more so.

Most surprising to Warren had been the response of DSI Grayson. When he heard that Warren, Susan and her parents would be taken to an anonymous Travelodge on the outskirts of Stevenage whilst their house was examined and then secured, he had immediately insisted that they use his own home.

The offer had been completely unexpected—and seemingly out of character. Or was it? Since day one, Grayson had struck Warren as the worst kind of self-serving political animal. Brought in as the interim senior officer in charge of Middlesbury CID after Sheehy's removal, he'd stayed in post after Warren's appointment to help him find his feet. That he also provided increased oversight for the largely autonomous unit went without saying, and rightly so. Nobody wanted another Gavin Sheehy.

At first Warren had been dismayed at Grayson's lack of involvement in the day-to-day running of CID. He probably spent more time at headquarters in Welwyn Garden City than he spent at his desk in Middlesbury; although nominally the senior officer in charge of all cases, in practice he invariably delegated the role of Senior Investigating Officer to Warren. Yet when it was time to speak to the media, either at the press conferences he so loved, or to announce significant breakthroughs from Warren's team, he would be groomed and polished in front of the cameras, soaking up the publicity.

But wasn't that what Warren wanted? He had made it clear during his interview for the job that he was hungry for experience and that he wanted to learn on his feet, to be prepared for his next rank. Well, wasn't that what he was getting? A baptism of fire it had certainly been—a major murder within a fortnight of taking the role, followed by a serial killer over the new year, plus countless other more humdrum yet equally challenging cases, had been combined with the difficulties associated with his first senior management position.

As for Grayson's unexpected kindness, it wasn't unprecedented, Warren recalled. He still remembered how he had bent the rules to grant Warren more personal leave to deal with the death of his grandmother and the man's insistence that a worn-out and still-grieving Warren take time off at Christmas.

So the question was: what were Grayson's motives? Was it an apparent act of kindness towards one of his officers, or was it something rather more sinister? The man had connections to the West Midlands Police at the time of Delmarno's arrest and had held a high-enough rank to have authorised the drugs raid that had allowed the planting of the gun that killed Frankie Cruise. And what about the golf connection? Grayson was an avid golfer. That was well known. But what club did he belong to? The Allingham Golf Club was refusing to release its member list without a warrant and again Warren didn't want to draw that sort of attention to his investigations. Was Grayson there the night that Liebig and his wife had been killed? Was he the mysterious man who had bribed Zachary Eddleston to spike the unfortunate coroner's drinks that night? The sparse description given by the young waiter couldn't exclude him.

Warren's polite refusal had been immediately dismissed. Grayson's three children had all grown up and left home. There was plenty of room. What about making Grayson and his wife a target for Bixby? Again, the notion was rejected. Grayson's house was far more secure than any Travelodge and the chief constable had authorised armed officers to mount a protection detail.

Yet the man was potentially involved in the killing of his father all those years ago and more recently the murder of several innocent victims—could Warren take his wife and in-laws to stay with such a person?

In the end, the decision had been taken out of his hands.

"Do it," Susan had instructed. "We need to end this. If you can find out where Grayson's loyalties lie, then we know where we stand."

"But what about your parents? They aren't involved in this."

But they were, Bernice had insisted. The shock of the attack had now transformed into a deep rage. As Warren had quietly explained all that happened—about the death of his father all those years ago and the conspiracy that had worked to keep it all hidden—Bernice's face had grown redder. Beside her Dennis, a man of few words normally, had finally spoken.

"You have lived with this for almost twenty-five years Warren. For the past four years I have called you my son. And if we can help you find peace and end this nightmare then we cannot—we will not—walk away."

And so it was decided. Tony Sutton had sided with Susan and pointed out even if he was wrong and Warren's suspicions were true, there was little Grayson could do to them whilst they were under his own roof without implicating himself—and this whole affair seemed to be about cover-ups. Furthermore, despite his training, not even Martin Bixby was likely to get past the armed officers sitting outside the detective superintendent's house.

Thus, with misgivings still weighing heavily on his mind, Warren, Susan, Bernice and Dennis had clambered into the back of an unmarked people carrier, with two firearms officers sitting up front, and set off for John Grayson's family home.

Refilwe Grayson was not what Warren was expecting when the people carrier pulled up outside detective superintendent Grayson's large, five-bedroom home on the outskirts of Middlesbury. Grayson had been correct when he said that his family home would be more secure than a local hotel. Set back from the road, the detached house was surrounded on all sides by a garden, ringed by tall, metal fences. Powerful security lights illuminated the four guests as they crunched up the drive. Behind them a powered metal gate whirred shut. Should Bixby track them down he would probably not even make it that far without being challenged by the two armed officers standing in the street. Another two officers were patrolling the grounds, with a canine unit for back-up. Warren shuddered to think what the bill was for such an operation, but he breathed a little easier. Beside him, Susan's face relaxed and the tight grip that she had maintained on his right hand eased somewhat.

John Grayson's wife was a complete contrast to her fussy, bureaucratic husband; she barely waited to be introduced before embracing the foursome in a big hug and welcoming them into the couple's spacious kitchen. A tall, striking woman of South African descent, within moments she was clucking over her house guests like a mother hen, pressing glasses of brandy into the hands of the four newcomers and announcing that there was plenty of food.

Despite himself, Warren was barely able to suppress a smile when his wife summarily dismissed Grayson's suggestion that the family might be a bit overwhelmed and he was dispatched to get some spare chairs from the utility room. As his boss meekly left the room, Warren reflected that Grayson and his father-in-law should perhaps compare notes...

Refilwe was a terrific cook, it soon transpired, and despite the traumas of the day, within an hour the six were enjoying a glass of wine in an atmosphere more akin to a dinner party. No mention had been made of the dramatic events that day and if one looked past the cuts and bruises, it was easy to forget what had happened. Refilwe Grayson was a very shrewd judge of character and a very intelligent woman, Warren was starting to realise.

John Grayson admitted as much later that night. An hour earlier, Tony Sutton had dropped off some clothes for Warren and Susan, and Bernice's and Dennis's overnight bags. The older couple had retired to bed, the stresses of the day finally catching up with them. Susan was having a long hot bath and Warren would join her in the guest bedroom later. In the meantime, he sat with Grayson in his study, enjoying one last whisky.

"She's the most intelligent person I have ever known." Grayson was in a mellow mood, and more verbose than Warren had ever seen him before. At the senior officer's insistence, Warren was calling him John. After all, it would be strange to have Warren calling him sir, whilst the rest of his guests were on first-name terms with him.

"She's a barrister, I understand." Warren knew pretty much nothing about the man and his family. He hadn't even known how many kids he had until earlier that day. However, there was a picture of Refilwe in silks on the wall, next to various photographs of the couple's three children.

Grayson nodded. "International human rights. She's currently representing victims of the Mugabe regime in Zimbabwe." Well, that probably helped explain the high level of security at the couple's house. A senior detective like Grayson would be careful about securing his home—more than Warren had been, he noted with some shame—but would hardly be considered a high-risk target. His wife on the other hand…

"It's a tragic reversal, really. When I first met Refilwe, she was involved in the anti-apartheid movement, here in the UK. She was born in South Africa to a white British father and black mother but her family managed to emigrate to the UK when she was young. She advocated on behalf of black political prisoners and Mugabe was still something of a hero to those seeking to overturn white-minority rule in countries like South Africa."

Grayson shook his head sadly. "She still describes her support of Mugabe as the biggest error of judgement she has ever made."

"So when did you meet her?"

Despite the relaxed surroundings, Warren hadn't forgotten that Grayson was still a potential suspect in the conspiracy. He'd held the rank of detective inspector back then and could have authorised a low-level drugs bust such as the one that had resulted in the planting of Delmarno's handgun.

"Christmas 1986," Grayson smiled at the memory. "I was working car crime with West Midlands—we had a few joint operations with the WMP back then—and she was in a bar with some friends. She really turned heads in those days, I can tell you. I was in with a few of the lads, getting into the Christmas spirit before I had the week off. Somehow my group ended up sitting with her group and before you knew it I was next to her in a corner of the bar." He shook his head. "It's remarkable really, the hand that fate deals you sometimes. I'm ashamed to say that back in those days, I lived up to a fair few of the less attractive stereotypes about the police. We all did. The only reason I ended up talking to Refilwe was because all of her white friends with big breasts had been taken by my rather more pushy colleagues.

"Anyway, I ended up with her phone number. The next day I postponed my train back to Herts for twenty-four hours and took her out for a meal. The rest as they say is history. When my secondment ended and I was recalled to Herts in October 1989, I decided to push my luck a bit further and asked her to come back with me. We were married on the twenty-third of December, the third anniversary of our first date."

The times and dates matched the limited details that Warren had gleaned from his service record, placing him in the West Midlands Police at the time of the conspiracy, but he claimed to have been working car crime—it seemed unlikely that he could have been in a position to have authorised the drugs raid. Nevertheless, it wasn't impossible—they could just have needed the signature from any old inspector and hoped that nobody looked too carefully.

"So did you work a lot of car crime, back then?" Warren asked casually.

Grayson nodded. "Yeah, it was a big deal. Car alarms and security systems weren't very effective back in the Eighties." He snorted. "You could pop the central locking on some models with half a tennis ball."

"Where were you based? I might have served there myself a few years later."

"Towards the north and the west mostly—up in the black country, Wolverhampton, Walsall, close to Staffordshire, that sort of area."

That was about as geographically far from Coventry as one could be and still work in the same police force. How likely was it that a detective inspector working car crime in the north-west of the county would have come into contact with teams working organised crime, such as drugs in the south-east of the area? Unlikely but not impossible—after all car crime was often facilitated by organised gangs. It was possible that there was some overlap.

Warren decided to pursue a different tack. He nodded towards the expensive set of golf clubs in the corner.

"I've seen those in your office; do you and Refilwe play together?"

Grayson shook his head. "No, Refilwe tried it a few times when we first met, but it wasn't really her cup of tea. I go on my own mostly, although Refilwe likes to come along for the charity days and presentation evenings. She's quite friendly with a few of the other wives and partners." Grayson smiled. "She doesn't play herself but she learnt long ago that it pays to sound as if you do if you want to get on in her chosen profession; she can talk about it all day and as long as you don't ask her to hold a club and prove herself, she'll fool you into thinking she's out every Saturday."

Warren's mouth was dry.

"So you're a member of a club, then?"

"Oh yes. Must be over twenty years now." He looked at Warren conspiratorially. "You should come along one evening; you never know who you might find yourself playing with. The police are quite well represented in the game."

Warren's heart was pounding. "I'll have to look into it. Where do you play?"

"Just locally, Middlesbury Golf and Outdoor Sports. It's the course that you see when you look west from the common."

"Do you ever play at the Allingham Golf Club?"

Grayson snorted. "Christ no! I've got three kids at university. The green fees alone would pay for a fourth one!" He shook his head slightly. "Besides which, we played them once in a charity match and comments from a few of the more conservative members of the club suggested that even if I wanted to join, my face—or rather that of my wife's—wouldn't fit, if you catch my drift."

So Grayson claimed he didn't play at the Allingham Golf Club. And he had said he'd been working in car crime on the opposite side of the county when the earliest days of the conspiracy had taken place. Yet Warren only had his word. Could the man be trusted?

Warren felt more isolated than ever before. At the moment, the people he could rely on could be counted on the fingers of one hand. And with his suspension his options were even more limited. He knew that his team at CID were loyal—and that they would follow his instructions, given via Tony Sutton, up to a point, but he had no idea how far he could push his luck before simple self-preservation would make them start questioning the wisdom of their association with Warren. It was ironic that the scars left from the Gavin Sheehy affair could be standing in the way of Warren getting to the truth behind it.

Then Grayson tipped his hand. "So have I answered your questions satisfactorily? Do you trust me enough to let me in on whatever the hell it is you are investigating? Because frankly, you need all the help you can get, and to put it bluntly having one of my officers suspended for running his own off-the-books investigation, then having his wife kidnapped by some fucking psycho ex-SAS type with links to organised crime, is really going to look bad at my next promotion review board."

Warren turned to look at the man in front of him. What was there to lose, really? If Grayson was part of the conspiracy to cover up Warren's father's death all of those years ago, then it was clear that he knew that was what Warren was investigating. If, on the other hand, Warren's gut was right and he had nothing to do with it, then perhaps Warren was about to gain a powerful ally.

Warren told him.

* * *

To say that Grayson was taken aback would have been an understatement.

The man's expression had remained neutral at first, before becoming sceptical. However, by the time Warren had laid out the evidence, he was decidedly angry.

"… so you see, I couldn't trust anyone who had been around in the Eighties. Especially after what happened with Pete Kent." Warren shook his head sadly. "I guess even Sheehy didn't see that coming; I wonder why he didn't name him when we had our talks. Loyalty? Fear? Or leverage. Perhaps he was still playing the long game."

"Shit." Grayson was pacing forward and backwards. In the end he sighed. "I guess I can't blame you for not trusting me. The question is: what do we do next? My instinct is that we should go to Professional Standards."

Already Warren was shaking his head. "We hit the same problem. That Markovich is old enough to have held a senior rank in the Eighties."

Grayson hissed in frustration. "Dammit, Warren, we can't dismiss every officer who held rank back in the Eighties. That's half the senior officers in the force. We need to find out who authorised that little operation, or find out who else was involved on the ground. Your father and Gavin Sheehy we know about. I guess Pete Kent must have played a role also—who else was on that team? Are they not listed on the court transcripts?"

Warren shook his head. "The team's names weren't read out in open court for operational reasons and West Midlands shredded the original documents after scanning them onto the system."

"And the key documents that named the officer who signed off on the raid weren't ever scanned?"

"Not as far as we can tell."

"And those same documents are missing from Hertfordshire's copies in Welwyn?"

"Yes. Gavin Sheehy almost certainly took them, but I've searched his house and couldn't find them."

"Do you think he destroyed them, or held onto them as insurance?"

"Well, I think it's fair to say that Martin Bixby thinks the documents still exist. He's clearly trying to track them down."

"Why? Surely not just revenge on behalf of his old buddy Vinny Delmarno?"

Warren tapped his teeth thoughtfully. "I've been thinking about this. What if Martin Bixby is behind the whole thing?"

Grayson frowned but gestured for Warren to continue.

"Look at the facts. When Vinny Delmarno went to prison, his best friend and right-hand man essentially took over from him. Could he have been the person who tipped off the police about Delmarno's gun?"

"I thought that was this gardener, Reggie Williamson?"

"Well, he stole the gun, but nothing in his past before or after suggests that he would have had the means or even the contacts to approach my dad or Gavin Sheehy, both of whom were based up in Coventry at that time. Somebody had to be the contact with Williamson down in Hertfordshire and to transfer the gun so that it could be planted."

"Pete Kent, presumably."

"He was almost certainly involved, but he was only a DC at the time, he'd never have been able to instigate the whole affair. And how the hell would he have known about the gun? What if the person who actually started the affair was Bixby? He arranges for Williamson to approach Pete Kent, who then passes it on to my father and Gavin Sheehy."

"And presumably Bixby was working hand in glove with whichever dirty senior officer decided to bring down Vinny Delmarno."

"Exactly."

"So the question remains: who was this person?" Grayson looked thoughtful. "My immediate thought is, 'who benefitted most from Delmarno's imprisonment?'"

Warren shook his head in frustration. "That's just it. There are no clear winners. The nature of the investigation was such that dozens of officers were given credit for bringing down his operation. And Gavin Sheehy has never benefitted personally from it as far as I can tell; Pete Kent certainly didn't. He'd been a DS for how long?"

"So either any benefit was material—say money—or they did it for other reasons. Such as ideology."

"Exactly, and that's what Gavin Sheehy said. He claimed that he and my father were absolutely convinced that Delmarno was guilty, that they just needed that last piece of the jigsaw puzzle to bring him down."

"Noble-cause corruption."

"Exactly."

Grayson snorted derisively. "Well, it's not looking too noble now. Reggie Williamson, Zachary Eddleston and Anton Liebig and his poor wife have paid a heavy price."

"You know what they say about the road to hell."

* * *

By the time Warren joined his wife in the Graysons' guest room, it was well past midnight. However, he couldn't sleep. Unsurprisingly, neither could Susan. He should have come to bed earlier, he knew. Susan had undergone the most terrifying of ordeals. On the surface she was bearing up well, although how much of that was delayed shock, Warren didn't know. In theory Susan was due to start back at school at the beginning of next week, but even leaving aside her safety with Bixby on the loose he wanted her to have at least one session with counsellors from victim support. However, he understood his wife well enough to know that she would object vehemently to any suggestion that she miss any school; it was the final half-term before many of her students started exam leave and he knew that as always these last few lessons would be crammed full of last-minute revision.

Despite his guilt at having neglected his wife, he knew that it had been unavoidable and for the best in the long run. He and Grayson had spoken at length about what to do, but their options were depressingly few.

Grayson was going to use his rank privileges to do some careful sniffing around Markovich and see if the man could be approached regarding an investigation into the conspiracy. If he couldn't be, then they would have to look beyond Hertfordshire for help. Grayson had only been half joking when he'd pointed out that Devon and Cornwall Constabulary would have a fully independent Professional Standards department.

In the meantime, their biggest hope for the future was a miracle recovery from Gavin Sheehy, or capturing Martin Bixby and persuading him that he should assist them with their inquiries.

As Warren hugged his wife tightly, the future seemed as uncertain as ever.

SATURDAY 14TH APRIL

Chapter 53

The smartly dressed man that accosted Warren on the front doorstep as he arrived home was nervous as he handed Warren the manila envelope.

"DCI Jones?"

Warren nodded warily at the stranger standing on his front path. How long would it take for his home to feel secure again? Grayson had pulled some strings and the force had immediately sent the contractors used by the Domestic Violence Unit around to secure the property and install panic buttons and a state-of-the-art alarm system. But if anything the large red button by the front door and the flashing panel in the hallway seemed to remind him of the violation, rather than reassure.

"I'm acting under instructions from Mr Gavin Sheehy to hand you this, should anything: quote 'happen to him' unquote."

"What's in it?" asked Warren, instinctively. The other man shook his head, quickly. "Not a clue, sir. I'm his solicitor and simply acting on his instructions. Please sign here."

Warren imagined that he probably received such melodramatic instructions from clients on a regular basis. No doubt he nodded gravely, resisting the urge to roll his eyes as he accepted his orders—and payment. He probably never thought that a client would actually be attacked in such a brutal manner.

Warren watched as the man pocketed the fine gold pen that he'd used, before scurrying across the road to the Mercedes Benz parked opposite without so much as a backwards glance.

It was obvious what was in the A4 envelope and Warren felt light-headed. He should take it straight into work and deposit it in documents analysis as potential evidence. But would that be wise? The envelope almost certainly contained evidence implicating senior officers—perhaps still serving—in murder and corruption. Did he want the fact that he knew who they were in the public domain? And what if the documents "disappeared"? He needed to know whom he was dealing with before he could decide on the best course of action. At the very least he should scan the documents on his computer as insurance.

Besides which, this envelope held the key to his own father's murder. Whoever signed the orders that authorised the drugs bust that allowed his father and Sheehy to plant Delmarno's handgun where it could be found had to be the one pulling the strings. Warren felt torn; his instincts as a police officer were in direct opposition to his desires as a son.

The son won out.

His decision made, Warren inserted his key into the door lock. A high-pitched beeping reminded Warren that he needed to disarm the alarm within the next twenty seconds or risk the embarrassment of his colleagues from the DVU arriving mob-handed, blue lights and sirens ablaze, sometime in the next ninety seconds.

As he stepped across the threshold he felt the shove squarely between his shoulder blades. Stumbling forward, Warren half turned, before freezing, the all-too-familiar barrel of Bixby's gun pointed directly at his head.

"If that alarm sounds it'll be the last thing you ever hear."

* * *

A sharp pinch on his earlobe brought Warren around quickly, the pain immediately followed by a wave of nausea. The moment he'd entered the code into the alarm panel, Bixby had flipped the gun over and pistol-whipped him.

The next few minutes had been an indistinct blur. He vaguely remembered hitting the floor, before being dragged into the living room by a foot. After a period of blackness, Warren's next recollection was of being lifted bodily onto one of the wooden chairs from the kitchen.

It was this that he was tied to now, he realised as he struggled to move his hands. Looking down, he saw that his wrists were wrapped in what appeared to be torn pillow cases, protecting his wrists from the rough rope that bound him securely to the chair legs.

"A little trick I learnt in the regiment. Stops chafing on the wrists, so the pathologist can't prove that the prisoner was tied up before death."

Warren said nothing. It probably wouldn't be wise to point out that modern forensics had moved on considerably in the thirty years since Bixby had left the army and that whatever crime scenes Bixby and his fellow soldiers were responsible for back during the Northern Ireland troubles had probably been taken at face value for political reasons.

Bixby squatted down in front of Warren, so that he was at eye level. He brandished the envelope like a trophy.

"You wouldn't believe the trouble that this has caused." He slipped a finger under the seal and tore it along its length. "Just one piece of paper with a single signature." He shook his head. "As soon as I destroy this, it's all over."

His eyes had glazed slightly. He wasn't talking to Warren any more.

"Over twenty years I've been under the thumb of that bastard. Twenty years, can you believe that?" He turned his attention back to his captive, but Warren doubted he was aware of who he was. "All I wanted was to live my life. With Jocelyn and Filipo. We were a family, you know? All those sins in the past, they were over. Nobody knew what we did; it was all buried." He waved the envelope. "It wasn't like he was going to tell anyone, was it? He grew fat off the back of that bust. The famous Vinny Delmarno behind bars due to the efforts of his team; no way he was going to admit he'd stitched him up or ordered the killing of a copper to cover it up. But then *he* had to come back, didn't he?"

It was obvious who *he* was: Delmarno. "He should have died in prison."

He stood abruptly, as if remembering where he was. Tugging the envelope fully open he slid a single, slightly creased, piece of paper out. Warren caught a glimpse of old-fashioned typeface, faded with age, and a scrawled signature in blue ink at the bottom.

Bixby smiled, humourlessly. "There it is. The only loose end in this whole thing and Sheehy had it all the time." He shook his head. "He figured it would be his safety blanket. Guess he was wrong."

"Who signed it?"

Warren's voice was scratchy, sounding as if it was coming from a long distance away. Suddenly it was the only thing that mattered. He was going to die—of that he was certain, but he needed to know who was responsible for the chain of events that had taken place so long ago, that had left a young Warren to not only find his dead father, but also to spend the next two decades despising him for something he had never done. He'd even robbed him of his surname as Warren strove to make his own way in the world without the influence of his father hanging over him.

Bixby stared for a long moment.

"No, I don't think so. I'm not going to give you the satisfaction."

He stepped over to the replica fireplace, before squatting down and removing the metal panel that hid the controls from view.

"It's amazing how even a modern gas fire can be a risk if you are careless. You wouldn't believe the number of IRA suspects who died in house fires back in the Seventies."

"It's April. Why would I have the gas fire on?"

Warren was feeling desperate. Bixby's mental state was even more fragile than Susan had described a few days earlier. He seemed to be occupying several timeframes simultaneously.

Bixby appeared momentarily nonplussed, before his eyes glazed over again.

"You were using it to burn papers and had an accident—embers on this lovely old rug. Yeah that'll work." He was mumbling now.

"What papers? I don't have any. You know that." If he could pick apart the man's logic he might be able to reason with him. A desperate hope, but it was all he had.

"Doesn't matter." He turned back to Warren and his voice took on an almost professorial air. "You see it's all about the misdirection. Throw up a smokescreen to confuse the enemy and use the time gained to exfiltrate the theatre of operations in a timely fashion, with the minimum of contact."

"So I was throwing paper into a fire whilst tied to a chair?"

Bixby sighed as if dealing with a small child. "I already explained that. By the time I'm done nobody will ever know you were tied up."

"And then what? I fell asleep in front of the fire? Perhaps I was drunk—you're good at that one." Despite his best efforts, Warren felt his voice rising. "You need to change your MO, this forcing people to drink then killing them is getting old. It's like a bloody calling card."

Bixby's lip curled. "Don't you worry about that. Me and my boys were faking deaths whilst you were still in nappies. We are the best of the best. Who dares wins."

His boys. Thirty years had passed since he was booted out and he still thought he was in the army. Present day or past—Warren knew that he needed the man to occupy one or the other. He couldn't hope to reason with him whilst he alternated between the two.

The clicking of the fireplace's ignition gave way to the muffled whump of the combusting gas.

"I think we can start with this." He held up the sheet of archive paper, waving it enticingly in front of Warren, the scrawled blue signature frustratingly out of focus.

"I'm curious about the name on that myself." The voice from the doorway was low and threatening and took both men by surprise.

Vinny Delmarno looked as if he had been sleeping rough. His eyes were bloodshot and several days' worth of salt-and-pepper stubble covered his jowls. His once-expensive loafers were caked in mud and he appeared to have snagged the left pocket of his trousers on something, the loose stitching revealing glimpses of his blue undershorts.

The gun in his hand was even bigger than the one that Bixby had tucked into the waistband of his trousers.

Bixby froze, the flames stretching towards the paper sheet, as hungry for the paper as Warren and Delmarno.

"Vinny…" Suddenly Bixby's confident swagger was gone.

"Did you think I was stupid? That I wouldn't find out?"

"What do you mean?" Bixby stood slowly.

"Jocelyn! You've been fucking her brains out, you bastard." Delmarno's face was bright red as he stepped into the room.

Bixby shook his head. "No way, I wouldn't do that to you. Why would you think that?"

Delmarno ignored him. "When did it start? The day I went to prison? The day after? What about before? Do you think I didn't notice? You were practically dribbling on her during our wedding." His face was turning even redder, purple tinges appearing along the edge of his ears, yet his gun hand remained as steady as an Olympic marksman's.

"No way!" Bixby repeated, more forcefully. "I looked after her; I tried my best to stop her but you know what she's like." He licked his lips. "You're right, she was sleeping around, but not with me."

"Who then?"

"Rubens."

Delmarno snorted. "Rubens? That greasy bastard? Jocelyn wouldn't cross the road to piss on him if he was on fire."

"A lot of things can change in twenty years, Vinny. The whole disliking Rubens thing—it was just a ruse. They've been together for years."

Delmarno paused in surprise, before lifting the gun again.

"So if that's true tell me why was Jocelyn round your flat—" he paused for effect "—and what about that white BMW I asked you to trace for me? The same fucking beamer that was parked in your parking space."

If Bixby was shocked by the revelation, he didn't show it.

"You're right, she did come around mine." He sighed. "I'm sorry,

Vinny, I've been trying to get her to tell you about Rubens for weeks." He reached out a hand. "She didn't want to hurt you. But I told her she had to come clean." He stepped forward. "Vinny, you're my oldest friend. And Rubens is my second oldest. And I love Jocelyn like a sister. The whole thing's a fucking mess and I just wanted to try and fix things. To make them the way they used to be. When you saw us together, she was upset. I told her that she needed to tell to you before the wedding, or I'd speak to you myself. She knew I was right and she just needed a hug is all."

The look of anguish on Bixby's face was so convincing that if Warren hadn't seen the intelligence reports about the couple he might have been fooled also. Of course, given the man's fragile mental state it was possible that Bixby was fooling himself as much as his audience.

Delmarno said nothing, the silence stretching between them.

"So what's on the sheet of paper?"

Bixby's face went momentarily blank, as if he'd forgotten what he was holding in his hand.

"The last piece of the puzzle."

"The person who was responsible for stitching me up. The fucker who gave the orders to his old man." Delmarno turned, acknowledging Warren's presence for the first time. His lip twisted cruelly.

"DCI Warren Jones—or little Warren MacNamara as you were called when you found your old man in that garage."

Warren bit his lip, not trusting himself to speak. He was only a small part of the scene that was playing out in front of him and he dared not say anything that would place him in a more central role. Delmarno pointed towards Bixby with his chin. "I guess you figured out who set that one up."

He leant forward over Warren. "But you know it's not enough.

Twenty-two years, your old man and his buddies stole off me. And I am going to make them suffer. One by one. That fucker Sheehy already got his. Then there was that bloody gardener." He shook his head in disbelief. "I can't even remember his name."

"So why do you want me?" Warren's voice was little more than a croak.

"Good question." He looked over his shoulder. "Martin, why do we want him? Surely he's more trouble than he's worth. I hope you've got a foolproof way of hiding his body, the last thing we want is this guy hanging around our necks; you know how the pigs pull out all the stops for one of their own."

"Leave that to me. He knows too much to keep alive. As to why—well, don't they say that the 'sins of the father shall be visited upon his sons'?"

Delmarno nodded approvingly. "I always loved a bit of scripture. So before you use that little piece of paper to burn the place down, let me have a look at it. I want the name of the bastard who set me up."

Delmarno reached out for the crumpled sheet.

The gunshot felled him like a tree.

Bixby stood and stared at the smoking gun in his hand, the shot reverberating around the room. Finally, his gaze shifted to the body of Delmarno—a man he'd known all his life, who now lay at his feet.

"Right through the kidney—how ironic. You brought it on yourself; you do know that, don't you?"

Bixby's voice was calm, matter-of-fact; he was clearly unaware of the tears trickling down his cheeks. Complete dissociation, Warren saw. The man in front of him had no idea what he was doing; it was as if there were two completely separate personalities occupying the same body and both were in control at the same time. If Warren had been concerned before, now he was out-and-out scared.

Bixby continued to address the crumpled form in front of him. "You're poison, you know that, don't you? Even when we were kids you were no good for me. You pretended to be my friend, but all the time you were using me." His eyes lost focus again. "Why was it always you on lookout and me nicking stuff? Why did you never get your hands dirty? And what about when I came back from the army? You said you wanted to help me—to give me a job. I could have been in charge of security at one of those pubs you owned or even driving a cab, but no, you wanted me doing your shit again. And then cleaning it all up. And if I didn't clean it properly, whose fingerprints were all over the place? Who was going to take the blame? Not you."

He crossed the room in two strides; ignoring the gun in his hand, he laid into the insensate body before him, raining kick after kick for almost a full minute. Finally he paused, his breath shaky, before speaking again as if nothing had happened.

"You never deserved Jocelyn, you know that? She was pure when she met you—" his face twisted, even as his voice remained flat "—but you corrupted her. I knew what you were doing. You claimed to love her, but you were using her as a cover. You and that slimy little bastard Rubens. If it all went tits up, Jocelyn was the one whose fingers would get burnt."

He swung another kick at Delmarno, smashing his boot into his face. "And that's for hitting her, you cowardly shit."

He turned on his heel and paced back towards the fireplace.

"At least she was an adult. She made her choices and she wasn't as big a fool as you thought. But then Filipo came along." Now he was smiling, almost wistful. "In all of the years I've known you, that boy is the only positive contribution that you've made to this planet. And I will *not* let you drag him down into your squalor and filth."

"Was that why you arranged for the gun to be planted?" It was a leap of logic, but Warren had spotted what he hoped was Bixby's weakness.

The look of startled surprise on Bixby's face caused the bound officer to flinch, as the man raised his gun—he'd clearly forgotten that Warren was even in the room.

"Yeah, it was time for him to go." He gestured back at Delmarno, lowering the gun again. "I wanted to kill him, but I knew that Jocelyn still loved him and she'd never forgive me. Then the diabetes finally caught up with him and promised to do it for me." He snorted. "When we were kids, we used to steal sweets from the corner shop. He'd shove them down his neck until he was buzzing—I've often wondered if that contributed to his illness. 'Course the arrogant bastard ignored all of the advice that they gave him." He shook his head. "The number of times I saved his life by getting Lucozade down his neck or injecting him with his insulin because he hadn't been watching his sugar levels. Not even that worked in the end. He was completely resistant. Christ, listen to me, I know more about his treatment than he does."

He leant against the fireplace, and again Warren doubted he remembered he was even in the room. "I should have let him die. Would have saved a lot of hassle and we wouldn't be here in this mess now."

"So why didn't you?" Warren needed him to stay focused, even if the last thing he wanted to do was draw the man's attention.

"If he died, I couldn't protect Jocelyn and Filipo. You see, everything was coming to a head. If he was out of the picture, then they would have started looking further afield. Jocelyn, me, even Rubens—although they can have that fucker. As usual, everyone else would have been left carrying the can."

"So you did a deal."

"Yeah, seemed like win-win. The pigs got Vinny; we got our lives back. Vinny was fucked anyway. His kidneys were gone. No way was he going to make it to the end of his sentence."

"Who did you do the deal with?"

"You mean whose grubby little fingerprints are on this piece of paper?" He smiled. "Wouldn't you like to know?"

Suddenly he clapped his hands and spun on the spot—yet another mood swing. Warren was struggling to keep up.

"Change of plan. It seems the fugitive Vinny Delmarno shot DCI Jones, who then bravely fought him off, shooting Vinny with his own gun, before tragically succumbing to his wounds."

"It'll never work, the angles are wrong. The blood spatter isn't right. Forensics will figure it out in a heartbeat." Warren fought to keep his rising voice under control.

Bixby waved his protestations off. "You let me worry about that."

"Why are you doing this?" Warren's voice was soft as he tried to reason with the man.

"Weren't you listening? The sins of the father and all that—your old man stole twenty-two years. He's not here, so you have to pay."

Warren's mind spun furiously. Bixby had finally snapped. As far as Warren could tell, Bixby was completely out of touch with reality.

"Pay who?" Warren nodded at Delmarno. "He's dead. And wasn't my father doing your bidding? You set it up." He licked his lips and decided to take a chance. "*You* were the one who betrayed Vinny.

436

My dad, Reggie Williamson, Gavin Sheehy, Pete Kent, Anton Liebig, even poor, young Zachary Eddleston—all of them paid that price. They're all on you!"

"No!" Bixby spun on his heel and Warren flinched—had he pushed the man too far?

"I never wanted any of this! I just wanted a normal life. For me, Jocelyn and Filipo. No more killing, no more violence." He wiped his face with the back of his hand, appearing surprised at the dampness. "I wanted to make something good, you know." Now his voice was quiet.

"All of my life, I've been killing people. First the army, then the regiment. The things we did in Northern Ireland…" His voice cracked. "I know they were terrorists. I know that what we were doing would save lives—but some of those targets were just fucking kids.

"You know, I couldn't even tell you who I killed back then?" He laughed bitterly. "Can you believe that? Me and the boys killed those lads—even tortured a couple—and I don't even have the decency to remember their names." His voice dropped, barely a whisper. "I've never forgotten their faces though."

He stood taller and walked over to Delmarno.

"When I left, I was an animal. I couldn't handle it any more. When the Falklands finished, me and the boys returned to Hereford. To train up for Northern Ireland again. But it wasn't enough. I was angry. I needed to kill people, to let it all out. I couldn't stand being in little rooms, having meetings, taking instructions from spooks who didn't even know how to remove the safety on a fucking Browning, let alone fire one at another human being. And so I got kicked out. There's only so many bar fights the regiment can cover up, especially if the poor sod you kick nine shades of shit out is a civilian minding his own and the police are already two doors down, dealing with something else."

"So then what happened?" Warren's voice was low, soothing.

"Vinny came to the rescue. Or so I thought. He gave me a job, sorted out a flat—he even helped me get a car." He laughed. "Hell, they teach you how to kill a man ten different ways and how to survive in the jungle for weeks with no food, but nobody ever told me how to sort out car insurance!"

His voice turned sombre again. "But he was just taking advantage. He was my oldest friend, you know? We met at primary school. Mum and Dad weren't happy—the old man fought in the Second World War against the fascists and he didn't like me being friends with a wop. But he was a wanker and when he pissed off with his tart and Mum started letting any bastard she could find who could put food on the table share her bed, Vinny was all I had." He snorted. "I probably had tea round his more nights a week than round mine and at least his mum could cook properly."

He walked back over to Delmarno and Warren expected him to start kicking him again. "There's something I've learnt over the years. There are two types of people in the world. Those who see a hurt, frightened dog and nurse it back to health, and those who see that same dog, take advantage of its fear and anger and train it to kill. Vinny Delmarno is the latter."

"So what made you realise this?" The conversation was heading in a direction that Warren felt more comfortable with, but he had to tread carefully.

"Jocelyn. And then Filipo." He nodded towards Delmarno again. "Vinny was never short of a tart or two. When he started making his money, they were like flies round shit. Don't get me wrong, I wasn't jealous. I got more than my fair share, and I always preferred the quieter best friends to the upfront slappers that Vinny used to attract, but still Jocelyn was different. Yeah, she liked a bit of a bad boy, but she was intelligent, you know? And funny. Vinny was used to being the centre of attention, making jokes, having everyone laugh at him. He thought he was like one of those Mafia dons you see in the movies, but Jocelyn was genuinely witty and she could have everyone around the table in stitches. That sort of thing would piss him off normally—but it just made him want her more." Again, he seemed to slip away into his own world. "It made us both want her."

"What about Filipo?"

A smile spread across Martin's face. "I never really wanted kids. But when Jocelyn had Filipo, things changed. Vinny was getting ill and spending a lot of time in the hospital, whilst at the same time the business was getting dirtier. Jocelyn would stay late with him sometimes and they'd leave me to babysit. In the end, I spent more time with him than his own father did. You know, I was looking after him one Saturday afternoon when he took his first step?" He laughed again, but this time it was the fond chuckle of a man reliving happy memories. "I've never told anyone that before. He did it again when Vinny and Jocelyn got home and I kept my mouth shut—they were so happy, I figured it would be wrong to tell them that I saw it first."

His tone darkened again and Warren held his breath. The man's mood swings were exhausting as well as terrifying.

"Thing is, I could see the writing on the wall. The police were closing in and even if they didn't end it all, did I really want Filipo to grow up with a dad like Vinny? We were already checking under our cars for bombs. Death threats were almost a weekly occurrence. Vinny usually kept his hands clean, but he had a few skeletons in the closet."

"So somebody approached you?"

"Sort of. I'd been a bit careless myself—left a few fingerprints lying around. They knew who I was, so I cut a deal. I put them in touch with Reggie Williamson, who stole the gun and passed it onto your old man. And Gavin Sheehy it turns out."

"So my father never contacted you?"

"Nah, too far down the pecking order. I never even met him until the night I killed him." His tone was matter-of-fact, as if they were discussing the weather. Warren fought the sudden surge of acid bile.

"So why did you involve the gardener? Surely that was just adding another person to the mix? One more person who knew the truth." Warren forced himself to treat the interview as if it was any other interrogation—to pretend that the man in front of him hadn't murdered his own father.

Bixby sighed. "Yeah, it wasn't my idea. Unfortunately, things were beyond our control. The case was stalled and questions were being raised about how much time and resources were being spent on something that wasn't going anywhere. I was working away in the Midlands, dealing with some suppliers, and Vinny would have been suspicious if I came back—he trusted me implicitly, but he was a paranoid bastard. And despite everything he still saw me as the hired help. I never set foot in his bedroom—Reggie Williamson had the run of the place.

"Plus, he was becoming sick. He just ignored the symptoms, but like I said, I knew more about his health problems than he did. I could see where it was going and the last thing we needed was for him to drop dead before they made the case against him and the blame was shifted towards me and Jocelyn."

Warren sighed. The gardener was a victim of little more than bad luck.

"So why did you kill him all these years later?"

A brief flash of pain crossed Bixby's face, before the mask slid back into place. He nodded towards Delmarno's body.

"Him. He wanted revenge. He wanted me to find out who was responsible for the stitch-up and sort them out."

"That's it? Surely you could have just claimed you couldn't find out? Why couldn't you just let it go? Claimed that everyone involved was dead—you were in charge of the investigation. Delmarno would never have known." Warren's voice started to rise in frustration. "Why did it all have to start again?"

Bixby said nothing, but his left eyelid started to flutter. Warren pressed harder. "Why Martin? Why couldn't you let it go?"

"Gavin Sheehy." Bixby's voice was thick.

Warren said nothing; he let Bixby fill the silence.

"I don't know if he had a touch of conscience or he was scared that Vinny would track him down and get revenge, but he started asking questions. He was looking for protection and I guess he figured that if he had evidence of who coordinated everything he could use that as leverage."

"So he asked DS Kent to help him find that evidence." The final pieces were coming together.

"Yeah, the stupid bastard thought that Kent would have the same worries he did, now that Vinny was looking for who stitched him up." Bixby shook his head. "Kent was furious that Sheehy was going to rock the boat. We'd kept it quiet for twenty-odd years; all we needed to do was keep our nerve. MacNamara's death was done and dusted; Liebig was never going to implicate himself; the gardener probably never even knew what he'd helped us do. Vinny was decades out of the loop—I was the only one who could help him join the dots and no way was I going to do that."

441

"I still don't see how this triggered everything. Even if Kent was worried and came to you, surely you could have locked everything down. Why all of the killing?"

"Kent didn't come to me. He never knew me until recently. I went to him." Bixby raised the piece of paper. "Orders from on high. He was livid. He figured that Sheehy was making a fuss about nothing and that it would all blow over."

"Who gave the orders?"

Warren tried to sound casual, to hide his desperation. Bixby ignored him.

"Kent tried to throw Sheehy off the scent. He played along with him, used his knowledge of police records and computer systems to control what Sheehy saw. Silly sod never had a clue. He trusted Kent completely. But he still wouldn't let it go. And so eventually I was told to clear it all up."

Warren's mind was racing ahead, making connections, but there were still a few pieces missing.

"Why didn't you get rid of Sheehy then? Why this elaborate plot to frame him?"

The twitch in Bixby's eye was getting worse—was it a sign that Warren should back off or should he keep on pushing?

"I was told to clean everything up. Not to leave any loose ends or it'd all come back on me and Jocelyn. So I did."

Warren decided to push. "But why didn't you kill Sheehy? Why try and set him up? Surely that's a huge loose end?"

"Vinny's idea. He wanted revenge. Reggie Williamson and your old man were dead, but it wasn't enough. He wanted someone to suffer. And he liked the idea that whoever stitched him up should get a taste of their own medicine."

"What about Jocelyn? What did she think?"

Bixby shook his head and said nothing. The twitch had spread to his cheeks and he had started to lick his lips. For a second, Warren thought he was about to say something, then the face went blank.

And there was the root of Bixby's dilemma. The man was mentally fragile from his war experiences and now he was being pulled in competing directions—the battered psyche that he and Jocelyn had worked to strengthen over the years was struggling to withstand a sustained assault from so many different sides. It was as if he was treading a tightrope, trying to please Delmarno and still keep his puppet master happy whilst at the same time protecting Jocelyn and Filipo and trying to preserve the happy lifestyle that he had worked so hard to cultivate for the past two decades. Add to that his conflicting loyalties—it was clear that despite everything he still loved Delmarno—and Warren could see that the only way his tortured psyche could deal with the conflict was to break apart, to shatter into different fragments, each with their own self-contained compartment.

Warren had spotted the compartment that could save him.

"Why are you doing this to me? Think about Filipo."

Bixby looked confused. "What's he got to do with this."

"You say that the sins of the father should be visited on his sons. That I should be made to suffer for the wrongs that my father committed. But what about Filipo?" Warren nodded towards Delmarno. "You've said it yourself; Vinny was a monster, but you didn't want Filipo to be tainted by that."

Bixby was shaking his head, but Warren could see that his words were having an impact. "And what about the sins of his real father? The man who brought him up as his own—who has loved him and his mother far more than that man lying over

443

there could ever do. What about his sins? Should Filipo have to answer for those?"

Sweat had started to bead on the former soldier's forehead. He crumpled the paper into a ball.

"Untie me, Martin. Tell me who started this all and let me bring *them* to justice. Let *them* answer for their crimes."

Bixby was absolutely still, but his face was a riot of different emotions.

"Tell me who did it, Martin. Let them answer for their crimes." Warren lowered his voice. "Do the right thing, Martin. Stop the killing; bring it all to an end. Give me the piece of paper—let's close it. Let Jocelyn and Filipo walk away from this. Vinny's gone. There's no evidence connecting them to the crimes he committed decades ago."

Warren held his breath. He could see the fight between the fractured shards of Bixby's psyche playing out across his face. Time stretched endlessly.

"No."

Warren's heart sank.

"You're right. It's time to bring it to an end—" he raised the piece of paper "—but this isn't enough. You know that. It's circumstantial at best. You'll never be able to deliver the justice that he deserves."

He crumpled the sheet still tighter and tossed it lightly into the fire.

Warren opened his mouth to cry out in protest, but it was drowned out by the sound of Delmarno's gun.

The bullet pounded into the former soldier, slamming him into the fireplace so hard that the mantelpiece followed him down as he slumped to the floor, the vases either side of the chimney smashing.

Warren turned in shock towards Delmarno, who lay in the

same semi-foetal position he had been in since Bixby had shot him minutes before. The man's face was a swollen, beaten mask. His eyes were barely visible behind the bruising—his nose a flattened, bloody mess.

The gun swung slowly towards Warren, who froze. He opened his mouth, but couldn't think what to say. His impassioned plea to Bixby had probably burnt all of his bridges with Delmarno. The killer's finger tightened on the trigger as he glared at Warren. Despite himself, Warren closed his eyes. A wave of exhaustion swept over him. *Just do it*, he thought, as he braced himself for the deafening bang and percussive force that would finally end a twenty-four-year story. There was no way that Delmarno could fail to hit him from such a short distance.

Unbidden, images that Warren had suppressed for the past two decades swam to the surface. Christmas day: Warren sat on his father's knee as he read him stories about Noddy and Big Ears. At his father's feet, Granddad Jack was helping James build a Lego spaceship. At the far end of the room Nana Betty was helping his mother lay the table yet again, the smell of warming sausage rolls from the kitchen teasing everybody's noses.

Susan squeezed his hand gently. That was impossible. He and Susan wouldn't meet for another twenty years, yet it seemed right that she was here as well, sharing the moment with everyone else Warren loved.

He felt the tears trickle down his cheeks. Who knew what could have happened if those terrible events of so long ago had never taken place? What else had little Warren MacNamara been cheated of on that terrible May night?

The bang when it came was quieter than Warren had expected. More of a clatter than an explosion.

445

He opened his eyes. The gun lay on the floor. Delmarno's face was slack, his hate-filled eyes turning glassy.

Warren took a deep shaky breath. It was over. Bixby and Delmarno were both dead. He slumped in relief, only the rope around his chest stopping him from sliding off the seat.

He coughed and turned back to the fireplace. Bixby lay half in, half out of the fireplace, his cheap suit now ablaze, smoke pouring from his body. As Warren watched in horror, the flames licked at the smouldering rug. They caught.

WEDNESDAY 18ᵀᴴ APRIL

Chapter 54

Warren steered Susan's car into Bob Windermere's driveway. Warren's Mondeo had been declared a write-off by his insurance company, but they were contesting responsibility, given that he had been responsible for the damage when he rammed Bixby's BMW. Grayson was trying to claim that Warren was on official police business when the collision occurred and due a payout from the joint liability pot, but the force's bean counters were taking some convincing.

The former detective had been busy since Warren's previous visit, he noted. A battered yellow skip had recently taken up residence in the front garden and was already half full of ancient kitchen units and an avocado bathroom suite. Warren barely had time to exit the car before his former mentor was at his side, his massive paws swallowing Warren's in a bone-crushing handshake. He stepped back and eyed the younger man appraisingly,

"Looks painful." He pointed to the left side of his face.

"It's not too bad now, no worse than a nasty case of sunburn." Warren dismissed the angry red burns to his cheeks, firmly pushing away the memories of heat and the smell of burning flesh and hair—most of it Bixby's, some of it his.

Following Windermere into the house, they headed for the

kitchen, stepping over the boxes of bathroom tiles and tubs of concrete that half filled the hallway.

"'Scuse the mess. I'm doing the bathroom this week. I got the old suite out yesterday and now I'm plumbing in the power shower." He paused. "Everything OK, Warren?"

Warren shook himself and forced himself to sit down on the wooden chair that Windermere had placed his coffee cup in front of.

"Fine," he lied. *It's not even the same type of chair*, he admonished himself. Nevertheless, he and Susan had used the fact that that they no longer had four matching chairs as an excuse to get rid of the three surviving pieces of furniture. Their replacements—on order from an obscure online furniture company—were ugly, overpriced and heavy but their solid frames provided little in the way of purchase to wrap a rope around.

He positioned himself more comfortably. The long drive had caused his left shoulder to stiffen again. He'd damaged the ligaments over the winter and the combination of the collision with Bixby's car and his desperate shoulder barge through the locked kitchen door, hands still bound behind him, as he escaped the conflagration in the living room, had left him using a sling again.

Windermere stared at him, his eyes searching Warren's face.

"Don't give me that. How are you holding up?"

"Really, I'm fine."

Windermere clearly wasn't convinced, but decided to drop it. "Have you spoken to your Federation rep recently?"

Warren nodded. "I'm due another hearing with Professional Standards next week. She thinks that given everything that's happened, they'll reinstate me. I'll probably get a black mark on my record and a formal letter of reprimand, but it's clear I didn't have anything to do with Billy Obsanjo's death."

"Good, I'm relieved. Have you decided what you are going to say?"

"No, I still don't know enough about this Markovich character to decide if it is safe to tell him what I know."

"I think you're probably right to be cautious. If he is involved, you don't want him coming after you. Or Susan for that matter. How is she, by the way?"

Warren shrugged. "I don't know. She's back at school, acting like nothing happened, but she had a really bad nightmare last night that she wouldn't tell me about. Bernice and Dennis are still staying with us. They insist that they want to help us redecorate, but I know they're worried about her. About both of us."

"So, any idea who was responsible?"

Warren shook his head in frustration. "Somebody senior enough at the time of the killings to sign off the drugs raid, but the records just aren't there any more. That piece of paper was the only remaining evidence; everything else has been shredded or deleted. And everyone who was involved is either dead or won't be talking."

"I take it Gavin Sheehy hasn't come around?"

Warren shook his head again. "We stopped Pete Kent from finishing him off, but it didn't really matter. He was already too badly brain-damaged. He'll probably never recover consciousness."

"What about Jocelyn Delmarno? Does she have any ideas?"

"No. Bixby never told her anything. We questioned her at length and she's still on police bail, but she's not got anything to give us. If she knew anything she'd have told us, I'm sure of it. She's scared that whoever this bastard is, they might see and her son as 'loose ends' that still need tidying up. I can't see it myself, but I can't blame her for being worried."

"So that's it then."

Warren's shoulders slumped. "It can't be, Bob. There must be something left. Something else I can do." He looked imploringly at his former mentor—the man he still regarded as the best detective he'd ever worked with. "I can't let this go."

He stood up abruptly, unable to sit any more. "Somewhere out there is the person who ordered the killing of my father. Bixby said as much. That person set this whole thing in motion." He closed his eyes, rubbing them wearily. "He could still be working for the police for Christ's sake!"

Windermere's hand was heavy, comforting, on Warren's shoulder.

"I'm sorry, son. I don't see what we can do. Even if you could figure out who did it, there's no evidence left. Short of a confession from somebody else involved, you'll never get the charges to stick." He squeezed gently. "I think it's over." He turned Warren to face him. "I think you have to face facts and accept that you'll never fully clear your old man's name—but the important thing is that *you* know that he was innocent."

Warren nodded miserably.

"You need a proper coffee. Go in the living room. This place is like a building site."

Following his instructions, Warren picked his way through the building material and made his way into the living room.

Since his last visit, Windermere had finished repainting the old-fashioned fireplace. Unbidden, his last images of Bixby, clothes on fire, sprung to mind. Warren breathed deeply, forcing down the horror. He closed his eyes. The side of his cheek stung with the memory of those flames, as he desperately tried to break free of the chair. He'd given up on freeing his hands, concentrating instead on getting his feet down on the floor and trying to stand. He'd finally succeeded in shuffling forward, curled over with his buttocks still pressed against the seat, his wrists tied firmly to the chair legs.

He'd managed only a few steps before he'd lost his balance, landing headfirst on the flaming rug. Throwing himself backwards in panic, he'd managed to break the front legs off the chair. Suddenly able to move his legs properly, he'd scrambled back to his feet, heading towards the kitchen. The air was already thick and the smoke detectors were screaming. It had taken three bone-crunching charges before the door finally crashed open and Warren collapsed, wheezing, into the arms of his next-door neighbours.

Warren forced himself to open his eyes and take in the fireplace. Getting rid of kitchen chairs to banish bad memories was one thing, but he couldn't afford to rip out the fireplace as well. The fire brigade had arrived less than a minute after Warren's escape and the damage to the living room wasn't nearly as extensive as it could have been. The fireplace would need a bit of paint and the carpet and rug were a complete loss—at least the fire meant that they didn't have to figure out how to remove Delmarno's and Bixby's bloodstains.

Windermere's mantelpiece was cluttered with pictures and trophies. Pride of place was a team photograph of CID, the day that Windermere was promoted out of the division. Warren stood next to him, grinning happily. Warren's eyes moved across the mantelpiece to a clutch of trophies. The blood started to pound in his ears.

"Warren, if you think it will help, you can speak to me." Warren hadn't even heard Windermere re-enter the room.

There was a metallic taste in his mouth.

"Tell me what actually happened in your living room on Saturday. There's been nothing in the papers and I'm not as in the loop as I used to be. Let me know what went down."

"I'd rather not talk about it." Warren's voice was thick, almost slurred.

"You really should." Windermere was pressing another mug of steaming coffee into his hand, the familiar smell of brandy suffusing the vapour. "I know it's hard, but you have to speak to someone. Someone who understands."

Warren felt sick. "I need to go."

"Jesus, Warren. You're as white as a sheet. You can't drive now. Sit down. You need to talk. Don't bottle it up."

"I'll be fine. I just need an early night. Susan is going to be back home soon. I need to see her." He was babbling but he didn't care.

"At least tell me what happened to Bixby. The papers mentioned one dead body, but no casualties apart from you. Was the stiff Delmarno?" Windermere's tone was slightly strained.

"Delmarno shot him," was all Warren could manage.

"Then why only one dead body? Did the papers get it wrong?"

Warren ignored him, stumbling towards the front door. "I have to go. Susan is still on edge. She'll be worried if I'm not home when she gets back from school."

The sun was bright after the dimness of Windermere's living room and Warren found himself squinting as he fumbled with the unfamiliar car keys. Windermere had followed him onto the driveway.

"Is Bixby dead?"

"I've got to go. Thanks for the coffee," Warren managed as he slid into the driver's seat. He pressed the starter button and the engine leapt into life.

The car's wheel's spun on the loose gravel of the driveway as Warren pressed the accelerator slightly harder than he intended. Within seconds, Windermere was a rapidly shrinking dot in the rear-view mirror.

Windermere's house was up a narrow, single-track lane and Warren drove several miles before he was able to pull over. By now, his shock had worn off, his agile mind making the connections, then trying to break them—to disprove what he knew was true. Warren had cried more in the past few weeks than he had done since he was a child. But this time his eyes were dry, even as his heart broke at yet another betrayal.

Nagging thoughts that had floated around his subconscious now made sense; how had Windermere known that the gun stolen by the gardener had appeared at the scene of the drugs bust a few weeks later? And what about his stating that Beno Richter, the pathologist who had performed his father's autopsy, was dead? Professor Jordan hadn't informed Warren of his discovery until after he'd met with Windermere. A slip of the tongue? It seemed unlikely.

Then there was Windermere's immediate recollection of the facts surrounding Operation Leitmotif. How many hundreds of operations had Bob Windermere been involved in over the past two decades? How likely was it that he'd be able to remember such intimate details years later?

He thought back to the day that Windermere retired—how he'd encouraged Warren to start looking for opportunities outside of the West Midlands. Had he known about Sheehy's upcoming disgrace? In fact, hadn't he drawn Warren's attention to it—an unexpected phone call a few months later. Sheehy's suspension wasn't a secret, but it was hardly being shouted from the rooftops and the force had moved quickly to block all but the most cursory reports from the media. How would a retired detective chief superintendent in a different force—even one as well respected and connected as Bob Windermere—hear that a vacancy was coming up? And why was he so keen for Warren to apply for the position?

Did he think that he could control Warren, to stop him digging too deep? Any other officer approached by Gavin Sheehy would probably have gone straight to Professional Standards. Warren had been played for a fool.

It was all circumstantial—each occurrence could be dismissed as coincidence, faulty recollection on Warren's part or any one of a dozen other innocent explanations. As could the final part of the jigsaw. The final, devastating piece that convinced Warren—if nobody else—who the puppet master was. Who the person was who had started the whole affair a quarter of a century ago, had stolen Warren's father from him and then, ten years later taken over that role, whilst all the while manipulating Warren as he worked his way through the police?

Moving quickly, Warren opened the driver's door as he vomited his breakfast onto the grass verge. Finally, he felt better. Wiping his mouth with some tissues that Susan kept in the glovebox, Warren leant back in the seat and closed his eyes. He knew that it would be a long time before the image that hovered before him would fade away.

A silver trophy, engraved in cursive script, "Winner: 2011 Men's Senior Individual. The Allingham Golf Club and Hotel: Robert Windermere."

SATURDAY 12TH MAY

Epilogue

Sunlight glinted off the wet grass as Warren waited by the entrance to the small cemetery. He'd been here for ten minutes and spent the time finding a watering can and using his penknife to remove the packaging and the tips of the stalks from the bunches of flowers he'd bought from the nearby florist. He could have gone ahead, he supposed, and made a start on tidying the graves, but he couldn't bring himself to make his way down the familiar pathway alone. Thursday had been the twenty-fourth anniversary of his father's murder. He had intended to take a half-day's personal leave to attend the grave, but he'd changed his mind at the last moment, unable to face the trip without Susan's support.

The quiet scrunch of gravel underfoot announced the arrival of his wife, arm in arm with Granddad Jack. Dressed soberly in dark trousers and an open necked-shirt, the old man's tread was slow but had a new lightness to it, as if the revelations of the past few weeks about his son had taken the last few years off him. In his left hand he held several bunches of flowers similar to Warren's and a pot plant; Susan carried a rolled-up newspaper.

"I thought you might want a look at this," she said, offering the newspaper by way of a greeting. Warren traded knife for paper and spread it open. Page three, lead article of the local gazette.

Death of retired policeman an accident, inquest rules
Coroner reminds DIY enthusiasts of the need to
use certified tradesmen for electrical work

The death of local resident, retired police superintendent Robert Windermere, 66, was ruled death-by-misadventure by Coroner Mohammed Asif today. The body of Mr Windermere, who lived alone, was found in the bathroom of his cottage by concerned neighbours on the twenty-eighth of April. Mr Windermere bought the cottage as an investment after he and his wife separated shortly after his retirement.

"Bob was a keen DIY expert and he bought the property about eighteen months ago as a project. The house had been empty for some time and needed lots of work done on it. He wanted to do it up and sell it as a profit, then move by the sea," said neighbour Stanley Addlemoor who discovered Mr Windermere's body after becoming concerned that he hadn't collected his milk and newspapers for a few days.

It was believed that Mr Windermere had decided to cut costs by doing all of the renovations, including electrical work, by himself. The cause of death was ruled to be electrocution by an incorrectly wired power shower that Mr Windermere had recently fitted. The incorrect wiring was compounded by a faulty circuit breaker that failed to cut off the power when the fault developed.

Dr Asif recorded a narrative verdict, in which he restated a 2005 change in the law that requires all electrical work to be carried by accredited professionals to stop just this sort of tragic accident from occurring.

The remainder of the article went on to praise Windermere's career in the police and his charity work, with quotes from the chief constable and other senior officers. Warren closed the paper, unable to finish it.

"Dangerous stuff, electricity," stated Susan flatly.

"Looks like it," responded Warren neutrally. "Shall we get on with it?"

Dumping the newspaper in a nearby bin, Warren slipped an arm around Granddad Jack's skinny shoulders. The worn path between the graves was covered in loose scree to help drainage and Warren worried about the old man's footing.

Two stones, side by side, the first engraved with his parents' names, the second with Nana Betty's—a space below was left for the name of Granddad Jack. Not any time soon, Warren prayed quietly. After all that had happened in the last six months he didn't think he could cope with the loss of Granddad Jack as well. He needed time to take stock and heal emotionally.

By unspoken consent, they tended to Nana Betty's grave first. It had been her birthday a few days ago and the spray of pansies were still fresh and bright. Susan plucked a few dead stalks from a previous bunch, making room for her and Warren's new delivery.

His parents' grave was less well tended and Warren felt a stab of shame. A few weeds had started to grow across the plinth of the headstone and a pot plant, probably from Granddad Jack, was now past its best.

"Let's dig them out and replace the plant," suggested Jack, producing a small trowel from the bag with the plant in it. The gathering lapsed into silence as Warren knelt down on a carrier bag to dig out the weeds and make an indentation for the pot plant.

"We should have filled the watering can before we came all the way down here," Susan stated, before squeezing the hands of both men and heading back to the standpipe by the entrance.

Now alone, it was Granddad Jack who broke the silence.

"We never believed everything they said about him."

Not trusting himself to speak, Warren could only nod.

"The truth's never going to come out, is it?" Jack's voice was sad, but held no bitterness.

Warren shook his head. He'd given everything that he had to Professional Standards, but it was all circumstantial at best. They'd look into it, he'd been assured, but he doubted anything would come of it.

Vinny Delmarno was dead. Jocelyn Delmarno and her son, Filipo, would never tell the authorities anything and all the other witnesses were either dead or vegetative. Judith Sheehy was deciding if she should turn off her husband's life-support machine. And Bob Windermere was a hero to many. Nobody was going to trample on his memory without rock-solid evidence.

Jack squeezed his grandson's shoulder. "Well, everyone who needs to know knows, and that's what matters in the end."

"Nana didn't." Warren inclined his head towards the adjacent grave.

"Yes she did, son. She always knew."

The two men lapsed into silence again, before Granddad Jack started again.

"I know it's wrong to want revenge, and I know that what Niall did was immoral, but I wish that the bastard who started this all off could have answered for his crimes. For his betrayal. But justice won't be done, will it?" The old man turned to Warren, his eyes narrowing, their gaze penetrating Warren's.

"Not in a court of law," was all Warren could bring himself to say.

Jack held his gaze for a few seconds longer, before grunting quietly.

It was a few minutes before Susan returned with the watering can, which Warren used to give the flowers on both graves a good soaking.

"Let's get rid of all these dead ends and wrappers before the wind blows them all over the place," suggested Granddad Jack, tying the handles of the carrier bag. He took Susan's arm, and they headed back to the entrance, finally leaving Warren alone.

As upsetting as it was that Windermere would never set foot inside a courtroom to answer for his crimes, Warren was more sad that he would never get a chance to ask his former mentor why he had done it. Had he benefitted in some unknown way, or was it really "noble-cause corruption" as John Grayson had suggested? Warren doubted he would ever know.

The padded envelope in Warren's breast pocket weighed heavily. It had arrived unannounced in the post earlier that week. No labels or card. It was completely anonymous. The address on the envelope had been handwritten. Perhaps the graphologists down at Welwyn could have identified the sender; they almost certainly had his writing on file somewhere.

But it wasn't necessary. Warren knew who it was from. He silently acknowledged the gesture with a nod. It wasn't an apology exactly—and he wouldn't have accepted it if it were—but it was something. The righting of at least one wrong. The newspapers had been right—there was only one body found in the remains of Warren and Susan's living room. The blood trails from the fireplace had continued over the windowsill and across the front garden. Still more blood had been found in the burnt-out wreck of Warren's neighbour's car, after it had been dumped, but that's where the trail had ended.

The search for Martin Bixby was active. The man was a multiple murderer. Specks of blood in the boot of his car had been positively identified as Reggie Williamson's, presumably from the blood-soaked clothing that he'd brought back from the murder on the common. Police forces across the UK as well as INTERPOL were on the lookout for him, but Warren doubted they'd find him. His passport was nowhere to be found and his bank account was empty. It might have been thirty years ago, but he'd been trained to avoid capture by the finest special forces outfit in the world; if he was in touch with Jocelyn Delmarno and his adoptive son, the police had yet to prove it and they could only keep them under surveillance for so long.

Warren no longer had the trowel, so he made do with his bare hands, taking care to pat the soil down when he'd finished.

"I'm sorry, Dad," was all Warren could think to say as he stood up. He could never clear his father's name. He'd accepted that. But at least those who mattered knew the truth—him and Granddad Jack. And if there was a heaven, Mum and Nana Betty.

And as for those who'd set it all in motion and caused nearly a quarter of a century of pain and suffering… well, justice of a sort had caught up with them all.

* * *

The old man with the litter-picker watched the man leave. He seemed a lot more relaxed than when he'd arrived, pacing around the entrance as he waited for the other two to join him. Good, that was what a cemetery was for. To bring peace to those still living, whilst the dead rested in peace for eternity.

At least they'd taken their litter with him, he thought as he completed his rounds. They'd done a good job tidying the graves up as well, he noticed as he got nearer. It wasn't up to him to maintain them, but he used to give a bit of attention to some of the more neglected plots. Perhaps when he eventually joined his beloved Violet, somebody would do the same for them he mused.

A flash of reflected sunlight caught his eye. Bending over he saw the edge of something white and plastic sticking out of the freshly turned soil around a new pot plant. Plucking it out, he turned it over in his hands in surprise. Over the years he'd found all sorts of strange things fluttering around the graveyard, everything from carrier bags and crisp packets to empty beer bottles and the head off a Barbie doll. But it was the first time he'd found an electrical circuit breaker...

Hooked on *Silent as the Grave*?

**Keep reading for an extract from
Blood is Thicker than Water, an electrifying
DCI Warren Jones short story...**

The old man wakes with a start. It's pitch black and for a moment he's disoriented. He's sitting upright; he must have fallen asleep in the chair in front of the TV again. So why isn't the light on? Has the electricity gone off? A blinking green glow across the room is slowly coming into focus—the clock on the video player. 01:27. So, no power cut but it did explain why the TV was off. It had switched to power-saving mode. Had he turned the light off before snoozing? He didn't think so.

Bloody eco light bulbs. They were supposed to last for ten years; he'd only fitted it six months ago. He didn't give a fig about global warming, but his daughter had shown him how much money he would save on his electricity bill and that had convinced him to pay the premium. Had he recouped his investment yet? He didn't think so.

His legs were stiff. He couldn't sleep here all night, he decided. Besides he needed the bathroom. The room was still dark; neither the green of the video clock nor the faint glow from the streetlamps through the curtains provided enough illumination for him to make out anything but the darkest of shadows. He thought about waiting for a few more moments to see if his eyes would adjust any more, but now thoughts of the toilet had taken hold and wouldn't be denied much longer.

Reaching forward he groped for the wheeled trolley. He still resented the contraption. It had a tray and all sorts of useful pockets, allowing him to shuffle around his house unaided, but despite what the brochure and his carers might call it, the damn thing was a Zimmer frame. His fingertips met nothing but empty air. Where was it? Had he kicked it away in his sleep? Some sort of leg spasm that sent it skittering out of his grasp?

He swept the air in front of him with his right hand, his eyes straining uselessly. Where was the bloody thing? The discomfort in his bladder was growing. He'd have to get to the bathroom soon. Time for Plan B he decided, turning in his seat for the wooden cane—he refused to call it a walking stick—that he kept hanging from the back of his armchair. His fingers brushed against the fabric of the wing-backed chair. It must have fallen on the floor he decided.

Reaching down he moved his fingers methodically across the carpet. After a few moments he gave up, his breath ragged from the pressure on his diaphragm, tiny stars sparkling at the edge of his vision. For the first time he started to doubt himself. Had he imagined hanging the cane off the back of his chair? It was something that he did every day—had he just assumed that he had done so last night? A chill ran through him. These little episodes were becoming more frequent. Was he just getting a little forgetful in his old age or was there more to it? Something more sinister? It ran in families sometimes he'd read somewhere. His mother had remained as sharp as a pin into her nineties, but his father had died too young for any of the symptoms of Alzheimer's disease to manifest themselves. However, both of his father's brothers had been showing at least some of the symptoms of dementia before the family curse of heart disease had taken them as well. He'd inherited the heart problems. Had he also inherited something else?

This time of year the sun made an appearance about six. Could he *just sit it out until it became light enough for him to see what he'd done with his mobility aids? A rumbling in his bowels joined the pain in his bladder, answering that question. He gritted his teeth. No chance. Old and infirm he may be, but he still had his pride—too much pride, even he could admit at times—and he would not be found sitting in his own piss and shit.*

Taking a deep breath, he shuffled to the end of the chair. He'd finally accepted the logic of a stairlift—it was either that or be confined to the ground floor of his own home, suffering the ignominy of bathing in the kitchen or downstairs loo and sleeping in the dining room, with a twice weekly trip to the upstairs bathroom to wash properly. He had, though, drawn the line at one of those tilting armchairs that delivered you to your feet. Not least because of the price. Eight hundred pounds for a chair! He regretted that now. Gripping the armrest with his right hand he pushed down, struggling to clamber to his feet. The chair rocked alarmingly as his full weight resting on one side threatened to topple it.

Finally he stood precariously upright, feeling a flash of pride in his accomplishment, followed immediately by a sense of shame at being proud of such a minor achievement. Maintaining a grip on the side of the chair, he shuffled his feet until he stood more firmly. His left leg was weaker than his right—not as useless as his left arm, fortunately, but it still made crossing the darkened room a time-consuming process.

The rug in front of the fire was an old, shaggy affair nearing the end of its fifth decade. It had been lying there since he'd moved into the house and had been the first piece of "luxury furnishing" his wife had bought. It had cost her a week's wages—not that she'd earned much back then, not compared to him—but it had been important for her. Her income had been little more than pocket money really. He'd been the breadwinner but it had been important that she felt she was contributing.

He was fortunate that it was his weaker left foot that caught the fold; it left his stronger right leg to help him regain his balance. He breathed out shakily. That had been too close.

And then he was falling. Time seemed to slow and then the stars were back, an explosion of light before his eyes from the sudden contact with the mantelpiece. They were beautiful in their own way, he supposed. He felt weightless, even as he continued downwards. There was no pain; there hadn't been time.

Then it was all over. A final crack as he met the stone hearth of the fireplace and that was it.

"Charles Michaelson, seventy-eight years old, lived alone," the young constable greeted Detective Chief Inspector Warren Jones as he stepped out of his car. He nodded in the direction of a middle-aged woman dressed in a plain skirt and woollen cardigan, talking to another uniformed officer. "That's his daughter over there. She discovered the body this morning when she came by to help the deceased get ready for the day."

"Anything suspicious at the scene?"

The policeman shook his head. "Nothing obvious. It looks as though he fell and cracked his head. Apparently he was unsteady on his feet after a stroke a few years ago."

The daughter was sitting on the steps of the ambulance's loading bay, her hands wrapped around a steaming mug. Warren decided to head into the house to see the scene for himself before speaking to her.

It was 9 a.m. on a Tuesday and the morning rush hour was well underway. In Warren's experience, the flashing lights of an ambulance elicited a curiousness that was usually tempered by respect. Nobody felt comfortable slowing down to stare as some poor soul was taken out of their home. However, the presence of a police car elevated the scene to an "incident" and all such restraint melted away. He turned back to the constable who had greeted him.

"Go and ask those kids why they aren't in school yet and tell them to stop filming or I'll confiscate their phones as evidence."

Leaving his empty threat to be passed on to the gaggle of gawking teenagers, Warren walked up the short garden path, towards the door. The house was a neat, terraced affair. The faint scent of air freshener and furniture polish spoke of a well-cared-for property, although he noticed that the paintwork on the windowsills and the front door was slightly faded, suggesting that the occupant was more interested in the interior than the outside. A glance back at the front garden confirmed his impression; the grass on the tiny lawn was recently cut, but small weeds poked their heads between the untidy rosebushes.

Another constable stood guard inside the narrow, dark hallway with a copy of the scene log attached to a clipboard. Behind him, Warren could see through an open doorway into the living room beyond, the bottom of a right leg encased in grey corduroy trousers with a bright red slipper just visible. Warren signed his name, noting that aside from the two officers he'd already met and a couple of paramedics, he was the first on the scene.

"The daughter found him this morning when she let herself in to make him breakfast."

"Did she disturb the body?"

"She says that she saw he wasn't breathing and touched his neck, but she couldn't find a pulse, so she called 999."

"What about the paramedics?"

"They came in, but they could see he was dead, so they backed out and called us in."

Warren nodded his thanks. The chances were that it was nothing more than natural causes, an old man collapsing of a heart attack or stumbling. Nevertheless an unexplained death was an unexplained death and Warren was the senior on-call officer this week. Reaching down, he slipped a pair of sterile booties over his work shoes and snapped on a pair of latex gloves.

The living room was old-fashioned. Aside from the large flat screen TV at the far end of the room, the décor probably hadn't been updated in the last forty years. The carpet, though clean, was faded, the three-piece suite slightly shiny from decades of use. Thick, dark curtains were still drawn, the electric light providing the only illumination.

The body of an elderly man lay face down in the fireplace. It had been a warm night and Warren was relieved to see that the fire hadn't been lit. Past experience told him that the smell of burnt flesh and the sight of charred features would linger in his dreams for weeks afterwards. Unfortunately, the man had soiled himself and the odour was starting to fill the room.

First impressions were that the deceased had fallen, face first, into the fireplace, striking the mantelpiece on the way down. The wood was cracked and broken picture frames lay scattered about the body. Warren recognised a photograph of the woman outside. Slipping his hands into his pockets to avoid touching anything, Warren stood still and moved his gaze slowly around the room.

The most useful piece of technology that any investigating officer has in his possession is the original, mark one eyeball, his former mentor was fond of telling his junior officers and Warren had found himself passing Bob Windermere's pearl of wisdom on to his own detectives. Until the technicians arrived with their cameras and briefcases crammed with equipment, it was all that he had at his disposal.

The cause of death was beyond Warren's remit. That was a job for the pathologist, but still he found himself looking for clues. The biggest question was why had the man fallen? Had he collapsed, falling towards the fireplace, or had he stumbled, the fall itself killing him?

A few paces behind the man was a wing-backed armchair angled towards the TV. A small table to the right of it—festooned in magazines, empty mugs and a selection of remote controls—suggested that this was the favourite chair in the room and probably the seat that the deceased had spent most of his time in. A little over an arm's length away from the chair was a wheeled Zimmer frame with a tray surface. On it the remains of a sandwich sat on a plain, white tea plate. Hanging off the left side of the chair was a curved, wooden walking stick.

Turning back to the body, Warren saw that the man was fully clothed, wearing a checked shirt with a sleeveless woollen pullover. The trousers were loose, but he wore no belt. The man's left hand lay at his side, his right was outstretched, as if to break his fall.

The body was lying on a threadbare, shag-pile rug. The furthest edge from the fireplace was curled up slightly. Warren measured the angles by eye. Had the old man tripped on the fold and fallen, catching his head on the way down? Careful not to disturb the area immediately around the body, Warren squatted down. Sightless eyes stared back at him disconcertingly, below a massive darkened bruise. A fresh-looking slice across his eyebrows hinted at a huge impact. A dark puddle of shiny blood on the gleaming, black tiles of the hearth indicated that the deceased had continued to bleed for at least some time before death. Warren looked up and saw, just as he had expected, blood smears and what looked like grey hairs embedded in the split wood of the mantelpiece.

The smell was beginning to get to Warren and he stood up. It looked like an unfortunate accident. An old man, unsteady on his feet, catches his foot on an old rug and takes a dive into the fireplace, splitting his head open on the way down. Nothing to get excited about, Warren decided as he left the room.

He glanced at his watch. The monthly budget meeting was due to start in fifteen minutes. He should really delegate, he supposed. If he put his foot down he could be in Welwyn within thirty minutes, but the thought of two hours in a stuffy room poring over spreadsheets was deeply unappealing on such a pleasant morning. Besides which his next most senior officer, Detective Inspector Tony Sutton, was away on a course, Warren was the senior on-call officer and the meeting was always minuted…

He decided to compromise. He'd speak to the daughter now, assuming she was in a fit state, satisfy himself that there was nothing untoward and then pass her off to a detective constable for follow-up. Then, if he wasn't too late, he'd make it for the last few minutes and pick up the highlights of the meeting. After removing his protective gear he pulled out his phone and dashed off an apologetic email to Detective Superintendent Grayson. His immediate superior generally did most of the talking in such meetings anyway.

Heading back outside, Warren made his way to the ambulance. It was always best to question witnesses as soon after an incident as possible, he told himself.

Kathy Mackay spoke with a local accent, as best Warren could tell, and she looked tired, the smudges underneath her red-rimmed eyes spoke of a long-term weariness that went beyond the stresses of the morning. Warren guessed her age to be late thirties.

"I believe you found your father?" Warren started, sympathetically.

She nodded and when she spoke it was as if she didn't quite believe what she was saying. "I let myself in about eight o'clock—I have a set of keys—and went into the kitchen to get Dad's breakfast ready."

"You didn't call out?"

She shook her head. "Dad's not what you'd call a 'morning person'. I figured he was awake, since I could hear the *Today* programme coming from upstairs, but he doesn't like to be disturbed."

"So you were expecting him to be up there?"

"Yes, we had a chairlift installed a couple of years ago. He insists on sleeping in his old bedroom."

"Do you make his breakfast every morning?"

"Yes. He had a stroke about ten years ago. His left arm is pretty much useless. I drop the kids off at breakfast club and pop in on the way back."

"So your father needed help with his day-to-day care?"

"Not twenty-four hours. He can walk with assistance but he was never much of a cook even before the stroke. I usually make him a spot of lunch at the same time then leave him to it until the early evening."

"You say that your father was not a morning person. Do you have any idea why he was already downstairs in the living room when you arrived this morning?"

She shrugged slightly. "He sometimes falls asleep in his chair in front of the TV. I've found him there once or twice, although I think he normally wakes up and goes upstairs to his bed." She paused for a moment. "I think those were the clothes he was wearing yesterday."

So Mr Michaelson had probably fallen on the way to bed the previous night, rather than getting up early that morning. The time of death should clear that question up.

"How did you find your father?"

"As I said, I let myself in about eight after I dropped the kids off. The living room door was closed, so I didn't look in there. After I made his breakfast, I went in to collect any dirty mugs and have a bit of a tidy-up. He spends all day in there and it gets a bit messy sometimes. And that's when I found him."

Her voice broke and Warren told her to take her time. The tissue in her hand was sodden and starting to shred, so Warren fished out a small packet from his inside jacket pocket. After a few deep breaths, she continued. "He was lying face down in the fireplace. I knew as soon as I saw him he was dead." Her voice cracked, but she continued, "You just know, don't you? He was too still. His eyes were open, staring at me."

"Did you touch him at all, or move anything?"

She shook her head. "I felt for his pulse—" she touched her throat "—but there was nothing. I walked out and called an ambulance."

She was looking tearful again and so Warren decided to move away slightly from the discovery of the body. The follow-up interview could answer any other questions. He cast about for the right choice of words. "Did your father require help with his more… intimate… personal care?"

"No fortunately. Dad was quite insistent about that. It took him a while, but he could pretty much dress himself and we had one of those sit-down showers fitted. He needs a bit of help with fiddly things, like his tie and button-up shirts if he's going out to the British Legion for the day, and about once a week we'd give him a proper wet shave instead of using his electric razor."

"You said 'we'. Do you have any other help?"

"No, just my brother, Tommy, and my husband. We split the rest of the duties between us: cleaning, shopping, odd jobs. We took it in turns to make him dinner." Her mouth twisted. "Dad had a good job and was always very careful with his money, so he doesn't qualify for any state care. He was—reluctant—to pay for help whilst my brother and I live so close." The speech was delivered in careful, neutral tones, but her eyes gave her away. Warren filed away her reaction for future analysis, if need be.

"Has Tommy been told about what's happened?"

"I phoned him about half an hour ago. He's on his way. He works in Stevenage."

"What about your husband?"

"His phone's off, but he'll pick up his messages when he finishes work in an hour or so."

"You said your father needed assistance walking?"

She nodded. "He could move around the house on his own and we got him one of those wheeled Zimmer frames with a tray fitted, but that's about it. His left leg was affected by the stroke and he wasn't very steady."

"So he was mostly housebound?"

She nodded again. "He didn't like going out. For some reason he was ashamed of his disability. He hated using a wheelchair."

"But he used to go to the British Legion?"

"About once a week. Funnily enough, he didn't mind that. I think it's because several of the others need assistance as well. They have a minibus that picks them up. I guess they're all in the same boat."

Nothing she had said changed Warren's mind about what had happened. Charles Michaelson had been unsteady on his feet; he'd either collapsed or tripped, possibly on the rug in front of the fireplace, and cracked his head against the stonework.

"When did you last see your father?"

"Last night. It was my turn to make him some dinner."

"What time was that?"

She thought for a moment. "I put the kids to bed about eight, then came straight around. I live about five minutes away."

"And how was your father?"

"A bit quiet. He's been a bit tired and under the weather for the past few days. He didn't say very much; he was watching some documentary on TV. He doesn't eat much in the evening so I just made him some sandwiches and a cup of tea and gave him his pills. I did a spot of ironing, then left."

"What time was that?"

"A little after nine, I guess." She paused for a second. "Yes that's about right. Whatever he was watching had ended and he'd changed channels to watch something else. Programmes usually start on the hour don't they?"

"And you went straight home?"

"Yes, Ian, my husband, leaves for work about ten. He works nights. I have to get back to look after the kids."

She suddenly looked exhausted. Warren wasn't surprised. Young children—an eight o'clock bedtime suggested they were probably still at primary school—an infirm father and a husband working shifts. Kathy Mackay had a hard life. There was nothing overtly suspicious here he decided. He'd get DC Gary Hastings to conduct a follow-up interview after the post-mortem.

Expressing his condolences again, he headed for the car. If the traffic was kind he'd make the tail end of the meeting. If he timed it right he'd miss the death-by-PowerPoint that finance loved and still manage to nab a custard cream.

* * *

Charles Michaelson's death remained a tragic accident until late that evening.

"Harrison here, sir. I'm out at the Michaelson death." Crime Scene Manager Andy Harrison's Yorkshire tones were clipped, his voice slightly tense. "I'm not happy with the scene."

* * *

The smell from the late Charles Michaelson hadn't improved any since the morning, even though the body had been removed to the morgue, pending autopsy. CSM Harrison and his team had been working in the small room for nearly three hours. Warren assumed that their noses had become used to the smell. Hopefully his would soon become accustomed to it also.

Harrison had turned up at the scene with his current trainee, expecting a routine unexpected death. He'd been anticipating an opportunity for Shaniya to try out some basic techniques in a low-risk environment, where there'd be no danger of jeopardising a prosecution.

"It's a combination of a few small things, sir." Harrison had photographed the body *in situ* before covering the hands in plastic bags to preserve evidence, then sending it away.

"First, I'm not happy with the positioning of the body." He pointed at the upturned rug. "If he'd tripped and gone straight down, I'd have expected the body to have landed a bit further back. He'd have still hit his head on the stone hearth, but probably missed the mantelpiece."

"He could have stumbled, caught himself, then gone down," suggested Warren, playing devil's advocate.

Harrison shrugged. "It's circumstantial, I agree. But I'm not

481

happy about him tripping in the first place." He pointed to the far end of the room. "He's supposedly unsteady on his feet and needs assistance walking. So why didn't he use his Zimmer frame?"

Warren gauged the distance between the chair and the wheeled frame. "It looks as if it was beyond arm's reach. Did he knock it out of the way in his sleep?"

Harrison shook his head. "No chance. Look at the design: two wheels at the front, rubber stoppers at the back. That's not going anywhere unless it's moved deliberately."

"OK, so somehow the frame is out of his reach. He was a stubborn bugger from all accounts. Maybe he chose to walk unaided, to prove to himself that he could do it?"

"But why not use his walking stick?"

Warren thought for a moment, before seeing what Harrison had already spotted. "It was hanging off the left-hand side of the chair."

"Exactly. Michaelson supposedly had no use of his left arm. He'd have had to twist around to hang it on that side. Why would he do that, when he can more easily hang it off the right side, which is where he usually placed it?"

Stepping over to the wing-backed armchair, he showed Warren a faint indentation in the overstuffed velvet.

"He hung his walking stick here for years, I'll bet. Within easy reach of his right arm. There's even photographic evidence." He pointed to a picture sitting on the TV stand and another one on the windowsill. Both were family shots, taken a couple of years apart. Both in the same room. In one he was holding a newborn baby in his lap, his face split by a huge smile. In another, he was flanked by a younger version of Kathy Mackay and a clearly related man of a similar age. An oversized badge proclaiming "70" and a coffee-tableful of greetings cards identified the occasion. In both pictures he was seated in the same wing-backed chair, the wooden cane clearly visible hanging off its right wing.

Harrison was right, the scene wasn't quite as one expected, but then they rarely were. He said as much to the veteran crime scene investigator.

"Again it's very circumstantial, Andy. I agree it's weird that he hung his walking stick off the back of the chair, pushed his frame out of the way then decided to walk unaided. But it's pretty clear his bowels were full. Maybe he got caught short and decided he didn't have time to shuffle to the bathroom? People do silly things all of the time."

Harrison still looked unhappy. The man was a highly experienced CSI and Warren could see the man's gut was troubling him, and that troubled Warren.

"You said on the phone that you had some concerns about the body as well?"

Harrison led Warren over to the broken fireplace. "Look at the pool of blood. What do you see?"

The puddle was larger than Warren had initially thought, the body having hid some of it. The blood gleamed, wet and shiny against the stonework.

"This probably happened in the very early hours; his temperature was already down slightly when the surgeon measured it mid-morning."

"It's still wet."

"Exactly. It should be sticky by now."

Warren thought for a few moments. Now his own gut was uneasy.

He was the senior investigating officer; it was his call.

"Let's call it an unexplained death for now and treat this as a potential crime scene."

Acknowledgments

Like all of my novels, *Silent as the Grave* couldn't have been written without the help and assistance of a great number of people.

The first thanks must go to my amazing beta readers, Dad and Cheryl, who put up with my foul-mouthed rants at my computer's steadfast refusal to print out a draft copy for them to read over, then dropped everything to go over the document in record time so I could meet my deadline.

Next is the long line of friends who have listened to extracts of the work during its gestation, giving much appreciated feedback and encouragement. I will never be able to list everyone who helped me, so if I don't name you, please be assured that I valued each and every suggestion and contribution.

A few who can't be missed out include my friends at the Hertford Writers' Circle, who have given me essential feedback on all my books, supplying thoughtful suggestions where necessary and giving me the strength to persevere when it all seemed a bit overwhelming.

Some chapters of this novel were written as an exercise for a creative writing class and the critical feedback supplied by Danielle Jawando and my friends at Hertford Regional College helped me raise my game enormously. Good luck guys and keep on writing!

As always, I relied on technical advice from many people: Elaine

Dockrill helped enormously with medical advice, Caroline and Dan kept me straight on the legal stuff and our close family friend Danny McAree generously shared his experience from decades in the police. As always, Crime Scene Investigator Lee Robson of Essex police was a source of both information and future inspiration.

My colleagues and friends at school have been wonderful, supplying both encouragement and feedback as well as acting as a useful source of interesting surnames and even more interesting character quirks…

Behind the scenes, I will forever be grateful to my publisher, HQ Digital, for taking a chance on me and for their support, from editing and feeding back on my manuscripts to the beautifully designed covers. Cheers, guys!

Finally, I must say a heartfelt thanks to the many kind readers who have taken the time to tell me what they thought of the first two books, either in person or via reviews. Releasing your 'baby' into the wild is a nerve-wracking experience and a positive review really makes an author's day.

DCI Warren Jones will return. In the meantime, I hope you enjoy his latest adventure.

Paul

Dear Reader,

Thank you so much for taking the time to read this book – we hope you enjoyed it! If you did, we'd be so appreciative if you left a review.

Here at HQ Digital we are dedicated to publishing fiction that will keep you turning the pages into the early hours. We publish a variety of genres, from heartwarming romance, to thrilling crime and sweeping historical fiction.

To find out more about our books, enter competitions and discover exclusive content, please join our community of readers by following us at:

🐦 @HQDigitalUK

f facebook.com/HQDigitalUK

Are you a budding writer? We're also looking for authors to join the HQ Digital family! Please submit your manuscript to:

HQDigital@harpercollins.co.uk.

Hope to hear from you soon!